Mattie,

Thank you

I hope you enjoy reading

This.

To Wrestle With Darkness

Alan D. Jones

A RISING SUN GROUP PUBLICATION
www.towrestlewithdarkness.com
Atlanta, Georgia, USA

To Wrestle With Darkness
By Alan D. Jones

Rising Sun Group Publishing
Copyright © 2009 Alan D. Jones

ISBN-10: 0-9666679-1-3
ISBN-13: 978-0-9666679-1-2

Cover image from NASA.
Image selection by author.
Editing Services: Terry Bozeman and Anita Diggs
Interior Page Layout & Design: Abena Muhammad for DetailsCount
Front & Back Cover Design: Abena Muhammad for DetailsCount

*T*hanks to the following whose support and understanding helped to bring this work to life:

Anika A. Jones
Lesley "Tafiti" Grady
Wilma Jenkins
Joshua Dickson
Eva Bird

Contents

What would you give to face the darkness? What would you give to avoid it? Or would you embrace it?

The first requires at least an ounce of faith, the second, a shortage thereof, and the third, a void of faith beyond measure.

Prologue: A Gift

I have this gift. For many years I did not know that I had this gift. I assumed that my experiences were not that much different than yours. I believed that your perception of reality was the same as mine. How would I know otherwise? And so it was during most of the story I am about to share. And what is this gift, you ask? Suffice it to say, that my dreams are not my own, but of those long gone and those yet to be. And while other gifts have been added to me over the years, this one true gift has remained with me across time and space. This one true gift, although seemingly an affliction at times, is most certainly a blessing to others in my life. For it affords me the opportunity to share their stories through their own dreams.

This book is an account of how I heard my own call and how the life of a man named Jonah helped to guide me to where I am today. Jonah lived in an age well beyond the time of my own birth, and yet the course of his life changed mine forever. And while this is very much a story of what happened, I hope also that it is a tale of why.

1: Slipping into Darkness

May the works of my life, and the words of my life, transcend my life.

I lie here composing these words as darkness thunders in and fearsome billows eclipse the sun. But rather than clouds of rain, these are plumes of ash. The four horsemen ride these last days with no regard for anyone. Here at the end of time hopelessness has few equals on this day made night by the deeds of mortals. Were it not for the despair in their cries, I would burst into tears of laughter at the rich irony of my being here at all.

I see through the smoke, past the haze and beyond the flack. Death and destruction are all around me as the wheels of war churn the souls of mortals, sifting spirits to grind out the most murderous ones, and yet I am not afraid. For I know things that these beings cannot even fathom, much less believe. My mind reels at the thought of where I have been and where I am. You cannot fully understand who I am in this future state, until you know something of where I've been.

Therefore, I have a story to share for those that seek the truth. I have a story to share for those who seek life. I have a story to share for those who seek the way. You can choose to believe what I have to say or cast it into the fire. But my charge is to tell it, and so I will. I hope you will hear me, for I know the Truth. It is a rich and layered thing that can be shared by deed, spirit and word.

For me, this journey began in earnest late one November afternoon of my junior year of college at Georgia Tech in Atlanta, Georgia. I'd just finished my morning Chemical Engineering class, when I received a voicemail message from my cousin Akina. Her voice was halting as she spoke, "Michael… Something has happened… something bad. Meet me at eleven on the bench at Piedmont Park across from my school… yeah, meet me there." There was something in her voice that I'd never heard from her before. It was uncertainty.

I closed up my cell phone and wondered to myself, what could she want with me? Admittedly, I was intrigued by the idea that perhaps finally I would get the real scoop regarding my family. My mother was always careful to block me from hanging with my cousins as much as I would have liked. Even so, ever since I was in the ninth grade I knew something was up. Were they in a cult? Was it drugs? Or were they working to subvert the government in some way? No, it couldn't be any of these, but something was going on and I was tired of sitting at the little kids' table not knowing. Yes, that cold November day was going to be graduation day for me.

Of course, there had been clues. The fact that no one talked about my dad seemed strange to me. Various family members would disappear for days or weeks at a time. Clergy of different denominations and faiths from all over would visit and I never knew why. The dearth of significant personal and historical information about my own family was maddening at times. Actually, the night before Akina called me, I rummaged through my mother's nightstand drawer (a taboo I know, but I had to do it nonetheless) looking for clues as to just what was the real deal with my family and my dad specifically. But what I found was an envelope of pictures. There were pictures of my mother and her sisters with my grandfather, who passed before I was born. But there were other pictures, pictures of people and places that shook my soul. Given the fact that I'd left the church and was a practicing atheist at the time, made shaking my soul quite a feat. The photos with "Uncle Paul" in them were particularly disturb-

ing to me. Actually, it wasn't him, but the people he was pho-
tographed with in these pictures that bothered me. I don't
know that I've ever seen such an evil-looking lot. Several had
the aura of death all around them. And one of the women,
while not possessing that presence, had eyes filled with so
much madness that I was forced to turn away. These were the
faces from my nightmares. At this time in my life, I had not
yet recognized the gift within me, so I suppressed the overwhelming sense of recognition creeping up my spine. It was a
reality that I was not yet ready to face. But there was one
reality that I could not escape. In all of the pictures, which
were labeled, Uncle Paul appeared to be the same unchanging
age, although several of the pictures were from the early
1900's, and still others were dated within the last twenty
years. In the earliest photo, dated June 11, 1903, Uncle Paul
was a grown man. In the last photo he should have been well
over one hundred years old, but you couldn't see where he'd
aged a day in all that time. If only then I had known the true
source of my dreams, I could have made sense of all this and
spared us all so much pain. And yet, even in my ignorance, I
knew enough to stuff the pictures into my coat pocket for
later review.

I zipped up my backpack and made tracks for the park. I
didn't have a ride. Being carless, I caught a school shuttle
that got me halfway there, and walked the rest of the way.

As I entered the mostly empty park I was surprised to see
my Uncle Paul, white cane in hand, sitting on the old wooden
green bench where I was to meet Akina. As I approached him
I could smell the snuff in his mouth and liniment all over
him. The moment I saw him, my thoughts immediately shifted to the pictures I'd found.

My blind uncle smiled when he heard me. "Michael, you
walk just like your granddaddy, God rest his soul." He actually knew it was me by my walk before I'd said a word. I al-

ways thought that I was a hard walker, with a rather large footprint in this life but Uncle Paul said disagreed. He said my walk was soft and yet unsteady. This was the first time in six months or so that I'd seen him. He moved his hat for me to sit on the bench next to him.

Uncle Paul was the closest thing to a grandfather I'd ever known. In recent years his faculties had begun to betray him. Although he could recognize me by the cadence of my step, he often lost track of the day or even the year.

I reached into my bag and pulled out several of the old photos and held them in my lap. "Uncle... Uncle Paul. I..." I stumbled, lost for words as I stared at the pictures. "I have these pictures of you that don't make sense. There's one of you at the Peacock West Club with five other people that troubles me. I don't know these people, but they're the same faces I've seen in most every nightmare I've had since I was a child. When I look at this picture, all I see is death. I see them in my waking and I see them in my sleeping. I, I see..." I sat for a second adrift in the surreal. Finally I composed myself enough to speak again, "On the back of this picture it says 'Paul Few at the Peacock West'". Beneath the writing was the date. "Uncle Paul, who are these people?" I asked.

Uncle Paul winced and answered, "Aw nawl, that picture's got to be at least fifty years old."

"But Uncle Paul," I retorted, "the Peacock West wasn't even built twenty years ago. In fact it had just opened the year this picture was taken. And that is it – I was just there last week."

Uncle Paul turned away and spoke tersely. "That ain't none of me at the Peacock, could've been any one of a hundred clubs back in the day."

The photograph was of Uncle Paul sitting at a table with three other men and two women, each of which had been haunting my dreams for as long as I could remember. That is, with the exception of Uncle Paul. He has always been cool with my cousins and me. But that was not the case in the previous generation. My two surviving aunts rarely spoke to him, but my mom still did. Aunt Cil, when she was alive, was the oldest of the sisters, then my Aunt Deborah and Aunt Ruth. My mom, Sarah, was the youngest. Uncle Paul, who I grew up believing to be their uncle, was older than all of them. So, it didn't add up. Uncle Paul appeared to be a very young man not even twenty years ago. What could explain the unaccounted years? The more troubling question for me was what manner of unspeakable deeds could have occurred creating such a rift in our family? And who were these people in this photograph? And why and how had just their mere image stricken me with such a psychosis?

Somehow I knew that this picture was the key to all that was unknown to me about my family and my place in it. It was the Rosetta Stone to my persistent nightmares and fears. And then the tears came, tears that I did not understand, streaming down my face. I felt like my whole life was in my hand, and I didn't even know the right question to ask. There I was, a twenty-year-old man, crying seemingly without reason.

Hearing the sobs in my voice, my uncle turned to me, reaching for my hand, speaking softly "Shhh boy and stop your crying. There is a reason this picture troubles you so. There is so much about your family and even yourself that your mother had hoped to spare from you. I see now that it is your time. So, let me begin with my own walk of discovery."

"Once upon a time I was given a great gift. At first, I did many good things in honor of this gift and the giver of it. But in the course of carrying this responsibility, I came to know some very dark things, a dark knowledge, if you will. It consumed me totally, taking me away from my family and leaving me a wretched man. When I was a child this gift from

Heaven was put upon me. By your age I was traveling between this world and the next on fire to do good. All that breathed, and some that didn't, obeyed my every word. These gifts gained me attention from the evil spirits of this world. Initially, I sought to infiltrate their ranks and to play their quest for me against them, but eventually, for the most part, I fell in with them. I have done some things, the likes of which I pray to God Almighty that this world never sees again. I have earned a debt that I can never repay, and on many days, I too sit in this park and cry. I cry for all those I have hurt. It is an endless river of tears."

"But Uncle Paul what is this power and what exactly did you do? What was so awful that your own sisters will not speak with you? And why does just looking at this particular picture leave me so empty and afraid?"

"Sisters?" He smiled at that choice of words, but went on. "That picture is of the Council of Nob. That's really all I want to say about them. The less you know about them, the better your life today will be. You will learn of them soon enough. But I will say this, the one on the far left is Matasis. He was our leader and my tempter into the darkness. As for your aunts, they were afraid of me with good reason and their strange anger was justified. They, not I, will have to choose whether to tell you of the blackness of my heart back when I fell from grace. It's not that I don't want to tell you, but I cannot tell you fully of my secret past without telling their secrets as well. It doesn't seem right to do without their permission. As for power, it is in our bloodline. Some say our forefathers were the magicians of ancient Kush and Egypt. Others say we were the Sons of God, modern day heroes of God. You will hear all kinds of things. As for me, I choose not to say. That answer I do know, but it is a solution that is best found on your own... Oh, there's Akina."

Akina is Uncle Paul's granddaughter and my second cousin... supposedly. She may be the cutest of my cousins, not in a sexy sense, but more like an African princess, fragile-like. Her skin was chocolate and fine, barely a blemish. Her smile could put a pitbull at ease. Her ever-present shades were a mystery to some, but her hair was the envy of many. She had an Angela Davis type of Afro and when she strode her five-foot-five frame across a room, her ebony halo bounced ever so slightly. She was a senior at the same high school from which I graduated, which also happened to be right across from the park. After class she'd often walk over to the park to meet Uncle Paul. Together, they'd ride the bus to her job, stopping to get a bite along the way. Other times he'd walk her the five blocks to her martial arts class and then ride home with her afterwards. Akina was the most well-adjusted teen I'd ever known, but not that day. As she ran to us, her backpack plopped up and down on her narrow back. It was evident, even from thirty feet away, that she was upset.

"Granddaddy, Mama's got Carla!"

Uncle Paul sat, head in his hands. "Avis, Avis!" he cried.

Avis was Uncle Paul's daughter and Akina's mother. Her name was taboo in my house. Carla was my Aunt Deborah's child. She had a twin brother, Darnell. The three of us, all being local college students, ran together quite often and looked forward to Akina joining our pack the next year. However, I suddenly knew all our plans were about to become secondary.

Akina, regaining a bit of composure and adjusting her sunglasses, spoke in a less rattled voice. "I called Darnell and told him to meet us at the sub shop. Granddaddy, you've got to help us get Carla back, please..."

Uncle Paul and I arose, and Akina took his hand and led us to the bus stop. As we boarded the bus and took our seats, a hot flash consumed my body and a flood of memories rushed into me; things that I had been trying to remember since I'd found those pictures in my mother's nightstand. I remembered a time when I was a child, after a rare mid-week Bid-Whist card party and everyone had gone home except for my aunts, hearing them and my mom discussing Uncle Paul. They called him "Brother". I remember Aunt Ruth saying "Y'all, I heard that Brother done gone and joined the church!"

Aunt Deborah, the loudest of the bunch and mother to Darnell and Carla, belted "What the hell did I tell y'all, that Negro is gonna try to slide into Heaven after all the straight-out evil he's done. Akina's born and boom, he's a saint. I ain't buying none of this crap. For God's sake, he's a demon!"

My mother interceded, "Now Deborah that's not a Christian thing to say. And he's not a demon."

Aunt Deborah, also the sassy one, replied, "Might as well have been one, the way he ran with 'em. And how can you defend the man, Sarah after the way he chased you?" She hooted, "He wanted you bad girl! If it weren't for Cil, he could have been your baby's father. He ain't, is he?" This was a very hurtful thing for me to hear back then, but it was an extremely hurtful thing to say to my mother knowing what I know today about the circumstances of my conception and birth.

Aunt Cil, who never seemed to particularly care for Uncle Paul, broke in then. "Deborah!" After a knowing glance towards my mother, Aunt Cil composed herself enough to turn to Aunt Deborah. "Leave Sarah alone, she's saying these things in love." Aunt Cil handled business for Uncle Paul and felt compelled to show him some measure of respect because of his blindness and what her daddy told her of Uncle Paul's days of fighting the good fight, even though growing up she'd never seen this Uncle Paul her father admired. Yet, out of respect for her father's wishes and his belief that Uncle Paul would someday repent, Aunt Cil kept the channels of communication open with *brother*, yet always keeping him at a distance. Best put, I guess you could say that she tolerated him.

Ruth, who was typically a bit more reserved, but had been drinking, responded to Deborah's comment adding, "The man was S-I-C-K, sick, but I don't think he was that sick. Deborah, I don't know how you can even say that or even think it!"

My mom, Sarah, finished the conversation with, "That's right. Yes, he's had some major problems, but I don't think any of us can say something like this about him. Surely, we all know that this mantle we all wear is a heavy one. But no, the boy wasn't right, or at least he wasn't back when Daddy was alive." She smiled a bit in some concession to her sisters. "But if we, who are blessed, don't minister to the afflicted, who will?"

Suddenly, I felt a hand on my shoulder and my memories dissipated. It was Akina. She spoke softly into my ear. "Michael, guard your thoughts and be of one mind. Now that you are with us, Avis will try to lead you astray." I glanced back over my other shoulder to see Uncle Paul looking about the bus as though he could see. He'd just smelled something in the air and seemed to be searching for its source. I tried to dry my sweaty palms on my pants legs as we rode to the sub shop. In the midst of the ride, I remembered whispered secrets about cousin Avis. Strangest of all, we were not allowed to mention her name. In fact, one of the worst "whoopings" I ever got came one Christmas Eve due to my doing just that. My mama and I were up late wrapping presents. I came across a childhood picture of my cousin Avis and decided to draw a picture for her. I thought I would give it to my Uncle Paul to give to her. As I sat there drawing, I softly repeated her full name over and over to myself as a part of a chant I heard Aunt Deborah saying once when no one else was listening. All of a sudden, Mama looked up and realized what I was saying. She moved like a force of nature, snatching me up by my arm, nearly dislocating my shoulder and smacked my bottom to the point that I still jump at the thought.

I screamed to the top of my lungs. She pulled me close to her bosom and held me, shushing me. I listened for long moments hearing nothing - no, less than nothing, a strange kind of nothingness. Suddenly the front door flew open, windows shattered and I cried out, "Mama!" She would not let me look up, and yet I could sense movement and hear whispers in the room.

My mother, on the other hand, was anything but awed, her voice booming like I'd never heard before. "Hear me Avis, I will say this once and I will not say it twice. If you touch even a hair of this child, I will abandon my vow not to use my gift against another human being and hunt you down, even beyond the gates of Hell. Demon child you know I do not lie. Heed this, my only warning, or your head shall sit upon my stake." Mama raised her free hand and I sensed a light so blinding that even with my mother covering me and my eyes shut tight, it felt as though I was looking into the sun.

I felt the presence leave and my mama relax. She put me down holding me by my wrist. She looked at me and said, "I love you, but..." and then with each word, she swung at my behind. "If...you...ever...say...that...again...I'll..." [You get the picture.] When she was done she picked me up again and walked over with me to close the door. She then carried me into the kitchen to get the broom for the broken glass on the floor. But when we returned to the living room, after getting up the glass, she looked at the rest of the debris, sighed and plopped into the big armchair. There she cradled me for the rest of the night. In the morning, I climbed down, leaving Mama sleeping. I remember reaching up to the doorknob, turning it slowly, first peeking and then opening it wide. The sun was so bright. Then I felt Mama's hand on the top of my head caressing me. She led me away and closed it again. She kneeled down speaking softly. "Remember you mustn't ever say that again."

"Okay, Mama."

We reached the sandwich shop and I saw quickly that we'd have to fight our way off the bus through the rush hour patrons trying to get on. Akina tossed her bookbag onto her back, the momentum nearly toppling her. I reached to catch her, but she righted herself. Glancing back, she called, "Granddaddy!?"

"Just a minute Baby," Uncle Paul said as he pushed his now somewhat frail body through the throngs and down the steps. All the while, his right hand was on my shoulder.

I didn't understand, but still I followed. That's what you do in a family sometimes.

The sandwich shop was just fifty feet or so from the bus stop. Akina, in her fury, flung the door open. She looked right and then left.

From off to the left, in the front corner, came a shout, "Akina!" It was Darnell.

She scurried over and slung her bookbag from her slender shoulders onto the table. I held the door for Uncle Paul and led him inside. Stepping in, his white beard was like a beacon to the afternoon crowd. As their stares faded we made our way over to the corner. I sat Uncle Paul next to Darnell along the wall and I slid in next to him on his left. Akina had seated herself across from me and next to Sandy, another cousin, sitting across from Darnell. Actually, Sandy was not a direct blood relation to me, at least not in a way anyone could explain to me. But supposedly, Sandy's dad might have been related to our moms some distant kind of way, but no one could ever tell me how. All our folks are from the same small town, so she was basically like family to me and it was killing me. Sandy was a freckled-faced cutie and a modest dresser most of the time. She was no Carla in the curves department although she was thicker than Akina. Sandy's vibe was slight; her presence was much more the remnant of a dream just lost at sunrise. Her transparency was the challenge of her life. Everything on her heart was shown on her face, and maybe that's why I loved her so.

"Uncle Paul, Carla's gone!" cried Darnell, as distraught as I'd ever seen him. He loved no one like he loved his sister; they've been through so much together. Darnell was brown-skinned and about my height, but he was built like a running-back. His athletic build didn't go unnoticed among the female population, however they would have to wait since Darnell had made a pledge of abstinence until marriage. "True love waits..." he would say. But still, he was very popular, especially in the Christian youth community. He was a man of faith, but his faith was being tested that day.

Uncle Paul leaned in Darnell's direction and spoke firmly, "Okay, okay, I know. Now, tell me what happened, as calmly as you can." His old hands reached across the table to Darnell's.

"About four o'clock this morning I felt this chill come over me. I just knew something was wrong. I got up and ran to Carla's room and she was gone...she wasn't there..." He paused for a moment. Just then I noticed the tears streaming down his face. I'd never seen him cry before. It scared me so to see him in that way. Looking up, taking a deep breath, he continued more slowly, "You see, last night at the library we read the New Orleans paper. Y'all have heard about the series of murders they've had. Well, we wanted to find out more about it, because Carla felt that Avis might be involved. The article we read seemed to suggest some type of seduction. All the victims were young men of various races, some of which had tattoos that read 'I commend my soul to Siva'". Siva, Avis backwards, is what she calls herself sometimes, especially those times she's feeling particularly malevolent. He continued, "We knew it was her. We tried to think of what we should do. Given that our mother and aunties were out of pocket, we decided we should sleep on it. I found this note when I got to Carla's room this morning." The note read:

Darnell, I'm sorry, but I cannot rest knowing what Avis is doing. I see no other choice. Before I go, I want you to know that never has a sister had a better, more loving brother than you. Even when I was unlovable and did not even love myself, you loved me still. Regarding Avis, I feel like God is calling me to do this, so don't be sad. I'm not scared at all. In fact, now that I've decided to go I feel more peace than I've ever known. I am going to call for Avis now. See you soon...

Love always, Sister

Sister was her nickname, or at least the nickname that the two of them used. Her nickname for him was Brother, the same as my aunts called Uncle Paul, but different. Carla's was full of affection without a trace of sarcasm, ever.

There are a couple things I should say here. Although my grandfather and his family are from Georgia, my maternal grandmother was from New Orleans, so we had some connection there. Secondly, several months before all of this happened Carla joined the church. It blew me away when I first heard about it.

Darnell, on the other hand, had been active in church since I could remember. He was the only one in their household to attend regularly. In fact, he was an acolyte once upon a time, which was a pretty good role for him, considering how he used to stutter. Acolytes don't have to say much. Deborah, their mother, while considering herself a Christian, rarely darkened the doorway of a sanctuary, save for funerals and the occasional wedding.

When they were younger, Carla and Darnell were very close but once puberty hit, they began to drift apart. She started sleeping around. She actually got a bit of a "rep", some of it earned, some not. Still, though there is certainly a double standard for boys and girls, there was no denying that she was out there. With it, in her case, came the drinking and the drugs. It wasn't until recently, like the last year or so since she got "saved", that they grew close again. Darnell couldn't be happier. He told me that it was like he'd found his sister again. I was a bit skeptical at first about Carla's newfound faith, but after this I knew the girl was for real.

Wrapping her arm around Darnell, Akina spoke strongly, "She's gone too far this time! We have to get Carla back." We all nodded in agreement. Then I thought "We?!"

As I tried to butt-in, Akina continued rambling on about how we'd pinpoint Avis's location and what our strategy should be. Sandy asked about Reggie and Kim, our cousins down in the country. Akina, said quickly, "I called them and left a message, but we can't wait on them."

Finally, I busted in, "What are y'all talking about? Why don't we just call our folks and when they get back they can...?"

Everyone stopped and looked at me as though I was the first ignoramus they'd ever seen. I was pretty sure they'd seen others before me.

Akina asked, "You really don't know?"

"It's coming to me, little by little. I know our folks are supposed to have these gifts. I don't know the details and stuff. But I know that Avis has got them and we're just ordinary folks."

"Are we?" Akina smiled and flashed her eyes at me. "If Avis, why not us? Why not you?"

As she lowered her shades, in her eyes I could see a well so deep that it must have reached back to the beginning of time. Her pupils were dark, seemingly bottomless, wells. Staring into the ages, I could not answer.

After adjusting her glasses back to their proper place, Akina continued, "I know you're not big on Sunday School but are you all familiar with some of the folks in The Bible? You know, like Samson, Elijah or Elisha? Or even Daniel? Not just the part with the lions, but how he seemed to be able to reach into the dreams of others? And even more meaning would this have for you, if you knew what dreams really are." A slight smile crept across her face.

Still, I could not speak.

Akina continued, "Could it not be that God would instill such gifts on whomever He chooses still today? Does He not have the right to impart these gifts and others as He sees fit? Some would say that any gift you've not seen in the Bible is not a gift from God. But I would say that there is far more in Heaven than mortal man has ever seen. If you truly knew the things of Heaven you would not, could not, be silent even now."

I scratched my partly cloudy to overcast head. This was all a bit much for me, a practicing atheist. But Akina was fond of saying that certain atheists like me were really Christians in denial. She would say that I protested the Faith, just a "little too much".

Akina continued on, "And greater than these gifts is the gift we do not mention. It flows between us, this force of life, this Spirit of God. We deny it at every turn because we do not understand it. But it understands us very well. And in reality, He is not an it... we are. We are an it into which He has blown His spirit giving us our being."

Darnell leaned forward to speak. "Uncle Paul, I've always wondered how Mike could not know who we are?"

"His mama did not want him to know. Michael, when you were very small your mother asked me to hide all this from you and using my gift, I did. She hoped to spare you from all this."

I was confused, but holding on to my point. "Still, let's call them. My mom left the number to the condo they rented in Nigril."

Darnell spoke up, "Condo in Nigril? Have you tried to dial that number?"

"Yes, in fact I spoke to her last night."

"Where's the number you called?"

"I've got it in here somewhere." I searched through my wallet, "See, here it is."

"Mike this is just a piece of paper with a bunch of seven's on it."

I took the paper back from Darnell, and dumbfounded, saw it for what it was. But I knew that I spoke to her last night. Akina brushed my shoulder. "Mike have you noticed that you haven't seen Darnell's mom around lately? In a nutshell she's gone AWOL and your mom and Aunt Ruth have gone after her to bring her back. That's probably why Avis has gone buck-wild. With Aunt Cil dying last year and the others gone, no one's around to keep her in check."

"What are you talking about?" I was still confused.

Uncle Paul took another shot at educating me. "If Carla is going to be saved it will have to be us. Your folks are out of reach right now. They'll be back, but they cannot get from where they are to here quickly enough to deal with Avis. It must be us. Now, since Akina was born I've sworn never to use my power again over spirits, but otherwise I will help you all I can."

"I didn't understand you in the park and I still don't understand. Can't anyone simply make all this very plain to me? Is this some kind of occult thing?"

Sandy turned her head slightly in puzzlement, "No, it is not, in fact, just the opposite. For whatever reason, God has chosen to bless your family with this mantle of power. And it passes between you much in the same way it passed from Elijah to Elisha. You have gifts. You can do things that the rest of us can't. But the problem is that demonic forces are always drawn to power. That's what has happened to Avis. She's given in completely to their influence. She has used her gift to gain dark knowledge, to the point where she now practices witchcraft. But there is no one here, at this table, casting spells."

Akina touched my hand. "But even if we were practicing Black Magic, what would it matter to you? You're an atheist, remember? Just meet us in the courtyard tonight at eight o'clock. We'll show you what we mean. Trust us." There she was playing the atheist card again, but I looked around the table and I knew. These were the people I loved, and they loved me. I didn't have that many friends. This was my family. They were all I had. If they lied or told the truth, it did not matter, for I was with them and they were with me. Thus it has always been and will always be. Ribbing or affectionate, true or false, they were my reality. I longed so much to be a part of them, to belong.

"I'll be there," I stated loudly. Perhaps too loudly given the subject matter and the fact that I wasn't the least bit certain of what I was agreeing to.

Akina left me with a parting thought. "If you really want to know who I believe we are, check out Genesis Six, verses one through four. I'm sure your momma left a Bible or two around where you could find one."

We departed the sub shop. Akina caught a cab with Uncle Paul. Darnell walked down the street back towards campus. Sandy and I walked briskly to the subway station. In fact, we lived off of the same busline, a mile apart, at least physically, that is. This brings us to the Sandy issue.

Sandy has always been the strangest bird in our flock. That's not her given name, but we all called her Sandy because in the summer she would get freckles. She had them all year long, but in the summer they'd really stand out. Really, any time of year they were the most adorable freckles I'd ever known. But there I go again, overplaying my hand.

When we were in high school together, the boys would try to catch her alone or trap her in a corner. They'd hold her against the wall, feeling all they wanted. She wouldn't raise her hands or say a word. She'd just stand there and take it, frightened and petrified like a little child. Eventually, if no one stepped in, the tears would come rolling down her face. Normally her tormentors, getting only tears and no moans of ecstasy, ceased their game. However, on several occasions she lost herself to them. See, when she was a child of eleven or so, an older boy molested her and she'd been messed up ever since. On her fifteenth birthday she was gang-raped. It happened one September after football practice. She caught a ride home with three of the players. I say "caught," but really it was more like coercion or Bullying 101. We took the bastards to court but they walked. Their defense was that she never said "no," all she did was cry. And the sickening thing is that half the school supported the players, saying she was stupid to get in a van with three football players, as though doing something dumb was a justification for rape. If doing something dumb was a justification to have someone abuse you then all of us would have a Sandy story to tell. That incident and the subsequent trial messed her and all of us up for a long time.

Sandy's such a squirrel, but still she was so much of my heart. Since we were little kids she's been the sweetest thing. When the other kids would make fun of me about the size of my head or the clothes I wore, she'd take up for me. I can remember sitting in the playground after the recess bell, crying, and there she would sit next to me until I was ready to go in or a teacher came out to get us.

We reached her house first. We stood on the front porch for a moment reminiscing about grade school days. With the mention of each name she smiled; those were mostly happy times for her. It was good, if only for a minute, to see her in good spirits again. Even I relaxed and shared a laugh or two. Then our impending agenda crept back into our consciousness. I gathered up my bag and kissed her quickly on the cheek. She gave me a curious look, opened the screen door a little, then paused and looked back at me again. She nodded slightly and went inside.

I was feeling a little awkward and unsure. It had been a strange week for us. Last weekend I had stopped over and after dinner (being a college student I rarely turned down a good meal) she decided she wanted to show me some of the moves she'd learned in the Judo classes we talked her into taking. Over the weeks, the course seemed to have improved her psyche. She was so much more confident. Unfortunately, my ego and lust got in the way. I guess I wanted to show her how much of a man I was. First she attempted a couple of thrusts that I deflected. Then she told me that's not really the way Judo works and asked me to rush her. She grabbed my arm and tried to flip me. But I stiffened, so when she turned and yanked my arm she succeeded only in landing me on her back. Amazingly to me, she carried me on her back for a few moments turning to the left a little. Then she crumpled to the carpet, with me still atop her back. Being the desperate, affection-starved individual I was, I lingered more than I should have, or at least that is how I remember it. Hey I'm not sure, but I did have a thing for the girl. Maybe I thought, no I hoped, she'd get caught up in the moment or something and profess her secret love for me. I told you I was a putz, didn't I? She lay beneath me, repeating "okay, okay," but neither moving nor taking action to remove me. Her body was so soft I couldn't help but hesitate. Was it even a second? If so, it was a second too long.

I know it sounds like I was so pathetic and maybe I was, but looking back on it now, and having learned more about myself, I'm not so sure what my intentions were. I think maybe it was a weak attempt to get the affection I was so desperate for. I didn't get much of that at home anymore with my mother being gone so much. Still, for that last week, and what I did, there really aren't any excuses. Are there really ever any for hurting someone you love? I mean, really?

So as I rolled off her onto the ivory-colored carpet next to her, I realized the full price for my indiscretion. Heaven forgive me.

Okay, okay... Okay, okay," she continued as she rolled over and pulled herself up resting her back against the beige wall. In that instant in which she lost control, Sandy was back in the moment of the rape, trapped inside of that van, with no hope. I pulled up beside her, offering my arm for her shoulder, but she was still panting and pushed me away. We sat side by side in silence for about fifteen minutes. When she finally got herself together, it was time for her to go to bed and I led her to the stairs. As she started up, she stopped, turned and stepped back down giving me a warm hug. That meant so much to me. It was like she was saying, "Thanks and you're still my boy." But couldn't she see what a jerk I was, what I'd become?

From what I learned much later, she and Carla stayed up half that night talking on the phone.

Now, a week later, she seemed better - or so I wished to believe. I went home to eat and let the dog out. I filled his food bowl with a week's worth of chow. I then took the bag over to a neighbor's house and asked them to check on him. When I was done I still had a couple of hours to kill before our rendezvous. So, naturally, I ate again. I toasted some bread and poured myself a bowl of frosted flakes. I clicked on the news. Before I could get two scoops down, there it was, on the national news: A story out of New Orleans about mutilated bodies found in the Mississippi. Damn it, Avis.

2: Reaching for the Light

Most of the crucial moments in our lives pass us by unrecognized. Only when looking back do we realize the true significance of each turn, each path taken or not taken in the life we have made. But sometimes we are in the moment and we know we are in the moment. This day was such a day for Jonah. He'd always had a sense of the future - not an exact knowledge of each event but a sense of what was to come. Before breakfast, something deep within him told him that this day was the day. All morning long nothing could dissuade him from this certainty. Waiting for lunchtime to arrive was sheer agony for Jonah, but it would prove worth the wait. During lunch he visited what was once known as the Smithsonian Museum. He had read an article about a new exhibit, which he knew instantly he had to see. As he entered the hall of the exhibit, he was sure his eyes were deceiving him or perhaps his wishful thoughts were deluding him. But his thoughts were true, as true as they had always been. There before him at lunch, was that which he had only heard whispered about as a small child, dreamed about as an adolescent and argued over as an adult: The Heart of Mystery, or The Princess Heart as it was sometimes known.

Jonah was nothing if not careful but that day he was so excited that all he wanted to do was run straight home to share with his wife of ten years, Monica. However, once again for Jonah, caution ruled the day and he kept off the main road, entering the brush.

At last, Jonah approached the fencing that separated the woods from the underpass. He slowly pushed through the precut opening in the fencing, which he himself had cut nearly eighteen months ago. He knew that it was time that they moved again, but this location had been working out so well that he hated the thought of moving. Moving was never fun and always risky and this time his wife, Monica, had really fixed up the little area they had excavated. That made it doubly hard to pick up and go somewhere else. Then again, he and Monica had stayed alive by being vigilant and smart in these years since the trouble started. He always had to pull her kicking and screaming, but she always respected his role as head of household and late at night she would curl up next to him and thank him for protecting the both of them. He did not enjoy making the hard decisions, but he decided long ago that he'd rather see his wife unhappy and safe than happy and in peril. Someone had to make the hard choices.

Reaching his destination, he knelt and rolled on his side through to the entrance. Lying prone, he inserted his key and turned the lock. Then pushing the door up, he rolled under it and once through, locked it back, knowing all the while that if the authorities came for them, that lock would only provide them time to make their peace with their Maker. Unlike their previous safe spots, this one had no back door, no hidden exit. He descended a small ladder to the dirt floor below taking a look around for his wife.

Rolling through the entrance always reminded him of the dream he had as a child. When he was a child of about four, Jonah remembered rolling down the large hill in front of his grandparent's apartment. The hill was at least fifty meters long and remarkably free of any sharp objects. As a child Jonah enjoyed the floating feeling he felt when he reached the bottom of the hill and extracted himself from the green summer grass. But on one occasion, on a certain day, things did not go as planned. At the end of that run, Jonah stumbled to his feet and inadvertently into a busy street, directly in the path of an oncoming truck carrying a load of sweet potatoes to market. As Jonah remembered it, as he stood he saw a young boy that looked exactly like himself standing across the street looking back at him. Then he glanced to his left to see the large truck as it was about to hit him. But in the next moment he was on the other side of the street standing where he'd seen himself looking back at where he'd stumbled into the street. The sweet potato truck sped on by and Jonah stood there dumbfounded. His rational mind could not accept such a thing so he reasoned that he must have been hallucinating. Or maybe it was a dream that was so lifelike that it became a false memory. After a time, Jonah accepted that explanation for what he'd experienced and the passage of time only served to reinforce that belief. Since that time he'd had other dreams that seemed real to him but these other dreams did not fit his waking reality either. He conveniently discounted all of them to some minor defect all his own, yet a part of him never let go of these dreams.

Jonah brushed off the grit he'd picked up rolling through the entrance before calling out for his wife. The surprisingly spacious room revealed no sign of her. Off to the left, was a latrine area, sealed off by a makeshift curtain. In the middle of the room was a couch of some sort. It was actually odds and ends pieced together to make something of a sitting apparatus. Since nothing of any size would fit through the entrance, everything inside was pieced together. To the right was a fireplace hearth, and though it contained ashes, neither he nor Monica had ever lit a fire there, nor would they. Along the back dirt wall were two lampposts shining dimly but brightly enough. In this room nothing was as it appeared to be, but all was as it was supposed to be. The toilet fed into the drainage pipe for the road above via a pump he installed.

The fireplace was kept full of ashes, but never used, because using it would create smoke and for people in hiding that would be bad. The ashes would lead one to believe that they had been there but were not now. And the lamps, they were nearly heatless. Nothing in that room had a heat signature beyond a meter or so.

Jonah studied his handiwork for a minute and then proceeded to the far right back corner. Stepping behind the lamp that was there, he reached into the dirt. He knew the spot so well that he no longer even needed to look. He smiled, as he did every time he found it. Turning the knob, a two foot wide, five feet high section of the wall swung slowly back. Slipping through the crack, he reached back around the door to smooth out the soil hiding that precious knob. He pushed the door shut, eclipsing himself in the blackness.

This most modest-appearing habitat had a most industrious attribute. Behind the back wall, half a level down, existed a twenty-by-fifteen foot room shrouded in total darkness. There were no lights in this room. No windows of any kind. Not only was there no piercing light, the walls were actually lined in a tapestry of lightproof, soundproof and heatproof fabric acquired by Jonah, stitched together by Monica and hung by the both of them. A device in the corner prevented scanning by x-rays and other forms of energy.

His eyes having not adjusted to the darkness, Jonah called for his beloved, "Monica?"

"Hmm...," slowly came a moan from somewhere in the darkness.

He stooped down a bit and then called again, "Monica?"

From the mat on the floor she sat up to meet his probing hand. "Hey, baby."

Like the knob, he knew this feel very well too and smiled. Without speaking another word he slid from his robes and into the arms of his wife who was reaching up to him. All the way home he had thought of nothing but how he was going to tell his wife about his great find. But now, in the moment, he was suddenly aware of what he had already found.

He had known her since he had known life itself. Born six months before him, her family lived two doors down from his. She was a thin little girl with dark brown skin, wavy hair and a captivating smile that would put anyone at ease. Her family was much more mixed than his. She thought she was mostly African-American and Indian, but some days, at least to Jonah she looked almost Mediterranean. The wavy hair made him think of Helen of Troy. He spent the first six years of his life chasing this girl. Then suddenly, right before his seventh birthday, she and her family moved away. He still remembered feeling like he'd lost his only friend. Their parents kept in touch at first, but as the years passed they eventually lost contact with one another. During most of his adolescent years he would think about her often, particularly when he was feeling low about his own social life, or the lack thereof. He would imagine that she was his girlfriend and how different his life would be if she were with him.

Then, in the spring of his senior year in college, everything changed. He'd just arrived at his second job interview of the week. Having been offered an engineering position with a company out of state, he was attempting to land a spot with one of the local firms. She, having opted not to go to college until her finances got a little better, was working at the firm to earn money for college. Walking into the reception area he noticed her as soon as she looked up, but he was very much unsure. Over the years he'd seen other girls on the street that looked somewhat like the girl he'd known before, so he held his tongue and his thoughts. Then, as he approached the desk to announce himself and his intent, she smiled and said hello. He knew in an instant that it was her. The very sound of her voice was enough but there was more.   The curvature of her lips as she formed the words trickling from her mouth, spoke explicit volumes to him of her identity. He could never doubt that smile. Looking down, he spoke "Monica?"

"Jonah?" she asked the same of him.

All the time he remained in the waiting area neither of them could contain their excitement over one another. His interview came and afterwards they went to lunch. [He can still remember how easily they spoke to each other. How he felt he'd known her all his life.]

They dated all summer and got married seven months later. Quite predictably, he was offered and accepted the position at the local firm where she worked. She quit her job and took a job working with disabled children, but she never began school even though Jonah encouraged her to do so.

Facing down now he thought about the Heart of Mystery, but then thought again. He pondered, in this world what gift to any man is there more precious than a woman? Monica was about five-foot-five in height and of medium build, but she was no longer "thin". And though she looked much more South Asian than African-American, a fact that came in handy during this new age, there was plenty of "sister" in this woman. Her mother raised her in a manner that she thought would be consistent with attracting a rich suitor. And that meant learning to hold her tongue, but that lesson never took. Monica had always been one to speak her mind, and her mother couldn't "fix" that. Also, her mother had been a bit underwhelmed when she married Jonah. Although she thought him better than average, he was in no way what she had in mind for Monica. "Better to be a rich man's mistress, than a poor man's wife," she always said to Monica. Jonah had been neither, thus she was lukewarm towards him. But behind closed doors she would whisper to her only daughter, "Well, you're a pretty girl; you can always trade up later. Just don't wait too long."

Some would say that Monica's husband was a bit "frosty". But she knew this wasn't true. He did not express his emotions as freely as others and she'd never seen him cry, but he was truly one of the most caring men she'd ever met.

Jonah slid down to the mat and kissed Monica. Curled behind her, he spoke softly into her ear. "How was your day?"

"How was my day?" she responded, twisting her head around to make sure he heard her. "You're the one. Coming in here all revved up and all. How was your day? What happened?"

"Well, you remember those crazy stories my old aunt used to tell? Remember the one she used to tell about the Egyptian, but not so Egyptian Artifact? The Heart?"

"Yeah, I think so. A little bit anyway."

"Well, I think I've found it. I went to the museum at lunch today and there it was, at last. Not in a special case or anything. It was just there sitting on a shelf with about five other religious artifacts. It was just as my aunt described it. It was three or four inches wide and about five inches tall, apple-shaped, and laced with four circular bands wrapped around an amber challis. Just beneath the amber was something dark. So dark that the object was not translucent, but only within the arcs of it could you see the amber catch the light. The bands that encircled it were gold and engraved with the words Auntie said. Baby, that's our ticket out of here!"

Even though their existence there was precarious and she knew it wasn't sane to think this way, curled up next to him, the thought of leaving saddened her a bit. She liked to think that no matter what their living conditions, her presence in his life would be enough to satisfy his needs, to make him happy. Upon returning to reality she asked him, "So what are you going to do?"

"I've never stolen anything in my life, but the thing was stolen from us, my family. It belongs to me. Besides, we're talking life and death here. We've got to get it."

"So how are you going to get it? You're not a thief. Are you sure you need to be the one to get it?"

"Who else can do it? Most of our family is dead and those who are alive and hiding like us don't want to be found. Plus, even if I could find someone willing to do it, how could I ask such a thing of someone else? It has to be me."

"Does it really? I don't know…"

"Monica, trust me. I can do this."

Gripping his arm more tightly she twisted onto her back and turned her head to face him, "Baby, it's just that with all that has gone on, all the killing and confusion, I don't want to lose what we have here. I blend in perfectly and Karun will look out for you. You make a lot of money for him, you know. It's not so bad here, is it?"

Kissing her on the cheek and pulling close again he answered, "No baby, it's not. But you have to understand, that while for now we still get by, it's only a matter of time before we get caught. Yeah, we got a better set up than most and we have truly been blessed. But what happens next year, or ten years from now? What about when we get old? What if something were to happen to Karun or the government should find a new way to find us? What then? Baby we have to take charge of this situation or it will take charge of us. So are you okay with this?"

"No, but what choice do I have."

"Hmmm, I really do have this all figured out."

"Oh, I know you do. You wouldn't have brought it up if you hadn't already figured it out."

"So what's the problem?"

"Okay, okay, but I want you to tell me the whole plan."

"Sure." Finally she had said the words he wanted to hear.

"You know we need to pray on this."

Sitting up he responded, "Heaven knows I know that."

They both stood and walked to the far corner. Jonah knelt while Monica picked up a wet cloth and wiped the Bindi from her forehead. She then knelt beside him and they began to pray.

When they were done they got back in the bed and agreed to talk about it in the morning being that the next day was an off day for both of them.

Lying there, Jonah was flushed with a feeling of excitement and anticipation. This was a new feeling for him, but he found that he liked it.

3. A Change is Gonna Come

Sandy and I arrived at the meeting site first, or so we thought. We proceeded to the open area in front of the high school. Stone benches lined the courtyard. There were two long benches, one on each side, and four benches on the top and bottom. The two benches on the top and bottom were split by a pathway from the street. That pathway led to the school's front door. I led Sandy to the bench where she and I always met after school when we both were students there. After the birthday thing happened to her, I always made it a point to meet her there after school. That is the one aspect of our past lives at this school that I do miss.

"Michael," (she seldom used Mike), "I think we're the first ones here."

"No, not quite," came a voice from above. We turned to see Darnell on a limb perched high above us. It was dark already and he would've been hard to see up there even in broad daylight.

I had to be the one to ask the obvious question, "What are you doing up there?"

"Making sure we don't have any uninvited guests," he responded with ultimate certainty.

"Ohhh-kay," I muttered, still not sure of what he was doing up there. I looked to Sandy, but she just shrugged her shoulders. Just then all three of us turned to see a yellow taxi pull up to the curb. Out of it popped Akina and Uncle Paul. Instead of racing ahead of him like she did back at the diner, Akina walked evenly beside Uncle Paul.

Akina smiled, "Hi." She was back to her steady, self-assured, but friendly self. She looked up to Darnell and waved quickly. He stood up, stepped off of the limb, and descended

41

rapidly to the ground, managing not to fall. It was as if you or I had stepped off of a curb, but for him it was thirty or forty feet. I was not given to fits of excitement or easily alarmed. I was a true cynic. Still, my jaw nearly fell off its hinges as I instinctively reached for him before realizing that he didn't need my help.

"What the...?!" I was left absent of a word to finish my thought. "Darnell, are you all right? You just... I mean..."

"I know," he laughed. "I think the fact that you saw me do it, means you'll be doing crazy stuff too after a while."

"What do you mean?" I asked, truly bewildered by his point.

"If you are called to be like us, then you will see, we all will," Darnell said as he grabbed my shoulder.

"Hunh?"

"Just wait," he encouraged me.

I followed them to the front door of the school building. Akina reached into her purse, pulled out a key and inserted it into the lock. She laughed as she punched in the codes to de-activate the alarm, "It pays to be student representative on the campus grounds committee." She gave me a wink as she ushered us in.

I hesitated to follow them. I'd never done anything close to this. I'm a joker, not a fool. She may have been authorized to be there off hours, still I was sure that I was going to visit the inside of a jail for the first time in my life that night.

"Michael, come on." Akina called back to me. Up one hall and down another to a tenth-grade English classroom we scurried.

"I bet we've tripped every motion detector in the building," I quipped, as I entered the room. Code or no code, I figured those things are always on down at the precinct. No one responded to my charge, they just looked at me.

Akina called out, "Over there...," while motioning towards a back corner. Immediately Darnell and Sandy cleared out the desks from the corner as Akina sat on the floor with her back in the corner. I helped Uncle Paul to the floor. He and Darnell sat to Akina's right. Sandy motioned for me to come over and sit next to her. I tossed around my bag banging my back against the wall and slithered down to the floor as I stared at her and then Akina.

"What's going on?" I whispered into Sandy's ear. I thought that we were all meeting at the school to drive down together to New Orleans, but at that moment it looked like we were getting ready to have prayer or something. I started to think that maybe my cousins were a part of some weird cult, and that this was going to be some kind of indoctrination for me. I didn't like that thought very much and started wondering how I was going to get out of this.

Sandy tilted her head towards me, "Shhh, you'll see."

Akina sat there in the middle looking as relaxed as ever and asked, "Is everyone ready?"

All nodded but me, as I was too busy glancing around the room trying to read just what the heck was going on here.

Akina started up, "Michael..."

Before she could finish, Sandy butted in, "Oh Michael, this is the important part. You must close your eyes."

"Okay?" I said, giving a hesitant surrender.

"Alright then, let's do this," Akina announced, as first Darnell and then the rest of them nodded in agreement.

They closed their eyes, and seeing them, so did I.

As I closed my eyes, my thoughts drifted to my mother.

It was just at that moment that I noticed warmth on my forehead and then my cheeks.

I opened my eyes to a crawling Mississippi river. In what seemed to be a blink of the eye we had found ourselves in the French Quarter of New Orleans. We were all sitting on the grass in front of a park bench facing the river. To the right was the Aquarium of the Americas and back to the left, Jax's restaurant. Behind us down below was a parking lot and just to the left of it a softly sleeping Hard Rock Café. A piece of waxed paper, still dusty from the Beignet it may have held the night before, danced by.

My cousins conversed causally, but I sprung up to my feet bedazzled by my apparent teleportation. "Uhhh, uhhh, where are we?" I knew where we were, but the words flowed from my mouth like some predestined force of will.

"As my girl Carla would say, we're in N'awlins," chuckled Akina. They all stood up, slapping their behinds and thighs to dislodge the blades of grass there upon.

Darnell helped Uncle Paul up. He then slapped me on the right shoulder once and then again holding his hand there and squeezing my shoulder muscles, "Pretty neat, huh? With a hook up like this who needs frequent flyer points?" Wheeling back to his left he spoke respectfully to Uncle Paul, "So does Avis still live in the Garden District?"

"Yes, I believe so."

"Well, I think we can catch a cab down here," Darnell quipped back.

Uncle Paul twisted his old head up, "Boy, you need to slow down."

Akina jumped in for Darnell this time, "What about Carla?"

"There's no need to go rushing off there. Anything Avis is gonna do to her she already did it last night or she'll wait until tonight. That's one thing she got from her mama. She don't do much spell casting in the daytime. Not that she can-'t, but she seems to enjoy it so much more in the darkness. I think you'd say she gets inspired. Plus, we gained a day coming here." Now this last part about us gaining a day just went right by me at the time. I didn't know what in the world he was talking about. I heard him say it clearly, but I figured he's old, so I let it slide. I found out later just what had happened to us.

Frustrated, Darnell mustered a stare back to Uncle Paul and the others, "But Uncle Paul... Carla needs us, and we're wasting time..."

"Darnell!" Uncle Paul raised his voice.

Finally Darnell relented. "Yes sir. So what are we going to do?" Knowing how Darnell loves his sister, even this moment-ary pause in his efforts was a major concession, and only accomplished by Darnell's sense of respect for his elders and Uncle Paul. This was made even more difficult by the fact that in the last year or so it was becoming clear that Uncle Paul's mind was beginning to slip a bit. But still, out of re-spect, he listened.

"Darnell, you know we need a plan." Akina broke in, read-ing Uncle Paul's mind it seemed. Their thoughts were so sim-ilar we sometimes looked at Akina as Uncle Paul II. It was al-most as though he were passing his mantle on to her and all her life had been preparation for this day when she would be-gin to shine, even as he began to fade away.

Uncle Paul turned to face the river, somehow sensing where it was, and spoke as quietly and affirmingly as the river itself. "See, there is something each of you must under-stand. There is more at stake here than your cousin Carla's freedom. I fought this day long and hard. I prayed never to see this day. But now we find ourselves at this crossroad. I was here before. I made a choice from which much good did come, but also a lot of pain. I pray that each of you chooses only as you are led, but I don't think any of you understands the weight of the cross you pick up today. In time you will understand."

Akina stood at Uncle Paul's side, staring out over the river as regal as anyone I'd ever seen. The question crossed my mind "...and I'm related to this child? She's so together and I'm so pathetic." Uncle Paul took the hat he'd been holding at his side in his right hand and in one smooth motion placed it on his head. With that, he imparted upon us a simple request, "Let's walk a bit."

As we walked back toward Bay Street, which ran parallel to the river, Darnell took up a position to Uncle Paul's right to lead him. Akina was to his left. Sandy and I followed. And while everyone else was on to the advanced question round, I was still stuck in remedial mode. So finally, I asked the question. "So Sandy, just what is the deal here? How did we get here?" I asked her with my jaw still hanging open.

"Mmmm... how can I say this? Your cousins have these talents."

"Talents?! Talents?!" I cried. "Playing the piano is a talent. Being able to juggle is a talent. But this... oooh, I don't think 'talent' quite gets it. Just what in the world did she do to us?"

Sandy swallowed hard then spoke cautiously, "Well I can't say that I actually know, not the details anyway. I know she can make us disappear from one place and then have us show up in another. I know that she can disappear right from in front of your eyes. You blink and she's gone. She does some other stuff too."

I cried again, "Other stuff too! What's that supposed to mean? Oh, don't even go there yet. Let's go back to us getting from Atlanta to New Orleans in the blink of an eye."

"Well, it was a blink of the eye, but remember we left at night and it's now morning. See we changed places and times. Actually, we've returned to this morning."

I leaned against a lamppost and exclaimed to the group, "Hold up y'all, all of this is making my head hurt."

Akina, turned and walked back to me. Then, grabbing my arm encouraged me to keep walking as she pleaded in my ear, "Faith Michael, have a little faith. You do remember that concept from confirmation, right? I know all of this is a bit much for you right now, but you will understand and you will have your role, at the appropriate time."

"Appropriate time? So, this ain't it?" I said as incredulously as ever.

Akina spoke in a quiet tone, which was meant to quiet me too. "Like we said, we all have gifts. That includes you too."

"So what is my gift?"

"Well, that's the funny part. I know but I can't tell you. But I'm pretty certain that this is the weekend you find out."

"How do you know that? What, tea leaves?" I cried.

"I really can't tell you that right now out here in the open. And I can't tell you about your gift at all. I mean I could tell you, but you wouldn't believe me. But just wait and before the sun sets tomorrow, you will know. Yes, you will know and nothing will ever be the same. Not you, not us, nothing in this world will be the same. This is your life, right here, right now." She stared intensely into my eyes for a moment and then dropped her hard grip on my arm, moving back to her position next to Uncle Paul as he walked on.

Sandy smiled at me and placed her arm on my shoulder, "Come on."

I started to think to myself, "So, this is how crazy people feel." I began to try to think of what could have all of a sudden made me snap like that. Maybe this was some sort of inherited mental malady that was hereto unknown to modern science.

Sandy continued to drag me down the sidewalk, while the others carried on in some coded dialogue.

I have to admit, I'd always felt like something was missing in my life, but I always thought like maybe I needed a girlfriend, a profession, lots of cash or maybe even whiter teeth.

You know, stuff like that. Needless to say I never imagined anything like this.

However, though on one level I was trying to accept what they said, most of my conscious mind was still spinning trying to figure out how they pulled this off. Surely not even these pranksters would have the nerve to pull off a hoax this big. Plus, with Uncle Paul here, that reasoning just wouldn't fly. Besides, if I were nuts, just how could I reason anything anyway? So, the whole exercise was pointless, right? Then there was still the issue with the photographs of him as well as lots of other loose ends that only seemed to have come into focus in the last twenty-four hours.

Little incidents that I had discounted as childhood imaginations and nightmares now seemed like puzzle pieces for which this was the final piece.

I felt an urge to look to Heaven for some sort of sign, but I knew that I didn't believe, so I didn't. I had taken great aim to bring about every cynicism regarding religion and faith that I could in recent conversations at school. In fact, I was beginning to gain quite a "rep" in that regard... but deep down I can't say that I felt good about any of it.

I noticed that they all suddenly seemed to be walking awfully fast... but then I realized that it was me slowing down. I grabbed a hold of the lamppost and called out to them, "Hey hold up y'all, I don't feel so good. I think all of this head-popping crap is giving me a migraine."

I tried to hold on to the post, but it was suddenly very slippery and I fell to the sidewalk, panting. I felt like I was in a sauna with a fur coat on.

They all walked back to me and rather than helping me up they just stood around looking down at me sitting on the sidewalk. Darnell spoke first, "I think it's starting to happen."

Akina placed her hand on my forehead, "Yeah. Son, I think you're right this time. This is it. Help him up."

Darnell grabbed me under my right armpit and wrapped his left arm around me supporting me. Akina hailed us a cab and they poured me into it. Then they all climbed into the cab as well. Uncle Paul gave the driver an address somewhere just beyond the Garden District. After that, during the remainder of the trip the only words that were muttered were "How much?" by Uncle Paul.

We all got out of the cab and I realized that I felt much better than I had ten minutes earlier.

The street we exited on was nice, but there was such a sadness about it. Not even knowing the worst of it at that point, I could have told anyone that no one danced around there. The Spanish moss was the only garland on a sad parade of dying 300-year-old trees and cemeteries up and down the street.

Uncle Paul reached out to touch one of the trees and then raised his right arm to point to a large two-story home that stood well off the street, "That's her house over there." It was as if even the trees had borne witness to Avis's deeds and somehow, Uncle Paul could hear their testimony.

There were six large white columns outlining the front porch of the house. There were no signs of life. No cats, no birds on the wrought iron gate surrounding the property, no blossoms on any of the bushes lining the porch. The wind swirled all around us sweeping leaves to and fro, but not a leaf stirred in that yard.

Akina spoke up, "Carla's in there. I know it."

But then Uncle Paul's face took on the look of a seasoned master inspecting the work of a protégé, "But how much do you feel it?"

She closed her eyes and breathed in deeply, "Only vaguely. It's like she's there and then she's not. It's like she's not all there. What is that?"

Uncle Paul stroked his beard as he answered slowly, but knowingly, "I suspect they have her bound down between two worlds. They can't send her to the next world, because not even they could bring a mortal like her back, but they dare not keep her in this one, because a telepath like Carla, even sleeping could be a danger to all of them. They'll wait until around midnight, when they're stronger, and feel that she is weaker, to wake her for their amusement."

Darnell twisted his head back as he peered back over his shoulder towards us, "So, does that mean we can go in now?" His hands tightly gripped the black metal rods surrounding the grounds.

Uncle Paul attempted to mellow him, "I don't know, but I don't think it would be wise to bust in there with Carla in her current state. We need her fully in this world before we take her back. The only thing is that they might be expecting us."

"What is this 'they' stuff? I thought we were just dealing with Avis." That didn't sound good to me.

Uncle Paul complimented me, "Good observation. Well, of course you have Avis, then you got all those she might have currently enchanted, maybe even Carla. Plus, you got whatever demons she may have conjured up."

"Conjured?"

"Yes, conjured," my uncle said back to me before turning and walking away. Sandy followed immediately, taking his arm, as Akina pulled Darnell from the fence. He would have stayed there the rest of his life, but he knew Uncle Paul was right and that there was little they could do now but make things worse. I was beginning to understand but I was still somewhat confused and still trying to digest it all. I lingered, staring blankly at Avis's house. How could it all come to this? I hadn't seen her since I was a small child, but I still had warm memories of Christmas and her entertaining me and the other little cousins. She wasn't much more than a child herself as she tried to raise Akina and still, still she was one of us.

I began to come to myself and turn away when a whisper came upon me. I heard the sound of a child calling my name, begging me not to leave. Then I heard an even more faint voice of a man pleading "Make it stop, please make it stop..." Hearing him startled me. I began to look around, trying to locate the voice speaking to me. Then, for a moment, and then another, the shade of a woman appeared before me, stretching her arms out to me. She cried to me, "Please take me with you. I could make you happy."

Those voices had me turning every which way. Although I saw nothing full on, every corner of my eyes held a glimpse of fear.

Suddenly, I felt a hand grab my arm and I jumped about four feet to my left, further out into the street.

"Whoa! Michael calm down. It's me Sandy. You okay?"

"Sandy, yeah.... Hey, did you see that?"

"See what?" she said in all honesty, her face somewhere between smiling and puzzlement, but innocent as always.

I tried again, "I just saw something... and I heard it too. It was right here calling my name asking me to take it, no her, or maybe it was them... I don't know. Oh my God, you didn't see what just happened?"

She said nothing, but the look on her face again, just flexed back and forth between emotions.

Akina had drifted back to us and couldn't resist a snipe at me as she smiled slightly, "There you go again, calling on the

Lord. I thought you were an atheist? Hmmm. Come on, let's go. We'll be back later." Then taking another look at my terrified expression as she dragged me along, she said, "Kid, you ain't seen nothing yet!"

4. See Me As I Am...
or Rather How I Wish To Be

Jonah awoke early that Saturday morning and after assuring his wife that he would indeed be back for their "discussion", he took off for that day's adventure. Like any man, he neither enjoyed nor looked forward to playing "Twenty Questions" with his woman, but he understood that it was just one of those things that had to be done.

Jonah got to his destination and just stood at the edge of the forest staring at it. It was the old plant he used to work at before everything blew up, literally. In the riots nearly ten years ago, order and structure at the factory had been a casualty. A mob of Blue people, the dominant class and harbingers of the current state of affairs, set the plant ablaze for being too friendly to "his kind", non-Blues. Not that they actually were, because he knew for a fact that they weren't all that nice as things broke down, but their ad campaign implied that they were. And isn't that what really mattered?

He worked in the new products division and often wondered about whatever happened to all the products he designed. He thought about the many product lines he'd worked on, but he thought most about the products that he himself had constructed. The two he cherished most were "The Excavator" and the "Wave Modulator". The Excavator was a relatively small hand-held device that could change the state of materials within its target area. It could change solids to liquids, liquids to gases or visa-versa and all the permutations in between. He thought the solid to liquid was a real coup although it seemed the marketplace thought otherwise. The device never saw the production line. The guys in marketing came back to him to build several prototypes to use in their pitches, but they'd never gotten an order. They claimed that they had trouble with it in the field. Jonah thought that perhaps the marketing guys were the trouble, by being a bit hard-headed in their sales approach. The Wave Modulator was his last big innovation before things broke down. The Wave Modulator could project a seemingly impenetrable field. The field could pretty much take on any geometric shape Jonah could think of. Jonah could use the protective field to encircle himself or project it into or around other objects as well. Thankfully for him and Monica, he'd been able to salvage two of each before the night of the fire.

Jonah stood there, breathing in deeply and then out slowly, letting go of all the self-doubt that gnawed at him constantly. It was time to move on. This was a new day and all those regrets would only hold him back from his future.

He climbed the pitiful fence with relative ease. The fence had now become a joke, but when he first started doing this it was quite formidable. Neglect had won out as it often does, neglect and a penchant of the locals to scavenge the barbed wire for their own purposes. The remainder of the debris was of little use to anyone but Jonah. He'd found many useful items here before and he was amazed at what a gold mine it still seemed to be. Then again he figured that most folks just assumed that there was toxic stuff buried all around there, and there was, but Jonah knew for a fact what was hazardous and what wasn't. He avoided the trouble areas. His biggest concern wasn't the toxins, but rather whether or not he'd gone to the well one too many times. And this time he really didn't know what he was looking for, but figured that he'd know it when he crossed paths with it.

Jonah needed something that would help him with his mission to get back the Heart of his family without too much ado. He had the Excavator (he'd given his wife the other one he took that night), but while it would ensure him an entrance, it wasn't the subtlest thing. No, he needed a way that would allow him some time, days or weeks, afterwards to fiddle with his loot, to see what he could do with it. After all he wasn't too sure of just what it would do. For a brief moment he began to doubt the saneness of all of this. "I must be a fool!" He laughed at himself, and with that laugh his mood lifted and he moved on. Every significant accomplishment in his life had been done by Faith anyway, so why should it change?

Besides, what Monica didn't understand is that more than actually finding the Heart, he needed to find a hope to hang on to. Despair was never too far away, even in the best of times. There were days when he'd feel the panic coming on so strong that he'd have to stop and pray just to steel himself. He avoided the silence, because it allowed the thoughts to creep in. Keeping busy had become his crutch. Deep down he knew that if he didn't keep busy, the darkness within him would devour him, or so he thought. Maybe it was good for her that she didn't understand after all.

Also, the story of the Heart had inspired Jonah since the first time his auntie told it to him. The tale about a foremother of his, who had become mad with power and how she sacrificed herself so that she might not hurt anyone else, was a very strong definition of love to him. Jonah was enamored with the affection she showed for those she would never meet and how she gave her own heart in a last act of love. The symbolism made quite an impression on him as a small child and so it remained to that day.

Jonah kicked and turned over everything in the yard near where his lab had been and then did it again. And still nothing came to him. But then he thought about the dreams he'd been having. He couldn't quite make sense of the dreams but he trusted that God would allow him to understand them in time.

In one recurring dream, Jonah found himself the shepherd of a herd of goats that had strayed dangerously close the woods. As the sun set, the wayward goats were headed for trouble. There were wolves in the forest and in Jonah's dream he could hear them growl. Jonah cried out for the goats to turn around, but they did not heed his call because he was not their master. And although he wanted to leave the goats to their fate, he remained with them into the woods, even as the wolves approached. But right before the wolves were to strike, Jonah heard the Master's call, "Are you ready?"

In his dream Jonah replied, "Yes, Master, but your goats will not follow me. How can I bring them to you?"

Again the Master asked, "Are you ready for whatever may come?"

"Master, my stick is sturdy, but there are so many and they are so scattered, how can I save them all?"

One last time his Master asked, "Are you or are you not ready?"

Up until about six months ago, that is where these dreams always ended.

But lately the dreams were different. For the last couple of months it was the same almond-eyed little girl asking him the same unfathomable question, "Are you, or are you not?" At the time he could not understand the question, much less accept the answer. As the weight of this question of what role he should play in God's plan weighed on him, Jonah looked up as he tried to accept whatever it was that God was trying to tell him. As he looked up, he saw a bird's nest and marveled at how after all that had come to pass in this land of evil, these smallest of creatures seemed to have hardly noticed. Jonah thought about how, in their nests, they'd escaped all the changes on the ground below. Then, just as if on queue, it struck him — a way to get in and out with the Heart without anyone knowing the difference.   He'd been going about this all wrong. It was so simple... so, so beautifully simple.

Jonah arrived back home, as carefully as ever, to find his wife cooking dinner as best she could given the circumstances. Due to their situation, they were forced to use low emission technology.   Basically, it was heat transfer technology that Jonah had pieced together from the scrap yard. Still it was a very manual process. Monica's moist hands held the peeled potatoes tightly, as she sliced them. No blenders, food processors or microwaves could be found in her kitchen. But there was love in every dish. Her head swung around as Jonah entered the room. She didn't waste a moment. "So, what's the deal? What did you decide?"

Jonah offloaded the few things he had carried back from the technical graveyard.   He figured this conversation would be the hardest part of the whole thing. Getting Monica to buy in just wasn't going to be easy. He thought for a moment that maybe while he was at the plant he should have been looking for a way to get her to not play Twenty Questions with him, but he knew much better men than he had tried and failed in that endeavor. He sat down at the little makeshift table behind the cooking area and motioned for her to do the same. He took a deep breath and began. "Here's the deal. It's so simple, it's beautiful. See, all I do is go in some time in the afternoon before the museum closes. I find someplace like a broom closet or restroom where I can climb up into the drop ceiling.   Then I wait until the museum closes. Once it closes..."

She cut him off, like a sneeze. Her words were like an involuntary reflex that she could not control. "You're gonna hide in the ceiling? How you gonna do that? Don't they check stuff like that?"

"No, I don't think so?" he said honestly.

"You don't think so! Have you really thought this through? You have got to be kidding me," she said with the most incredulous look on her face.

"You haven't heard the rest of it yet...." He attempted to retake the floor.

"I don't want to hear anymore. Just what you've told me is not going to work."

"Well, just listen and let me finish..." Cut off again.

"Don't you think if it were that simple, folks would be robbin' and stealin' from there all the time? Huh?"

"Can you just let me finish?"

"Why? It's a bad plan."

"But I haven't even told you the plan yet!"

"You told me enough for me to know it's a bad one."

"Why do you always do this?" he said with some firmness. "You just jump all over my ideas. Haven't I done, by God's grace, pretty good by us? Huh? Sometimes you talk to me like I'm stupid."

Sensing his hurt, Monica reached out a bit. "Baby, I do appreciate what you've done for us. And I think you are really bright. But that doesn't mean you know everything. And as your wife I think I have a responsibility to say something when you're going off track a little bit."

"But you haven't even heard all of the plan yet. How do you know it's a bad plan? I mean you just jump in and cut me off. I'm your husband; you should at least let me finish a statement."

"That's just it; you made your point. What more could you say that could fix what you said in the beginning?" Monica retorted.

He sat quietly, holding his tongue as best he could. They both sat quietly for a moment. And it wasn't that Jonah was without thoughts. He had them, but they were mean-spirited, bridge-burning thoughts that were better kept to one's self. In their marriage he'd tried to avoid saying things just to win an argument. Jonah figured out early on that the win-at-all-costs approach in an argument served only to lose all in the long run. Then Monica broke the silence. "Okay, go ahead. I'll be quiet."

He could tell that she had become a bit emotional about the topic and he knew that their current predicament and his wanting to change things might be freaking her out just a bit. So he saturated his words with as much compassion as he could. "Once I'm in the ceiling, I wait until they close..."

"You said this already..." He started to object and she cut in again. "Okay, Okay, but you're taking too long." Her patience was thin that day.

"When they're closed, I'll slip down and grab the Heart and use the Excavator to cut a hole in the wall to escape. I'll use the Wave Modulator to hide me from their cameras and motion detectors. Sure, once I cut a hole in the wall, I'll set off a bunch of alarms, but at that point who cares. They'll be looking in the building and I'll be long gone."

"That's it? You're done?" she asked looking at him intently.

"Yeah, pretty much." He wanted to say more but felt like he couldn't.

"And what is it again that this thing is supposed to do?" she continued.

"You know what it does," he replied, somewhat under his breath.

"Supposed to do," she said with inflection. "Please just tell me again."

Now speaking even more under his breath, Jonah replied, "It's supposed to be able to teleport you."

"Teleportation! That old rusty thing is supposed to teleport you? To where?" she queried, not that there was going to be a right answer.

"Anywhere you want to go... Really."

"And you believe that?" See, there was no right answer. "You're willing to risk your life for that? For a fantasy?"

"I don't believe it's a fantasy." Jonah gave his most sincere answer.

"Teleportation? Come on, let's get real. Jonah, that's not reality."

"Baby, I understand your concern." Jonah was now trying a little charm where logic was failing. "Don't you remember what Auntie told us?"

Monica gave an unenthusiastic, "Hmm."

Jonah continued, "Don't you remember the gifts she had, the things she could do, the way..."

Monica cut in again, "You mean those tricks she used to do? They were the tricks any magician could do. Plus, we were children. I'm sure our memories make more of it than they ever were."

"But I was still there after you moved away. And until she left, she was still doing those things. Monica, baby, I tell you with all my heart, I really do believe that there is something to this."

"Hmmm. Well, if you're so sure why don't you just go in there and grab it when the place is open and just poof away?"

He thought she might ask this. It was a very good question he thought and one that might show she was beginning to soften. "Well, I think I'll need some time with it first to figure out how it works."

"So, you do have some doubts?" She hadn't bought in completely he could see.

"Well, I am certain, that if I can get some time with it, that I can figure it all out."

"Jonah, this is not one of your lab toys. I can't even believe that you are considering this."

At that point, for a moment, he regretted even telling her about his ambitions. For a moment, he thought that he should have just gone ahead and done it. But then he remembered that he had always tried to include her in everything he did. They were supposed to be one, one mind and one flesh. "I know, it sounds a bit out there. But think about all the incredible things that are going on today. Even the Excavator twenty years ago would have been thought impossible."

"But darling, all those things were based on science. This is not. Are you really willing to risk your life for this?" She was careful not to mention her life as well. She wasn't ready to go Nuclear on him emotionally with the tears and the whole nine... yet. She was still willing to reason.

"Well, baby," and he hesitated even to say this. "There are some things that you can't explain, but you know in your heart that they are true, because you have seen evidence of them or felt them. You know like..."

"I know you're not trying to compare this to our Faith, are you?"

"All I'm saying is that I know there is something to this. All my adulthood, I've tried to discount and wash away those things I saw as a kid, the things that happened and those things I feel now. But I can't. It's like denying my own existence. I realize how hard this is for you to understand. So, tell me how can I prove this to you? How can I make you understand?"

Monica looked at him in silence for long moments, trying her best to see things as he saw them. But in those same moments a part of her didn't want to see things as he saw them. She held on to the part of her that said this is foolish, and this man is a fool. Smart but completely foolish, that's what the voice in her head said. So in some dialogue within, from her subconscious, the thought appeared of an alternative. It led her to suggest, "Okay, tell you what, can we do this instead? Can you at least discuss this with Karun? He's really smart too, like you, and together I'm sure you can come up with something. If not this plan of yours, then something else." There it was, said as smoothly, logically and convincingly as she could have dared imagine. She had shown compassion for his point of view, while maneuvering her demand of having Karun review it. She knew Karun very well, and she was certain that he'd see the plan for the foolishness she knew well that it was. She banked on the certainty that the two of them objecting to his scheme would shut it down cold and she would avoid once again being the heavy.

As for Jonah, he knew this was going to come up at some point in their conversation. Karun was Monica's friend first from her early teens. After Jonah and Monica reconnected, they began hanging out with Karun and his then girlfriend, Manisha. And while Jonah's friendship with Karun before the meltdown had been through Monica, they'd formed a bond of their own. When things turned ugly, Karun was willing to risk all to protect Monica and Jonah. But still, although Jonah liked Karun very much and thought the world of him as a person, friend and employer, he had no delusions; it was Monica that held a special place in his heart. And in fact, he believed with all his heart that if Karun had not been earmarked for someone else back in India or if Monica had been of his caste, he would have pursued a relationship with Monica, with all the desire that he himself once had. Karun's name was mentioned often in their home, and Monica respected him and his views so much (more than his own he felt), that it discouraged something deep inside of him. He could never say anything about this secret pain, because he was ashamed of it. Karun was a good man, the kind of man whose heroic deeds if discovered many years later, would be glorified in plays and movies, as they should be. How could he resent this man?

In the end he conceded with a soft, "Okay."

It wasn't the outcome he'd hoped for, but it was progress. And knowing his wife, this was actually quite a start to things, or at least that is what he tried to tell himself.

Monica was pleased. She'd gotten the end result she'd hoped for at the beginning of the day.

5. In the Shadows

Cut lilacs lie like the dead, giving no measure but taking none, save their scent and your soul, if you are in New Orleans and you yield it to them. Dead yet living, their fragrance remains long after they've been cut. Not so different from us I suppose. Are any of us any more than cut flowers, even the living? You know, beautiful, giving the appearance of life but already dead? So why should it be so hard for me to believe that the dead are so near to us? Or is it we that are so near to them? Are they the natural state and we the aberration?

That was the gist of what Akina and I discussed as we strolled through the darkness. I was always, at least on the surface, such a sullen boy, to the point that I truly felt that happiness was a delusional state (in which one actually believed everything was going to be alright). Akina spent many an afternoon trying to reel me back to shore.

I attempted to call out to Darnell who was walking just a bit ahead for his input, but before I could do more than blurt out his name, he called out his mantra. "All I know is that now I am living, I will be dead sooner than I would like to think and someday I will rise and walk again. I don't see where I need to know much more than that." I could hear his feet rustling through the dried leaves that covered everything.

"You wouldn't!" Akina laughed and snapped back. "In all my days I don't know if I will ever see you ask for more than you already have."

Darnell replied, "So, is that a bad thing?"

Akina conceded, "No, I guess not. In fact, it's beautiful. I wish I could be more like that." Then she postulated on, "I think maybe my soul is too old for that. Seems that day is long gone for me. Anyway, what I was saying is that it's okay that you heard them. Avis is going to attract them no matter where you find her. They hang around her because just like us, the dead, especially those without God, want someone they can talk to. And Avis is that person. Someone who can understand them is like candy to the dead. Their incoherent pleadings are mostly intolerable even to each other. But the living can give them context to who they were, if not what they've become. Without God they really can't move on. Their spirits are like broken records, stuck on whatever was incomplete in their lives."

I nodded like I understood. And I did, kind of. But I had lots of questions. "So you all have seen these dead folks before?"

"A time or two," Akina answered with a smile.

Timidly, I posed my next question, "...Have they ever tried to hurt you?"

Again Akina yielded, "Well, not in the way you might think. They can't really hurt you physically, but I would suggest that you not talk to them, that is, if you value your sanity. Now, Avis is quite another matter."

I thought for a minute and then almost a block later a thought occurred to me, "So is that how Avis lost her mind?"

"I don't know. None of us knows for sure," Akina said. Darnell and Sandy nodded in agreement. But then Akina, seemingly in a darker place, added "Mama has always had her ways. And today it troubles me particularly. Yes, it does."

Continuing, I asked what seemed to me to be an obvious question, "So, what now? I know we're not just gonna show up and take Carla out of there. Right? I mean surely Avis is expecting us."

"Yeah, that's what we're thinking. When she took Carla, she knew we'd have to follow. And Uncle Paul is beginning to think that maybe this whole thing, the killings and all were just a game to bring us all here. But he's not sure and neither are we."

We stopped in a Waffle House for a dinner of pecan waffles and something akin to orange juice. As we all sat down with our snacks we joined hands to ask a blessing upon our meal. Then, as a part of the blessing, my cousins prayed over me. Their hands joined as they asked God that my gift be revealed. They ended the prayer with "...and greater things than this you will do in My name."

As we sat, they began to discuss just how we'd go in, who would get Carla and all that kind of stuff. Meanwhile, I began to drift off. I started to think about my mother and where she might be. Then I realized that the presence of my mother had enveloped me. I'd felt this way before only to later find out that at that moment my mother was praying for me. At first it distressed me as one fighting to wake from a dream. But then I saw that face and felt her presence, and something within me yielded to the flood of her comfort. A sense of warmth soaked through me. I came back to clarity of my surroundings, sweating from every pore.

I reached for the glass of water right in front of me, while the others stared at me as I gripped the container. The glass itself felt soft, almost gooey in my hand. And the water within it began to swirl. As I lifted it to my face it began to bubble. I would say that it was boiling, but the glass, putty though it was in my hand, remained cool to my touch.

Akina smiled at me and said, "It is beginning, the Spirit is upon him." Uncle Paul grunted in reluctant acceptance. Darnell just took a breath and stared at Uncle Paul looking puzzled, but I didn't know about what. Sandy stretched her arm out around my shoulder and held me. At her touch, the glass firmed, but when I placed it back on the table my imprints remained casted in the glass. This meant that it had not been a dream or just my imagination. And although I'd had a good four hours to digest all they'd told me, my mind scrambled for an explanation I could live with. I found none.

While I struggled to rebuild my world, they returned to their discussion.

Then Uncle Paul made his feelings known. "Y'all need to calm down. Akina twinkling back and forth, here and then. Darnell and Carla done both got caught up. And now y'all dragging Michael into all of this. And what's the point? Y'all need to wait on Reggie and Kim. Not so much Kim, her little butt should be out playing soccer or something. But Reggie does this kind of stuff for a living. He's older than all of you and he knows what he's doing. Plus, Avis's little tricks don't seem to bother him none too much. I've been down this road y'all is on now. It's been so long and my mind is starting to slip, so I can't tell you everything, but I remember enough to know that y'all should not be so eager to jump into all of this. I almost wish I'd come by myself."

"But Uncle Paul," Darnell pleaded, "How can I wait on them? That's my sister in there! We don't know if Reggie even got the message. He might be in Angola for all we know. And Kim doesn't know any more than we do. So what's the point in waiting? This sitting around is just making me crazy."

"Have you forgotten everything that I've told you? All things in their proper time," Uncle Paul replied sharply.

Darnell sat still, and for just a second he appeared to be calming just a bit, then he bolted upright to his feet and began to pace back and forth. Uncle Paul let out an enormous sigh and shook his head. It was only 9:30PM and I just knew that Darnell wasn't going to last until midnight. Anyway, I was dealing with my own challenges.

I picked up the glass again for another sip. This time it felt like a zip-up freezer bag filled with water. The whole thing became fluid in my hands. And still, at first the water was contained. Then the whole thing became goo dripping through my fingers onto the tabletop, the water and silicon blending together becoming a syrupy type substance. Sandy gripped me tighter around my shoulders, saying quietly, but excitedly "See, your change is coming. Don't be afraid."

I can't say that I was convinced about that "Don't be afraid" part. In my swelling panic I interrupted the others. "Hey, y'all are all so calm and I'm dying over here, or at least I think I am. Did y'all see what happened to that glass? What if that happens to me? What if this starts happening to me on the inside, my organs, heart and stuff are gonna just stop. I already feel short of breath. Oh God, I think I'm really dying!"

Akina reached across Sandy and placed her hand on mine, "Hey relax, you're short of breath because you are hyperventilating. Your body will not hurt you. We all went through this. Think of it this way, when you first started growing facial hair, your body knew not to grow it on your brain, right? It's the exact same way with this. So just chill and see where it takes you." I remember thinking that was very easy for her to say, but for me the stars were very different.

I took a deep breath and released it trying my best not to think about anything. This was the toughest assignment of the whole experience up until then.

The waitress, in black pants, a white blouse and a yellow and black apron stepped back over towards us and upon seeing the mess I made just stared in disbelief, not knowing what to make of what she saw. By this point the water and glass had separated again with the water running off the table and the glass spread across my half of the table like some oddly shaped work of art. Finally, after having a moment to smack her gums and to place her hands on her hips, she grabbed an additional napkin dispenser from the next table and handed it to us. I wanted to order another glass of water, but I didn't think that was the right time.

Akina smiled and laughed just a bit as the waitress turned to walk away. Akina looked my way once again and queried, "So what did it feel like when the glass began to melt?"

"It felt like jelly," I snapped.

"No, stop and think for a moment. What did you feel at each point?"

I responded thoughtfully, "Well, at first I noticed that the glass began to feel like putty. Firm but textured and pliable. Then the sides of the glass began to wobble and at that point it was like Jell-O. Until finally, it was running through my fingers like syrup."

"Good," Akina said. "Now take this fork and tell me what you feel."

"Okay. Well, oh there it goes again. It's starting to feel rubbery. See, it's beginning to droop."

Akina pressed again, "But what do you feel? Close your eyes and focus on the feeling."

Darnell interjected, "Hey maybe that's what he does. You know, melts things?"

Akina gave Darnell a look which said "Hush." It was a knowing look that I would later come to interpret very well, but at that moment it puzzled me.

I closed my eyes and began to tune everything out but the fork. In doing that I began to feel something movable to my touch. Like writing on an Etch-a-Sketch, but it wasn't like I was seeing it change, I was feeling it change as I stroked it. I continued to rub it and felt it change some more. Then I heard a gasp from Sandy and my eyes sprung open. There in my hand, what had been stainless steel was now copper in color.

Sandy let out a, "Oh my gosh! Look at that!"

Darnell took the fork from me and held it up to the light as Uncle Paul leaned closer to him to get a better sniff. Darnell took a new penny out of his pocket and held it up next to the fork. He then declared, "I say it's copper, at least mostly."

Uncle Paul reached out, took the fork and placed it below his nose, "Dang, if that don't beat all. I've seen this done before a time or two, but it was an all day thing. I've never even heard of anybody performing alchemy by just rubbing a thing." My typically expressionless uncle was clearly impressed.

Sandy continued to stroke my forearm as Akina sat there, arms folded, with a smile beaming so brightly she would have blinded anybody walking through the door. Finally, she just couldn't hold it in any longer. "Hallelujah! Score one for the Good Guys!"

With that they began collecting and bringing to me little odd pieces lying around the Waffle House that they wanted to see me work my way upon. For the next hour or so, that's what we did, until the staff got curious (although, I did return most of the objects back to their original state before anyone noticed). But until then, with each turn, I became more and more aware of what this gift was. It seemed that I could change most any element into another one, as well as change the state of it, be it gas, liquid or solid. I was floored and kept doing it just to make sure it was really happening.

6: A Day in the Life

Jonah pondered the magnitude of the challenge before him as he prepared to go to town; it weighed upon him like some ancient curse. His fears seizing him around his shoulders and blinding him to the hope he had just moments before. It was a fear that closed his eyes to all that seemed so possible only a day before. A fear that, in the end, he was from a line of people doomed to suffer failure. But in that moment he looked upward and whispered "You and me, Lord. You and me, always." As he did so, he stepped carefully from his hidden underground abode.

As Jonah slipped into the woods, doubt crept into his mind again. He had often wondered whether he and his wife had any realistic chance of escaping this place alive. But he learned long ago that it was more helpful to focus on the challenge of surviving each day rather than worrying about tomorrow. He had even reasoned and taken comfort in that even in another land, tomorrow is not promised. His wife, Monica, reminded him of this constantly. But what was constant in his mind was that each "goodbye," each "I'll see you this evening," each "I love you, baby," could be their last. That is what hurt him most. Of his own life he could reason that everyone must die sometime, so why be afraid? But the life of their union seemed a much more fleeting and fragile thing.

Jonah exited the woods about half a mile from his bus stop. He'd tied his turban on about a mile back, just in case someone spotted him tracking through the woods. He laughed often that the Blues did not or could not distinguish between Sikhs (of which he was more closely adorned) and Hindus. It

71

was always amazing to him how simply dressing the part, even the wrong part, benefited him in his guise. And as he expected, the bus stop was packed. The crowd helped him to blend in. The more cramped the bus, the better. The bus was old, as usual, and he knew that more than likely it was a hand-me-down from the masters. Still, he reasoned, even this worked all the more to his advantage in his role as a Hindu, or at least not African-American. Since the new National Security chief had taken over, there had been a real persecution of men and women like him. As the bus rolled up, Jonah saw an ad on the side paneling that read, "Nothing matters, and what if it did?" It was one of the many ads plastered in locations where the "underclass" could see them. Technically, the Blue Faith, the state religion and philosophy, applied to all residents, but you rarely, if ever, saw one of those nihilist propaganda signs in the more affluent communities of the "upperclass".

Jonah was standing on the bus, hanging on to the overhead rail, bouncing back and forth with each bump in the road. He was near the middle exit door, on the chance he might have to bolt from the bus. Yet, he could have almost slept like that, and early in the ride to work he did tend to drift. On the trip home he tended to be more alert, so as to not miss his drop off point. It was key that he vary his drop off point so that his goings and comings were not clear to any of the daily riders. That morning had his mind wandering just a bit. And then, like a speeding driver just noticing that he just sped past a highway patrolman, a fright ten times worse hit him as he noticed a Blue Blood stepping aboard the bus. He prayed that his eyes and expression had not given him away. He looked down and away towards the back of the bus as the Blue Blood made his way to and past him, or so he thought. Feeling the danger had passed him, he lifted his head to spy where the newcomer had landed. He was startled to see the young Blue Blood male standing right next to him. To move away then would have been too obvious and the bus was so jammed that it would have been hard to do without knocking someone down. Jonah had to stay right there, at least until the next stop.

The young man searched for and found Jonah's eyes and sensing his fear, spoke to calm him, "Brother..." With that first word he nearly killed Jonah right there, his heart wanting to leap from his chest but held down only by the total constriction of his throat. Jonah wondered was his disguise really that transparent? The young man continued, "Say Brother, does this bus go by the federal works center?" The second time he said "Brother" Jonah realized the context.

Jonah lifted his head slightly to answer him. Avoiding eye contact, he spoke softly but firmly enough not to run the risk of having him not hear and having to ask him a second time. "Yes."

Jonah's eyes danced away, but the "Bluey", after looking up toward the bus system map posted along the top of the bus above the windows, retrained his gaze on him. "So do you know where I should get off?"

Jonah began to realize that this Blue Blood was every bit as young as he looked. He knew that the Blue Bloods had engineered themselves to stop aging around twenty-eight for the men and twenty-six for the women, but this guy had an air of being new to the world. So he might have actually been twenty-something, Jonah figured. But his confusion regarding the transit system seemed a clincher that this was indeed a kid. "You have to get off right after we pass Fourteenth Street."

"Thanks dude. Hey, my name's Dave. What's yours?"

Double shock. First he used the word "dude", which Jonah hadn't heard since the riots. Then he actually asked for his name. "My name's Murali," Jonah lied. He had to. Murali was his assumed name after all of the trouble broke out. Plus, as always, he was afraid that this was finally Trouble come to hunt him down.

Jonah's new friend continued, "So Murali, where do you work?"

"At the Food Mart." Jonah lied, again. He actually worked at the Gadget Depot. Sensing that Dave wanted more, he added, "I work in the stock room." He actually worked in the service department of Gadget Depot repairing electronics, if indeed you'd really call it that. Many a time, he had redone whole system architectures just for the challenge of making them run better or perform tasks the owner may on some odd day be surprised to discover. Most of it was just stupid stuff. In his careful world this seemed his lone opportunity for humor. His customers never saw his face, because he worked in the back or the basement of the store. He was happy with Karun taking credit on the occasions when ecstatic customers sang his praises. Save his wife, this was his single joy those days, in that world.

"Oh, wow my old nanny shopped there sometimes. That's on Eighth Street, right?"

"Yes sir." From the moment he said it, Jonah instinctively knew it was a poor choice of words, or so his spirit told him.

"Oh, Murali you wound me. I'm no Sir. Just call me Dave. Okay?"

"Okay," Jonah muddled back as cheerfully as any fraud could under such circumstances. He looked up to see Sixth Street pass by. "Dave," he said softly, "I have to go now."

"Oh wow, that's right. It's cool. Hey Brother, have a great day."

Jonah, having pressed the stop request button, re-gripped his lunch bag and prepared to turn towards the exit door behind them. Then something moved in his heart and he relaxed enough to say "You take care, brother." Jonah then slipped past a couple of other riders towards the door. But before he did, he glanced at Dave to see him smile. Jonah had been taught that the Blue Bloods were the devil's very own, and for the most part he didn't doubt it. Still his reasoned mind could not truly accept that all of them were.

He watched the traffic pass back and forth in front of him, barely lifting his head. Besides his adornment, Jonah had taken to playing the role of a fool. During the day he didn't look anyone in the eye besides Karun and some of the other staff that worked with him at Gadget Depot. He revealed whatever light remained in his eyes for those who already knew of his pretense. The traffic light changed and he began to cross. Blues to his left and his right, for all their supposed intellect, were ignorant of him.

But Jonah was not ignorant of them and what they had done. The "Blue Bloods" had been around since well before Jonah was born. A genetically altered species of human, the Blue Bloods, as they were called, were the Holy Grail of genetic engineering. They were impervious to most disease and birth defects. Each of them had a, supposedly, superior IQ. And most significantly, they did not grow old. As to why they were blue (actually, like a chameleon, they could pretty much tone it down to the point that no one could tell, or they could turn it all the way up, which they often did for special occasions) that was pure business. Branding, baby. There were other bio-tech firms which beat Blue's patent right holder (AAA Technologies) to market. However, AAA Technologies niche was established by their marketing strategy. After all, what good was it to have a perfect child, if no one knew it? Unlike their competitor's babies, AAA babies were the most spectacular blue anyone had ever seen. And since they could turn it on and off, their babies became the "gold" standard in human genetic engineering. Every couple that could afford it, wanted one... not that much of, and in many cases, none of the baby's DNA came from the parents. Pretty much all of the DNA was replicated and synthesized from existing stockpiles in Jonah's time.

As the last century had progressed, the Blues gradually rose to controlling positions in most western governments in Europe, North and South America. They would tell you that they rose to power because of their superior ability and performance. Non-Blues would say that their extended lifespan gave them an unfair advantage. Either way, they were certainly in charge of most things. However, for the most part, naturally born humans and those engineered and cultivated in a lab lived peaceably side by side.

Around ten years ago, slightly more than two years after Jonah and Monica wed, all hell broke loose. After nearly two decades of passing progressively more restrictive laws governing the behavior of non-Blues (like childbirth penalties, revocation of all church permits and the termination of all public education) the last straw was the lifetime income tax cap. As with all of their other moves, the Blues reasoned that this system was unfair to anyone with an infinite life expectancy. Naturally born humans would pay no more than fifty to sixty years of taxes, where the Blues could go on paying forever. This was deemed as unfair and a cut off was placed at fifty years or an earnings total equivalent to fifty years of average wages. And since most of the best jobs went to the Blues, most of them (besides the slackers) would reach this goal in less than fifty years. On top of that, they grand-fathered it in. That really added insult to injury.

The other cultural assaults, for better or worse, had been tolerated. Supposedly, the banning of religious organizations was due to the high historical correlation between them and political unrest. These groups were then deemed as being subversive, and as subversive they were subject to the "Threat to the State Act" passed when the Blues came to absolute power. It was the passage of this bill that led to the creation of a Christian State known as New Jerusalem (God's New Peace) beneath the northern ice cap. And although New Jerusalem was the official name, most people called it the Circle. At that time a large number of Christians left for this new refuge during the grace period, but the majority stayed. Most who stayed did so because they could just not fathom living beneath the Artic Circle. Jonah, however as a significant number of others, distrusted the visa process. Most were granted, but if your visa was rejected you were not just prevented from leaving the country, you were arrested... and those were the lucky ones. The Blues claimed that those being punished possessed some sort of criminal record, when in reality it was merely a matter of what sort of threat they felt you were.

Besides political foes and the typical enemies of the state, they also arrested and subsequently slaughtered anyone they determined to be in the top four percent intellectually or that they felt showed superior achievement in an area of expertise that they felt was or could be a threat to the state. So, no Nuclear Engineers or as in Jonah's case, Molecular Engineers, were spared or allowed to leave.

The Blues also had a ruling body of governors called the "Sapphire Illuminati", a name partly reflective of their blue blood and partly a part of their consistent practice of incorporating icons of the past to put fear into the populace. This Sapphire Illuminati was supposed to be supernatural in nature. And though Jonah wasn't really buying any of that, there were things he'd seen or heard about that were hard for even him to explain away. Jonah had seen some things in his very own lab that had given him glimpses into a new world that few could ever imagine.

The reason it was safer to be Indian was two-fold. Firstly, the Blues had a long-standing treaty with India (they also had one with China). The second reason, simply put, was that they needed them. Yes, the Blues kept the best jobs for themselves, but given their life spans and their high opinion of themselves it was hard to find a Blue willing to do any really hard work. Actually, India and the Indians had quite a say in how things were run in the west. In the treaty they signed with the Blues they actually negotiated an exception for Hindus in regard to the ban of all non-Blue religions. The official position however was that the Hindu faith was more accepting of one's position in life and less likely to spur civil unrest. In fact, the Blues had actually adopted many aspects of the Hindu way of life into the official state religion, the Blue Faith. Karun was quick to point out that it was nothing like Hindu, but their own perverted concoction, through which they had defamed all true Hindus. In the Blue version, they placed themselves as the final step on the reincarnation pyramid. They were the final and best caste, that is, according to all the new education propaganda. This generation and this age of Blues had, in their words, achieved nirvana.

Jonah swung around taking the long way to work, stopping at the Food Mart for just a second. He looked around before coming back out to the sidewalk. Just as he was stepping out he noticed an average sized woman with blond hair. It was Sara, a good friend who worked two doors down from him in her husband Ashok's bank office. She gave Jonah a quick smile and Jonah responded. She was attractive, in her late forties and in pretty good shape. She wore her blond hair up most days. She was a rarity, in that she was so clearly not conformed to the Blue way. She wore all the clothing and accessories, but if you ever had a conversation with her, you just knew she was just putting on appearances. She was a Christian and it was thinly veiled that she was not Hindu. Jonah believed if it were not for her being married to a very influential Indian in the business community, surely she'd be either in prison or dead. However, her husband being the leading non-Blue banker in the city, she got certain privileges. Although Jonah never dared to step foot in her place of business or even have a conversation with her in public, he had often seen her in the electronics store. She and her husband Ashok on a number of occasions visited Karun's shop bringing dinner as well. At those times, she would also conduct Bible study with Jonah and Monica, and sometimes Karun and his wife. Only half the group was Christian, but they enjoyed the fellowship nonetheless.

Walking a few feet behind her and in silence, Jonah followed Sara as they turned the corner approaching her bank. Sara stopped and began to use her key to open the door. She glanced around not looking specifically at Jonah and then touched her heart. In this time that was a Christian symbol for "Go in Love." Jonah, aware of several acceptable responses, touched his own heart, which basically meant "Go in Love as well."

Finally, Jonah arrived at the electronics store. He slipped in the employee entrance, which opened into the lobby. It was only five minutes before opening and Karun was behind the front counter reading the paper and swearing to himself while his coffee grew cold. Most of the other workers were standing around him gasping and giving comments on the headline, which had so disturbed Karun.

"Jonah!" Karun cried out. "Have you seen this?"

He shoved the paper into Jonah. Jonah pulled it back a bit to see the whole page. It was an underground paper, but the print was clear:

CHINA TO COMPLETE SPACE PORTAL BY YEAR'S END

As he skimmed through the article, it dawned on him that things really were going to come to a head, and real soon.

The Chinese and Blues were at peace because the Chinese were actually going to leave. Yes, leave as in actually leaving the earth behind. Seems when the current ruling party in China came to power some seventy years ago, they made a commitment to build a star gate and colonize the heavens within seventy-five years. And doggone it if they weren't five years ahead of schedule. In theory, they and the Blues agreed to live in peaceful coexistence as long as China was making progress towards leaving. The rest of the world hated this arrangement. China and the Blues were both 1A superpowers, with India just slightly below each... or at least it was assumed. The Blues controlled North and South America. India ruled all of the sub-continent plus most of the Middle East. China's domain spanned from what is now China, north of what is current day Russia, south to Australia and the outer edges of Antarctica, where they did most of their beta testing for the Space Portal. Europe and Africa were a different story. So caught up in ethnic loyalties they missed the boat when the three Super Powers were taking technological quantum leaps forward. Europe was mostly at peace because they seemed to be more accepting of foreign rule, although they were brutally taxed. Plus, there was an additional issue with most of Africa. They seemed incapable of submitting for any extended period of time. There were constant revolts followed by ever progressively harsher crackdowns. To make matters worse, none of the three Super Powers wanted to see Europe or Africa unified to any measure. In the big picture, each reasoned that those two continents mastered the world for the better part of recorded human history. They were due to be plundered themselves for a change. Totally rationalized if not totally illogical, but it allowed the masses to sleep easy at night. Strangely enough, this was also part of the official reasoning behind why the rest of the world did not intervene when the Blues first began to persecute Christians.

Whereas the Blues, in what used to be the Americas, had focused inward, spending a full ten percent of their national GDP in healthcare, the Chinese had spent just as much looking outward on their quest to roam the stars. Needless to say, the two societies had totally disparate technologies.

The West, or at least its leader, believed that they had achieved heaven on earth. The West believed that star travel was pointless given the amount of time it would take to travel from system to system even at the speed of light. What they didn't see was that a manmade device would someday bend time and space. The East believed any search for immortality within this life was a fool's quest. What they did not see or understand was that the thirst of an empty people could never be quenched.

Jonah finished the article and handed it over to Sridhar who stood next to Deepak. Sridhar was a short heavyset man in his thirties, possibly forties. Deepak was twenty-something, tall and lanky. He was athletic but not overly muscular. They were both in Jonah's inner circle with Karun. As Sridhar searched for a particular section of the article, Deepak posed a question to Jonah. "So, my friend, what do you think will happen? Do you really think they're leaving? Do you think the Blues are going to let them leave?"

Jonah shrugged and offered a soft response, "Well, to be honest, I really don't see the Blues stopping them at first, but once most of them are off the planet, I see the Blues rushing in to steal all the technology for themselves."

Deepak smiled and puffed out his chest. "See Sridhar, even the underground genius agrees with me. There is no way the Blues will honor that agreement."

Karun turned back from the register to the group to restate his opinion. "And all the more reason for India to act now. We must strike now. Sridhar, you are a fool if you think the Blues will honor their agreement with India and China. They will see this as a green light to do to us what they've done to others.   Look at Jonah here, this is what awaits our children if we do nothing."

Sridhar defended himself, "The only certain war is the one you start.   Yes, appeasement is foolish and past policies by China and India have only made matters worse. But still, you must think as your enemy thinks to understand what motiv- ates him and what he will do. Yes, they are an evil people, but the one thing the Blue man wants most is to live forever. Warfare makes this a tentative possibility at best.   India is strong and there are millions of us throughout their society. Surely, the reasoned intelligent man would realize the cost of subduing India would be quite high. Surely, they are not such big fools!"

A couple of the younger salespeople shook their heads in agreement.

Jonah picked up his vest and casually mentioned as if only in passing, "Well, I hope you're right.   No offense intended, but are you certain it's truth that has swayed your reasoning, and not wishful thinking?"

Karun jumped in again, "Yes, Sridhar, how can you say this? After all the Blues have done, after every agreement they've broken, what could possibly persuade you that they will be honorable this time?"

"My friend you are right in part. No, they are not an hon- orable people. History shows this clearly. But history also shows that they do respect power. You forget my friend, they have honored their current agreement with India and China, not because they are honorable, but because they realize the cost of going to war with either of these two nations."

Karun responded, "Well, I hope you are right Sridhar. But remember the Brazilians, all of Africa and Europe said the same thing, and now they are dust and all they worked for, merely a footnote in history and soon to be forgotten. Countless lives lost and a generation from now, who will know it?" The Blues had a habit of rewriting history books to their liking.

It was times like that, that made Jonah the saddest. He thought of all the loss and hurt and almost in tears asked himself how God could stand by and let this happen? They all saw his sorrow sweep over him and each of them showed compassion in his own way. And all the more did Karun's heart go out to Jonah, for he knew the painful particulars that the others did not. They all knew of the brother Jonah once hoped to be living among the Christians beneath the Pole. But Karun also knew of the other brother he had not heard from in nearly two years. Not a word or rumor, secondhand, thirdhand or otherwise. He knew of his sister working in China and now a Chinese national. He knew of the many other members of his family who disappeared in the riots and how the more recent crackdown on people like Jonah, had brought him even lower. He knew how desperately he sought to have better and do better by his wife, Monica and the child they hoped to have some day. He also knew that all he could do was reach out and grab his friend's shoulder and offer words of comfort.

Deepak gathered up the paper and handed it to Karun who, as was their ritual regarding the underground press they received, pulled a lighter from his pocket and set the paper afire. Before placing the torched pages into a wastebasket, he briefly disabled the fire alarm. Deepak laughed to Karun and Sridhar, "We disagree, but it could be worse. You know my wife still thinks the Sapphire Illuminati are gods." The three of them snickered. A large percentage of the public believed that the ruling body were truly supernatural beings or at least possessing those types of abilities. No one there, nor any true "techie" worth his weight in salt, bought into that. The staff enjoyed working there in part because this was one place that they could have an intelligent conversation free of superstitions and hysteria.

Jonah chuckled at the three of them and requested, "Karun, please remind me to ask you something the next time you are in the basement."

"Sure, my friend."

Before Jonah reached the elevator en-route to the basement, Karun issued one last word of encouragement, "You will get out of here someday my friend. There is a better day for you." He used to tell him he'd find his brothers someday, but he no longer did that. He, as did Jonah, realized that his brothers were likely dead by then. Plus, what news Karun had heard had not been good. The one source he had heard from mentioned the worst, but could not be certain. And although he had not told Jonah what he heard because of the uncertain identification, he personally trusted the competency of the source. He knew in his heart that at least one of Jonah' brother was dead. He knew that Jonah knew it too, or at least felt it. But he knew that Jonah could not bring himself to talk about it just then. So, he waited for that moment in which he must be a friend. He didn't know what he would say, but he knew he must be ready.

Karun took one last look around his store and then walked smiling to the front door. In this advanced age he could have opened the door from behind the counter, but he preferred this ritual of unlocking the door personally and greeting that first customer with a smile. Typically there were two to three people lined up waiting for his doors to open. These people held a special place in his heart each day. Karun liked helping people, and these early birds were usually the one's who needed it the most. He raised the blind, unlocked the door and swung it open. He saw that there was only one waiting that morning when he raised the blind, but upon opening the door he saw a familiar-looking woman. And when she looked up, he gasped.

"Hi Karun. How's it going?" Her name was Vicki. She was a ghost, a part of the underground. They never came out during the day. But if any of them would, this would be the one. "So, are you open for business?"

She breezed by him as he continued to stand there stunned. Finally, he managed two words, "Oh my..."

7: 'Round Midnight

At about ten 'til midnight we departed the Waffle House and headed back to Avis's place. The sweats I'd had earlier were gone, evaporated somewhere into the New Orleans night air. They were replaced by a quickening in my blood, more anticipation than excitement. For a moment I thought of the voices I'd heard before outside of Avis's house, but this time I was more curious than afraid. More was changing in me than the fact that matter yielded to my will.

We rounded the corner of her street to the greeting of a strong stiff breeze that quickly became a windstorm. "What the....!" I cried out, taken by surprise. The others then grabbed the wrought iron fencing along the walk, and so did I pulling up the rear. Avis's house was, thankfully, next door to the corner house. I looked up to see the front door of her home open and I realized that the gale we faced was coming straight from her door. It went not right, nor straight ahead, but turned left at her front gate and directly at us. I also noticed for the first time that the inlaid stained glasses on the windows were placed in such a pattern to make a crucifix on each one. Some were red, some blue, some white and some black. The large wooden front doors were flung open and flailing. We could see the inside of them and the crosses carved into them so deeply that even the darkness could not hide them. Considering what we believed to have taken place here, even I, the professed atheist found this a bit perverse.

The gale subsided just enough for us to move forward. When we reached the front gate, we found it locked. As Darnell reached for the lock, Uncle Paul restrained his hand saying, "Boy, let your cousin have a look at that." He was nodding towards me.

I knew immediately what he wanted. I reached out my hand taking the padlock in my hand. With a little concentration I began to feel texture within the metal hoop that locked us out and away from Carla. I felt the inside of the substance move as I rubbed it. First it changed colors, but I continued to rub. Then suddenly, I rubbed it to a state that it became a vapor, strangely sinking to the ground rather than rising. It was a matter I would have loved to ponder right then, but my immediate desire was to have the gate open and that it was. Uncle Paul gave me a second nod. This time it was an affirming nod. He walked by me leading us into the front yard. Weeds dominated the landscape, but scattered about were a strange collection of other plants I'd never seen before. I looked up to the tree branches and saw what looked like a face staring back at me. Then something clicked and I looked again at ground level and realized that the bushes and stunted tree-like objects around me were petrified torsos and other odd body parts. They stood like statues of petrified wooden warriors guarding a prize no one could want. But then I looked above again at the fruit hanging above me and saw through the darkness vague shapes of heads without bodies. Then in my spirit the warriors around me became symbols of some defeated army. Like a parade of dead flies caught in a spider's web, these empty carcasses marked the passing of life not yielded freely. Even in death, each of these faceless ones still cried out in some personal agony that only Heaven could now heal. And would it ever? I used to wonder about these things, but right then, perhaps for the first time in my life, I understood something about Hell.

I fell to the back of the group again, my newfound confidence now flown off after a mere twenty feet.

An angry Darnell reached the doorway first and gave out a call. "Avis!" Given his soft-spoken way, the strength of his voice shook me.

A voice from the darkness inside came back, "Nobody's home."

As he dragged the rest of us inside, he cried out again even more powerfully than before. "Avis!!!"

Again she mocked, "I'm sorry, I already belong to a church. It's called the New Orleans First Church of Me-myself-and-I. I think you know our pastor."

"Avis, don't play with me!" Darnell shouted.

A moment passed and then a simple whispered "Okay," passed through us. Then a second later a ghoulish creature with no visible eyes or mouth, but with two sword-welding arms, came out of the darkness so savagely that I backed up so quickly that I hurt my shoulder on the doorpost. Before I could reassert myself correctly and exit out the front door, white-hot fire burst out of Darnell's eyes towards the beast and it was engulfed in flames. The fire from his eyes was only visible once it reached the darkness. The creature stumbled around until a second, narrower burst of light from Darnell cut him in half.

Darnell cried out a last time, "How many of these do you want to lose?"

She called back, "You're right. That one couldn't cook worth a damn, but he was hell in the yard, if you know what I mean." Then the candles located around the great room began to burn more brightly, gradually lighting the whole room as Avis walked out of the darkness towards us. When the lights went up, I could also see that all of the walls on the first floor had been knocked down, making the entire area like some makeshift throne room. Bookcases lined the main hall. On the shelves closest to us I could see that some books had red jackets with gold crosses on them. Again, I found this strange.

But given our hostess and the duality of her upbringing I wrote it off as part of her sickness. "Evening," she said with a smirk. I noticed that she did not say "good" or even "bad," but simply "evening." I also noticed that her hands were covered with blood. So much so that it dripped from her fingertips.

Darnell still in front, spoke again without hesitation, "I came for my sis..."

"I know who you came for, darling," she cut him off. "But let's see who you brought with you first. Oh, it's Aunt Sarah's child, Michael all grown up. I haven't seen you in what? Ten years? More I think."

She smiled at me and continued as she walked to the other side. "And I see that you brought 'the Prize,'" referring to Akina, her only child. "Hello, daughter."

"Hello, mother." The civility of her reply surprised me as much as Darnell's shouts earlier. This scene was not new to either of them.

Avis continued, "Oh, and who else have you brought? Is that Sandy?"

Sandy did not respond to her acknowledgement.

All this time, Uncle Paul had remained silent until finally, he spoke. "Avis..."

"That's Siva to you!" she raged back to him. "You have no right to call me Avis!"

"Child," Uncle Paul tried again. "About Carla.."

"Yesss, about Carla... Why don't you just command me to let her go? You still have the gift, don't you? Oh, that's right, you made a pledge before God, that you would never use that particular gift again. Unto death, I wonder? Eh, Poppa? I hear that your mind is slipping, so will you even remember your pledge a year from now. Such a gift in the hands of a senile god, unfathomable calamity awaits us all."

"Avis!" Darnell said attempting to regain his agenda.

"Ah, yes, your sister. Here she is." Suddenly to the right of what I guess you would call her throne, an illusion of banal tapestry dissolved revealing a gagged and unconscious Carla tied to a stake. A stake that sat upon a pile of wood topped with straw. Avis laughed, "The stake is real, but the kindling is mostly for effect. I mean it wouldn't make much sense for me to start a bonfire inside of my own house would it? But I do find the irony funny. I mean with my being a witch and all." Then her face turned serious. "But make no mistake. If I don't get what I want, she will wish she had been burned at the stake."

Darnell shot out another fireball at a second minion of Avis's that got too close. I did not even see this one until it burst into flames. I was staring right where he fired and did not see a thing. The creature must have been invisible, at least to me anyway. Darnell, did not miss a beat. "What is it that you want?"

"A one for one trade - your sister Carla for my daughter, Akina. See, very simple." She almost hissed the way she said "simple." She continued, "You know a girl belongs with her mother." She laughed.

Darnell held his ground. "You know we can't do that."

Avis took on a kitten-like tone to cajole him further. "Don't you want your fine sister back? And she is fine isn't she? All the fellas in your school thought so. And very agreeable too. Remember how she was even back in Junior High? How'd it feel to have such a tramp for a sister? Mmmm, is that why you're doing the whole chastity thing?"

Without hesitation Darnell shot back, "Avis you're sick. Let us help you."

Avis smiled and carried on her interrogation, "I always wondered about you two being so different. You know her being so free with her body and you being so pure with yours? Is that why you went to see a counselor? Did her ways freak you out? Is that how you wound up in therapy? Did the stress of it all give you bad thoughts? Hmmm? Did you want to kill yourself? Was that it cousin? Having a twin like that and all the guys laughing at you? My being an only child and all, at least that's how I was raised, maybe I just can't relate. Then again this is a night for confession. Ain't that right, Pa? See Darnell, if you want to dump on your sister you will come by it honest, because it runs in the family. When things get tough, cut 'em loose. Right, Pa?"

Uncle Paul cried out, "Avis!"

"No, daddy. You brought them here, they might as well hear it all. But Akina, you already know don't you? You have traveled space and time, how could you know all these things and not know this one thing? What granddaddy allowed to happen to me. About how he sold me like a whore just so you could add another notch on your belt? Surely, you know who your father is don't you? Hasn't he told you?."

Uncle Paul pleaded, almost crying, "Avis, if I have hurt you..."

His daughter cut him off, repeating his words back to him. "If? If I've hurt you? You have got to be kidding! Poppa, I have always been this family's sacrificial lamb and you, senile or not, have the gall to ask if you've hurt me?" With this she flew into a rage and the entire house began to tremble. Even her ghouls, which guarded Carla, lost their balance. All of her attendants, six young men, scurried behind her throne. The disturbance also awakened Carla.

A groggy Carla began to call out "Avis" over and over as she drifted in and out of consciousness.

"Momma!" Finally, Akina raised her voice. "Momma you have to stop. Look at what you're doing. Who are all these boys? Why are you hurting them? Look at them. And how can you tie up Carla like that? That's Carla over there!"

Now sweating profusely, Avis turned from her rant to answer Akina. "Darling, I'm just paying the world back for what it did to me. As for your cousin, she's free to go anytime she likes, just as long as you stay with dear old Mom. What do you think I'm going to do? Put a spell on you and use you to plunder the universe? Would I do that? Come on baby, stay with Momma. We don't pimp our kids that way in this family, right Poppa?" Her fingernails appeared to become long, warped claws as she spoke.

Darnell stepped in front of Akina, "No Avis, we're all leaving here together."

With that, Avis's hellish henchmen surrounded us, even blocking the doorway out. I began to crouch just a bit trying to look in every direction all at once. As I turned to face a horribly disfigured looking spawn, I heard a piercing of air, followed by a short muddled sound, then half a second later a loud thud. I turned back to see the two demons that had been blocking the door, lying face down on the floor with a long rod sticking out of their collective backs. It was like they were some giant demon kabob. Another figure, bigger than either of the two demons, stepped sideways through the door. He would not have fit through the one open door full on with shoulders squared.

It was my cousin Reggie. The silhouette of his Afro gave the appearance of a halo around his head. He reached down, placing his huge foot on the back of the second ghoul and pulled his stick from their stacked bodies. It was in this process that I noticed a small slight figure to his right coming around him now into full view. The second figure was our other cousin from down home, Kimberly or Kim as we called her.

Reggie was a large dark-skinned brother who stood at least six-foot-five, with a deep heavy voice to match. He was also a bit of a ladies man. Kim on the other hand was quite small, the smallest in our group. I thought she was half Filipino and half African-American, but whatever she was, she was a real cutie-pie. Like Akina, she was a senior in high school and ready to join our ranks in college the following year. In the darkness there she seemed to almost glow.

Having dislodged his rod, Reggie twirled it a bit as he laughed, "Now, Avis what I done told you about cuttin' up?"

Avis snarled, "Damn you, Reggie. If you get in the middle of this, I'll take you out too! You don't have the Aunties to back you up this time."

He laughed again, "Avis, when's the last time I had to call one of them to handle you? Hmmm? Get real."

It turned out that in a strange kind of way Reggie had become Avis's keeper. As I was to find out later, he was pretty much impervious to her spells. I had gathered from the others earlier in the night that he was probably bulletproof too.

Regarding Kim, I really didn't know much. I'd seen her no more than nine or ten times before that night in my entire life. She was one of those relatives that unless you're in the inner circle, you'll never know the full truth about. I had never even heard about her until I was in the fourth grade. Then Reggie started bringing her around to the family cookouts down in Newnan, Georgia, where they both lived back then. I guessed that her dad was the illegitimate son of one of our aunties. I'd never met or even seen a picture of him or anything, but I assumed that or something like it to be the deal. Heck, knowing my Momma, my aunties and all their secrets, there was no telling what the truth was. Given what I'd learned that evening, I thought she might even be Uncle Paul's child. But one thing was becoming very clear on my second take of her in the darkness, it was not my imagination that she was glowing. I began to notice little sparks around

her, especially from her hands. At that moment I definitely
knew that she was one of us.

From out of the darkness where the light of the candles
did not reach, every sort of nightmare crept. They began to
circle us, criss-crossing between each other. One of them, a feline type of beast sprang at Darnell and he caught it by the
throat in mid-air and using its own momentum, slung it
across the hall. With that, all hell broke loose. Avis had been
expecting us and had conjured up all sorts of demons to anim-
ate lifeless objects, although I think some of them were physically straight from the gates of Hell.

Right after Darnell had slung the first one, a second one
lunged at Reggie. He dodged it and I heard him shout back to
Kim, "You stay behind me!" right before he swung his rod into
the mid-section of the beast.

Kim, who was also known in certain circles as "Arc", in a
bit of forced laughter mocked back to him, "Yeah, right..."
She then stuck out her hands and a bolt of electricity arched
from her hands into the flesh of the beast Reggie had just
felled, toasting it very well.

Akina had drawn quite a crowd, but they seemed more
bent on catching her than killing her. Four or five of them
circled around in some vague attempt to corral her away from
the group and further into the darkness. But her moves were
deft and from nowhere a sword had appeared in her hands.
She flipped, jumped and danced around them eluding them
while in the same movements, slicing them with her blade.

As for me, well let's just say that this was my finest moment, in a dodgeball sort of way. I tried to stay in the middle
scampering behind Reggie mostly. In the midst of this I noticed that none of these creatures even seemed to notice
Uncle Paul. I began to wonder why this was. Not out of sheer
curiosity, but in a sense of what it might be that he was doing
(or not doing) that I could do too to avoid these things chasing

me. It was in that moment of reflection that I was suddenly grabbed from behind and lifted up into the air. It was that feline creature. It lifted me to its mouth with its left arm while its right arm dangled from its shoulder held on by strands of pseudo flesh. Thankfully for me, the whole front of its snout, with which it was attempting to gnarl on me, had been smashed in by the collision with the column Darnell had tossed it into. But still, there were some teeth left in its disfigured head and on the one good hand it had, the claws were over an inch long. I was too surprised to cry out at first. At that moment its claws merely held me, but at anytime I knew that they could cut me into bite-sized pieces. I reached for its upper arm in an attempt to free myself and then, as before in that evening, I felt more than the surface matter that most feel. I felt beneath it, the gooey inside; the sliding, changeable inside. I began, quickly, to thumb through the Periodic Table of possibilities, then sensing somehow that I'd come upon what I needed. At that instant its arm began to vaporize and I was free. I fell to the floor. The beast, now basically armless, continued to make some pathetic aggressive attempts towards me until Reggie noticed it and decapitated it with one swing. Its catlike head fell to the floor and shattered, dislodging hundreds of maggots from its confines. I'm sure they were glad to be free too from that special hell. I gave Reggie a nod of gratitude and then immediately ducked in behind him again. I may have had certain gifts but I couldn't see where they were much good in this hand-to-hand combat thing.

Apparently Kim had come to a similar conclusion. She shouted out quickly, somewhat out of breath "They're moving too fast, and too close in."

"I know. Both of you against the wall, I can protect you better that way and you can watch my back." This last part about us watching his back was some gesture on Reggie's part for us to save face. I don't know if it worked for Kim, but personally I had no problem with Reggie being the "Man". I had kind of gotten used to breathing and any dude that wanted to prolong that activity got big props from me.

Standing next to me against the wall, Kim continued to fire out arcs of juice whenever an opening around Reggie appeared and there was a nightmare in sight. As for me, I just kept diving anytime something came my way. I did look up to see that Darnell was still going strong about twelve feet in front of us. For the most part, he was swapping blows with Avis's minions between dodging bursts of energy from the queen herself. I didn't know what would happen if one of them hit Darnell, but I figured that if he was avoiding them it must be bad. Avis was floating in the air trying her best to get an angle on Darnell, but he was too quick. Then he moved to the shadows on the left and took to the air himself. Moving within the darkness he began to fire back at Avis.

Off to our left, past Uncle Paul and the doorway, was Akina. She had cut down all but two of her assailants. In the midst of all her maneuverings, Akina took glances at us, then Darnell, and finally to where Carla was tied up. Following her gaze to Carla, I saw a second figure behind Carla. Finally it hit me like a ton of bricks. Shamefully, in all of my self-preservation I had failed to notice that Sandy wasn't with us anymore. But as I looked to Carla, I saw that the figure behind her was Sandy. She was working feverishly to free Carla. When the fighting had broken out while I had run for cover, Sandy had somehow worked her way through all of this chaos to free Carla.

Carla slumped momentarily as the bands that had held her captive fell to the ground. But then, looking up she noticed Avis and Darnell tussling in the air and this look came over her face that I'd never seen before, and she screamed out, "Witch, get your hands off my brother!" as she slung herself into the air, across the floor, into the rafters and into the back of Avis. They both fell to the floor. As Avis and Carla regained their footing, Darnell flew down to assist her, but Carla motioned for him to stay put. "Oh, no I owe this heifer! I came over here trying to be nice and you tied me up and tried to torture me? But it's my turn now."

But before Carla could make her move, Avis spoke some words in Latin and a drawing on the wall behind her sprung to life and towards Carla and Darnell. However, in the blink of an eye Carla reached out her hand towards a column to its left, pulling the column down as though she was pulling a string tied to a tower of children's building blocks. The marble column crushed the beast before it had taken three steps. Then, just as suddenly, large chunks of the resulting rubble rose into the air. "Girl have you lost your mind? Don't you know I will kill you?" Then the stones moving to Carla's command, hurled towards Avis. For the most part she eluded them through some kind of mystical barrier and just good old-fashioned bobbing and weaving, but one stone was true and felled her to the floor. Carla immediately hopped on top of her and began screaming at her. "What is wrong with you? Huh? What is wrong with you?"

Having no more terrors to slay, we all gathered around the two of them as Carla continued her rant. "Answer me! What is wrong with you?" Then the strangest thing began to happen. I noticed that Carla was crying and her demands were now pleadings as her tears began to fall on Avis's face. "Don't you remember when we were little and you used to take us to get ice cream? And now you're trying to kill us? What is wrong with you?" Carla had collapsed and now her face was pressed against Avis's. "Don't you know we love you? How can you do this? We love you."

Avis tried to turn her head away. And there I saw perhaps the most perplexing thing of all - the look of shame that came over Avis's face. It was as though she did not want to look at Carla. With her head turned and tears now rolling from her own eyes, I realized that Avis was no longer whispering incantations, but confessions of her own. "I'm sorry, I'm so sorry... I am such a horror, that I am not worthy of my life. Have no mercy on me, I beg you. Spare me of this life and what I have become." Carla's tears pierced her soul more than any stone or anything else that night. These were tears of condemnation of someone who truly loved her.

Darnell lifted his sister up into his arms, as Avis curled into a fetal position continuing to murmur.

Reggie asked the question, "So what do we do with her now? Usually the Aunties would put her on house arrest or restrict her for some time or something. None of us really has the power to do what they did and secondly what's she's done this time is much worse than before."

As Reggie began to pull a ball with straps on either side from his pocket to insert into Avis's mouth, Carla gestured toward him to stop. "No, let's not do that. I have a better idea. Sandy, go next door and have the neighbors call the fire department. Tell them there's a fire here."

"But there's no fire," I chimed in, really trying to be helpful.

Carla and Akina smiled at each other as Carla said to me, "No, not yet there isn't."

This got Avis's attention as she lifted herself from a prone to a sitting position on the floor.

"But my books! Take my life, but not the books!" Avis hastened.

"Yes, I'm sorry. Really I am, but this knowledge has been a curse to you. As of now, what you don't already have memorized, you will never know." Carla said as kindly as she could. "See Avis even though you had me bound and dazed I could still see enough to realize that you really don't have that much committed to memory besides your spells of self-protec-tion. Everything else you have to look up. I think this will help you to move on with your life."

Akina augmented, "Or at least you will have the opportun-ity to move forward. You can choose to search the world over to build this temple back again, but this is your chance now Momma for something better. If you want me in your life again and by your side, willingly, then you have to make a change Momma. It has to start now."

Ignoring his cousin's protest, Reggie proceeded to insert the marble ball into Avis's mouth and tie her hands behind her.

Before he secured it Avis gurgled out, "No, you don't un-derstand..." Her eyes bulged and her drained body bucked and lurched like a wild stallion, between moments of rest. But secure in Reggie's arms she quickly realized the futility of it all.

As he looked off, ignoring Avis and taking in what all of this meant, Reggie offered a thought, "Mmmm... we never did this before." He pulled at his goatee and lifted an eye towards the others.

"That's right! And you know why don't you?" an excited Kim offered as Avis scampered to her feet.

Akina, giving her mom a serious look said sarcastically, "I think we all know why."

Darnell quickly clued me in on their belief that the Aunties liked the idea of having such a vast library of mystic knowledge. Supposedly none of them practiced in the dark arts. The explanation given was that it was good to keep this library for research purposes. "Every good exorcist should have one," they argued, but my cousins had their doubts. Either way, it was clear that Aunt Deborah had delved into dark mysticism, or else they would be here cleaning up this mess. And that whole situation with Avis, just confirmed that this place should burn.

Reggie moaned in concession. "But hey, all I'm saying is that they ain't gonna like it."

Carla replied, "Well, they aren't around to agree or disagree with much of anything these days. Are they?"

Uncle Paul gave a nod of approval to Carla's summation. With that, invisible fire erupted from Darnell's eyes again, although the emissions from his eyes were clearly visible once they reached the books in the dark recesses of the room, and electricity arched from Kim's fingertips to the books that lined the walls of Avis's great room.

As the fire began to catch and take hold, Uncle Paul moved towards the door calling out, "Y'all it's time to go." To my surprise, given all that I had learned that night, they all moved without hesitation. Not that they shouldn't have, given that all the bookcases were now engulfed in flames, but I was thinking that if Uncle Paul was such a slime, how could any of them not bring up what he'd done to Avis, or allowed to be done to her. I felt at least someone should address the accusation... whatever it was. Avis spoke so vaguely that I wasn't really sure what it was he supposedly did or didn't do. It was then that I realized that Avis was right about one thing. Everyone, with the exception of me, already knew the truth for the most part. Apparently, even Kim, although this did perhaps explain why she always seemed a bit cold towards him.

I tried to ask Darnell what the deal was regarding Uncle Paul and Avis and he replied in a low voice, "It has been and still is an issue. The fact is that Avis was raped at thirteen and the man who did it was an acquaintance of Uncle Paul's. But how it happened or was allowed to happen is a matter of debate. To hear them speak of it is like hearing from two different people from two totally different worlds."

"Huh? What does that mean?" I was still dumbfounded. Why couldn't he just give me the whole story?

"I will holler at you later about it all," he whispered to me. Still unsatisfied, I let it drop for the moment.

We walked down the path towards the street with Reggie still holding tight to Avis.

Avis, now looking somewhat saner and more controlled, began motioning towards the house, but Reggie continued to drag her along.

Noticing her butt bouncing and legs dragging along the walkway, my attention turned back to Avis. "So what are y'all gonna do with her? Turn her into the police?"

Reggie laughed. "Yeah, right. Every time we do that she enchants the guards to let her out. I'm telling you, y'all better watch this girl. You can't give her a break. She'll try anything." He tossed her up unto his shoulder like a bag of potatoes. He argued that, "We can't be soft with her. I know from experience that you can't give her an inch."

Akina countered, "I know she's my momma and all so maybe I'm not objective, but haven't you and the Aunties always done that and now look at her. She's worse than ever!"

"Yeah, let's try to think of something different," Carla agreed.

Darnell, holding the gate open for everyone, mentioned softly to Carla, "How about Dr. Sitgraves?"

"Who is that?" Reggie asked.

Carla answered him, "She's a therapist I've been seeing. She counseled Darnell some time ago and she's worked with Akina. Hmmm?" Carla stood there for a second thinking as Reggie and Kim looked at her puzzled by the fact that this was even a consideration. She began again, "That just might work. I'll have to clear it with her first, but she already knows about..."

"What? You're kidding, right?" Kim could hold her tongue no longer.

Reggie was incredulous as well. "My God, this Dr. Sitgraves is not one of us and you're telling her all about us? That compromises all of us."

Carla tried to ease his concerns. "Don't worry, I didn't tell her about you and I've never mentioned Avis by name. She only knows about Darnell, Akina and me. No one else. I wouldn't do that."

Reggie thought for a second before asking, "So is she the one who told you come over here and try to talk to Avis?"

"Well, no not really. I thought of that on my own, but I did call her before I came, just to get her input." Carla conceded. Dr. Sitgraves had played a very important role in Carla's life to that point and she would, in a day to come, play an equally important role for each of us.

Sandy came running up to us and stopping just short, confused by the tone of disagreement she saw and felt. "I called. They're on their way," she announced before sliding back a bit. How can anyone be so shy of conflict and still so fearless?

Reggie continued with Kim nodding by his side. "So, what are we saying we do? Let her go and just have her get some therapy? I can't believe this."

Uncle Paul stood silently like some mute stone god, as though he had total faith in the outcome... regardless of what it might be.

Darnell, supporting his sister added, "Well, at least it's a start."

Reggie became enraged. "You all know that if the Aunties were here Avis might not live to see the morning. They've done it before for reoccurring problems that didn't have a resolution in sight. If she wasn't their niece she'd be dead already. Makes me sick! For all of this she has to be punished. This cold-blooded witch has killed who knows how many and tried to kill you. Who are we just to let her go? She walks just because we don't know how to hold her? Hell no!" he said, tossing Avis back to the ground and lifting his hand as though to slap Avis.

Carla grabbed his arm by the wrist and cried out at him, "The one's she has killed cannot speak but I, the one she tried to kill, can and today I say we spare her life. I do not know about tomorrow, and justice must be served someday but today I will show mercy, because I can and I have the right. Understand?"

As he drew back his hand his words were relentless, "Dear cousin that sounds nice, but I must disagree with you. We have a responsibility here and we cannot allow Avis or any one of us to do these things and live. You know that no human prison can hold her. At the very least we ought to cut out her tongue and turn her in to the authorities. Anything less than that makes us a party to the crime."

I have to admit I was seeing Kim and Reggie's side better than Darnell, Carla and Akina's side. But to follow them begged a question, which Sandy then asked. "I understand you Reggie, but who among us would actually kill Avis or even cut out her tongue? Could any of you really do that? Has anyone here besides Reggie ever killed anybody? I mean of all the assignments the Aunties have sent us on, we never had to kill living people. And Reggie, I know as a mercenary killing is a part of what you do for a living, but could you really mutilate, much less kill, Avis?" She stared at him like the disbelieving child she was.

Kim jumped back into the conversation. Her tone was compassionate to Sandy's complaint, "I understand you Sandy. I really do. And I know that I wasn't around much back when Avis was sane and all. But we have got to do something. Look at this yard. Look at all the lives she's taken. If it's not a matter of vengeance and it's not a matter of punishment, then at least it is a matter of taking responsibility to protect others."

Carla argued back. "I feel you Kim. But are we then the police, judge, jury and executioner? Who, besides the victim of a crime, has all those rights? Do we, if we do this thing, make ourselves gods? Why stop with Avis? Why not do that with everyone we battle? Do we decide everyone's worthiness and then punish accordingly? In this land the accused have rights. Are we above the law?"

Finally, we stood across the street looking back at the house being engulfed as we continued our debate. Then, suddenly Akina grabbed Carla's arm. "Look!"

Earlier in the night I saw spirits floating in and out of the midst of the house, but now in the flames I could see countless spirits scattering skywards, but a number of the spirits did not continue upwards, but instead took the shape of red fiery tongues in the front yard. One of them walked towards us as we began to hear sirens in the distance and the neighbors began to stir. The one flaming creature walked through the closed front gate. With each step it took on more flesh and more form.

Somehow Uncle Paul sensed this and cried out "Matasis!" It was his old mentor alive again. This ancient demon walked the earth again.

He reached out and pointed towards Uncle Paul, "You old blind fool, did you not know that when the sisters defeated me that they tied my soul to and within this old house, and that I have been locked within the pages stored therein? But of course you wouldn't have known, they didn't trust your pitiful mind with that information. In fact, even Akina, who surfs the very streams of time was kept unaware. Very impressive of them, but ultimately so very foolish." The fire trucks rounded the corner as he gave them a quick look. "Oh well, there's my cue to leave, but do not worry I will be in touch. By the way, you've also managed to free some other very interesting things. I'm sure you'll enjoy the next century or two trying to recapture them. But I must tell you I am really enjoying the double irony of it all. First, the sisters keeping everyone in the dark actually leading to my freedom. And Paul, the master puppeteer being played so well." He laughed and then began to fade into nothingness as he moved into the shadows.

Carla let out an, "Oh my God!"

Akina added, "That's what Momma was trying to tell us."

Reggie continued the collective stream of consciousness, "And that's also why the Aunties kept Avis around. They used her like a pitbull to protect all of this. Avis kept the demons on a leash and I was her leash. For all her power, she could never beat me. I was immune to her powers. I can't believe I didn't see this! And Avis played along because she had a vested interest in keeping all these things on lockdown. It kept her in charge."

I chimed in, "That also explains the crucifixes on the windows and the book jackets. This was a prison for evil spirits they couldn't send back to Hell. And we just burned it down and set all the inmates free."

Darnell, now void of all false pride, as were we all, made a suggestion. "Wherever the Aunties are, I suggest we go find them... now!"

As we continued to stare across the street we could see dozens of beings taking form and slithering into the darkness.

Kim summed it up for all of us, "Oh, shit!"

Reggie just then removing the ball from her mouth, a hard breathing Avis looked at Akina and exclaimed as she fought back the tears, "Baby, that was," speaking of Matasis, "your father."

Kim, now doubled over and slowly dropping to her knees, sighed just as slowly as she fell, releasing a second, "Oh, shit..."

8: Choose Your Weapon

"Vicki..." uttered a confused Karun as he locked the door back and pulled down the black, lightproof shades on the adjoining windows.

"Yes," she replied.

"What are you doing here? This is not the meeting place. Plus, it's eight o'clock in the morning."

"Yes," she replied again.

This time he just stared at her, dumbfounded.

"Yes, I am fully aware of what time it is and where I am. Don't worry, I was careful, as I always am. And I would like to stay until dark and leave through the tunnels." She pulled the scarf from her head, revealing a head full of somewhat straightened hair. She straightened her hair from time to time to aid in her ruse, but truth be told she would rather wear it natural, and in fact she did when she was at home back in the Artic Circle, home to the remaining Christians and displaced Muslims and Jews. On that day however, it would be clear to any that saw her that she was an African Queen. Cinnamon brown and strikingly beautiful, she had a walk and way so confident that surely she must have been royalty. What she was, was a field research operative for the Circle. Her primary job was to gather technical information from field operatives and to relay it home. A former engineer herself, she was well suited for this role.

However, today she hadn't come to Karun's shop for any such inside scoop on the enemy. Today she had come to visit an old friend. "Is Jonah in?"

"Yes, of course he is. Is something wrong?"

"No, everything is fine. Relax Karun. My schedule pretty much boxed me into pulling this stunt. I'm sorry if it upsets you, really. I'm on Resistance business. I have to ask him a couple of things." She browsed Karun's newest gadgets. "Hmmm, this is interesting. Oh, how's your wife?"

"Manisha is fine. She'll be down later." Karun stated matter-of-factly, almost like a threat. They both knew that Manisha couldn't stand Vicki. Perhaps Vicki had similar thoughts about her, but Vicki was not one to ever play her hand in such a way.

Vicki paused and then as if it were a second thought asked Karun, "Oh, and how is Jonah's wife?"

"Yes, Vicki. She has a name. Her name is Monica. You know this."

She smiled and looked up at him. "Yes, I do." She looked back down at the device in her hand barely suppressing a giggle. Although in the back of her mind the "stunt" Monica played back when she and Jonah were getting married, was still a source of irritation for Vicki. She saw it as a power play to either drive her away or force her to bow down. Vicki had never forgiven Monica for this "transgression".

Vicki had come to this life in an odd way. She never signed up to be a spy. She signed up to be an engineer. But after things broke down and having lost so many of those she loved, Vicki was an easy one to recruit. And although she was striking in her beauty and sharp mind, Vicki was just one of the faceless believers who over the years have sacrificed their own moral beliefs on behalf of the whole. Her role at times seemed to place her own soul at risk for the lives of others.

Vicki continued to mill about as Karun swapped glances between her and the front door. Finally, his patience ran thin and just as he was about to speak Vicki spoke first. "I know. You want to open your store. Sure go ahead. Given that it's daylight, do you mind if I spend the day in your safe room?"

Karun conceded, "Certainly. What choice do we have now? It is still in the same place. In the parts and repair room. I will buzz you in from here once you get down there. I'll call Jonah and tell him you're on the way down."

Abruptly she stopped him. "Oh no, don't do that. I want to surprise him. Thanks." With that she turned and made her way to the back of the store and then down below.

Once downstairs she stood in front of the sealed door for a good five seconds before the access light flashed green and she pushed the door open. Sliding through the door, she first thought the place seemed a mess. But then she noticed that all the repair items scattered around were tagged with tracking numbers and that the part's bins along the wall were sorted and equally labeled correctly. She proceeded to the opaque partition that separated the parts area from the repair area. This partition was largely to give Jonah a chance to flee or do something should someone discover that he is down there. Any life-sensing device would not be fooled by the partition but it gave Jonah a more secure feeling while he worked.

Vicki stepped past the partition and spying Jonah, she just stood there and waited for him to notice her. He was firing an ion laser into a device to achieve some very precise soldering. However, while he was consumed by this task, he had sensed that someone else was now in the room. At last he looked up and was nearly floored by who he saw. He sat back at first almost in disbelief then sprung to his feet and across the floor to meet her. Usually reserved, Jonah embraced her and lifted her up into the air to her unrestrained glee. "Oh wow, I can't believe it's you. You're alive!"

From above him, still lofted into the air, she questioned, "Oh, had you heard otherwise?"

Putting her down, he conceded, "Well, no, but you know I hadn't seen or heard from you in a while. I would think that I would hear something if anything happened to you, but so many people just disappear, well you know, it's hard to keep hope."

She smiled at him, "Yes, I know." Vicki was slightly taller than the average girl, and although her caramel-brown skin was slightly lighter than Monica's, she was more clearly of African decent. Typically, beneath her head wrap was a full Afro of kinky hair. Her build was a little leaner than Monica's, mostly due to her height. She was curvaceous, confident and clever.

For just a second, a single comment she made nearly ten years ago flashed in Jonah's head. Right after he got married he ran into her at a basketball game where in the midst of their conversations she blurted out in a tone of regret, "You got married too soon." At the time he was so stunned that he didn't know how to respond. He danced around it and to this day those five words still on occasion entered his mind and caused doubt, not about being married to Monica, but about Vicki's true feelings for him. Was she regretful for him or herself? In college he and so many others adored her, but she always treated him like a kid brother. But that day at the arena had been like blowing life into cooling coals. Having this thought, an uncomfortable moment later, he took his arms from around her waist and attempted to smooth out his smock. "I just can't believe you're actually here. Where have you been? What happened?"

She smiled almost laughing, "The reason you haven't seen me around, is because I haven't been around. I went up north to the Circle. Since that last Purge, when they broke our codes, all critical information has to be delivered face to face. Even with my cloaking device it took me a while to get up there. And once I did get there I spent a month spilling my guts to the Horton-Hears-a-Who crowd. Then, I decided to take a couple of months for myself. Hey, even spies, need a break every now and then."

Jonah was totally impressed that she was able to move back and forth so deftly. "Wow, that cloaking thing of yours must really work big time. Can I take a look?"

Even before she began to voice a response she was already handing it over to him. "Well, you know I really shouldn't, but since you helped to design one of the original models, I guess you earned it. It can make me completely invisible on three sides, up to 270 degrees, and translucent on the other. Used with the goggles you're always aware of where your exposed side is."

She studied him admiring her latest toy while pondering her next words and how she would broach the subject. She decided that a little more small talk was needed. "Jonah, why don't you build a cloaker for yourself?"

"Well, obviously early on I had one, but I really don't get enough of the Intelligence info down here to keep it current. Heck, the very phase wave I send out to mask myself, if not up to date could be like a beacon to anybody with new detection gear. Anything I build here powerful enough to make me invisible to the eye would show up like a blowtorch without the correct settings. I find it much simpler to fool the electronic eye than the human eye." He studied the device for another moment and then handed it back to her.

She nodded. She had thought his reasoning would be more about a lack of tools, not information. She hadn't really thought about that. Being in the loop you sometimes forget that most folks are outside of it. Finally, she decided it was time to make one of her reasons for being there known. The second reason she would play close to the vest for now. "Hey, dude you know we are still using your Wave Modulator as a shield to protect the entire Circle." This was the hand held device he'd developed years earlier before everything fell apart. The Circle had used to it create an impermeable shield around the Artic Circle. One of the prototypes that had left his shop in the time before had been supped up with more juice, but was really ninety-nine percent the same device he'd created with just different parameters supplied. Although it always had an effect zone, it was just that now, rather than punching in meters, there were thousands of kilometers being keyed in. It ran continuously, but with no moving parts it just simply seemed to never quit. Like the cloaking device it was all wave theory, of which, Jonah was a master developer. He was one of, if not the leading wave technology developer in the world before everything fell apart.

With some sense of pride he responded, "Yeah, it's still working. After all of these years it's kind of hard to imagine, huh?"

"Yes, it is. But that's partly why I'm here. There's a growing concern that the Blues will crack the barrier anytime now. Every other month we catch sight of another undercover team of theirs at some point along the barrier trying out some new technology to pierce it. We don't have any concrete evidence that they're close, but given the time that it's been in place even our most generous algorithms say that they should have developed some sort of counter measure by now. The Elders are so concerned that they sent me to invite you come with me when I return to the Circle. They have a couple of upgrades in mind that they feel certain could ensure the survival of the Circle for generations to come."

"So, they want me to come up there, huh? What about all that stuff about it was too risky to move me... to move us?" Jonah corrected himself to include his wife. Vicki winced a bit at the mention of her, but tried to hide it.

Vicki looked down, to hide her face a bit. She felt that maybe her emotions might betray her. "Well, they still think it's risky. But only three people outside of The Elders know that the man who designed the shield is still alive. That's me, you and Monica." Karun knew about the Wave Modulator and

Jonah's other toy, the Excavator. But, like so many who did know Jonah was alive, he'd never made the connection between it and the Circle's protective shield. Vicki continued, "They think it's worth the risk now. Moving you does increase the risk that you'll be found. It takes a network to move a person across the border and we try our best to keep our operatives in the dark as to the importance of any one refugee, but sometimes it does get out and we all know that the Blues have their counter-intelligence agents just like we do. But still, given the need, they think it's worth the risk. As long as they don't know you're alive, it should be okay."

Jonah untied his apron and placed it on the table. "So when are they thinking about moving us?"

Vicki looked down again, "Well, see that's the thing. They really don't want the both of you, just you."

"Just me? Why? What's with that?"

Vicki, feigning perplexity, replied, "I'm not completely sure, but they seem to think she's a security risk." What she did not tell him is that she, Vicki, was the one to plant the seed of doubt in their minds via her report. She mentioned the fact that Monica had been a member of the Blue Guard in her youth. This was an organization similar to the Boy or Girl Scouts, but its focus and mission were to inspire each child to live up to their genetic potential. Monica had not wanted to join such an organization. She resisted, but when she started middle school her mom enrolled her. Her mom thought it was a good way to mix with the "upper class". Godless though they were, Monica's mom felt like they would lead to unlimited connections for her daughter in the years to come. She rationalized too that placing her daughter within a group of sworn anti-Christians was some kind of evangelical statement... or at least that's what she told her friends. It was all for naught anyway because within three years the Blues pushed through a new law allowing segregation and discrimination by private organizations.

"A security risk? That's crazy. My wife is the most devout person I know. Her faith and honesty are without question." He thought for a moment about how he was lacking in the former and at least emotionally questionable in the latter. "Obviously, I can't, I won't leave here without my wife."

"Obviously," she replied. In the fishing game this is called "giving the fish some line." In other words she showed complete agreement with him, going totally in his direction. She would now begin the process of working his thoughts back to the place she wanted him to go… into the boat with her.

After a moment Jonah looked up at her and asked, "So what's going on up there? Really."

"Hey, if I could tell you anymore about what they're thinking I would. I'll let them know that you're not coming. They'll be disappointed." She also left off the fact that a couple of members of the council actually mentioned the idea of "terminating" Jonah if he refused to join them. The thought being that he was a security risk living behind enemy lines. But then, showing some moral fortitude, the body felt that his service warranted tolerating some amount of risk. Plus, they have other operatives like Vicki in place that could pretty much get to him anytime if the need arose later. They had time to fish too.

Jonah thought for a moment, then rolled his shoulders and went on to his next thought. "So, what's with you? I can't believe you came at this time of day. You'll have to stay till dark, right?"

In a seemingly begrudging tone she responded, "Yeah, I guess I will. The schedule we worked out for me kind of boxed me into spending the day here with you."

"Well, that's good for me because I get to spend some time with you, like back in the day," he said honestly, relating the sheer sincere pleasure he found in her company. "But it's gonna be hard on you to be cooped up in here all day."

"No, Jonah, it's fine, really. I mean I enjoy your company too." She smiled at him. She'd seen the way he looked at her and knew there was still a spark for her within him and she was determined to fan that glowing ember into a raging fire.

Changing the subject, Jonah asked about the Circle, "So what's the deal in Circle-ville these days?"

"Oh things are really happening. All the regions have sports teams now. We even have league games broadcasted now!"

"Oh, wow…"

"And you won't believe what else is going on." He had fallen right into the hole she hoped he would. She leaned back and began to tell him of all the advances and choices that had come back to life in the Circle. She knew that the sense of normalcy would remind him of how life used to be stateside. With full intent, she planted the seeds of desire for a return to how things used to be. She fully intended to harvest in a season of her choosing.

As always their conversation was effortless. Like back in the college, he could be witty with her. With Monica it was different. Sure they joked around, but she seldom got his jokes or the irony in some of the things he said. Jonah missed this give and take, this dance of the mind he and Vicki often played so many years ago.

Vicki was pleased too. She smiled more in the first twenty minutes with Jonah than she had in the last month. Not that she wasn't one to find humor in life, but her current occupation didn't really lend itself to such frivolity. But then for a moment both of them grew quiet as their walk down memory lane took a turn down the alley where her ex-boyfriend stood. Vicki had found herself in an abusive relationship with a guy named Buster. At first, he was everything Vicki wanted in a man. He was clever, attractive and financially secure, considering that his family owned a number of restaurant franchises. But once Buster got comfortable in their relationship, he developed a habit of showing Vicki the back of his hand whenever she said something that he disagreed with. In hindsight, she realized that there were signs early in their dating. At first, she took his aggressive, controlling ways as a sign of a real man who knew what he wanted. She was happy to have a man at last that could stand up to her. He was a man who felt passionately about her and having her. However, by the end of the first full beat down, with her eye blackened, she'd so gotten over that desire. Embarrassed and confused, she didn't call the authorities and instead she called Jonah with the intention of asking him to gather her class assignments from her professors to bring to the apartment she shared with Buster. But when Jonah arrived it was obvious that this wasn't a case of the flu. Without a moment of conversation Jonah dropped the lunch he'd brought her and grabbed her hand saying, "Uh-unh, this ain't gonna work. We're out of here." They packed up her essentials within twenty minutes, but before they could finish loading up Vicki's things into Jonah's vehicle, Buster showed up.

Buster immediately tried to walk up to Vicki as if to grab her. But Vicki twisted her body to avoid his grasp. In doing so she cowered behind Jonah like a little child hiding from an overly angry father. Jonah stood between them and shouted at Buster, "Look, unless you want me to give you some of what you gave her, I suggest you get out of my face, now!"

Buster could see that Jonah was serious and he appeared to concede for the moment as he went back into the first floor apartment. However, not a minute later, he returned outside walking briskly towards the couple and carrying a baseball bat. Vicki screamed as he raised the bat and moved towards them. Jonah, without really thinking about it, launched himself into Buster landing a right cross before Buster could bring the bat down. The blow staggered Buster sending him backwards. Jonah followed that with a combo that separated Buster from his bat and sent him reeling into the bushes. That concluded Buster's day and he never said a word to Vicki after that. Vicki and Jonah drove off with the bat for safe measure. Vicki, with Jonah's backing, threatened to file charges unless Buster left school and left town. Buster's parents made the decision for him. He was gone in little more than a week. Jonah would say later that he really didn't think about what he was doing, but there was such a foulness about the whole act that Jonah's entire being almost convulsed in striking Buster down when he returned carrying a bat.

Vicki spent her first night away from Buster with Jonah back at the student center. The two of them spent the night cuddled up on one of the couches. She vented, cried and slept in Jonah's arms all night. Jonah never told Monica those particular details. As the years went by, Vicki became more and more enamored with the moment. That night she learned about friendship, realizing in the years to follow that what she really learned about that night was love and that really there is no difference in the two. And there, so many years later, in the basement of some electronics shop, behind enemy lines, her appreciation was no less. In the years that passed she'd learned to love everything about Jonah.

For Jonah's part, he was filled with embarrassment by all the praise Vicki heaped on him. As he toured her around the lab, showing her each new device he'd perfected since her last visit, she responded with the wonderment of a child on Christmas morning. Hearing such accolades from her, someone with the same schooling as himself, meant a lot to Jonah. So many times, in those days particularly, he felt so worthless. But here was Vicki praising him and telling him of how the Elders of the Circle were continually amazed with the wave technology that protected their northern enclave. They were also impressed with the many gadgets Vicki brought back from her visits with him. Mostly, she was telling Jonah the truth. They were amazed, but then again nearly half the stuff he invented they found little use for and dismissed. But Vicki kept it all. Vicki truly believed in her friend and the products he produced. In her heart she knew that he was so far past what they were doing in the labs up north that many of these advancements were beyond them. She didn't see the point of telling Jonah that there were those back home who discounted his work. But the fact remained that the top five technologies decried and listed by the Blues as a threat to peace at the peace talks were the work of this man's hand. It pained Vicki to hold her tongue when debriefing the scientists back home. She told them that the works she brought back were from many different men. Their jealousy was such that she felt forced to do this. She knew in her heart that if they knew these things were mostly from Jonah they would not give each advancement fair consideration. Only she and the Elders knew the truth. So, she smiled at everything he showed her. Most she understood. Some she did not, but he was patient to show her and in those rare cases where she still didn't get it, she still smiled. In between these showings, they spoke of days gone by and she made sure to keep him laughing. That was something for which she truly had a gift and she gladly shared it with him. Her heart went out to him tolling away there day after day, year after year with no one who truly understood, to affirm that his labors were not in vain.

$$\infty$$

As Jonah and Vicki talked the hours away, upstairs Karun's wife, Manisha had made her way from the storeroom to the main floor.

"What? Vicki is here, downstairs, in our store? Why would you let that terrible witch into our store? If I'm going to be hauled off and executed by the Blue Lords, I do not wish to do it for aiding the likes of her."

"She is here to see Jonah."

"I know she is here to see Jonah. That is obvious. That still does not explain why you let her in. How long has she been here?"

"All day. She was standing at the door when I opened the store."

"And didn't you find that the least bit strange?"

"Well, I was surprised."

"And nothing beyond surprised? Did you not think about why she came so early?"

"She said it was the only time her schedule allowed and..."

"Her schedule! Is it not obvious that she came by so early to force you to allow her to stay all day, to spend all day with Jonah? You men are all so simple..."

"But she is on official business for the under.." He froze mid-word from the gaze that she leveled at him.

Manisha started in again, "Does Monica know she's here?"

"No, I do not think so. She..." Karun attempted to answer.

"Of course not. This is the one day of the season that Monica would never stop by. Oooh, that evil bitch!" With that she stormed towards the back of the store headed for the stairs that led to the maintenance area below.

Karun gave a quick whispered shout to her to get her attention. "Manisha!" Then he walked briskly to catch her and grabbed her by the wrist. "Where are you going?"

"I'm going downstairs to throw that hussy out! I do not want her in our store," she protested as she squirmed to free herself from his grip.

"Manisha, we cannot throw her out in the middle of the day. You know this. She would be spotted immediately. None of her stealth-wear works in the daylight. You know this. Manisha, please. We have customers."

She looked around a bit relaxing her scowl, not that she really had much of one anyway. "Okay, I won't throw her out," she whispered, "but I do want to go down and talk to her."

"Later, you are too steamed right now. Cool off a bit first. Okay?"

She relented a bit, but then refocused, "Well, have you at least checked in on them?"

He laughed, "They are not children!" His laughter was drowned by a second red-hot gaze, inferring that the fact that they were not children was exactly her point. His bowed head gave a more acceptable reply, "Alright, I will go downstairs straight away to check on them. You wait here." He departed for the lowest section of the store.

Upon reaching the bottom floor he paused for a second before entering the repair area. He had laughed at his wife's suggestion, but still he thought that if it were true he'd rather not know. So, he cleared his throat rather loudly before going in to give them some warning that he was approaching. Pushing the unlocked and slightly ajar door fully open he saw no one out front, but he heard them talking in the back work area. Rounding the corner, he saw Vicki sitting up on the far end of one of the workbench tables with her legs dangling in the air. Jonah was to her left leaning against a second table that was perpendicular to Vicki's table. "So, how are you two making out?" He smiled warmly mostly because he was relived to see that he could give his wife a good report.

Vicki smiled back warmly, "We're just fine. I was just catching Jonah up on what's going on up north. Is your wife in yet?"

Karun replied looking down a bit, "Yes, she is upstairs."

Vicki lifted a brow genuinely surprised that Manisha had not made an appearance. She sat frozen for a moment not knowing what to say next. Finally, she blinked her eyes and gave a stilted "Okay..."

Karun gave her a look acknowledging the awkwardness of the situation.

Vicki began to slowly swing her legs again. "So, I guess I will be staying down here."

"Yes, that might be wise," Karun conceded.

Jonah bowed his head in mild disbelief and utter concession to understanding women. Almost all of the women in his life hated Vicki and for the life of him he couldn't understand why. He found her exciting and entertaining. Her honesty could be brutal sometimes, but her charm more than made up for that, to him at least anyway. Occasionally he thought that maybe his affection for her glazed over her faults. But then he'd think isn't that true of everyone you care for? He smirked a bit and then re-engaged Vicki. "So, what made you decide to come out today of all days? You know what day it is, right?"

"Oh, I'm very aware of what day it is. It's execution day. Actually this is the best day of the week to move about, especially around here. Sure there are more people in the street during the day, but once they round someone up and take them off to the Central Square, it's actually almost deserted everywhere else. The Blues are either with the mob in the Square or they're at home watching the broadcast. So, once night falls I shouldn't have a problem sliding out of here."

Jonah and Karun both laughed at her moxie. The gall to come there and to hide in plain sight so close to the authorities both amused and impressed them. "You are certainly the girl!" Jonah acknowledged.

The rest of the afternoon passed with a lightness none of them had known in some time. Jonah and Vicki both laughed at the numerous, and now funny, tales of Vicki "the spy", while Karun flashed upstairs to check on the store, but always returned quickly to rejoin the banter. Given that his wife wanted him downstairs as much as possible, his being away from the sales floor wasn't a problem.

At about five o'clock, they turned on the evening broadcast. A three dimensional talking Blue head babbled on about several national events, some local stories and a token feel good story about an Indian festival to be held that weekend. Lastly, they reminded their viewers that today was the first day of what the Blues called "Alignment".

"Alignment" was a euphemism for the almost quarterly practice the Blues had for publicly executing a select number of detainees accumulated over the last period. The detainees to be executed were supposedly composed of persons who would not conform to the "natural order" of things, that "natural order" being that the Blues were now the highest caste and as such, their way was to be "the way". Most of the people convicted of this crime were Christians, supposed Christians, and political enemies of the state.

As the broadcast ended Vicki turned to Jonah and Karun and announced, "I think that's my cue to beat it out of here. Karun, is your tunnel secure?" There was an abandoned subway line that ran right in front of Karun's business. Unfortunately, it was a dead end at one end and lead to the Main Square on the other end.

A slightly mystified Karun replied without doubt. "Of course, but..."

"I know, it lets out into the Square. If I leave now that should put me there just about dusk, but before the mob gets

there. My cloaker should get me to the safehouse just fine.
Oh, Karun I think I left my goggles upstairs. Without those
I'll never be able to see in that tunnel. Would you please run
upstairs and look around for me? I hope nobody picked them
up."

Karun nodded his head and departed for the upper parts
of the establishment. Vicki turned back towards Jonah.
"Strange, isn't it Jonah, how this whole world has turned
around on us in just ten short years."

His sigh acknowledged her point. "Yeah, sad isn't it? And
what's worse I think we are just at the beginning of a long
dark period in our lives here on earth."

Vicki looked down and continued, "You're right. And I
really don't think any of us will live to see this country or
much less this world free of the Blue way." She walked over
to him to give him a hug. "Hey, think about what I said. I will
let the Elders know about your reluctance to leave your wife
here. Come on now, give me a tight squeeze. That tunnel is
going to be cold and wet, and besides we never know if we'll
see each other again."

Jonah hugged her tighter, tight enough to feel the definition in her body. His emotions were mixed, but he needed the
hug as much as she did, maybe more. Like her, so much of his
past had slipped away and here was something tangible,
something real from his past that bore proof of a better day
now gone.

She held on to him for a long moment and then with her
mouth close to his ear whispered, "Thanks, I needed this.
Sometimes it's really lonely out there on my own." Then half
a moment later her body stiffened just a bit as though she'd
just remembered something. "Oh, snap. I need to run by the
restroom before I go. I can't be doing my business in the
streets." With this she slowly pulled herself from his grasp.

He looked at her as if slightly under the influence of some new strange drug. She smiled a shy smile, "I'll be right back."

As she ran off to the basement restroom his heart tugged and he struggled to regain his composure. He thought he'd overcome it, but there was still something there. This was something that had preceded Monica's reintroduction into his life right before he graduated his senior year of college. Perhaps it was something that had preceded even his meeting Vicki. While Monica was his better half and closest friend, there was something about Vicki that he had longed for long before he ever met her and she gave a name and face to it that day freshman year. It was always a pleasure to see her, just as it was always a torment. He thought those days were over, but they were back, just down the hall in the ladies room.

While Jonah was lost in thought, Karun rushed into the room. "Where is she?"

"She ran down to the restroom for a minute. What's up? Did you find her goggles?"

"No, I didn't. I looked and looked, but I could not find them anywhere. So, I brought her a pair we sell up on the third floor. Not regulation and it won't help with the use of her cloaker, but it's the best we have here."

Karun looked over his shoulder to see Vicki breeze into the room. Seeing the brand new pair of night goggles in his hand, she smiled and exclaimed, "Oh, thank you Karun. You are so sweet, but when I went into the restroom, I found my goggles in the bottom of my bag, stuffed beneath my night wrap." She gave him a quick hug and pulled away telling him, "Please tell your wife hello for me. I think it best that I not go back upstairs with all those customers wandering around." They exchanged conceding glances of relief.

She stepped to Jonah, extending her hands to grab his, pulling him close enough for her to kiss his cheek and whisper to him, "I'll be in touch later, okay? You be careful. As of right now, the Blues still don't know that you're alive, and much less where you are. Let's keep it that way." She took a step back still holding his hands together with hers. Saying nothing, she made eye contact and froze him there, and then, facing away from Karun, gave Jonah just the slightest nod, and then a slight smile as she released his hands from her lingering fingertips.

Karun grabbed a small dinner bag of food packed in an airtight bag and handed it to her as he led her out of the room. As he put his arm around her shoulder to lead her down to the other end of the hall to the tunnel entrance, Vicki glanced back one last time mouthing one last "bye."

Jonah suddenly realized that his heart was racing again. It had raced that morning when she first walked in and during the early morning awkwardness until their conversation became more natural towards the afternoon. But here he was all hyped up again. In his next breath, he thought about his wife, Monica. In his third breath he felt shame that he had not even thought about her all afternoon on that most dangerous day. In some ways she was safer than he was. On a Blue holy day like this one she carried one of the Excavators and could really level anything in her line of sight with it. Plus, she was half Indian, and could pass any of the genetic road blocks that occasionally popped up on days leading up to days like this one. Still, he knew he was remiss in not offering up the first prayer for her since he arrived that morning. Vicki had totally consumed him. Interestingly enough, it wasn't that Vicki had done it to him, but he felt he had done it to himself and he was at fault. And although Jonah's faith had begun to wobble a bit as of late, he still fell to his knees right then to pray for forgiveness and safety of his wife.

The bad part about days like this one was that he was unable to leave until well after the executions were finished and the crowd had dispersed. It would surely be past 11:00PM before he could safely head home. The location of Monica's job and her path home meant that she had to leave before the event and he had no way of contacting her without increasing the chance that she would be caught or their home discovered. He hated days like this. It would be very late before he would know that she made it home okay and that would be far too late to do anything about it.

Nearly an hour passed by in perfect quiet. Then about 6:15PM Jonah heard the rumblings of activity somewhere down the street through the pipes that ran along and through the basement. About 6:26PM he began to hear the chants. They were chants of detestation and devastation. He'd heard these chants before and they'd gotten close before, but always as his heart had begun to race, the sound of them would begin to fade. As the chanting and rumbling through the pipes got closer he stopped working and stood completely still. He stood there looking up as though through the floor, listening. Jonah listened for some tell-tale sign.

Unlike before, the steady progression did not abate when his heart neared his throat. His gaze grew steady on the ceiling above him. He began to hear angry words and loud talking above. Not that Jonah could make any of it out, but the tone of what was being said transmitted easily thorough the metal pipes above him. As the confusion seemed to close in around him, Jonah glanced around the room to consider what he might use to defend himself. He dare not try the tunnel at that moment because the door only locked from the inside and if they were coming for him he'd be trapped with few tools to defend himself. Of course he had his Wave Modulator and the Excavator. But there in his shop, he could certainly go out with much more of a bang. He had the basics like an electrical arc welding torch, plus a number of very flammable gases hooked to his other torches. Besides that, he had some industrial lasers and pseudo fusion devices. These assisted in his molding matter to the proper state to meet the needs of the array of specialty, gray market devices that Karun made such a killing selling. Many a day Jonah thought that if push came to shove he could rig one of these devices to set off a small nuclear explosion. It would be a reaction that would just send out radiation, similar to the tactical nukes that were so popular in modern warfare. He knew that this same wave shield he used to hide and contain radioactive materials in his workshop could protect him and anyone else in the room, but in his heart he knew that he could never do that. Although knowing he could do such things had given him a certain comfort, he knew he could never do that, never kill so many just for his own survival. The lasers were flashy but really not very effective at stopping people. The heat was beyond that which a nerve could feel and though it would put a hole in you, it often cauterized the wounds it caused, allowing the target to continue aggression. No, the arc torch was the best offensive weapon he had. And the pseudo fusion could power the torch for a thousand years. He knew he would only go so far to save his own life, and these items were his best hope given his personal constraints. He gripped them tightly in his hands.

Looking up again, he heard a large crash, and he instinctively ducked. He heard a woman screaming in protest. Was that Manisha?   By reflex he called out "Karun!" The two of them had discussed this before and in such situations he was to remain hidden in the workshop area until he heard directly from Karun. But there was more screaming and tumbling that sounded like someone was being dragged out to the street. But surely Karun would call for his assistance if it was his own wife being attacked. Then another thought occurred to Jonah - what if it was Monica up there? He began to reason that maybe she had come over to discuss with Karun his plan to steal back the heart-shaped "Artifact" from the museum. Surely she had better sense than to come downtown on this day. Surely. Surely? Doubt began to seize him to the point that he put down the torch and ventured beyond the secure area and towards the door. The sounds were so muddled that he couldn't really make out if that woman sounded like Monica. As the crowd began to move away he wanted to bolt up the stairs and out the door to follow them. Jonah moved quickly to the stairwell, but before he'd climbed three steps, the door swung open. It was Karun at the top of the stairs.

Karun was soaking wet from perspiration, his eyes flashing wildly. "They took Sara from two doors down! They broke in and took her!"

Jonah rocked back, "Oh my God! Not Sara... We can't let them do this to her."

Karun still breathing hard, his hands on his knees, replied, "My friend, what can you do now? They have already taken her."

Jonah looked around, considered and then made a decision. "You call her husband and let him know that the mob took his wife. I've got an idea." Jonah grabbed one of his pocket reactors, a micro laser and his energy Wave Modulator.

Karun glared at Jonah, "What are you going to do with that? Are you mad?" he shouted.

"Yes, I'm mad! But not as mad as you think I am. Just lock the tunnel door behind me." He held Karun's gaze for a moment and breathed a calming sigh. "Look man, this is not a suicide mission. You just have to trust me on that. Okay?"

Karun yielded. "Okay, my brother. Go in Peace."

They gave each other a quick hug and Karun departed. As Jonah gathered his tools, he gave a quick shout to Karun who by then was back at the top of the stairs. "Hey dude! Make sure you lock this thing back. I'm gone."

Jonah threw on his boots, cape and wrapped his face as best he could. He walked along the basement hallway the length of the building, his backpack strapped across his back and his night goggles dangling from his mouth, their strap clinched within his teeth, while he put on his gloves. As he paused at the tunnel gateway, a prayer convulsed from his lips. "Lord, help me."

Jonah pulled back the façade hiding the gate and then he flung it open to reveal the darkness beyond. Placing his goggles over his eyes, he paused again and reflected for another moment. "Lord, I pray for the shield of your hand over Sara. And regarding myself, I place myself in your hands. Your will be done." At that he stepped down and pulled the large metal door closed behind him. He guessed that he had about fifteen minutes... Fifteen minutes to save someone dear... Fifteen minutes to risk so much in doing so... Fifteen minutes to control his fears... Fifteen minutes to join his brothers.

9. Into the Pit

"Oh shit!" Kim sounded very much her age. She sounded like the typical high school girl when mommy and daddy get home from vacation a day early.

The rain and wind were now in full effect. With rain coming from the direction of the house, it was hard to see. Were it not for the street lights no one could have seen more than two feet in front of themselves.

We all made our way back to the Waffle House. A stray cat huddled behind the newspaper bin beside the entrance as we entered. It was empty inside except for the cook and one waitress. We took up two tables. Reggie told the staff that he was a bounty hunter, which he was, and showed them his credentials. He said that Avis was his prisoner, which she was, and they let it go. The two points together were a lie but taken separately they held some truth. They assumed the gag ball, which was then back in Avis's mouth and tape over her mouth was to prevent her from biting anybody. That worked just fine for Reggie and he let them believe it.

We sat at two booths directly across from each other. In the booth next to the window, Avis sat on the left next to the window. Across from her sat Kim. To Avis's right was Uncle Paul. Across from Uncle Paul was Reggie. You could tell from Avis's expression when she first sat down, that she hated being next to Uncle Paul, although her face loosened a bit after a minute. On our side of the aisle I sat in the left corner with Darnell to my right. Across from us the three girls, left to right, Carla, Akina and Sandy sat scrunched up together. Carla's butt was a little big to be trying to sit on the end, but since she wanted to be in the middle of the conversation it was her chosen position. It was past two in the morning so we

130

pretty much had the place to ourselves and would for as long as we wanted to be there. We sat there drinking coffee and tea, trying to calm ourselves and weighing our options. It was storming outside, so it felt good to be inside, given the circumstances.

Reggie looked towards Carla then Akina and responded to the question of how we could find these escapees, "I can spot them when I'm in close proximity, but that's about it."

Akina looked up from her nervous habit of biting her nails. "I can track them, but I have to know what I'm looking for. I'm sure that I can find Matasis, even though he's a shape shifter. But I think he may be the last one we want to find right now."

Carla added in for herself and her brother, "So, what do you want to do regarding the others? We can deal with them once they reveal themselves, but that's about it."

"Maybe we should go after Matasis?" Reggie offered. "Hey, he has already said that he was coming after us. The best way to deal with that is to take it head on." Kim, as usual, nodded in agreement with him.

Akina replied, "Hmmm, I don't know. I mean if we have to deal with him now then we do. But I think we, working as a group, need to work up to someone like him. From what I know, besides being able to change his appearance, one touch from him can be fatal."

Then I, from off in the corner, got the nerve up to state my opinion. "Maybe we should ask her?" I stared straight at Avis.

Everyone kind of readjusted themselves in their seats as they tried to readjust their thinking.

Reggie was the first to reply, "I don't know about that." But he really couldn't back it up with a reason besides he just didn't trust her.

Carla answered him, "Do we really have a choice?"

Uncle Paul, remaining silent, simply nodded.

Kim, who was sitting next to Avis, started to remove the tape from Avis's mouth, but then gave a glance back at the lone waitress and chef on duty. "What about them?"

Akina offered, "Carla why don't you give them a suggestion."

Closing her eyes and entering an almost trancelike state, Carla responded "I was just about to do that."

Then suddenly the waitress blurted out, "Hey Rob, cover for me. I gotta run to the bathroom."

"Okay," he grunted.

Again Carla closed her eyes and then a few seconds later the cook hollered out to us. "Hey, could y'all please tell anyone that comes in to just have a seat?" He headed to the back as well.

Carla opened her eyes looking somewhat upset. "That guy was tough. He doesn't trust us. Anyway..." She looked at Kim to proceed.

I coughed up a, "You can make people do things?"

Reggie grimaced, "So do you only ask obvious questions?"

Carla smiled at Reggie and then shrugged it off. "Well, it depends. Among other things, I have this knack of making people feel like they got to take a dump. What a skill right? But it comes in handy."

Kim leaned across the table to remove the tape and ball from Avis's mouth. All of our eyes were transfixed on her, except for Darnell, who jumped up to lock the door.

Avis rubbed her mouth, and somehow more modest now, she looked more like one of us than earlier when she looked like something unfit for this world. "Some night huh? Well, I know what you need to do. You need to go get your parents. Nobody here is able to deal with this. Yes, I can summon some of these free spirits, and maybe we could deal with those, maybe. And even my daddy who has the power to summon all of them, does not know who these cats are and he needs their names to call them. Only the Aunties know for sure, and I hope they've got a backup copy somewhere of who these guys are. The hard fact is that we alone cannot find these guys, let alone recapture them. Now, what daddy doesn't want to bring up is going into the Pit as we call it."

Uncle Paul interrupted her. "Avis! Let's think about this."

Avis replied, "Poppa, you've been thinking about this for the last hour. We have no choice. As you know, one of your aunties went on a bender. Imagine that in this family?" She smiled and laughed at her own instability. "Sorry Darnell and Carla, let me restate that. Your mommy, Aunt Deborah started dabbling more and more into the dark arts, especially calling spirits up from the Pit. I don't know everything about it, but I know that if you spend too much time in it or dealing with it you can get caught up like Aunt Deborah. It's not a place for those made of flesh and blood. You have all sorts of things prowling around there. It's a place where you can lose your immortal soul. Really. And don't go getting all religious on me. I can't explain why such a place exists but it does.

Uncle Paul broke in, "That's where I thought your aunties had sent Matasis. But in hindsight I can see their reasoning now. Your Aunt Cil, the oldest, who died last year, had banished him there once before, before I changed my life... but he came back. So, I guess this time she decided to keep him close, bound up in that old house. Plus, since her health was bad I guess she didn't want him to come back when she wasn't around. She didn't know that she'd live another sixteen years or that someone like us would be fool enough to burn the house down. Avis was young, and had a vested interest in keeping the house. They told Avis the deal, but I see why they didn't tell me. They thought I might backslide into my old ways one day, especially with my mind going bad. I understand it now."

Uncle Paul continued, "These gifts can be intoxicating. But your Aunt Sarah and Ruth are very gifted and yet they remain humble. Not so for Deborah, she's been looking over the fence her whole life and now she's finally gone over. And how strong are any of you? What if you get caught up or maybe have your soul devoured?"

"Devoured?" Kim questioned, with a doubtful look. Kim definitely had issues with Uncle Paul.

"That's right, devoured. You don't have to believe me. Go there yourself and you will see why that may be preferable to living an eternity there. I was there and if it weren't for divine intervention, I would still be lost. And truth be told, the true blessing of my old age, besides my salvation, is that I have forgotten so much of my life, including my time in the Pit. What a blessing that is."

Kim rolled her eyes and let it go. Avis added in, "He's telling the truth. I've never been there but I've seen into it, and I have no desire to go there. The best way I can describe it is as a place somewhere between the living and the dead. Looking at it though, I'd say mostly the dead."

Darnell, sitting next to Kim on the aisles asked, "So, let's say we do decide to go. How do we get there and how long will it take?"

Carla added, "Yeah, I don't know if now is the time to skip town for any length of time."

Avis, after taking a sip of water, shook her head until she could swallow. Her curls danced across her face. She really is quite attractive when she's not trying to kill you. Regaining her voice, she clarified for us, "No, you don't have to worry so much about time. See regardless of how much time you spend there it really doesn't have much to do with how long you're away from this reality. But you could be in there for years and only have a week pass by here. Now, as far as how you get there, well that's not so much of a problem. I mean if you invite certain malevolent spirits into your home, they'll be more than happy to take you there. The really hard part is getting back. That's where Akina comes in. Your girl-friend here should be able to take you and bring you back. See she goes places she doesn't want to tell y'all about."

"Mama, I've never taken this many through," Akina pro-tested.

"I know, but you can," Avis chimed back.

Uncle Paul reclaimed the floor. "Avis, you make it all sound like a trip to the beach. They would be far safer fight-ing hand to hand with every demon loose on earth than to go there."

Avis replied back, "So, you're saying they shouldn't go?"

Reggie, who had been hard at work on a couple of pork chops he pulled off the grill, took a break to address the group. "I don't know why y'all discussing this. We all know we've got to get the Aunties back here from wherever the heck they're at to nail these suckers again. I mean who else besides us can do this? It has to be us and that is our only real option. There comes a time when you have to step up and this is it. Case closed." The lightning flashed outside and the lights inside began to flicker, but Reggie was undeterred from continuing his meal. He liked to eat.

Sandy, stretching her upper body around Akina to see Uncle Paul, asked him, "So Uncle Paul, do you think we can do this?"

Turning his whole body from the window to face us all, he added, "Children, I tell you the truth, I have seen the very gates of Hell and I would not wish it upon anyone, even my worst enemy."

As the lights flickered on and off and back on again from the last lightning bolt, a heavy voice replied back to Uncle Paul's statement, "What Paul, not even me?" It was Matasis standing on the other side of the glass window pane from Kim and Avis.

Kim bolted up from her seat and the window, back into and over Reggie. As she rose up she flashed a bolt of her own lightning into and through the window. Simultaneously, Darnell jumped from our booth towards the window, invisible fire raging from his eyes. It flared towards the window, only becoming visible once it reached the darkness outside. However, his blast was redundant since Kim's knee-jerk charge had already blown glass shards out onto the sidewalk beyond. Darnell leaped out through the opening into the night air. Reggie grabbed their table from the end that had been next to the window and tossed it up and away nearly hitting those of us still at the other table. But we were all up on our feet anyway, peering into the darkness for this bold dark opponent.

Within five seconds we were all through the opening and standing in the darkness, raindrops and wind damping our view. Then, Akina shouted, "Over there! To the left in the trees, five trees from the corner."

There he was, barely visible in the darkness and driving rain, but there nonetheless. He was just standing there, waiting. Darnell took a step, at which Uncle Paul grabbed him by the arm. "Hold on there. He's testing y'all. He can sense whose children you are, but he don't know anything about you or what you can do. He wants to see."

Darnell, still in attack mode and not wanting to turn it off just yet, replied, "So, why don't we show him just a bit?"

Reggie grabbed Darnell's other shoulder and cautioned, "Uncle Paul is right. If he really wanted to fight he wouldn't be playing peek-a-boo. He would have jumped on us right off. No, he's hoping we'll chase him into the woods. He's thinking that if he can knock one of us off, great, but if not then at least he'll know more about us. Let's keep him in the dark as long as we can. Though the next time we see him I'm sure he'll have a couple of buddies with him."

"So maybe we should take him now," Carla added.

Avis, who had stepped out front for a better look, glanced back at Carla. "No, we don't have a plan or anything. He's very slippery. If we do catch him without a plan, I can guarantee you that he'll take one of us with him. If we battle him now, no way do we all go home. We need to fight him on our own terms." It was heartening, at least for me, to hear Avis say "we." I knew that I would feel a lot better with her on our team, than against us, but who knew who's team she was really on?

Then, without warning, a flash of blue light erupted towards us from out of the darkness. I ducked but saw it dispersing around us along some, until then, invisible shield. A second bolt came from the tree line illuminating the outer barrier. At that moment I didn't know what that energy could do and I didn't want to find out. Also, I wasn't sure who was protecting us until Kim spoke up. "Thanks, Avis."

Darnell turned to whisper into Reggie's ear. "We may still have a fight here tonight. That stuff doesn't affect you does it?"

Reggie answered, "No it doesn't, but he doesn't know that. And I don't want him to know it until I'm right up on him."

Uncle Paul called out, "You may have taken my sight, but I can still smell one as foul as you, Matasis." That was the first I'd ever heard about how Uncle Paul lost his sight.

We watched him, or at least a shadow we thought to be him, move through the woods. Someone called out, "Look, there are others with him!" Standing in the back, trying not to be seen by whatever was firing at us, I heard something behind me. I turned to see the cook's empty car starting on its own and then lurching towards us. Kim spun around quickly and stretched out her hand towards it. Sparks flew everywhere as she fried the car's electrical system. It smoldered for a second and then burst into flames. I hoped the rain would douse it, but at that moment the fire began to rage and fight the rain.

At that, Uncle Paul announced, "He's gone and so are the rest of them. The thing he fears most is to have his existence documented. The fire will bring cops and firemen. People like that file reports. He doesn't want this world to know about him until he's ready. Besides, he got some of what he wanted. He knew about Avis, but now he's also seen a little of what Kim can do."

At long last we looked back toward the Waffle House. The cook and waitress, having both exited the bathroom, poked their heads just above the counter top. The cook had the phone in his hand. Darnell looked at Carla and said. "You've got some damage control to do." Soaking wet, she nodded in acknowledgement to her brother and trudged off towards the unhappy couple, forcing a smile all along the way.

Akina and Sandy, on the other hand were stooping behind the newspaper bin to fetch out the cat that had been hiding there. They pulled its limp body out and held it up to the floodlight looking for a sign of life and found none. Sandy took the cat from Akina and continued to stroke it. Kim mentioned that she should put the cat in the fire. Sandy held it close for another silent moment and then did as Kim asked. The unearthly energy from Matasis' hands that Avis had blocked from touching us, had drained all life from the kitty. I realized right away that that could have been us.

Eventually, we all made it back inside. Uncle Paul stood in the small double-door foyer facing the night. Carla convinced the cook and waitress that they really didn't remember much of anything and to tell the police that when they arrived. But still we knew our window to depart unnoticed was small and shrinking. I took the opportunity to join Uncle Paul in the foyer.

"Uncle Paul, I know this may not be the time, but I have just got to ask you. What was all that stuff Avis was talking about back at the house?"

Uncle Paul adjusted himself just a bit and took in a deep breath. "Where do I start? For a period of my life I served the darkness and what happened to Avis is just some of the harvest of the seeds I sowed. I sought to ingratiate myself with more powerful evil spirits that I might learn more about them and somehow betray them all someday in some sort of ultimate checkmate. But it was I who was played. People like your grandfather tried to warn me, but I wouldn't listen. At my estranged wife's request, I even allowed my daughter, my last child, my youngest child, Avis to be taught in the ways of witchcraft to prove myself.

See, I had the ability to bend most anyone to my will. Even most spirits obeyed me. I corrupted good people in the insanity of my cause. I cannot count the number I've led astray. Nor can I count the number of demons I've placated and suffered in my grand delusion. Along the way I began to entertain spirits and command them to carry out my bidding. That is how I ran into Matasis. I was seeking control of a minister, but there was resistance. Not from him, but from another dark spirit that already had possession of him. That spirit was Matasis. Initially, we battled. When neither of us could dominate the other, we decided to work together towards our common goal. We came upon the idea of forming a league of like-minded evil-doers. We recruited many over the years, but the ones you saw in that photo were our last group. During this time in the wilderness, your grandfather battled me tooth and nail, and I'm thankful that he did. Were it not for him, my legacy would have been far worse. I know for sure that he saved many lives, including my own in some ways.

I left the group within a month of the date on that picture you found. See, even though Matasis and I were working together, we were still in competition, I just didn't know it. We defiled one sacred thing after another until soon after that photo was taken I found out that Matasis had been forcing himself on Avis. I went to the annual gathering of Avis's mother's order. I knew Avis would be there too. That day, when I saw Avis she was obviously pregnant and instantly I knew who the father was. I confronted her mother, my wife, but when I saw a part of his spirit on her, I realized that she had been with Matasis too and had condoned this thing. As soon as Avis's mother confessed, I saw Matasis. I ran towards him my arms stretched out to his neck, but he disappeared into nothing but laughter in the shadows of the arena. The whole brood of witches laughed at me as I lay there sprawled on the floor clutching nothing. In my anger, I summoned up a destroyer from the Pit and he slew so many of them that witches of that sect around the world offer up a drink offering on that day every year in honor of those who died that night."

I broke in, "So, is that what happened to Avis's mom?" I glanced towards the others huddled by the broken glass.

Uncle Paul did not answer, except to shrug his shoulder. "Anyway, your aunties took Avis and tried to finish raising her. She was fifteen when Akina was born."

"And what happened to Matasis?" I asked him, as I began to see activity way down the street.

Uncle Paul continued to talk to me as we made our way outside again and down the street just behind the others and away from the direction of the approaching flashing lights. "Well, initially with your aunties we banished him back into the Pit. Your Aunt Cil could send folks there. I was a fool to work with a demon. He was a fool for not knowing what we could and would do. Maybe he did know, but just didn't care. That kind of demonic evil can't help but do evil, regardless of the consequences. That was the last I saw of him until tonight. When he escaped the Pit a couple of years after this all went down, your aunties were waiting on him. Before he arrived they sent me off with my friend Ray overseas. Matasis, in addition to having a couple folks with him from that picture that were still loyal to him, also had at his side some demons he'd brought back from the Pit. And still, your mom and three aunties defeated them. Matasis had been imprisoned in that house until now. And until this day, I don't know exactly how they knew when and where he was coming." He thought for a moment and then added, "Yes, on the floor in that witch's coven I realized just how perverse I was. Soon afterwards I made a commitment to change my life.

But in regards to using my gift, I just don't trust myself. For your mom and your grandfather, this walk seems so easy, but for folks like us it seems such a struggle."

"Us?" I thought. He's assuming an awful lot I thought, but I let it all go. I looked over my shoulder to see the fire trucks pulling up to the burning car. In front of me the group had come to a stop. They were looking at a figure lying along the edge of the bushes. It was a corpse, a disfigured one.

Reggie was kneeling down and looking up at the others, "Yeah, his heart has been ripped out. Uncle Paul, is this what Matasis does to his victims?"

Uncle Paul stood silent for a second and then replied. "No, not so literally, at least not in the past. It could be the work of one of the creatures he hauled back from the Pit. No, disfiguration and tumors are the mark of Matasis. Even the foliage he brushes against take on an odd shape. As for this man, there's nothing we can do for his poor soul now. I suggest we keep moving. We need to find a place off the street where we can talk and finish planning out our next move."

"You're right Poppa," Avis agreed.

The comfort at which she said this caused Uncle Paul to pause. I realized that it had been a very long time since he'd heard his little girl call him that without a lethal dose of sarcasms attached. We started to walk up the street again as he turned to me, "Where were we? Oh, yes I was telling you about Ray. He was such a good man. I always kind of wished that he and your Aunt Cil had gotten together at some point. Later on, they were both alone, you know."

I still had questions, so I continued. "From all the things I've heard that Aunt Cil had her hands in, I'm surprised she even had time to raise Reggie. So, let me ask you this. Why, back at Avis's house, didn't those creatures attack you?"

"They were afraid of me. See, back when I was doing my thing, even the demons were afraid of me. They knew me from that other realm. Before I returned to this world, before I lost my way, I spent many, many years in the Pit fighting evil. And even though I can't remember much of it now, I developed quite the reputation back then in that place. And since these demons have no concept of time, I am still what I was then. What makes it complicated is that in a sense they're right. Back in the Pit where time holds no ground, yesterday is today, and today is yesterday."

"So, you've been there?" My words jumped from my mouth.

"Oh, yes I have," he confessed.

"So, why don't you just take us to where the Aunties are?"

Uncle Paul reminded me, "You forget, I do not have powers of my own like that. I just have the power of control. I summoned and controlled something that could get me there and back when I was done. And since I don't do that anymore, I can no more get there than any man off the street." He took another couple of steps and then a breath. "The main thing you must remember now that you have begun this walk is that abilities like ours attract the dark spir-

INTO THE PIT   143

its of this world and beyond, like ripe fruit draws flies. If you're not careful, you'll be consumed like I was. Keep your heart pure. In my desire to infiltrate their ranks, I became one of them. You cannot play with the darkness, for in truth it is a fight to the death."

We rounded the corner and ventured through a gap of a fence into the back parking lot of the local "no-tell-motel". We waited near the dumpster while Reggie got us a room. The dumpster was closed and it was still raining just a bit, but Akina took one look at it and exclaimed "There's a body in there."

Darnell and I opened it to see a young man lying on top of a heap of garbage, his face hidden by newspapers.

Kim took a small flashlight from her backpack and shined it into the dark dumpster. "His chest is open. They must have taken his heart too!"

"Why are they taking their hearts?" Darnell asked the crowd.

Kim, Darnell and I gave our opinions as Carla walked off from the group having no taste for dead bodies. And then Sandy spoke up. "Maybe they're looking for a particular heart?"

At this, Avis gave Uncle Paul a quick glance and a knowing passed between them, a knowing that I did not understand at the time.

Akina, walked past Sandy to close the dumpster door. "Perhaps you are right Sandy." The subject was dropped for that day. Uncle Paul, perhaps in an attempt to change the subject, made a suggestion. "If y'all do go to find your aunties, leave Avis here with me."

"Say what?" I blurted out, nearly gagging on the words. "After all that's happened, how can we do that?" I said this like I'd done something to actually help in catching her.

"Things have changed," he replied.

Avis explained, "What I think he's saying is that since Matasis is back, there is a wee bit more to worry about than me. Besides the whole world domination eternal damnation thing, he wants to see us dead."

Kim turned from peering into the trash bin again, "What do you mean by us?"

Laughing a bit, like someone not all the way back from her insanity, Avis offered "I mean he wants to see all of us, the cousins, dead. I think he's worried about some prophecy being fulfilled. The Aunties know the full deal. My daddy here should know, but I think he's got rocks in his head." She tried to rap her knuckles on his head, but she missed as he repositioned his Kangol. Sobering from her laughter, she continued, "I think Poppa here plans for us to play a little cat and mouse with the old boy until you guys can get back with some help."

Reggie returned with the keys to a second floor room in the back of the property. I'm sure the night manager had no idea that all of us would be filing into that one room. Reggie flicked on the light switch to the scurrying of a couple of six-legged guests whom had taken up residence on the near nightstand at the site of what I hoped was a fruit juice stain. Akina and Kim tossed their bookbags onto the bed. Kim also laid her skateboard there as well.

Carla asked the question. "So, okay what are we doing?"

Reggie replied, "I guess we have no choice but to go and get the Aunties. It's a punk move, but we're way in over our heads. I mean I'm way ahead of the rest of you in this life and I don't even know where to start."

"Uncle Paul, what can you tell us?" Carla asked.

He rubbed the side of his face and spoke slowly, "Well, baby I'm sorry to tell you I don't remember much of the Pit. It comes on me in dreams and nightmares now. All I can tell you is that it's on the edge of Hell and that I cannot go back there."

Avis jumped in, "Yeah, it's funny that he can't remember the place, but I told you before, Akina has been there. Ask her about it." She gave a stare and nod to Akina.

Sandy turned to Akina and asked, "Is that true? You've been there?"

"Yes," Akina confessed unwillingly.

Avis followed up, "Yeah, in one of my many poor moments as a mother I had my baby go there and fetch something back for me."

I didn't particularly like the nuance I thought I heard in her "something." When you're the one that has constantly been left out of the loop, you tend to read volumes into every nuance.

Reggie laughed, "You know we are one really screwed up family. Come on let's do this." Reggie, knowing how Akina worked, took a position on the floor with his back against the side wall. He also knew that it was pointless to continue this conversation. In this auntie-driven world there were many secrets that we would never know. They never told any one cousin the whole story. Reggie had alluded to this many times before at family gatherings, but only within earshot of the cousins. I didn't have a clue that he meant anything like this. To a large degree he was right. Although I would have liked to have known a little more before we set off, the fact of the matter was that it wasn't going to change our objective and given our time constraints, we didn't have time to really make any detailed plans. Whatever came at us, we'd just have to deal with it.

Sandy asked, "So, what happens while we're gone. And also, how long will we be gone?"

Avis answered as best she could. "Well, my daddy and I here will try to think of something while you're gone. As for how long you will be gone, well that's hard to say. See, time does not move lockstep between here and the Pit. You could be there for a couple of days, then return here and not a moment will have passed or on the other hand twenty years may have gone by."

"What the *heck* are you saying?" Carla caught herself, but her point was made. Kim looked so exasperated that she couldn't express herself likewise in a timely manner.

"Hey, I have to tell you the truth. Why do you think I don't go there? Besides being dangerous, I mean. But you have Akina, so I don't think you'll have a problem there. That was why I sent her there. I knew that she could go and come back in a timely manner, so to speak."

I imagine it crossed all of our minds that if anything happened to Akina we would all be left to roam the Pit forever.

From his position sitting on the floor, Reggie instructed, "Okay, y'all let's go." With that everyone, with the exception of Avis and Uncle Paul, took their places in a circle arced to his left and right.

Akina grabbed her bookbag and told Kim to do likewise. "Hey, anything you want to take with you, you need to grab it now." Kim got not only her bag, but her skateboard as well. It was a funny-looking board. It was a real throwback with plenty of metal reinforcement.

Akina looked up as she began to squat, "Momma and Granddaddy, y'all need to leave the room now."

Avis clicked off the light as she pulled the door closed leaving us in total darkness. For a moment I thought about those roaches, and for the first time in my life I thought that perhaps it would have been better to be one of them than to be one of us going into this place... this place, that just two days ago I had no doubt was just a fable.

Hands joined, we all looked to Akina. She nodded and bowed "Okay, everyone. Close your eyes and I'll guide us through this." Then she removed her shades and stuck them in her blouse.

Everyone closed their eyes except for me. I instinctively watched Akina and waited for her to close her eyes. She stared back at me. "Don't you close your eyes?" I asked.

"No." she replied. "I have to drive. But you, you need to close yours. This whole process is like staring into the sun. It could fry your brain. I'm not saying it will, but it has happened to others before. Okay?"

"Okay," I acknowledged and closed my eyes.

Just then to my left I heard Reggie say, "He would be the one to ask the stupid questions. Is she going to close her eyes? Incredible."

For a moment I was offended but then I couldn't help but smile, as a couple of the others chuckled.

Then, with my eyes closed I could sense that the boundaries and confinement of the room were no more. I felt an openness, but I didn't dare open my eyes. I felt a sense of movement, but could not tell the direction. This turned into a floating sensation which very quickly transformed into one of rapid movement bracketed by rumblings I didn't care to know the origin of. The rumbling grew closer. But just as I began to lose faith, the floating feeling came back. And not a moment later I realized that the feeling of actually sitting on something returned to me. I hadn't noticed that it was gone, until it returned.

All was quiet, and somehow I knew we were done, which Akina confirmed. "Wake up everybody, we're here!"

10: Salvation

Jonah didn't know where in the order of executions Sara's execution would fall. He didn't even know the method of death de jour. But he knew he didn't have much time. He guessed he had fifteen minutes to get down to the Square and set up before the first execution. The water in the tunnel, unlike in the afternoons, was now knee-deep. He reached the Square in less time than he thought given the depth of the water. Under the Square the tunnel opened up into an area where at least ten different tunnels converged to feed into one very large tunnel, which ran to the ocean.

Jonah scouted around just enough to be certain that he heard the mob above him. Then he traced the underground electrical cables along the ceiling to the stage, marveling all the while that in that day and age, power was still being transmitted via hard cables for the average Joe. Transmitting power through the air made bootlegging a little too easy.

A small stone pillar protruded up from the water to just above Jonah's waist. He sat his equipment atop it.

Jonah worked frantically to get set up. He knew that he would have to time this well. Do it too early and Sara and the others wouldn't be on stage yet and he wouldn't begin to know where to find them. Take action too late and there would be no point. He initiated the pocket reactor's start up sequence. The plan was to create an Electro Magnetic Pulse (EMP) via a small nuclear explosion; not a huge one, but more like a neutron bomb, a small tactical anti-personnel nuke. Uncontrolled, the device could and would kill a lot of people, but Jonah intended to use his energy Wave Modulator to control the blast. It could be set to contain harmful radiation while allowing the magnetic waves to pass through. The explosion would magnetize everything for ten blocks in each direction. Nothing mechanical would work. Not vehicles, phones, broadcast cameras and especially not any of the execution devices typically used for this spectacle. However, Jonah wasn't sure that this was actually going to work. His concern was not the effectiveness of EMP, but the absolute effectiveness of his energy Wave Modulator at such close range. Due to his proximity, Jonah was the only one in any real danger.

Jonah saw the reactor turn blue and he knew that it was ready. He checked the connection between his personal computing device and the energy Wave Modulator. He keyed in the needed parameters to hopefully control the blast. Before engaging it, he waited for several moments while listening for activity above him. Over the loudspeakers he heard the announcer for the evening calling out the crimes of the condemned. He could also hear the prisoners being lead up to the stage. However, between the ranting crowd, boisterous announcer and dripping water, he heard the most unexpected thing... singing. It was Sara and the other prisoners singing a hymn. Jonah began to sing with them. Nearly a minute passed while the guy on stage thanked his sponsors. As the maniacal host called out Sara's name for a second time, that being for her to die first, Jonah engaged the countdown sequence, and initiated the energy wave. A warm light enveloped the reactor and Jonah in a gentle glow. Suddenly, he was in a soundless glowing world. Given his line of work, Jonah wore contact lens that would shield him from any flash from the blast that escaped his modulator's control (they also doubled as a night vision enhancer, changing function instantaneously). Then, in the eerie silence, a quiet sun flashed. In that flash was Jonah's whole existence it seemed. The difference between life and death was this warm yellowish hue. Being at the center of the blast he didn't have to worry about items flying towards him and his modulator was capable of preventing the parts of the pocket reactor from striking him. He did a quick check of the radiation level and then lowered the shield just a bit.

Suddenly, Jonah could hear screaming above. For a moment he thought the worst and his heart sank. Then, looking up through a grate he saw that the whole Square was pitch-black, with people running everywhere. In their panic they began to trample each other. Jonah hadn't accounted for that. Ironically, the only safe place was up on the stage. Jonah twisted around in an attempt to get a look at the stage. He still had a yellow glow about his body (the modulator was strapped to his right wrist), so he was a little concerned that in the darkness someone might see him looking out, but they didn't. He'd brought a laser to cut through the grate or whatever might be in his way to complete this daring rescue. Just as he was about to start cutting his way through, he turned down his glowing protective shield so that his special contacts would switch to night vision mode. This granted him a better look. Jonah could see the stage now but he didn't see any prisoners. That gave him pause. Suddenly he realized that right in front of him in his near vision stood Sara and the other prisoners. Like an eruption he called to her, "Sara, Sara!"

She turned but with her eyes darting here and there, she did not see him. Jonah called again, "Sara, down here." He flashed his laser into the ground near her feet. At last she saw him. Kneeling down to the drain grate she tugged and motioned the others to follow her. Jonah pushed the grate out for them to slip by. For a moment his mind hesitated as it occurred to him that, with the exception of Sara, he really didn't know these people. Four of them came down. Sara introduced the others as Pam, Jared and Bruce. Of those three, Pam was the only one he'd met before. Leading them back to Karun's was out of the question.

After Sara hugged him to near suffocation, Pam said thank you and then feeling that that was not enough, gave him a sudden hug. Jared likewise thanked him with a hug.

Bruce, the last one down, was less gracious. He was still concerned about his safety. "So, how do we get out of here?" he asked.

After giving Bruce a glare, Sara pulled Jonah close and whispered into his ear. "It wouldn't be fair to Karun to bring all these folks back through there. We'll need to follow this large drain out to the ocean. I know where we can find help there."

Jonah grabbed her shoulder and whispered back, "I think you're right." Then, speaking to the group, he said, "Listen up. We're going to need to get moving quickly. This large tunnel here will lead us out to the ocean. Once we get a there, away from the city, we'll plan our next move. But we do need to get away from here."

No one argued with that. But as Jonah turned his Wave Modulator back up again, its yellow glow worried Bruce. "Hey man, that light's gonna show up on their infrared!"

As he swung his backpack over his shoulder, Jonah answered him, "Don't worry. It actually helps to hide us from them. Not only does it not give off heat, it blocks their infrared scanners from picking up and imaging our body heat. Though given what I've done, there isn't a scanner within ten blocks that works."

As Jonah began to walk, Jared followed him and asked "Hey man, just what did you do?"

Jonah laughed and said, "Oh, I could tell you, but then I'd have to kill ya!" mocking the failed execution attempt.

Along the way through the tunnel he came to find Pam was very conservative, while Jared was very outgoing. Bruce for the most part was just very angry with his captors and the events of the evening.

For nearly two hours the yellow glow accompanied them all the way to the end of the tunnel. With every few steps that they came closer to the end and the outside world, Jonah reduced the intensity of the shield, until it was completely turned off. Exiting the tunnel, they climbed back up through the weeds, over the dunes and back up into the woods. Jared let out a "Praise God!" and gave a tentative Pam a high-five.

Bruce asked the obvious, "Where are we?"

Sara let out a slow "Well... I'd say we're in the woods by the sea." In this future age, sea levels were high enough that the outskirts of D.C. actually met the bay.

Bruce glared back at her grudgingly acknowledging her attempt at humor.

Sara looked around for a second then pointed, "There's the old lighthouse three clicks north of here. There is a meeting there tonight. I think that's our best bet now until we can find out what's going on. We need to find out how much they know about who we are."

The meeting she was talking about was an irregular get-together of Christians and those affiliated with them. For safety reasons, the time and location of the meetings varied quite a bit. In fact, they typically were not arranged until the day they were to occur. Tonight's meeting was actually to have been a prayer vigil for those who were going to be executed. Since the mobs randomly abducted people, no one who planned to attend knew whom they'd be praying for, or, as in Sara's case, if that night's prisoner being prayed for might be them. Jonah had attended one of these before, but the boldness of it scared him. It seemed foolhardy to him for so many of them to gather in one place, especially on those hunting days. And occasionally these gatherings were raided, but it was surprisingly rare that that happened. Jonah believed that there must be some kind of unspoken agreement between the higher ups and these outcasts. Take Sara for instance, everybody on the block where he worked knew she was a Christian. She lived her faith out loud, but this was the first time she'd been hauled off.

Jared called out to the group, "So, what are we waiting for?" and he began to trudge off towards the lighthouse. The others fell in line behind him. Tracing just inside the tree line towards the old lighthouse Jonah could hear and see the waves breaking along the shore. Every fifty yards, he caught a glimpse of the night sky. As always, the stars intrigued him. Somehow, he'd always felt that he'd be among them one day. Now that desire seemed like such a foolish fantasy. So many dreams it seemed had vanished with the morning vapors.

As they made their way out of the woods and onto the small peninsula upon which the old tower stood, they found themselves working their way through thick brush and leftover debris from the age before. "Here we are!" Sara called out.

Jared ran to the front again with Pam not far behind him. As they got close they could hear the music and feel the glow from inside, although to the outside world, all was dark.

Jared, while having never been to one of these meetings at this location, was a frequent guest at others and upon reaching the door knew the admission procedure. The guy opening the door saw Sara not far behind Pam and Jared. Upon seeing her, his face broke into a huge grin and the door swung all the way open, welcoming all five of them in. As Sara passed the doorman she asked him if the broadcast had gone out yet. He replied no. The Christians had a broadcast that went out most every night. The process was quite clever actually. After recording the thirty minute to an hour broadcast, they'd record it into a self-contained transmission capsule. These capsules were about two feet long and maybe four inches in diameter. The cool thing about them was that they could be inserted into the ground and then a set numbers of minutes later begin transmitting. Being inserted in the ground they were hard to see. The time delay was to allow time for the person placing the nightly capsule in the ground to make a clean getaway. There was no way to tell how much of a delay there had been. The Blues would eventually triangulate the location of the capsule, but by that time the courier would be long gone and there was no way of knowing just how far away the courier might be because of the random delays. Sara wanted to make sure that the news got out as soon as possible that Bruce, Jared, Pam and Jonah were safe and sound. She was sure that their families would want to know. As for her own husband, Ashok, Sara knew that with his connections that he already knew that she'd escaped the execution, but she thought it would be good to let him know where she was.

The doorman replied to her, "No, they were just about to leave when they heard the news of your escape. We were waiting to send it out until we had more information on your condition. It is so wonderful to see that you are all alright."

Sara glanced around as the crowd began to realize who they were and began to storm towards them in full elation. "Where's Heru?" she asked the doorman.

"Over there, helping the band set up on stage." He pointed across the room at the men and women on the stage, who were just looking up to see what all the commotion was about. Heru, originally from California, was a big man, though not overly heavy. He was built like a lumberjack. He was obviously of Mexican decent, but also of African, of European, and a little from somewhere else. Before things fell apart he used to wear dreads, but his hair was now cut short.

"Sara! It's Sara and the others!" he yelled out to the crowd. "Praise God, our prayers have been heard and answered!" He continued to shout as he made a beeline towards her. Jared glad-handed in every direction given that he knew most of the folks there already. Pam knew two or three in the crowd. Bruce didn't know anyone there. While Jonah knew a few more than Pam, he'd been out of touch so long he'd forgotten most of their names.

The buzz was so loud by the time that Heru reached Sara that they had to scream just to hear each other. Sara started the introductions. "Heru, you already know Jared, right?"

"Oh, for sure!" He reached over and gave Jared a hug.

"And this is Pam, from the northwest part of town," Sara continued, pulling Pam over to Heru.

Heru, reached out and took Pam's hand. "Hi I'm Heru. It's a pleasure to meet you Pam. I feel like I already know you. I've spent most of the evening praying for you." Both he and Pam laughed at that.

Sara tugged at a slightly reserved Bruce. "This is Bruce Cain. Bruce this is Heru. Bruce just accepted Christ a couple of weeks ago."

Heru reached out to him, "Congratulations Bruce!" he shouted.

Bruce shrugged his shoulders, "Yeah, but look at all the trouble it's gotten me."

Heru tried to console him, "Well, you're among friends now. Relax and have a good time."

Sara reached around a couple of people to grab Jonah. "And here is Jonah, our hero of the day. You remember him don't you? You know his wife Monica."

"Oh, you know I know him. I knew him before I knew Monica. How are you Jonah?" Heru said. The truth of the matter was that they were very tight back in the day.

"Hi Heru, I'm fine. Just a little overwhelmed right now. I haven't seen some of these folks in at least three or four years," Jonah confessed.

"Yeah, I know. Sara, Jonah and I used to attend the same underground church right after the Blues took over. But through the years we've kind of lost touch." He gave Jonah a knowing look. Jonah knew that it wasn't by chance that Heru had cut him some slack. Jonah had intentionally pulled back from the group. Jonah felt like his chances and his wife's chances were better not being a part of the group, especially this group. Too many "out there Christians" he thought. He could pray on his own he had reasoned or rationalized depending on one's view. Monica on the other hand, took every opportunity to maintain contact with the group. Jonah had his suspicions, but Monica always downplayed who she'd run into or where she'd stopped on her way home. She didn't work the hours that he did and could make a lot of impromptu dinners. In fact, many a night he'd eaten other people's dinners brought home for him by his wife, who because of her visit, didn't have time to cook. He didn't sweat her too much about it all. Still he had this sense that what he viewed as her cavalier attitude was going to get them both killed one day.

Heru led Sara and Jonah over to a prime table in that night's set-up. He sat them right in front of the stage. Heru leaned over to Jonah's ear, and yelled into it, "I'm going make sure that the broadcast has news about you guys. We won't even have much of a delay tonight. I don't want your wife or anyone to worry any longer about you than need be. You two order anything you like. It's all free anyway, but we'd like to serve all five of you at your tables like the guests you are."

Jonah looked up and said, "Thanks. I really don't want my wife to worry about me. Maybe I should just go."

Heru reached over and grabbed his shoulder. "Dude, relax. I don't know where you're living these days, but if you live as far out as I think you do, this broadcast will beat you seven ways to Sunday letting her know you're okay. So just chill and take a break. You've had quite a day. Besides, knowing your wife, she already knows exactly what happened."

Jonah did not share that his real concern was just the opposite of what he expressed. He wanted to make sure that his wife was safe. Every day this was his concern. Even though he knew that in many ways she was more suited to blend in than he was, he still worried about her. He was her protector after all. Monica and her well-being were his life. He knew that he would not be comfortable until the moment he could leave this place and head home.

Jonah and Sara attempted to have a conversation while the band tuned up but person after person approached them both to comment on their escape. Most of them asked Jonah how his wife was doing. One of them asked how he liked the apple pie she's sent to him via his wife. "Oh, that was great. Thank you," he replied.

Then a short Latino woman stepped up to him as he was finally taking a sip of tea. "I saw your wife today," she exclaimed.

He stopped mid-sip. "You did?! Where did you see her?"

The stout woman replied, "On my way here. I told her about what happened at the execution ceremonies. We both shouted, but neither of us knew that you were involved. It's just so, so, wow. If we had known you'd be here tonight I know she'd be here now."

"Yeah, I didn't know I'd be here either. What's your name again? Is it Marta?" Jonah asked her.

"Yes, that's right," she answered him. He'd met her before and knew that she and her husband lived somewhere near him and Monica. In fact, she and Monica often ran into each other when out in the woods foraging. The women in the community knew much more about what was edible and what was not, so they did most of the "nature shopping". Meats and certain other things you had to get in a market, but most folks strove not to be dependent on them because of their openness and exposure.

"Thank you, Marta." Jonah now knew that Monica made it to within at least a couple of miles of their home. He felt a little better now.

Sara leaned over to Jonah, her blonde hair now unencumbered by the wrap she wore most days to cover it. "Jonah, you're quite the celebrity today. You've really fired these folks up."

"Yeah it looks that way, but I really didn't do that much," Jonah honestly said to her holding out his hands.

"Well, it was a big deal to this group and you did save my life today," she said.

"Okay, yeah maybe I played some part in that but it wasn't like a hero thing. I knew I couldn't just sit there and do nothing," Jonah conceded.

"See, Jonah that is the thing for all of us." Sara smiled at the implication that everyone does their individual part.

Heru, having made his way to the stage, spoke to the group. "As we all know, we have some very special guests here tonight." The cheering of the room broke up his introduction, but he began anew. "Tonight we also have special guests from Atlanta here to bless us with their music."

Bruce, sitting at the table next to Sara and Jonah on Sara's side, said loud enough for Heru to hear, "I thought Atlanta wasn't there anymore?"

Heru answered him curtly, "Yes, we all know that, but the community is still there. And from that body these gentle folks have traveled all the way up here to be with us tonight." Heru went on to introduce the band and they began to play several very inspiring acoustical selections. Live music held such a special place in Jonah's heart. He longed to learn to play someday and that made his wonderment even greater.

The allure of playing music was to him what someday being able to read must be for the illiterate.

In the transition between the first and second song, Sara leaned over Jonah again. "Oh, by the way I heard that Vicki spent the day with you. What did she want?"

Jonah looked off for a second embarrassed by the question, but he didn't know explicitly why. He hadn't done anything. He looked back at Sara a second later. "Well, this is what she told me. She said that the folks in the Christian Circle up north want me to come up and join their technical team."

Sara laughed and said, "So, it took her all day to tell you that? Ha!" She rolled her eyes.

Jonah defended her, "Well, you know her cloaker doesn't really work during the day. So once she was there, she had to wait until dusk."

Sara stuck her head up and actively looked around the room, and then back at Jonah. "I don't think anyone in this room has one either and every one of them moves around during the day. Pretty good I might add."

Jonah continued his point, "Yeah, but she's a bonafide spy, a regular subversive."

Sara smiled, "Okay, okay, so maybe it's plausible, but still it smells to me. Anyway, are you going to do it?"

"Well, as of right now, no. She said that her bosses don't want Monica to come with me because she was once a part of one of those Blue youth groups. And you know they don't let anybody like that in up there." Jonah grimaced a bit.

"Yeah, that is true. I know I could never go as long as I'm married to Ashok. But come on Jonah, doesn't all that sound a bit strange to you? I mean yeah she needs to move at night and yes the folks up there would have an issue with Monica, Lord knows that's true but together doesn't that sound a bit funny?" Sara probed him.

"I hear you, but I really don't think Vicki is up to any-thing. Plus, what she said does make sense. But I told her that I'm not leaving without Monica. Actually, I'm surprised they want me." At that Jonah took another sip of his herbal tea.

"Mmmm... I don't know..." Sara shook her head.

"Sara, you know my goal has been to get Monica and me out of here, and if I play my cards right this may be the way. And besides, with them wanting me to work on their tech team I'd really be able to help in the fight against the Blues."

Sara smiled and placed her hands over his hand on the table, grasping it. "But Jonah, why would you leave? Can't you see? Can't you see that the battle is here? Tell me Jonah, how do you treat the sick if you are not among them?"

"Sara..." Jonah began to protest, but Sara cut him off.

"I know with your earthly eyes it makes total sense to leave here. Let's face it, you are in the belly of the behemoth. And I know you're afraid, not for yourself, but for Monica. You're afraid that one day the Blues will overwhelm you and then who will look after Monica? I know your concerns, but I'll tell you what else I know, as long as you're alive no one will harm Monica. Secondly, the Blues will never defeat you. I see the aura of God upon you. This evening just confirmed what I already knew. God has blessed the labor of your hands." Sara held his hand and looked to connect with his eyes.

A modest Jonah replied to her with an understanding lowering of his head, "Yeah, I hear you."

"Besides," Sara continued, "you wouldn't fit in there. The two of you are so dysfunctional, but in a very fearful and won-derful way. She is so open that she needs someone to protect her and you need someone to take care of, so that your thoughts do not consume you."

A non-sequitur thought about The Heart of Mystery entered Jonah's mind, but he chose not to tell Sara about it. He thought, how do you tell your spiritual mentor that you plan to break into a museum and take something out of it? On top of that, some would call the Heart an object of the occult. Jonah knew that to be untrue, but who would believe the fantastic tale around it? Would Sara have that much faith in him and the stories his Auntie told him? He didn't think that way about it and didn't consider it as stealing either since it had belonged to his family in the first place.

Looking around, Jonah's gaze fixed suddenly on a young guy at the juice bar. The shock of what he saw nearly froze his heart. It was Dave, the young Blueblood he met on the bus that same morning. Trying to hide his alarm, he leaned back over to Sara, "Sara, there's a Blueblood at the bar. Over there, the second guy from the left."

Sara turned to look, "Oh, that's Dave. Yeah, he's a Blueblood, and I'm sure he's not the only one in here. I told you we were now witnessing to the Blues as well. In fact, quiet as it's kept they are the fastest growing group among us but mostly on the hush-hush."

Jonah sat back up. "Yeah, I knew we witnessed to them now, but you never told me you were inviting them to safe houses and gatherings."

Sara confessed, "Yeah safe houses, but not the really, really safe houses, not yet anyway, but to gatherings, yes. A handful of them have been attending for a while. This is not Dave's first large group gathering. He's actually quite the evangelist and he's an attorney. He's handled a number of cases for Christians who have been unfairly treated or detained. The firm he works for is real Christian friendly which is a little surprising considering his dad is some kind of big shot in the Blue administration here in town. He's actually taken care of a couple of things for Monica too."

Jonah sat up again. "Whoa... I didn't know any of this."

"I know. I wanted to tell you, but I was hoping that Monica would. I think she was afraid to tell you, because she knew you'd be concerned."

Jonah was silent as he stared at her and then off into space. He wondered if he had done anything that might have caused his wife not share this with him.

Sara continued, "But Dave there is cool. How do you know him?" Sara waved at him. Dave lifted his smoothie to the two of them. Jonah waved in acknowledgement. It occurred to Jonah that Dave may not remember him, since when he was on the bus Jonah was heavily wrapped and gave Dave a fake name. A name different than the one they announced tonight.

"I don't think he knows who I am, but I met him on the bus this morning." Jonah confirmed. "Things have changed so much!"

"Yes, they have Jonah, but if you came around a little more often, it wouldn't be such a shock to you," Sara informed him.

"Yeah, Sara, I know. Oh, but you know the Circle doctrine states that Blues don't have a soul. Not that I buy into that."

Sara's piercing blue eyes held a steady gaze on Jonah. "Make sure that you introduce yourself to him before you leave here."

"Sure. Actually, I need to do it now, because I need to be going." Jonah took a sip of tea.

"Jonah, you've only been here twenty minutes. Why can't you just relax? Marta told you Monica made it out of the city just fine, and you know she'll listen to the broadcast tonight, she always does. She'll hear that you're fine. Actually, it should be transmitting now." Sara said with an encouraging smile.

Jonah checked his watch and then shook his head again, "I don't know Sara."

Sara touched his arm and asked him softly, "Jonah, will you ever find your true joy? Listen, there are two types of people in this world. There are those who can't wait to live each day and those who spend their lives waiting around to die."

"I know Sara. I try to be different. I try to be cheerful or whatever. Each year, each day and each moment I think it will be different, but it seldom is." Jonah ran his finger around the rim of his cup. In his heart Jonah knew that that certain prevailing sadness would never leave him. Even happy times were tinged by it. His sincere hope was that his good deeds could somehow cover this stain on his entire existence.

Sara looked at him again trying to make eye contact. "You know I don't make light of how you feel. I can tell that someone or something must have really hurt you in the past. I don't know what it was and you probably don't either. But you have to reclaim your life before you wake up one day and find that it's passed you by without a moment of joy. Don't let the joy of this gift of life pass you by. You must discover how to live, rather than just waiting on death."

"I'm really trying Sara. I really am..." For a moment Jonah's emotions almost spilled over. "Maybe I'm just supposed to be this way. Maybe God wants me this way..."

"Hush, don't say that. I sent a message to my sister asking her to send me a couple of her books on depression. I think we're going to have to just work a little harder and smarter to get you right. Okay?"

"Okay." Jonah took a last gulp of tea. "I guess part of my problem is that sometimes I can't help but think about how many have died."

"Yes," Sara conceded, "but look at how many have been born and reborn. Unless a seed falls from a limb and dies, how else can a tree be born? No one, not one, in our struggle has died in vain. Nor, do any of us, not one, live in vain." Jonah looked up to see Sara smiling and then he looked around the room. It warmed him from his head to his toes. Then Jonah took out a tip and laid it on the table.

Sara pushed her cup and saucer from between herself and Jonah. "You know something, and we've talked about this before, life is a balance. You feel such an emptiness inside of you. The emptier you get, the more you use caring for your wife to fill that void inside of you. Now should a man be passionate about his wife? Yes, he should. But should his whole life be wrapped around the well-being of his wife? No, I don't think so. You weren't put in this earth just to take care of Monica. You are hiding in that because of the lack of purpose you feel otherwise."

"Sara, I know you're right, but without her I don't know what I would do. I have to keep busy, or else, you know, I start having those feelings and thoughts"

"My brother, I think you miss the point of this life we lead, even in your prayers. Your prayers are To and From, when they should really be With. Sure you pray to God, but when you invite the Spirit within you, you are praying with God. You are then on one accord and in doing that you will learn to let go and trust God."

To this Jonah could attest. Sara was so filled with the Spirit that she seemed to actually glow from a light within her very flesh.

"And do not believe this lie the darkness tells you. You are not empty. Not that you don't have demons that you wrestle with, we all do. But don't ever lose sight that you are a child of light. Even in your darkest moments, don't lose sight of that. I know you want to run away to the Circle, but God has a claim on your life and it's here in the land of your enemy. And yes a life here will bring a day of hard choices." She reached out again grabbing his arm right above the wrist shaking him firmly.

Suddenly they both noticed a commotion to their left, back towards the entrance. It was Sara's husband, Ashok pressing his way past the doorman and through the crowd towards them. "Sara!" he yelled out. She jumped to her feet and they flew into each other's arms. Then he forced himself to push her away far enough to get her attention. He spoke rapidly and forcibly, "Darling we have to get out of here. The Blues are really upset this time."

She smiled and replied, "So what? Like every other time, they'll get over it."

"No," he said. "Apparently, they are very upset about a nuke going off right downtown, in their capitol no less. From what I've heard, the head of Blue National Security is coming down himself." Ashok looked at Jonah.

Bruce bolted up from his chair lunging at Jonah grabbing his collar. "You set off a nuke? Is that what that was? Are you crazy?"

Ashok, a big man, pulled Bruce from Jonah. Holding each of his wrists, one in each hand, Ashok spoke plainly to him. "And I would have it that he set off a thousand more if it meant the life of my wife."

Bruce relented for the moment, at least physically, that is. He shouted again at Jonah, "You set off a nuke?"

Jonah, after adjusting his shirt and after the shock of Bruce trying to throttle him passed, became a little angry. He answered Bruce, "I told you I created an EMP. How do you think those things are created? But the reaction was very contained."

"My God man, do you realize what kind of heat you've brought down on us?" Bruce said loudly as he turned to the crowd looking for support.

Jared, who was sitting at the same table with Bruce and Pam, to the right of Jonah and Sara, attempted to calm him. He reached to place his arm on Bruce's shoulder to comfort him, but Bruce brushed his arm away and went for his coat resting on his chair.

Heru, stepped in closer and then after inadvertently shaking his head at Bruce's behavior, asked, "Ashok, did I hear you right? Are they rounding folks up?"

Ashok spoke calmly as he helped Sara with her coat. "Yes, I'm afraid that is the case. You know they all prefer to believe that all non-Blues are only semi-literate and something like this just blows their minds. The masses are shocked that a nuke went off in their city. I would imagine the fact that it was contained like it was is of more concern to the Blue leadership, because that shows real power!"

Heru, patting Ashok on the shoulder, made his decision. "Okay, I see." He turned and stepped up onto the stage taking one of the microphones. "Okay, everyone I need your attention. This is a Scatter One Alert. You know the drill. Captains make sure you know who in your block is still in the building. Also, make sure they're all accounted for, before you get outside. God be with us all. Let's move!"

With that Heru motioned to a man behind the juice bar. The man threw a switch and the house lights went off, and black lights went on.

Hurried goodbyes, tossed clothing, occasional shouts across the room to straggling parties is all that was heard away from the door as one by one, the pre-assigned groups left the building. Each group left going in its own direction, at its own pace, in its own method. Some had all-terrain vehicles. Some had boats and some had personal transportation devices but most just had their two feet.

Dave, the Blue, had no group, so while they were queuing up, Sara called for him to join her. Her group would leave in her husband's multi-person transport. Bruce was a part of that group too. He lived on the same side of town as Ashok and Sara. Dave, didn't live that way, but his parents did and he could spend the night there. Jonah was actually in the group right in front of them. He didn't really know any of the people in his group besides Marta. He was so out of touch. His group would be going by foot for about five miles and then hopefully somehow, get upstream to the part of town they needed to be. Jonah had some thoughts as to how they might expedite that effort. He prayed to God that Monica had not gone out looking for him, or worse had decided to come out to the lighthouse. Jonah's anxiety about his wife must have shown, because Marta took care to comfort him. "Jonah," Marta said, "your wife is fine. I told you that already. I saw her go home myself." Finally, it occurred to Jonah that with all the Marta this, and Marta that in his house and her comments tonight, his wife and Marta were actually pretty close. In fact, he realized that Marta had indeed likely been inside of his house and Monica inside of hers. That made two breaches in security. The first was Karun's wife, Manisha. Monica had invited her over just to see the place on one of the many days that Jonah worked late. While Jonah and Monica had visited Karun and Manisha's place on many occasions, Karun and Jonah both agreed that it would be foolish for them to come out to Jonah and Monica's place. If they were ever interrogated it would be best that they didn't know. Knowing Manisha, Jonah doubted that she could find her way back there if her life depended on it; although she was a very bright woman, her sense of direction was notorious among her friends. On the other hand, Marta and her family were very close. They were a different matter. Still, in that same moment he realized there in the crowd the real price his wife was paying being isolated as they were. In that moment he understood the longing for human contact and fellowship.

Those thoughts prompted Jonah to turn behind him and get Dave's attention. "Hi Dave, I'm Jonah. You met me on the bus this morning. I gave you a different name though. Sorry about that."

Dave smiled and answered him back, "Hey man, no sweat. I thought that you might be the same guy, but I didn't want to make you uncomfortable or anything. So, I just kept my distance tonight. But looking at what happened this evening, I understand completely. I would have done the same. God bless you, man."

"And may He bless you too, Dave. May He bless all of your days."

Sara smiled at the two of them.

The band was to leave with Heru and the doorkeepers after everyone else had been led out. The band was busy moving its equipment downstairs to Heru's boat, while most everyone else was going out the side door.

Jonah, Marta and the three others of their group reached the doorway. They stood there with the doorkeeper waiting for a signal from the spotter who was sitting up in a tree that it was clear for the next group to go.

Jonah looked into the clear night sky and the quiet dark trees below. Though peaceful they appeared to be, his spirit told him that something was amidst. When he had these feelings in the past that something was about to happen, it usually did. His group got the all clear signal from the spotter and headed out across the somewhat overgrown clearing behind the lighthouse and towards the woods. The groups were leaving in timed intervals to improve their dispersal pattern and better each group's chances of making a clean getaway.

Plus the different zig-zag directions each group took would hopefully help prevent any captured group's direction of travel leading anyone back to the group still at the light-house.

As Jonah and his group passed across the field, past the tree line and began to make their way away from the others, Jonah still felt like something was wrong. Then, without warning, a bright light appeared in the sky behind them, right above the clearing. Jonah stopped and looked up. The clearness of his view froze him. Up in the sky was a blue/white almost translucent figure of a man standing in midair. His skin was like the shell of a pearl. He had no eyes or ears, but he had a mouth and when he opened it both light and sound erupted from it. "Mortals!" the floating semblance of a man cried out to Ashok, Sara, Bruce and the others below him. They stood halfway between the lighthouse and Ashok's vehicle. "Today is the day that you all shall know the number of your days!" With that, he reached out his hand towards Ashok's vehicle and fire erupted from his hand setting the vehicle ablaze.

Their transportation now in flames, they huddled back a bit towards the cliffs. The man of flames floated unchanging above them. He called out again to them and the few others still in the lighthouse. "I am Demon, Herald to your Destroy-er." He reached out his hand again, this time to the sky bey-ond him. Immediately the entire sky was filled with light as a glowing plume of clouds billowed and rolled in from the northwest sky.

At the front of the plume, standing on the leading cloud stood a giant about 4 to 5 times the size of the Herald. His skin was metallic blue and his beard a blazing hot shimmer-ing translucent white like his Herald. He had the very ap-pearance of everything you might think a Greek god would be. Energy crackled around him as his chiseled body stood at high attention.

His Herald Demon, smiled a wicked grin, and gleefully announced to those below. "Behold your judgment, of the Sapphire Illuminati, the Blue lord Matasis!"

II: Oh, Oh...

Cold. Silent Cold. A darkness that knows no relief. From the moment you realized its existence, you felt its call, its insatiable desire for your own presence.

To our left, to our right, behind us and in front of us, nothing but bones and shadows as far as the eye could see; cold lifeless bones casting shadows on our lives and the breath escaping from our lungs.

Akina's eyes blazed as she beheld the sight all around us. "We've got to move, we're in a killing field!" she cried out to us. Standing and looking around, she then pronounced, "This way. Reggie make a path for the others." She headed off towards a hill to our left passing right through the bones. Not so for the rest of us. Reggie did his best to break apart the larger bones with his staff, but we still found ourselves tripping over the carcasses. Most of them appeared to belong to animals and still, chillingly, a good number of them appeared to be human skulls.

Akina called back a warning to us. "Watch your feet. There are scavengers called Ungazi that slither all around in here. They don't know the living from the dead. Secondly, this is a killing field where some of the larger residents here corral some of the smaller ones to make the killing easier. We don't want to be here."

Our pace quickened. Akina and Reggie were up front, followed by Kim, then me. Sandy was behind me. Behind her was Carla with Darnell bringing up the rear. I was close enough to Akina and Reggie to hear their discussion. Akina seemed exasperated, "We need to get to higher ground. We shouldn't be down here. I don't know how we wound up here."

Reggie tried to reassure her, "Hey Cousin, it's okay. We're fine. Let's just get out of this bone yard and up that hill over there and we'll be fine."

Akina, speaking quickly and still walking forward, looked down and spoke behind her to Reggie without turning completely around. "No, you don't understand. I can feel these types of things when I make my moves. It's not conscious, but I know safe places from bad places. We should not have shown up here. Not only are we in a killing field we're a long way from where we need to be!"

Glancing at the side of his face, I could see that Reggie had confusion. "So, you know where they are?"

Looking back Akina answered Reggie. "Well, not in the way I could show you on a map, but yes, I can sense where they are." Akina turned and again faced fully forward.

Reggie looked around at the peaks that lined the valley and the ungodly vastness of the carnage. "You go then, girl. I got your back." On a peak some distance away we both caught sight of a very large winged beast as it flexed its wings. Reggie flinched and regained focus on keeping pace with Akina.

Something slithered across Kim's leg causing her to scream and jump backwards into me. I stumbled and Sandy reached out trying to catch me with only limited success. I also felt an invisible hand helping me back up. That was Carla's doing.

"Forget this," Kim announced and took out her metal skateboard. I was totally confused until she stood on it and it began to levitate.

Akina glared back at her, "What are you doing? We have to stay low so that they don't see us."

Reggie defended her, "Well, she might as well fly. I mean if she's going to scream, they'll hear her anyway."

Kim circled back around and picked up Sandy who stood behind Kim on the board holding her tight. Darnell picked me up. Carla landed herself onto Reggie's shoulders. Levitating herself for an extended period would have really strained her. She needed to save her strength for whatever might be coming.

Akina tried to reason with them that no sound they made could travel far enough to reach that winged thing everybody saw. But by going airborne other things on the ground beyond the field of bones could now see them coming. The bones were actually a good cover against anything in the valley with us. We were small compared to most of the skeletons. Akina said all this to no avail.

At last we reached the edge of the valley, which was also the base of the hill we looked to climb. Akina was the first to clear the bone yard. As she stepped past the last thicket of large bones, two large hound-like creatures flew into her from the right. She toppled over and they were on top of her. Reggie, with Carla on his shoulders broke the last tusk in front of him and slung his staff into one of the dogs spearing it like a steak. After retrieving his staff, he reared back to throw it into the second beast, when a third hound came flying through the air towards his head. Carla instinctively put up her hands to fend off the attacker as Reggie swung his stick at a fourth canine. These things, whatever they were, stood about three to four feet high at the shoulders, slightly larger than lions and as fierce as any feline.

The rest of us who had been hovering low and behind Reggie and Akina rushed to the front. Darnell dropped me on a large carcass. Kim did the same for Sandy.

Darnell grabbed the beast from Reggie's back that was attempting to maul Carla and tossed it, impaling it on a large pointed rib bone.

Akina's second attacker was becoming frustrated as she had regained enough focus to make herself completely ethereal. The creature's lurches and lunges passed right through her. She had daggers, one on each hip. She firmed her hands just enough at the time of impact to stab the beast simultaneously on both sides of its neck. That did not kill it, but being practiced at this she became a ghost again after pulling the blades back into the air. Again she thrust down, this time hitting a major artery causing something akin to blood to pulse from the beast.

Meanwhile, Kim was circling and shooting bolts of lightning at the pack. In total, there must have been at least ten to twelve of them and their hunger was unquestionable.

Carla, having composed herself, climbed down from Reggie's shoulder and mentally set up a telekinetic barrier around us. I was shocked. I had no idea she was that strong, then I remembered how she had toppled that column in Avis's place. She spoke low and quick to Darnell and the others. "Okay, you guys take your shots… quickly please."

Darnell, with beams of fire flashing from his eyes and Kim, with bolts flying from her fingertips, began to pick off the dogs. Kim's bolts only jolted them, and while they weren't particularly flammable, Darnell's efforts were more permanent and in this place the beams from his eyes were always visible, not just in darkness. At last, the dogs apparently realized that the current state of affairs was not beneficial to them. Thankfully they did not realize that Carla could only protect us like that for so long.

As the remaining hounds began to trot off, we heard clapping coming from above us. "Well done!" We all looked up at once to see two very large black men. The taller one stood about twelve feet tall. The shorter one stood about ten. The taller one wore an Afro. It was like a crown upon his head. It gave him an appearance of some kind of African god. The shorter wore dreads, no, they were tendrils that seemed alive and although there was no wind, each tendril moved constantly. They appeared to move independent of any outside force we could see. Otherwise, he had the look of a prototypical Rastafarian.

The taller one replied back to the shorter one's comment. "Yes, but they let some of the dogs go. That was a mistake. Care to wager on their mistake tolerance, brother?"

"Wait a moment dear brother, let us find out more about them first. Surely, you've noticed they are like us?" At first I thought he meant our race, but then he added, "And their complexion as well." Then the shorter brother turned again towards us to address us. "I am Dread. This is my brother Shamus."

Darnell moved to the front of us, slightly up the hill, his eyes still ablaze and ready for action.

The one called Dread threw open his arms and said laughing to Darnell, "Relax."

His brother Shamus added, "Hey, if we wanted to attack you we would have done so while you were fighting the dogs. We are scavengers like the dogs, but unlike them, we are pure to our craft. No offense, but you all look more like bait, than a good meal." At that I noticed that the bigger one, Shamus had some kind of leash extending from his hand. It was tied to something small that was dancing back and forth behind him.

Dread turned back to us and continued, "We're what you might call long term guests here. However by the looks of things we may be of some mutual benefit."

Akina broke in to tell us, "Rule number one. Don't trust anybody you meet here."

Shamus chided Dread, "Your reputation with the ladies does again precede you little brother. You will have to work hard to catch this one. You saw how easily she passed through those bones. Is she flesh or spirit?"

"The hunt has not even begun and already you discount me? Truly, she is flesh and unspoiled! But I say there are two ladies in their party who have not known a man! On such a day in honor of them I shall tell them only the truth and still prevail," Dread exclaimed to his older sibling.

Reggie did not take kindly to their attitude and let them know it by stepping forward and swinging his staff down splitting a boulder. "You two need to get to steppin'."

Shamus laughed and pointed mockingly at Reggie. "I think you've upset them brother. That overgrown one is going to stop you from speaking, if he has to split every rock down here."

Carla grabbed both Darnell and Reggie by the shoulder and urged them, "Come on let's go. We don't have time for these clowns."

Dread looked back to his brother speaking quickly, "Oh, that one is feisty." Then he addressed Carla. "Young sister, time is the one thing you now have plenty of."

Akina looked them square in the eye, asking, "If you two don't mind, can we get a look from up top there? We won't be here but a minute."

As we marched up the hill I noticed what seemed to be shadows passing in front and between us. Not like from clouds, for there were no clouds or even sun in the sky, the shadows between us were more like drifting shades.

Dread stepped back allowing all of us to pass. "Pretty women are always allowed on our hill." The hill was not close to being the highest peak around, but it was high enough and positioned such that we could get a good look at the plains below.

As we reached the top, the little creature tied to the other end of Shamus' leash stepped forward still darting back and forth.

While Akina, Carla and Sandy walked onto the opposite edge to scan the landscape, Darnell, Reggie and Kim stood in front of the brothers. Oddly enough, I asked the first question. "What is that?"

"I am not a that," the creature replied to our surprise. It looked like a dog or maybe a lynx, but totally unlike the pack that attacked us before. "I am Nihil Spei, but you can call me Nihil."

We all looked at each other in amazement. Reggie replied first. "We thought you were a pet or something."

Nihil replied sharply as he stood up on two legs, "Obviously, I am not!" It was then I first noticed that his other arm was chained to Dread. He was at the center of a chain between them.

Darnell ventured forward with a question. "So, why are you on a leash?" We all awaited the answer.

The leashed beast spoke, even more strangely. "Let's just say that I lost a bet. So why are you here?"

Darnell began to speak, "We're looking for some..." but Reggie stretched out his hand motioning for Darnell to be quiet.

The dog took a step towards us and continued, "So you're looking for someone? Everyone here is. Are they lost? Everyone here is."

I could see the girls on the far ledge pointing and coming to some sort of agreement. Typically Reggie or Darnell would have been over there with them plotting strategy, but they were more concerned with these three peculiar characters. Together Akina, Carla and Sandy turned and headed back towards us. Akina spoke for the group. "We need to head over that way through this other valley and just to the other side of those peaks. We might be less visible if we track along the range around the valley, but that's three times as far." I was a Chemical Engineering student, but I knew enough about geometry to know that it couldn't be three times as far, but looking at all those peaks and troughs I realized that it would take at least three times as long to go around.

As we were coming to a consensus, a rumbling grew from down below to our right. Tumbling down the path between our mound and the valley of bones was a white rhinoceros. Its path would surely take it towards the dogs that attacked us. Looking at the rhino gave me a chill. I saw that I wasn't the only one. Carla, who had her jacket tied around her waist, wrapped her arms around herself and shivered a bit.

Our collective gaze held on the rhino until it had fully passed us and forged into the mist that lined the valley floors all around us. Reggie got our attention. "Come on. Let's get moving y'all," he said.

As we started down the other side of the mound from where we had walked up, Dread, Shamus and Nihil began to follow us. Dread called out "This is number two."

Kim stared hard at them and then tugged on Reggie's sleeve, or what there was left of it after the hound attack. Reggie stopped dead in his tracks, and turned back to them. "What the... why are you guys following us?"

Dread spoke for both of them. "We are scavengers. Quite honestly we're just looking for a meal. Given the path that you are taking we expect there to be plenty of killing and therefore by definition for us, plenty of food. Do not be alarmed. That is how we survive here. In case you haven't noticed there is no life here besides the life you bring when you arrive. Nothing grows here, no seed or any type of germination, be it plant or animal. So, what you kill we will eat. Plus, having us with your party will make you appear bigger and fewer of these beasts around here will think you're dinner."

We all looked at each other, and then surprisingly Sandy blurted out a question on all of our minds. "Why do you keep counting?"

"Yeah, what's up with that?" Kim asked.

They looked at each other apparently puzzled. "What do you mean?" Dread declared.

Carla demanded, "Don't play dumb with us. You remember, right after the rhino passed by..." Her voice trailed off as she looked off in distraction, in the direction where we last saw the rhino. Although we were no longer actually in position to see down into that first valley, in the distance we could hear the encounter; the dogs attacking, the rhino rumbling back and forth. I could only imagine the teeth of the dogs sinking into the flesh of the White Rhino.

Dread cleared his throat and conceded "Oh, that counting. Again, since this is a special day, I will tell you the truth. We have a little wager going as to how many mistakes it will take before you are all killed. It's the national pastime down here between thinking creatures. Not killing all of the hounds, once you gained the upper hand was a mistake. And going through the valley is your second mistake. The beasts in the hills are fiercer, but there are fewer of them. If you are careful you may be able to sneak by most of them. Plus, you are so small you are like grapes to them, not very filling. But going through the valley you will certainly encounter many beasts. That bodes well for us, for in your wake we will dine greatly."

Darnell posed the question none of us wanted to ask. "So, what if we are the one's killed?"

The two brothers gave a knowing look to us and from it we knew that they'd be just as happy to eat us as well.

Carla let out a "Y'all are some sick freaks!" and turned back down the hill.

As we marched off, Dread replied, "There is no other choice. We feed off of death down here."

Carla raised her hand and waved them off like "Whatever!"

$$\infty$$

The further we descended down into the valley, the denser the mist became. The shadows still passed all around and between us. I guess they had before when we were in the valley of bones, but given our state of mind then it was not unreasonable to think that we would not have noticed.

We figured that it was somewhere between five and ten miles across the floor of the first valley to the opposite side. We figured that at a good pace we should be able to make it in three to six hours. It took us at least eight.

The first attack came about twenty minutes into our trip. Through the mist five giant Stickmen approached us. They stood about fifty feet tall; so tall in fact that their shoulders and heads passed in and out of view as the mist flowed by. Their legs looked like the trunks of bamboo or birch trees. Unlike the three scavengers following us, when they conversed we couldn't understand a word they said. But when the one in front threw a spear that suddenly appeared in his hand we understood them completely. The spears they threw were quite large and would have smashed us rather than pierced us.

To that point I wondered about the full extent of my cousins' abilities and here they did not disappoint. Reggie swung forward and quickly toppled the one in front with a strike from his staff. The leader fell back but was caught by one of his brethren. Kim, atop her board, took to the air. High above us, soaring in and out of the mist, she tossed bolts of current towards the eyes of all five of them. At the time I wondered how she could zoom in and out between their heads so deftly without falling off her steel-lined skateboard. I was later to find out that she can mold the current she generates to magnetize the board to her feet. Carla, realizing that she could do little offensively, defended Sandy and me via her telekinetic abilities, by invisibly deflecting their spears, which continued to appear out of thin air into the hands of the Stickmen. Akina stood off to our side. All objects hurled her way passed harmlessly through her. She attempted to give direction to the rest of us, but I don't really know if that was needed. Honestly, Akina tended to overmanage sometimes. Darnell however, was the ringer in this fight.

Darnell floated closely to Sandy, Carla and me. It was at this time that I realized more about how Darnell's gift worked. In the first few moments of the battle he had been "focusing." He doesn't have to do that, but given the size of the task and what he was about to do, he needed to go there.

While he had been staring blankly, looking within, his sister Carla had been protecting him as well. Suddenly, his face and eyes became focused again. Carla gave a knowing look as her brother floated slightly higher. They were so in tune that she knew when he was ready without him saying a word. A split second later he unleashed a firestorm from his eyes that not only engulfed the mid-drifts of each of our adversaries, but also lit up the dark sky. The fire seemed almost suspended in the nether firmament beyond. Closer in, the fire caught to the Stickmen and began to work its way up their torso. They stumbled and lurched until one of them attempted to move to his left as if to run, but the inertia of his upper body held it firmly facing forwards. As his legs went out to the side, the Stickman's upper body toppled to his right. His legs being still somewhat connected to the falling part of his body careened back to the right following his other limbs to the ground.

Then another one went down like a tree felled by a lumberjack. Kim came back to the ground and stood next to me. Reggie backed off, rejoining the rest of us. We all stood and watched as one by one they fell. We could see Dread and Shamus talking, whispering to each other a short distance behind us. But even from where we were, we could tell they were impressed. As we began to walk off, and the last Stick-man fell to his knees in flames before falling completely over, we saw Dread, Shamus and their attached friend Nihil move in towards our fallen attackers apparently in search of something edible. Reggie shook his head and commented of the Stickmen, "They thought we were dinner."

Within fifteen minutes, our unwanted accompanists caught up with us again just as I first noticed the most un-nerving event to date. Off in the distance, about fifty to sev-enty-five yards from us, I saw a decayed evil-looking hand protruding from the ground. In its grasp it held tight one of the shadows that had passed between and all around us since we'd arrived. I could hear no sound, but we were close enough that I could see the distorted shadow form struggling to free itself.

Nihil, noticing my interest, commented, "Oh, we failed to mention that besides the various carnivores running and fly-ing around here, you must also be on guard for those below. They'll reach up and snag most anything. That's an addict that one has." He grinned. Then we saw a second grotesque hand extend up grabbing a hold of the struggling ghost. "Oh, it looks like we've arrived just in time to see the end. These things can go on for quite some time. At times they escape through death's door, other times not. You never know, but in life they are bound in this way. You really are privileged to see one of these play out, to see a not so fortunate addict as he is dragged below."

Dread continued, "Yes, the things below are all around and they are hungry little buggers. We've lost our share of free meals to them. But hey, what can you do?"

Nihil shouted ahead to Akina who was leading up front. "Akina, why haven't you told them about this place?" Akina scowled and lifted up her hand without fully turning around. Nihil continued to the rest of us, "You really should ask your cousin about this place. She knows more than she's sharing. You should ask her why she doesn't tell you more. She has you all here and you're just supposed to trust her? Do you even know where she's taking you?"

At that point, none of us paid that little dog any mind. We all had full confidence in Akina, although she seemed a bit out of sorts. But given where we were, that was to be expected. I for one, wondered just how she knew where the Aunties were. I didn't ask, because none of it made sense to me anyway. That was just one more thing. However, though none of us quizzed Akina as Nihil suggested, given what he said about the "ones below," we all began to spend more time looking down than up.

About a half hour later, I was of more use in a less spectacular second skirmish. I'm not sure that words can adequately explain what confronted us next. Looking something like giant leeches, a countless number of these things stretched as far as we could see. Although they were unique individuals, they moved as one. We moved to the right and we could see their collective form moving with us. Going to the left they did the same. I imagine we could have worked our way around them if we had run or certainly if we risked flying again. When we finally determined that they were behaving aggressively with bad intent towards us, Reggie swung his staff at one of them felling it. To our amazement, the blow caused it to split, forming two new creatures. Kim's electrical shocks did the same, even making three from one in some cases.

Dread commented, "Ah, I see that you have come upon the Legisdoctor. My brother and I don't really care for them, but Nihil finds them quite tasty."

"I most certainly do! Their flavor is unmatched. Notice how each one could satisfy a palette in its own way, still collectively they move together for the consummate meal. The perfect blend of pluralism and relativism, they are a fine treat anytime." Nihil licked his lips, his split tongue flicking wildly.

Then, and this is strange in that from the start I thought to do this, I placed my palms on the ground. I felt the dust in my fingers and then like before I began to feel layers. I could actually feel the energy levels of the atoms within the molecules and like pulling a switch or rolling a dial, I could change them. I reflected inwardly and felt outwardly as far as I could. Then from my very hands spreading out past my cousins and to the ground beneath our enemy beyond, the brown dust turned pearly white. I had transformed the dust into salt. While it had no physical effect on us, it clung to our opponents. The more they squirmed, the more it worked its way all over their bodies. Like a slug covered with table salt, they began to whither.

As they began to drop, my cousins all began to turn back towards me thoroughly speechless save Sandy, who, once she smiled generously, hugged me. I was reminded that she is not actually my cousin. "Wow! That was great." She spun around releasing me and began jumping up and down. "That was amazing!" Everyone smiled and took their turn patting me on the back.

Our peanut gallery once again offered their take. Dread, was first "So the guy with the glasses can do something. I was beginning to wonder if he was as much dead weight as he appeared to be."

As the leeches continued go to through the throes of death, Nihil danced around while Shamus reached down and whispered something into Sandy's ear. I touched her shoulder and asked, "What did he say to you?" She rolled her shoulder and literally brushed me off; deciding to keep whatever it was to herself.

Reggie posed the question to Dread, "Well, aren't you guys going to eat?"

Dread, his serpent hair disturbingly animated upon his head, laughingly replied, "Oh no, we told you, these guys don't taste so good. Nihil will eat enough for all of us. But hey we were right. We knew there'd be a whole lot of killing whichever way you guys went."

As we began to walk through the shriveled parasites, continuing on toward our destination, all around us we could see hands reaching up and pulling down what remained of these newly deceased. And just as quickly, I started to feel sorry for these guys. Somehow, I knew what was happening to them was far worse than death. And all the while Nihil danced between Dread and Shamus as they followed us.

We defended ourselves five more times across the valley floor. I wasn't much help in any of those attacks. And as Dread had predicted, they ate well in our wake. Their appetite was insatiable.

We snacked on trail mix we'd packed for the trip. On that first day none of us tasted the flesh of a single inhabitant of the Pit. Towards the end of our trek across the valley I overheard Nihil tell Dread and Shamus, "I never would have thought that anyone in their generation could make the straight and narrow across the valley this far."

A good bit later we reached the opposite edge of the valley floor. And right there before us was a mountain crowned by what appeared to be a city. There was a loosely defined path zigzagging up the face of the mountain. And where that path began was a large marble tablet at least twenty feet high and fifteen feet wide. Into it was etched an inscription. It was written in Latin. It read:

OMNES QUI TRANSEUNT HINC OMNIA
RELINQUANT. URBS FRACTA SUPER TE

TESTIFICETUR STULTITIAM HOMINUM. QUID INVENTUS EST IN HAC NOVA EDEN, NON POTEST DISINVENIRI, NAM HAC EST IANUA ILLA SINE REDITU.

Sandy, having studied Latin, read it to us. "Let all who pass here forsake all. May this broken city above you be a testament to the foolishness of man. What was found in this New Eden cannot be unfound, for this is the door of no return."

"Mmmm..." from beneath us we heard Nihil say. "You might want to heed this one."

At the bottom of the tablet there sat the impression of a handprint blazon into the stone. Sandy made a movement to place her hand into the inset, but Akina reached out and pulled Sandy's arm away. Akina then pressed her hand into it and a coldness swept over her that was visible to all of us. As it did, the words on the stone began to transform from Latin to English and an appendix appeared at the bottom of the block at our eye level. The additional text in much smaller print read:

To those of my bloodline, who now read this text, greetings. My dreams have told me that one day you would come here in search of answers. The city you see above is an epitaph to the arrogance of man. Man sought to reach beyond time and look upon the face of God. The results can be found above in the wreckage. Neither you nor I can do anything about that now. And although I cannot see the future clearly, this riddle has haunted me all my years here and I know that it is for you to answer.

One will live and die by the sword, while another shall die and live by the Word. One shall find life. One shall lose her heart and be swept away. One shall perish this very day. One shall reach the end and begin again.

It is my fondest wish that these words would provoke you to remove all sense of pride and run to the womb of your own world and time, but my dreams tell me you will do otherwise. They tell me that you will press on and that these things, in their proper time will come true. My dreams do not tell me your names, but they do tell me that you know my name. I hope that, in spite of who and what I may have become that my name might have meaning and caution for you,

In your service,

Paul

Confused as ever, I shouted out, "Hey! What is...?" before I realized that Akina, stricken, was recoiling from the tablet, her right hand firmly covering her mouth and her left hand outstretched and looking for comfort. She was beyond confused and obviously stunned by what we had all just read. Akina was not only shaken by the words but also the fact that rather than leading, it was clear to her now that she was being led.

Shamus called from behind us, "That Paul was clever hiding that riddle like that all this time."

Nihil, on two legs, danced between us up to the writing. "Yes, and I wonder what other secrets Paul has for us in the City of Man? I'm sure there are plenty of other things he's hidden from all of you. Surely, it is your destiny to find out? Surely, your fates have not brought you all the way here to turn around now? And then there's the matter of contacting your aunties. Plus, going back now means seven more battles and who wants that today?   Then of course, you could just walk around this mountain. You'll reason that the mountain is wider than it is tall and that the quickest route will be up and through the city. But in reality it's that you're curious, isn't it? You can't resist seeing what it is Paul does not want you to see. You're curious; you've always been curious."

Reggie and the others discussed the matter, while I stood off to the side staring at our three parasites with everyone else focused on the towers above us.

That was the first moment in all the time that we were in the Pit that it occurred to me that maybe we ought to dump these guys... at any cost. In all the hours of my life, if there had ever been an hour in which I should have spoken my mind, it was that one. Now the pain of that dismissal will live with me until I die.

12: Secure Yourself to Heaven

What would you give to face the darkness? What would you give to avoid it? Or would you embrace it?

The first requires at least an ounce of faith, the second, a shortage thereof and the third, a void of faith beyond measure.

Jonah felt himself to be a member of the latter two, but for the second time that day he found himself in the first grouping.

Seeing Matasis, his Herald floating at his side, and the screaming beyond the tree line led him to a quick prayer of supplication as he raced back towards the clearing. "My God!" Jonah uttered.

As he broke free of the trees, Jonah heard the tail end of a pronouncement by Matasis, but at the time he had no idea what the Blue god was saying. But what he did know and witnessed as he pushed past the last branch, was that Matasis was firing at will. People were running and scattering in every direction, but Matasis was without mercy. White-hot beams erupted from his hands disintegrating whatever they struck.

Without hesitation or fear, Jonah dropped to his knees, pulling his handheld computer and Wave Modulator from his backpack as he fell. The two items were still hooked together. In the chaos he spoke deliberately, but precisely to his devices. "Awake Computer. Two targets, seventy-five degrees above the horizon, ten to twenty meters above the ground. Envelope completely, zero emit."

Immediately, sunlit spheres began to form around the two floating combatants. The spheres then darkened until they were opaque. The firing ceased. No beams, no sound, no nothing. Then it became apparent on Jonah's monitor that the inhabitant of the larger sphere was firing into the now black shield as patches of white appeared on the surface of the image before him. But still none of these attempts breached its shell. Both globes moved to and fro but to no avail, as the spheres moved with them. The larger one, which contained Matasis, landed on the ground, but the sphere stayed with him.

Jonah was pleased, but not all together surprised. He had figured that if this wave technology of his could contain a nuclear blast, then it ought to be able to contain these pseudo gods. All the same, he kept his hands and eyes on his equipment as the running and screaming slowed. With the bubble containing Matasis on the ground, everyone was careful to stay far from his blind darting back and forth.

While the Herald remained motionless in the air, Matasis took to the air again himself. This eased Jonah's mind a bit because these two were less dangerous floating around than on the ground. Suddenly Matasis zoomed off towards the horizon. This concerned Jonah, but still his sphere followed him. He knew his device had distance limitations. Matasis was flying blind. In his frustration, Matasis mostly just went up and down, left and right as though he were trying to jerk the sphere off of him. After a minute, while a small crowd gathered around Jonah, the shimmering black spheres ran into each other and merged. Then after an apparent conversation between the two, the spheres split and both headed off to and beyond the horizon. Suddenly, Jonah felt a tap on his shoulder. It was Bruce. Jonah, in his immersion into the task at hand had failed to notice that a crowd had formed around him. "Dude!" Bruce cried. "That was awesome!"

Coming to his senses, Jonah thanked him and asked "So where is everybody? Where's Heru and Sara?"

Back towards the center of the field, near Ashok's vehicle another crowd had gathered. At first Jonah walked towards them, and then began to run as he realized whom he didn't see. Breaking through the circle of people, he stumbled to his knees to witness Heru and Jared attempting to comfort Ashok as he knelt before a small, smoldering pile of ashes. Jonah mouthed silently in disbelief. "Sara? Sara?" He felt a presence to his right; it was Pam, the other woman he'd rescued earlier, kneeling beside him.

Pam stroked Jonah's shoulder to comfort him, as she murmured, "Lord, Lord..."

But she could bring him no comfort. Jonah, if nothing else, was unflappable. His friends marveled at his consistent measured response in most every situation, though no one ever considered the role his general depression played in that aspect of his character. But this moment was different. Jonah was stunned like never before. Outside of his body he could see Heru and Jared leading Ashok back to his vehicle. Jared slid in to drive. Bruce, looking mad, climbed into the back seat. Bruce shouted out a response to something Heru said, "Alright, you're right. We should all get out of here now. But, we have to make those bastards pay!"

Seeing and hearing this brought Jonah back to his body. Jonah wobbled to his feet and reached to help Pam up as well, even though she was a good five to ten years younger than him. Realizing that Pam was relatively new to the group and the chaos that had just transpired, he asked Pam, "Hey, do you have some way to get home?"

She stuck one hand into a back pocket and stretched the other one out as she replied, "Well, I had a ride. But..." Her vision spanned the nearly empty field. Many had run during the battle. One was her ride.

Heru, broke in. "Hey, we have room in our boat for another. Why don't you come with me?"

"Sure. Thanks," Pam said and then took a step back to pick up her bag.

As Jared started Ashok's transport and an obviously despondent Dave climbed into the rear storage area, Heru reached out his hand through the front window to grab Jared's arm. "Hold on a minute." Then turning to Jonah he asked, "Hey I saw what you did earlier. Can you do anything to help cover us and those still in the woods?"

Not looking directly into Heru's eyes, Jonah answered softly, "Yeah, I think I can." Heru gave him a pat on the shoulder before he turned to gather the people going by sea.

Jonah drifted back, backpedaling as he continued to take in the scene before turning completely to walk towards his gear and backpack.

Then, like a ton of bricks, with each step a new level of hopelessness fell upon him. Levels of despair that he had never known before assaulted him with every breath. He wanted to cry. He hadn't cried since before his mother passed in his childhood. As he collapsed next to his devices he felt wetness on his cheeks and thought that he might be crying. But then he realized that it had begun to rain. The heavens were crying for Sara so he thought. The raindrops ran down his face so rapidly that he could hardly punch in the proper codes. Through his pain he tried to set up a shield that would allow his comrades to disperse undetected. He set the shield at a fixed perimeter so that his moving would not cause its boundaries to move with him. This would make it more difficult for the Blues to pinpoint his location. Tears continued to fall from the sky onto his instruments, soaking them in anguish. Kneeling, Jonah watched the water drive Sara's ashes into the ground. Some of the ashes floated on the water and ran towards the sea. As everyone pulled off and went their separate ways they all looked at him, their hearts broken from their solitary pain. None of them could have consoled him even if they'd tried and besides, they could not invite him to join them because no one remaining was going his way. Everyone realized that there wasn't time to offer shoulders for crying. Jonah realized this as well.

Once regaining his feet, Jonah was paralyzed with the magnitude of what was before him. This was the same feeling he had had in the junkyard when planning his retrieval of the family heirloom and when he was in the sewer preparing to rescue Sara. And then, as before, he came to himself and stretched out his faith to Heaven despite the sea of sadness that was threatening to drown him. His fear abated and he was able to take that first step towards the woods, and then a second. By the third step he was running, backpack flapping on his back.

He knew exactly where he wanted to go, but he knew he couldn't take a direct route there. Being the last one out and the only one of the last group departing on foot, he knew that he had the longest odds of escaping. But Jonah never was one to think that way. For reasons known mostly only to him, he always felt empowered as if it was his divine gift. For whatever reason, God had given him the ability to get things done. Losing Sara and facing her death had floored him, but fear of the Blues was not an issue for him. In fact, about ten minutes into his trek into the woods he had to fight off the temptation to act when he heard their fighters flying above him headed for ground zero. He pondered whether or not to blind their navigation equipment and send them crashing into the sea or each other. Not wanting to shed innocent blood, he refrained knowing that if one of them happened to spot him, then he'd have no choice but to defend himself. It wasn't vanity, but he knew what the Blues thought of his class and he knew they had no clue who they were messing with when fooling with him.

While he did not think long on crashing their interceptors, unless they attacked him, Jonah did consider for a quarter mile whether to go home at all that night. He reasoned that if the Blues were indeed on his trail, that it would be safer to go somewhere other than home. That way, at least Monica would be safe. But Jonah knew his wife, if she got even a whiff of what had gone on that evening and he didn't come home she'd be out looking for him and that could make things even worse. She was fearless too. He wished for all the world that he had one of the communication beacons on him that he could have dropped along his way. He could have set it to broadcast a message later that night that he was safe, long after he'd gone from wherever he dropped it.

After moving through the woods, upstream parallel to the river, but away from the roads, Jonah came to fencing which bordered the rear property line of an apartment complex. Like always, the most dangerous part of traveling through the woods is when you come out of them. That is when you are most likely to be seen and asked questions you'd rather not answer. Although he remained electronically cloaked, Jonah thought it far safer to scale this fence and emerge onto the street from the front entrance of the complex. The Blues relied too heavily on their technology to invest a whole lot in street patrolmen, but still Jonah had found it wise to take every reasonable precaution. And now that the Blues knew or would soon figure out that the masses could cloak themselves, it was going to get even harder.

Jonah climbed the fence, backpack and all, swinging himself over the top as quietly as he could. Landing in the darkness he looked around at all the back porches, balconies and windows for the slightest hint of response. Seeing none, he walked quickly through the parking lot and towards the front entrance. He noted that this complex was built in a time when the common man could afford personal transportation and needed a place to park his or her vehicle, but those days were long gone. Now they served mostly as a hardtop playground for only the most resilient of children. Passing the main office he noticed a group of youths playing basketball, seemingly oblivious to the aircraft streaking back and forth, the sirens in the distance, or just the general state of high alert by the authorities. Jonah knew these boys; they had nothing to lose. He knew them well enough to know that in their own way they were far more dangerous than the Blues could ever be. The hopeless have no regard for life, not even their own.

Reaching the street, Jonah made it to the bus-stop just as a bus was pulling up. He melded into the crowd and thanked the Lord that he happened to have the correct change on him.

Moving towards the back of the bus he found an open seat, and swinging his bag to his lap, collapsed into it. He slid to the window being careful to pull his cap over the better part of his face. Closing his eyes for a moment to think of Sara and what he'd lost that night, he hoped that this would be the end of his losses, at least for the night. He was not bold enough to hope for anything beyond that night. Opening his eyes as the rain began to fall again and the bus passed from one streetlight to another, he was again struck with the urge to cry. But no tears came. It was as if the rain outside did his crying for him. He told himself that was good, because crying would draw attention. But in reality, there was never a good time to just let go behind enemy lines. He couldn't remember the last time he had. In his dreams he'd cry, but never in his waking life.

∞

Two buses, two trains and nearly three hours later, Jonah arrived at his exit. Clear on the other side of town from the shore, he felt reasonably safe in assuming that if the Blues were on to him, they'd have nabbed him by now. Entering back into the woods he walked briskly, and then began to run, sensing something within himself that was reminding him of the urgency to get home.

Less than twenty minutes later he approached his homestead to see a small group of people standing and speaking briskly to each other. Within a second he realized who they were. He broke into a full run yelling out, "Monica! Monica!"

She broke away from Marta and Marta's husband Jorge and ran to him as he ran to her. They flew into each other's arms falling to the ground in a storm of leaves.

Marta and Jorge, laughed just a bit before they wandered over with Marta exclaiming, "See Monica, I told you that if anyone got out of there it was your husband. Jonah, your crazy wife was going to go out looking for you. We couldn't stop her, so Jorge and I convinced her to let us go with her. You came up just as we were fastening our packs on and locking the kids down." Their oldest, who was fifteen, often watched the brood while his parents were away.

Monica, slobbering and kissing every inch of his face repeated over and over, "Oh, baby. Oh, baby."

Then like a bolt of lightning, a sense of recognition came over Jonah as he realized by their very air that none of them knew all of what had happened that evening. "Monica..." he tried to interrupt.

Monica began firing questions, but didn't wait for answers before she fired off the next one. She wanted to know how he'd gotten away. Marta had told her how the Blues had come and everyone ran, but he ran back.

She continued her litany, but Jonah closed his eyelids and rolled his eyes inside as he searched the strength to tell her the news that Sara was gone. He reached up with his right hand and touched her softly on the outside of her arm. "Monica…"

She looked at him sensing something was coming. "What is it? What's wrong?"

Jonah grappled desperately for the right words, but submitted to a muted "Sara. Sara. She died." He spoke it almost as if it were a question.

Monica covered her mouth and fell towards him, her eyes darting back and forth as though searching the leaves for answers. Marta, not hearing or choosing not to believe what she heard, rushed towards them. "What did you say? What did you say?"

Jonah's tearless and vacant eyes looked up, and confirmed to her, "Yes, Sara. I'm sorry."

Marta's husband held her as her knees gave way and she cried "Jesus, El Senor!" Jonah, who had not cried since childhood, could only sit with his arms wrapped around Monica, as she wept on behalf of both of them for their friend.

There in the darkness, the four of them sat for the next half an hour as Jonah tried to explain what happened. Each of them in his or her own way tried hard to find gaps, possibilities that might offer some hope that Sara was indeed not dead. But patiently Jonah went over every fact twice and some three times. In his heart he too hoped that he'd missed something, something that would reverse what he now found so hard to believe.

Then their focus changed as Monica asked the question, "So, who all knows this? Has anyone told Karun or Manisha?"

Jonah had not thought about his employers since he first freed the hostages and led them through the tunnels. He reasoned that since Ashok and Sara's place of business was just two doors down from Karun and Manisha they'd heard somehow, but at that moment he didn't even know if Karun had gone home or stayed through the night. (The couple had an apartment above the store that they often used during the week.) He'd listened to the airwaves all the way home and hadn't heard any news whatsoever. Not that he would, given all that had gone on that night. These types of events didn't make the papers or the authorized airwaves. You hear this kind of news in the streets. If Karun and Manisha had indeed gone to their suburban home for the evening they might not know yet.

Monica, still weary from the news, suggested, "We need to go down there and let them know, especially Manisha."

Jonah realized she was right. Karun might be okay, but Manisha and Sara had grown very close over the years. Despite the cultural and religious barriers, they were the best of friends. Jonah picked up his bag and tossed it over his shoulder, pondering the coming morning. "We need to get there early today; that gives us maybe an hour to sleep."

Marta offered, "Well, if you don't need a fresh set of clothes you're welcome to take a nap here at our place. We have plenty of room. You can have our bed."

"Oh, thanks Marta, but the couch will be fine. We get in a bed, we'll never get up in an hour," Jonah replied.

Marta acknowledged his sentiment and led them all back to her and Jorge's place. Climbing down the hidden stairwell, the four of them came to a landing where the couple's four children lay sleeping. Their living area was much larger than Monica and Jonah's, but most definitely low tech. The only real protection they had was the matting from above that covered the ground above their room to block any infrared heat-sensing cameras. But that was it. Jonah offered many a time to share some of what he'd thrown together, but Jorge had often rebuffed him, saying all that stuff wasn't necessary, and were just things to get him in trouble. He felt it best to keep it simple and right rather than complicated and wrong. Jonah couldn't really argue, because in all their time there neither family had been found out.

They rested.

An hour later, Marta offered Monica and Jonah snack packs for the road. With that gesture of care, they departed, waving back at their friends and neighbors. Once they reached the main thoroughfare they'd have to split up. They might take the same route and even the same bus, but they were apart, rarely even making eye contact. But on this day, they walked hand in hand through the woods. They spoke softly to each other, remembering the good times with Sara and all she'd done for the both of them and the community.

As they approached the point where they'd have to walk separately, Jonah worked up the courage to broach the subject his wife cared the least to discuss. "Baby, how would you feel about leaving this place if I told you that I could get us into the Circle?"

Her reply surprised him. "Well, my love, I'm with you. Whatever you think is best. But how are you going to do that?" On another day she would have added a question as to whether he was just going to go up and knock on the door, but not today.

"Well, I'm hoping that Vicki can do something. She stopped by the shop yesterday."

Monica rolled her eyes and stopped. "Vicki?" Slowly she began to walk again as she continued, "What can Vicki do for us?" Then she thought for a second, "…and why is Vicki stopping by your shop?"

Jonah, now realizing his mistake, attempted to answer, "Well, she…"

Monica jumped in again, "Did she actually say she could get us in?"

Something within Jonah tweaked. He didn't want to sink this proposal completely, but something within him, until that point unacknowledged, did not want to tell Monica the specific offer Vicki made. "Well, not exactly. She did mention that the council of elders was considering bringing us in." The "us" part may have been a lie, but he reasoned that it might not have been. Vicki had not mentioned anything about "us," but he figured that surely in their discussion of bringing him up to the frozen north, that they'd considered his wife as well. He wasn't going otherwise, so why veer off into such a potentially messy conversation?

"Jonah, she lies for a living. For gosh sakes, she's a spy, and that's what they do. They lie, lie and lie some more. She might get us up there in the middle of the artic and leave us to the polar bears and things."

Jonah laughed. "Things? Surely, we have more to worry about here than something like that, even if it happened."

Monica relented, just a bit. "Well, okay maybe we should consider it, but I don't know that I'd trust Vicki to make it happen. I know she's your girl and all, and y'all go way back, but I don't know." She looked up and pronounced, "Hey, we're getting close."

"I know," Jonah said grabbing her arm and pulling her close to him. They kissed quickly, but held each other longer.

Monica walked off ahead of him, as was their way, so that he could keep an eye on her. Often she'd ask him, "So, who's watching you?" and always he'd just smile. He loved her as a wife, but so much of how he loved her was as a friend. Jonah could not even think of what he would not do to protect her. Often he suffered the pain of having to watch her walk away as he waited for her to leave his sight, so that no one might know that they're together. Today he waited as well, but when he did come out of the woods he quickly closed the distance between them so that he could, for the most part, keep an eye on her.

Merging with the throngs of working class people, he dared to board the same bus as his wife. He boarded in the rear, she in the front. They would, in these instances, look at each other on occasion, but always without emotion. For moments at a time they would stare with opaque faces. Yet what was cold to others was passion between them. These steely guises masked sensual transmission that spoke of lovemaking that would come that night. How they would share this same stare the moment the second one arrived home that evening. How without a word or expression, they would engage in the God given right of a husband and wife.

After making their connection and arriving at the pre-discussed spots, they both exited and headed towards the electronics store. Monica took the direct path, Jonah the long way. When Jonah arrived, Monica was standing behind the counter with Manisha. Karun stood next to Jonah, between him and the others. He saw Monica grab Manisha's hands and realized that Monica was already working her way up to giving Manisha the bad news.

Just as Jonah dropped his bag Monica began to get to the meat of the matter. "Manisha, you see, during that incident last night something very bad happened."

"Yes...?" an obviously frightened Manisha replied timidly, with the trembling of a thousand earthquakes in her voice.

Monica continued, "During the attack Sara was hit and ..."

"No, No!" Manisha broke in not letting her finish.

"She died," Monica ended.

"No, No don't say it! Don't say it!" Manisha continued to shout over her.

"Manisha..." she tried again, but Manisha was now stomping her feet and shaking her head as she worked her body lower in denial. Monica tried to hold her up, but was failing. Karun stepped back behind the counter attempting to hold his wife as she wailed and convulsed. The futility of it all did not discourage him until his friend Jonah touched him lightly on the shoulder. At that he let his wife fall to the earth. Monica descended with her, holding her all the way.

With each employee that entered thereafter, there was renewed pain, as they were told the news. Each of them cursed the news. Some had heard rumblings on the way in, but all where shocked at the reality of it all, the finality of it all. What measure can any man take against that day? To die in the most feared way of any oppressed people, at the hands of your oppressor, made such a loss even harder for some.

For some it was an awakening to the folly of their predicament - to be here, in the midst of a society, that at this point had shown its fangs and that would someday devour, if not them, then their children. Surely anyone smiling in such a land was a fool. Anyone laughing was a lunatic. The pure evil of this place had come to the surface and none could deny it.

Later in the morning, Karun and some of the others cornered Jonah to commend him on his efforts the night before, busting up the execution during a live broadcast and giving one of the biggest Blue bullies a lesson in humility. They all wanted to know the details and the technical tit for tat. But that would have to wait for another day. With Sara gone who could claim victory? Who could claim any accomplishment? Who could rejoice at anything about the night before?

While Monica and Manisha were on the floor, Jonah could hear them quietly conversing and he even joined in at one point adding facts to help clear up some unanswered questions. Afterwards, Jonah continued stocking shelves and preparing to head downstairs while Monica and Manisha continued their conversation and sipped one cup of tea after another.

The day would go on, but things had changed and Jonah knew it. The very air was charged. The evil deeds of last night would not go quietly. Without a word from anyone, he was certain of this, more than ever he was willing to give his all for whatever must be. And he also knew that tomorrow would be a day of reckoning.

13: Perils

Oh Lord, what have you purchased with thine own blood? Such a worrisome and weak lot are we. I can't speak for others, but surely you are due some refund when it comes to me. Lord, I am afflicted. Can you not see how diseased and damaged I am? Why have you not cast me out?

Reggie led us up the path leading to the mountain's plateau and the towers that stood upon it. Behind Reggie walked Akina. I followed her. In line past me were Kim, Carla and Sandy, with Darnell bringing up the rear. Our overgrown, uninvited guests drifted off into the mist, but I knew that they were still somewhere nearby. I could feel it.

About thirty yards past the stone tablet with the message from Uncle Paul that had so thoroughly rocked our worlds, stood a slender metal tower. It stood about twenty feet high. Looking out to the left and the right I could see similar monuments in various states of disrepair stretching out as far as the eye could see. Reggie spoke out to no one in particular, "They must have used these to set up some type of electronic barrier all around the mountain top. There must have been a transmitting tower on the very top as well. It might have been very clever, but from the looks of things not clever enough."

"No, I'd say not," Akina added.

As we gained altitude, apparently we also gained notice. Some of the smaller-winged creatures began to buzz around us with increasing intensity. All this set Reggie's instincts on edge as well. "They're sizing us up. We need to send a message. Darnell, drop a couple of these buggers."

As we all stood still for a minute, Darnell searched the sky for the next incoming beast. I could see clearly the larger creatures on the peaks and the foulness occasionally spewing from their mouths. However, in the poor lighting, these smaller ones were hard to pick up once they got any distance away from us. Then in a flash of light I heard a cry. While I was looking the other way, Darnell had indeed nailed one of the suckers. It crashed into the mountain a short distance away from us. Then a second one swooped down just over the middle of our line and Darnell fired. This time he literally decapitated the creature.

Reggie hollered out, "Excellent, Darnell! That should give these rascals something to think about."

I couldn't help but ask, "What about the larger ones?"

Reggie replied, "I wouldn't worry about them just yet. I don't think there's enough meat on our bones for them to get up off of their perch. And the smaller ones don't concern me individually, but collectively, if they were to get into a feeding frenzy, then they could be trouble. During our trek across the valley I noticed how they feed."

I don't think that had the comforting effect on me that he had imagined it would. Plus, even though Darnell had shooed them off, I by no means was ready to stop watching the skies or flinching at every crumbling rock.

It took us nearly two hours to reach the plateau at the summit. At the top we stood beneath a thirty-foot high wall that appeared, at least for the most part, to circle the city. I say "for the most part," because it didn't take long for us to realize that there were multiple breaches in the wall. Whatever purpose this wall served was long gone. It was now just an annoyance at best, and a testament to futility at worst. Once inside the wall we could see in the distance a tower in the very center of the town. The spire on top of it was tall enough to be the broadcast point for whatever type of electronic fencing they'd had.

It was also much cooler up there. Not cold by any means but coming out of the heat of the valley, it was a noticeable change.

Reggie pointed to the tower, "There. I figured there'd be a transmitter up here." Even from a distance you could see the disrepair. Whatever purpose it served, was long gone as well.

Looking around, we saw building after building. Some high, some low, but all dirty and dusty. The area to our immediate left looked to have been a military compound. To the right, was what obviously at one point had been a shopping district. Straight ahead and as far as the eye could see was residential housing. There were single family units, apartments and a hotel.

Darnell stepped up to Reggie, "So, what do you want to do?"

Reggie took a deep breath and held it for moment, and then releasing it, spoke matter-of-factly. "Well, it's obvious that things did not go well here."

Exasperated, Akina mocked him loudly, "Ya think? Could they have gone any worse?"

"As I was saying..." Reggie continued, "Things didn't go well here, but I think we can salvage something from these guys that might help us, since it looks like we might be here more than a day." Akina glared at him, as though that comment was meant for her. He never glanced her way, but he did reply to her glare nonetheless. "Akina, you said you don't know how far this place is that we're going to nor do you know what we might run into along the way. All you are certain of is the direction we should go. I'm not pointing fingers, but that's not a lot to go on. So I think it wise that we prepare ourselves for the long haul. There are things here that can help us survive. We've got to find the Aunties and take them back to deal with Matasis and the others. Plus, given that time doesn't flow the same way here as it does back home, for all we know, regardless of how many days we spend here, we may still return just a moment later."

"Or fifty years later," Akina quipped.

Carla spoke up. "But that's not likely. Right?"

Akina said nothing, but just stood with her arms wrapped around her body.

Reggie continued, after a silent glance towards Akina, "I see four targets that could really benefit our cause here. To expedite things I think we need to split up. The barracks over there, Kim and I will search them for any weapons we can find. Darnell and Carla, since you two can travel quickly, you guys fly down to that central tower. I'm sure it's a command center of some sort. Akina since you can pass thru walls and zap your way out of anything, you get to search through the living quarters. That would be the most dangerous assignment for anyone but you. So just stay misty and let us know what you find. Mike and Sandy, you guys stay here where I can see you from over there. You can go into that grocery store right there and bag up some food for all of us. Since it's obvious they still have power, I'm hoping that you can find something that's still edible. Kim and I will switch off checking on you two, since we'll be less than a hundred yards away. Any questions?"

At this point I was about ready to puke, but I'd been such a wimp to this point (besides throwing salt on those leeches), that I really didn't want to sound like I was scared, although I was. Darnell did speak up, but his reply, "No, just tell us when to meet back here," really didn't measure up to what I wanted to hear.

Everyone dropped their gear into a pile right at the front of the grocery store, so that Sandy and I could hopefully fill their backpacks with delectable goodies. In this action, Sandy tried to make eye contact with Akina when she stepped over to drop her load. Carefully she asked, "Are you okay, Akina? It's okay to be a little scared. I know I am."

Out of character, Akina brushed off Sandy's hand from her shoulder. "Not now Sandy. I don't have the time for you right now." She sounded really aggravated and irritated with Sandy, even downright patronizing. Neither she nor any of us was ever mean to Sandy, which is what made it so odd. Sandy didn't say a word but the crack in her face told the whole story. As Akina turned and walked away, Sandy began to reach out to her again, but I grabbed her arm and pull her away saying, "Let her go. She's just in a bad mood with all this stuff that's going on. Come on, let's see if we can find some food."

"Okay...," Sandy conceded.

With that, Sandy and I walked the short distance to what was at one point a grocery store of some type. The building was largely in poor condition and what wasn't broken, like some of the glass panes in the ceiling, were dingy. Kim and Reggie headed off to the left and into the armory and person-nel barracks. Darnell picked up Carla in his arms and they flew off together towards the tower. Akina walked off straight ahead and through the side wall of the building in front us as though she were walking through a breezeway.

I took this opportunity alone with Sandy as a good thing. Through all the complications I was still crazy about this girl. We walked through the doorway into a disaster area. All the shelving had been turned over and everything that had been on those shelves was now scattered all about. All of the fresh food bins were empty or torn apart. However, amidst the rubble were thousands of cans. Sandy and I began searching through them. At first most of them seemed to be empty or at least open. And opened by some pretty sharp teeth I must say. But then I heard Sandy call, "Here's one that's not open. It's a can of tuna fish. I wonder if it's any good?"

As I dug deeper, as Sandy had done, I too began to find unopened cans. I found a can opener. As I began to use it to grind through the lid of the can, I became acutely aware of how much warmer it was in here than it had been out in the open. Then finally the lid snapped and I took a whiff. "Sandy, I can't smell anything."

She shouted back across the store, "That's a good thing. I am thinking that this place is somewhat out of time, ya' know. It's like stuff here doesn't age or decay like it does back home. A lot of this stuff may actually be edible." Sandy stepped over to me and stuck her fingers in the can I'd opened to pinch out a bite. She smiled letting me know that it tasted fine.

"I hope you're right. I'm amazed that there is this much food left. I would have thought the locals would have eaten it all. They seemed pretty hungry an hour ago. With those claws I'm sure they don't need a can opener." I continued to stuff one of the three backpacks I had with me.

Sandy thought for a minute and then barely looking up and only slowing at her task, she replied back half in answer, half in question. "Maybe they don't like this stuff."

"What do you mean? They don't like potted meats?

"No," she started thoughtfully, "I am not sure that most of the residents have much interest in anything that's already dead."

I started to laugh; in fact I chuckled so hard that I had trouble catching my breath to form the words I wanted to say. "Girl, what are you talking about? Because these cats don't like beef stew you figured all that out? Maybe they just don't know how to pop tops."

Sandy, still moving deliberately, "Oh, I'd say they definitely know how to pop tops, just not like you think. Look around you. Look at the walls and the floor. See all of this brown stuff?"

"Yeah... Looks like standard post food party crud," I said as I started filling my second backpack.

"Mike, it wasn't that type of party. This is blood; dried blood. I think this place, this store, has become a de-facto human lure. I think these creatures lie in wait around here like spiders in a web just waiting for the next victim. This is just as much a killing field as the valley of bones we landed in. These guys up here are just smart enough to clear away the bones once they're done to reset the trap."

I stopped hording for a second to think through what she was saying, searching for a flaw in her logic. "You're kidding, right?" was all I could muster. Sandy was certainly the quiet, shy type, but every now and then she'd throw you a curve ball just to keep you on your toes.

"No." The simplicity of her answer left me no quarter. We sat there again, saying nothing. We were so quiet all you could hear was the hum of the empty freezers.

I ventured another question, even though each question I asked seemed to only make me feel worse. "So, why are the freezers empty?"

"I don't know. I haven't figured that part out yet."

Again we sat in silence. Sandy picked up a can and held it in her gaze while she pondered. I had decided by this point that I really didn't like Sandy pondering anything, anymore. She began to speak, but just as the words escaped her mouth, we both heard a sound from the shadows of the pharmacy. We both spun our heads around in that direction. It wasn't loud - something like "whoosh" or a perhaps the flap of a wing. Again there was silence. Next was the sound of a plastic vitamin bottle bouncing once, then again, then rattling on the floor, as too did it contents. From the shadows it crept. It walked on two feet with a basically human-like form, but it was not human, not even close. It stood between fifteen and twenty feet tall. Its head was something straight out of Hell. With daggers for teeth and shears for fingernails, it was easy to see why this room was washed with blood. As it stepped completely from its dark nest it spread its gigantic wings to a span in excess of twenty feet.

Sandy and I both stood up. I was at a loss for what to do. In the valley my lone contribution had come a minute or two into the situation. But this time there was no luxury of time to think. Fleeing was not an option at this point because where the gargoyle stood was nearer to the entrance than either of us, and Sandy was even further into the store than I was.

Then to our amazement it spoke. "Gezuzala, nil pes." We didn't understand a word he said, but the cheese-eating grin told us all we needed to know. This escapee from someone's nightmare intended to have us for dinner.

"Sandy," I called out, motioning her to come my way. Instead she picked up a metal shelf. She intended to fight this thing. "Sandy!" I cried out again, "Let's go!" But she stood her ground.

Never taking her eyes completely off of me, she motioned in my direction. "Look behind you."

I turned to see a second one of these creatures standing in the doorway. He was just as ugly as the first one but wider, not as tall and holding a very nasty-looking axe whose handle was long enough that it straddled both his hands. "Oh...," before I could complete my call for divine intervention, glass shattered from up above us. As the glass fell to the floor two flashes of light filled the room and the first gargoyle cried out as smoke billowed around him. I turned just in time to see

Kim zooming between us on her skateboard and straight for the first gargoyle.

"Kim!" Sandy called out. I looked behind me at the second gargoyle. He started towards us and then seemed to hear a sound behind him. Just as he turned around to spy its origin, Reggie's shoulder flew right into his thighs as Reggie's arms locked up the gargoyle's knees. Down went the monster with a force strong enough to rumble the whole room.

Reggie got up and unclasped his club from the band arched around his back. He reared back to strike his fallen foe, but saw out of the corner of his eye Kim take a spill when her gargoyle stretched out his hand to swat her like a gnat on one of her fly-bys. "Here, you take this one!" he yelled out. And Kim, never the one to take orders from anyone except Reggie, hopped back onto her board and made a beeline to the front of the store.

Meanwhile, Reggie walked back towards the larger creature. As he walked he tossed his club back and forth between his hands, twirling it every now and then as the monster watched intently. Just as Reggie got within striking distance, the large gargoyle took a swing, but Reggie danced to the right avoiding the talons and then counterpunched with a mighty blow to the back and side of the beast's left knee. The force of his strike caused the knee to buckle. For an instant the monster fell to one knee but quickly bounced back to its feet, a little wiser if a bit bruised from Reggie's attack. It had underestimated Reggie, but would not again.

As for us, we had our own troubles. While Reggie had felled the shorter brute, we'd been unable to keep him down. Kim danced around him on her skateboard. In and out, up and down she deftly avoided every blow. A mistake like she made the first time with the other one would surely be fatal this time. I knew I needed to help because her bolts seemed little more than annoyance to him, most of them striking his axe and flashing down its arm and into his hands. Each two-fisted swing seemed sure to be Kim's last. It became very obvious that Kim had done this sort of thing before, but still I needed to think of some way to contribute.

As unoriginal as it was, I reached down to the floor again, as I had done on the valley floor and felt my way through the molecular chains for an opportunity. Turning, turning, turning, finding the effect I wanted at my fingertips and closing my eyes and then imagining it flowing out from me towards the axe wielding menace. The effect I sent was one of fluid. The floor beneath the creature became a pool of liquid, muddy liquid. He began to lurch and swing out of balance, surprised by the change. In this instance Kim had the advantage, but it lasted only a moment. The substance of a madman's lament, extended the claws on his toes to dig into the solid rock below that which I had transformed.

Kim swung out our way on one of her passes, yelling to me, "Good try!"

Before Kim could speed off again, Sandy yelled, "Hey, what if Mike freezes it?"

Kim's eyes danced at the thought. "Yeah guy, give it a try."

I reached back down a second time sticking my hands into the goop for another change of state. I was able to twist and turn until I felt the effect I wanted and watched it cascade beyond my own hands to the bay beneath our enemy. The result was at first amazing. The gargoyle this time had no answer for the ice on which he stood, or on which he tried to stand. He slipped and slid and would have been comical except for the fact that he was swinging this six-foot axe and meant to chop us all into little bite-sized pieces.

Kim flew back to catch her breath next to us. Breathing hard, she spat out, "Hey, I've got an idea. Can you see that large freezer in the very back of the store? Looks like that might have been the meat department's freezer. I am going to try to lure him back there. You guys open it up and then hide on the backside of the door. Once I get him inside, slam the door shut."

"Slam it shut?" I yelled perplexed by the thought.

"Yeah, shut. Once we're in I want to you do whatever you can to make it as cold in there as possible. Don't hold back, give it all you got."

I began to speak. "Well, that might be pretty..."

"We understand." Sandy cut me off, as she grabbed my arm and dragged me off to the rear. The debate was over. Before we broke into a full run to the back of the store I took a quick peek in Reggie's direction. He and the larger beast were still going at it. It wasn't nonstop toe-to-toe action. It was like a heavyweight-boxing match. There would be a spurt or series of exchanges in which each of them attempted to take the other out. And then they'd separate and take measure of each other looking for weaknesses or areas to exploit.

Sandy and I reached the freezer door. Thankfully, although the store was fairly automated, the lock for the door was still an old-fashioned latch. Sandy grabbed the handle and pulled. I reached in behind her and pulled too. At first the door seemed to be stuck, but together we swung it open and pulled it to ourselves full open as we hid behind it. As covertly as I could I managed to spy on Kim's progress. She was playing way too close for my comfort. She led the beast off the icy patch I'd created, but now she was playing dodgeball with the business end of a very evil-looking axe. She danced in and out of the rows of fallen shelves, all the while working him back in our direction. The stockier gargoyle growled a deafening call and spoke out audibly for the first time, "Persta pugnare, miser scortillum!" Again, I had no idea what he was saying, but I think Kim found it amusing. She looked in our direction and smiled.

Thirty seconds later, they had progressed this dance of death to the door of the freezer. Kim flew in. But the gargoyle hesitated at the entrance. Did he sense a trap? My heart began to beat so loudly as he stood virtually next to us, that I was sure he could hear it. Then, from the darkness of a door swung fully open, I watched out of the corner of my eye as the monster took one step in. A moment later he took a second step and just stood there. Still he wasn't far enough in for us to slam the door without him stopping us. He needed to go further in. Kim knowing this too, took action. She landed in the far corner of the freezer out of reach of this would-be assassin. She shouted in Latin "Juste me timeas, ultra ianuam istam, tibi clunis calcitraturus est." From the corner she fired off several bolts of juice that so enraged our opponent that he instantly overcame his inhibitions and rushed towards her.

Sandy and I, hearing and seeing that the fight was on, slammed the door shut. On the side of the unit was a double paned glass from which Sandy and I could see the battle inside. Kim was circling around him twisting the giant. Still, I did not feel good about this plan. Then I realized that Kim, on each pass, was looking at me. Before I could respond, Sandy touched my shoulder. "Do it Mike. Do it now!"

Again I touched my hands to the metal and began to reach in deeply, even to the molecules beyond the metal casing. I twisted them, feeling them slow to my efforts. Colder and colder they became until some of them were even motionless. I looked up to see everything in the room frosted over, except Kim. She was spinning around the gargoyle faster and faster, sparks flying all the while. In fact, she moved so fast that viewing her was like looking into the spokes of a bicycle wheel. You could no longer tell her direction or path, but you could only see appearances of her as often as the neurons in one's retina could fire off images through to the synapses of one's brain. Then suddenly the revolutions climaxed and the

gargoyle exploded into a cloud of dust. And there in the freezer stood Kim alone. On her last turn she'd flown right
through the chest of the beast causing his frozen matter to
shatter into millions if not billions of dust like particles that
now covered everything in the freezer, including Kim.

An understated Sandy said quietly to me, "That was intense." We ran to swing the large stainless steel door open to
let Kim out. As the door flew open, out tumbled a dust-
covered Kim, coughing and hacking down to her knees. Sandy
took her blouse off and immediately began to wipe her face
with it, trying her best to clear her mouth and nose areas. I
knelt down too and I began almost instinctively wiping Kim's
face with my hands. Almost miraculously, water appeared
from my hands. I was turning the very air around us into water.

Almost as miraculous as that, was that Kim was kneeling
there quietly allowing me to help her. She never, with the
possible exception of Reggie, allowed anyone to help her with
anything. And it was more than that. Although it was hard to
tell, this powerful fearless young woman seemed to be crying.
Maybe it was a natural bodily response to the dust in her
eyes, but I could feel the emotion within her. Somehow the
water or my touch had released her from something I knew
nothing about. It was at that moment the mystery of this girl
became personal to me. When we touched I was stricken with
a firm desire to know her, to be more than a cousin, but a
friend to this child hiding in a woman's body.

Kim's coughing eased just enough for her to sputter, "Reggie... Please see what happened to Reggie."

Sandy motioned for me to go back up front to check on
him. I seriously doubted that if there were an issue that Reggie couldn't handle, I would be of any help.

Up front there was now a brand new hole in the wall. Out
in the courtyard, Reggie and the taller gargoyle continued to

slug it out. Then, as I took another step I saw that the stone god had something, no, someone wrapped around his neck. It was Akina. She was almost translucent. Going in and out of phase, the two daggers which had been in holsters on either side of her slender thighs flashed and danced in her hands as she twirled them like circular saws. Then I saw the pattern. Every time the beast lifted his hands towards his head to remove her, she would go out of phase and his hands would pass right through her. At that moment, Reggie would whack him again on his knees and his hands would come down. When they did, Akina would stick the blades back into their foe and extract them as she became more solid tearing at the monster's stony flesh. Were it not for her unique ability, the knives would have surely broken on impact.

The beast was calling out in my direction, in an effort, I later surmised, to enlist the aid of his axe-wielding companion. But seeing me come outside instead must have confirmed to him the true nature of his predicament, because when I appeared he began to retreat. He actually began to run before spreading his wings and taking to flight. As he started to take off, Akina did a back flip off his shoulders, somersaulting several times before landing perfectly. She went to one knee only to cushion the landing. When she stood up, Reggie applauded as she slid the knives back into place.

"Well, done cousin." Reggie laughed as she walked back over not even breaking a smile. "Thank you."

"Not a problem," she said, not even looking him in the eye. She continued to look around in apparent distraction.

Reggie reached out and grabbed her arm turning her back to face him. "Hey, you aren't going to continue to hold that little spat we had against me, are you?"

Akina continued to look down as she shook her head no. Then she looked up, "It's not so much you, it's this place. Yes, I have been here before, but this time is different; it's weird."

Reggie laughed. "No kidding, Sherlock!"

"No, you don't understand. It's my spirit. My spirit is never troubled, but it is here." Her words matched her expression.

Reggie tried to comfort her, "I know this place has us all on edge. It's far worse than what the Aunties told us or any of us could have imagined."

Akina, looking nervous, acknowledged his words, but added, "I hear you, but I've been here before and something is different this time. It's not just the pressure to find the Aunties and get back. It's something else."

Sandy, with Kim still hanging on, her right arm wrapped around Sandy's neck, emerged from the grocery store. She whispered to me as she passed, "If Akina is worried, we should all be concerned," as though that wasn't already the case. Personally, I was way past concerned and hanging out in a neighborhood somewhere between distraught and paralyzed with fear.

Reggie let out a "Hmmm..." and raised an eyebrow (he's good at that kind of thing) while he made his way over to check out Kim. Then as he picked Kim up and quickly put her down due to her protest, he reconciled it all, at least in his mind with a, "Well, I don't know that any of that really changes what we need to do here. We want to see if there's any helpful information here, stock up and get back on the road. That hasn't changed. Unless you're telling me you aren't certain on where we need to go?"

Akina conceded, "Oh, no. That hasn't changed. The aunties are like a beacon to me."

"Alright then," Reggie exclaimed, picking up his rod, "Then let's get moving. Looks like Carla and Darnell have found something."

It was then that I realized that the buzzing in my head causing me to keep looking back to the tower, was Carla in my head saying "Come here." In fact, it was also Carla that had alerted the others that Sandy and I were in trouble. The girl has got skills; when those she loves are in trouble she can feel it. It took us twenty to thirty minutes to reach the center of town. For once we didn't have any trouble getting somewhere. It seems that a lot of the bad elements hung out around the grocery store. I guess it was their rendition of a watering hole in the Serengeti.

The central tower, once we reached it, looked even taller than it did from a distance. The footprint of the base must have been a couple of acres alone. It extended upwards about forty to fifty stories with a circular floor on the very top. That level was enclosed in glass and looked to be a very large observation deck and possibly a command center. Glass on all four sides was etched with the same symbol. The translucent image looked like a star or maybe even the sun. And rising from the very center of that glass challis was a metal-framed tower that at some point long ago, reached into the darkness of the sky. It was broken and whatever it transmitted was a secret, part of the cosmic background and food for stars. But even the fact that it was broken betrayed some of its secrets.

I looked up to see someone waving out of one of the broken windows high above us. She was waving at me. It was Carla. Her waving at me made me feel good. She was such an "it" girl. An alpha female, if you will. She'd always been popular, even with the girls, despite some of her past behavior. And for me, (the prerequisite socially-challenged "loser" that every asylum, excuse me, every high school must have), it was really inspiring to know that someone like Carla could care about me. That someone with that much going on, wanted to know how my day was. And yes, things had changed greatly since I'd been in college. But still, it warmed me that someone with so many options took the time, on that day to send a wave my way.

As Carla called out my name and we all looked up, we saw her motioning for us to come on up. I, for one, was suddenly aghast at the thought of my having to hold on tight to little bitty Kim and her little bitty skateboard while she took me straight up forty floors. But Carla was pointing at something just at the far corner from where we were standing. There was a lift of some sort. It turned out that it was totally electromagnetic, like one of those high-speed trains. This meant it had no moving parts to fall into disrepair. The same was true of the elevators inside. This lift had apparently been used to haul large equipment that wouldn't even fit through the front doors of this place, let alone on the elevators, to the top floor.

We happily scampered down to the corner and rode up to the observation deck. Once there, we could see that it was much, much more.

For one thing, along the perimeter was an almost countless array of outward facing stations. From here an operator could see every valley and hill out to the horizon, which must have been at some points, 150 miles out. This was indeed a command center and from these workstations a commanding officer could see firsthand the placement and possible predicaments of his charges. We could see all of the surrounding peaks too. Down below where we could see through the seemingly ever-present mist, we saw nothing but chaos. All of the inhabitants here were in a never-ending battle to consume one another. And though there were other creatures flying about, it appeared that the large-winged beasts ruled the sky. From what I could see, flying abominations would launch from one of the peaks below us and dive into the mist. Sometimes the mist would glow red from their scorching breath. On other occasions their icy breath would freeze their prey and the mist alike giving a snapshot of the kill before the surrounding mist filled the void again. Still most of what was going on below was hidden from us. Then Carla flipped a switch and wherever there was still glass turned blood red. Peering through the frame now, we could see images dancing about beneath the fog. Carla nodded her head in concession to the feats of these who came before us and said, "Infrared windows. These guys were tight."

Kim was ecstatic with the view. "Oh my goodness!" she proclaimed.

The usually cheerful Akina couldn't help but question back "Goodness?"

Darnell called out from across the room, "And look over here." He was looking gleefully at a series of flat screen computer monitors. Unlike the other monitors in the room that were hooked up to very impressive looking, but most likely dysfunctional devices, these monitors were not obviously hooked up to anything, which in effect meant that they were in a sense hooked up to everything, or at least everything that we wanted to know. As we all cruised over and smiled, seeing the screens flicker at his touch, Darnell said with confidence, "I think this is where we're going to find the 411 on this place."

It turned out that some potentially helpful materials were password protected, but by and large, a lot of general information was readily available. I guess in the Pit they don't worry about hackers and such.

Darnell was almost entranced. While I leaned towards the sciences and was a chemical engineering student, Darnell was a hard-core computer geek at heart. He looked like he belonged more on a gridiron, than behind a keyboard but there he was hacking away "oohing" and "awing" at every piece of the former inhabitant's lives that he found. And I, more than any of the others, sat there behind him witnessing the retelling of their lives. Sandy stood by one of the windows scribbling in her pad. While the others milled about, Akina pulled up a chair to look over Darnell's left shoulder and I remained peering over his right. I leaned back and asked Akina, "So what did you find in the homes?"

She let out a sigh and took in a deep breath, "Well, it was all a bit much. I mean it was so obvious that they left or were taken, in a hurry. There were plates and dishes lying about. There were pictures and keepsakes on mantles that surely they'd have taken if they had had any kind of time at all to pack. All we can do is hope that when they left they went home and weren't devoured by this place."

"Yeah," I let out and nothing more. It seemed as though I should have had something more to say, something profound that might sum up the accomplishments, the sacrifices and perhaps even the folly of these people, but I was speechless. Maybe it was the newfound but constant thought that we all might meet similar destinies as these poor souls that dimmed my spirit to further discuss the matter.

These were indeed men and women, like us, who'd built this place. Somehow mankind had learned to apply mathematics as a means to access these formerly dark equations. Men had reached beyond the seemingly great beyond to reach a place of nightmares and horror stories. And though it was obvious that they ultimately lost this fight or gave up, these men and women for some time actually "lived" here and survived. There were pictures of men and women on file. There were faces and names now that brought a whole new level of compassion for what must have happened here. But still all I could muster were moans and grunts of sympathy and sadness I'd not known before.

Reggie strolled over as Akina began to whirl in her chair, "Found anything?" he asked.

"Well for one thing," Darnell began, "it looks like they were definitely from our world. They've got all kinds of national news sound bites detailing the global debate on whether they should be here or not. Seems that scientists finally developed a workable Unified Field Theory."

"A what?" Reggie exclaimed.

"A Unified Field Theory. It's like the Holy Grail of science. One mathematical algorithm that explains the relationship between all four of the cosmic forces: gravity, electromagnetic, strong atomic force and weak atomic force."

Reggie laughed and patted Darnell on the back. "Well, doggone it Darnell, I knew there was something missing in my life. Now I can die in peace."

Darnell turned slightly and was beginning to offer a more detailed explanation when Reggie cut him off. "Man, I know what you're saying. I was just messing with you. I know what the Unified Field Theory is. Figuring it out was supposed to explain all creation."

"Yeah, that was the thought. It was supposed to show us the whole space time continuum and unlock an infinite number of doors."

I finally had something to say. "Sort of like how mapping the entire human gnome was supposed to lead to the cure of every disease known to man."

Darnell nodded his head and continued, "Things like time travel and other dimensions weren't really deemed to be credible realities, but a unified field theory would prove or disprove the possibilities of such things once and for all. I guess we know how that discussion ended."

"You got that right," Akina added.

Reggie pointed his finger at the monitor and asked, "So is there anything in there we can use now?"

Darnell hit a couple of keys. "Yeah, here's a map showing this entire region. Let me display this for the whole room." Darnell hit another couple of keys and a three-dimensional image appeared in front of us in the middle of the room. "You can see that they've tagged and named all the major landmarks. There's a lot to tell here, but I think what's most important to us are the armory depots. All of those blinking green areas pinpoint stockpiles of arms and supplies that they stored in the field. The string of letters and numbers above each one is a key code to open it. If Akina can tell us where we're going, we can map a route that allows us to restock along the way."

Akina started to get up, but Reggie lightly placed his hand on her shoulder causing her to remain seated as he asked another question. "But what makes you think these storehouses have anything in them?"

"Well..." Darnell held down the control key and hit yet another key and a separate image appeared above each site as he tabbed to it. "This shows you the current inventory levels at each site."

Carla, a business major, laughed out "I can't believe it, they've got supply chain management in Hell too!"

Akina smirked as she stood up, "Makes perfect sense, if you think about it." She walked over to the suspended image as Darnell reached in the drawer and pulled out a very fancy-looking laser pointer that highlighted the areas of the map that pleased her. "Looks like we're here and where we're going is over here. Does that thing tell you how far that is?" Akina asked looking at Darnell.

"Hold on," he called. Several wrong choices later, a vector appeared between the two points Akina had marked. "Says it's 129 kilometers, which is just about eighty miles."

Akina followed, "So, if we do about twenty miles a day we should be there in four days. Right?"

Reggie didn't quite agree. "Twenty miles a day? I don't know about that given all the obstacles out there. We'd be doing good to do fifteen miles a day. That would be more like six days. On top of that, if we want to take advantage of the storehouses, it's going to take longer. Why don't we map out a course through them?"

Akina reluctantly tagged the two flashing green points generally along the way. Once Darnell did a refresh, a new number popped up. The number was over 180 kilometers. Our collective hearts sank. Akina said to the group, "I say we just make a beeline to where we need to go and get out. Going by these depots is going to add what, another thirty miles or so to our trip? That could be an additional two or three days."

"How do we know that the food in these weigh stations is any good?" asked Carla.

Her brother, Darnell, already had the answer. "See that red number next to the food item counts? That's a spoilage percent number. I have to believe that if the refrigerators were still working in that burnt-out looking grocery store, there is every chance that these numbers are correct. Plus, they've got some sort of packing technology to preserve food that is beyond anything we know." Sandy and I thought it more the case that these food stuffs, like us, were out of their naturally occurring place in time, and thus did not age as one might expect, but we didn't argue the point.

Sandy spoke now. "But might these places also be more likely to have creatures like we saw in the store, who prey on humans looking for food?"

Reggie replied, "I guess that might be true, but our trip over here was no picnic either. I think any route we take is going to be a challenge. Trust me, we'll fight better on a full belly and a full clip."

Kim smiled, "I'll second that!"

Akina looked to Carla for support, "What about you Carla? Do you agree with them?"

Carla hesitated and then spoke as kindly as she knew how. "Well, it's a bit longer trip to stop by these places but it would mean we'd have to carry less stuff out of here. I think we need to be light as possible. Maybe if we're light, we'll make up the time."

Akina looked to me, but somehow knew that I wasn't going to say anything. I hate it when people do that to me. Although, I will say at the time I was feeling Reggie's viewpoint more than hers. Maybe she could see it in my face. "Okay," she said at last, "we'll go the long way. If I thought I could safely teleport us all there I would but it would be like pin the tail on the donkey. Something is so off center here this trip that I don't trust myself to teleport more than a few feet. I've got such a funny feeling here this time that I just want to leave as soon as possible."

I asked Reggie, "Did you guys see any cars or trucks in the barracks?"

"No, we found plenty of fuel cells, but no cars, bikes or anything," he answered me.

"So maybe they did make it out of here," I replied almost as a question.

"Maybe. That fact could be read a lot of different ways. Either way it looks like we'll be on foot unless we can figure something out. Darnell, can you bring up a map of this building?"

"Yes sir." A layout of the building appeared.

Reggie moved to the center of the room. "Here we go. Mike, you and Darnell head down to the science lab to see what you can find down there that might come in handy out in the field. I'm sure there's a terminal down there that you can both use. Kim and Sandy, y'all come with me; we're going to scope this place out some more. Akina and Carla, you two stay up here. If either one of you senses something or someone up to no good near one of us, let us know. If something comes after you up here, just pop down to the lobby and we'll all regroup and take it on together. With all of us in the building, there's no sense in anyone trying to go it alone. Okay?"

Akina had a comment, "So, what time are we leaving?"

Before Reggie could respond, Kim asked, "And what about sleep? You can't tell by looking outside, but by my watch we've been up for almost twenty-four hours straight. I don't know about anybody else, but I'm fried."

Carla jumped in, "And we're talking about heading off on a hundred and something mile trip across this godforsaken place."

Reggie thought for a moment, then threw up his hands. "You know what? You're right. We do need to rest up before we head out. Let's do this then. We can all stay up here together and sleep for a minute. All of us need to eat something quickly and then bunk down right here in this free space in front of the main monitor. I'm Sorry Carla, but you'll have to stay awake and watch over us. Darnell you stay up with her, since you don't need sleep anyway. But I want you busy. Michael you tell Darnell the kinds of things you'd likely find in this place to take on the road and he'll search the inventory listings in the computer. Then when you wake up, the two of you can go pick up what you need... assuming it is still there. We'll sleep for six hours and then be out of here an hour after that. So, I have 10:00PM on my watch. That means we need to be up by 4:00AM and out of here by 5:00AM. Carla, you're gonna have to somehow catch some sleep on the road. I don't know how, but we'll work it out. Cool?"

Everybody finally nodded his or her head in agreement. We searched around and quickly found some materials to make some kind of a collective area in the middle of the floor that we could all sit and lounge on. We went into our backpacks and each of us pulled out something that we brought with us, that is, with the exception of Reggie. I think to some degree he wanted to eat something that we'd found here as a sign to the rest of us that it was okay. I guess you'd call that a leadership thing or something. As for the part about Darnell not needing sleep, well he needs sleep after a time. It's just that with his recuperative abilities, he doesn't really get tired. That Darnell is a different kind of cat.

Just as we were getting into the seemingly mandatory food swap, as we always did on family camping trips, Reggie cleared his throat and offered up a blessing for the food.

I grabbed some juice and went to speak with Darnell a bit before I laid down to take a nap.

After about a ten minute conversation with Darnell in which he jotted down a list of items we hoped to find here, I laid down next to Sandy, who had dropped her pack next to mine after we laid down the bedding. Resting my head on my backpack that I was using as a pillow, I glanced at Sandy as she was repacking her bag. I'd eaten just two fruit pies I'd stowed away, but she had broken out plastic-ware and napkins. She handed me one to wipe my mouth and hands. "Thank you," I said as I sat back up and finished my abbreviated clean up.

Sandy, in words that my affection-starved mind read way too much into replied softly, "No problem." The only objective thing I can say about her reply was that she did say it softly. Real softly. But everything else racing through my mind was sheer fantasy. Here I was in a place I never really thought existed and still my crush on this girl consumed me. She laid her head down on her backpack and said "Goodnight..." before closing her eyes. I, still in a sitting position, stuttered back, "Goo... goodnight," and slowly lowered myself down beside her. I rolled over onto my back in hopes that my affection for her was not too obvious to her or anyone else. Before I closed my eyes I looked down below my feet to see Darnell sitting at the keyboard smiling at me and forcing back a laugh. I smirked in a "give me a break" sort of way and then drifted off.

When I awoke the group was buzzing. Apparently there had been just a bit of drama during my six hour blissful and admittedly deep sleep. As it was told to me, about four hours into our slumber, a whole pack of winged things, though not like anything we'd seen before, began to circle our building buzzing our rooftop lair. These other creatures, which we would begin to call Night Terrors, were the stuff of nightmares. We'd not seen them before and apparently although they were quite frightful, the siblings were not afraid of them. They were like flying shadows. They floated and flew in and out, through and about, not caring for the boundaries of glass, rock or steel. Carla and Darnell watched them circle in and out for nearly an hour but never did they land. Now Carla was attempting to tell Reggie why she didn't wake the entire group.

"I don't know. There was something I sensed in them. It was like they were afraid, or at least cautious. Those big winged things don't enter here because they seem to be concerned about not having a perch to support them should they attack. And to some degree, they respect our ability to retaliate. I sense from them that they would prefer to attack in the open field. But these winged black vapor things, they flew wherever they pleased. Some stopped for a moment but then took off again. Mostly they just flew around. Maybe they were waiting for Darnell and me to fall asleep too."

Reggie, exasperated, threw his arms up. "But that's what you were supposed to do last night. Wake us up if there was any trouble."

"But there was no trouble," Carla defended herself. "You wanted me to warn you if there was trouble or we were going to be attacked. Well, it was my job to make that judgment. That's why you had me on point and that's what I did. And, we're all alive."

Reggie leaned in, "Okay, I hear you, but the next time you see these guys just let me know, if for no other reason than to let me see what we're dealing with."

Carla capitulated and conceded to do that going forward, although at that point she just wanted to end the inquisition and get some sleep.

Akina walked over and gave me a tube of toothpaste before I could even finish yawning. "Hey bro', you need this."

I took it and went off to brush my teeth.

When I returned to the main room everyone was beginning to scatter. Darnell called to me, "Come on Mike, let's head downstairs. The testing lab is one floor down. I think we'll find more ready to use stuff down there." We made our way to and down the corner stairwell. "Dude!" Darnell nearly shouted as we exited the stairwell into a lobby area, "Check it out!" He pointed to a sign hanging above one of the doors off of the lobby. It read "Chapel". Some may hear me on this, but when you roll with these born-again guys like Darnell, you come to understand what puts a buzz in them, whether you believe or not. Then he went on to explain, since by my look I did not get the full significance of the matter. "That Chapel is right below where we slept last night. Maybe that's what kept those things from attacking us last night."

"Oh..." I acknowledged his point. "That's good, but where's the lab?"

"Over here." He led me over back behind the reception desk and down a hallway. Then he ambushed me. "So, what's up with you and Sandy? Did y'all talk?"

"Hey man, give me a break. This isn't the most conducive environment to make a play or have a conversation like that."

"Yo, Mike I feel ya. But there's never going to be a perfect time. I mean you don't hit on girls like at a funeral or something like that, but besides that, in war and in peace you have to keep living. That is part of living, you know, looking for the right woman. Of course you know that you can't play Sandy. The girls will all jump you if you if you try anything funny."

"Darnell, you know I'd never hurt Sandy. She's like the nicest girl I've ever known."

"Plus, you think she's a cutie pie too. Right?"

"Most def."

We reached the end of the hall and stepped into the lab. It was what we'd hoped, a smorgasbord of tools and gadgets. All the little things you need to go "MacGyver" on a situation. There were lens, pen-light lasers (not those toys you use during a slide-show presentation), pocket PCs that we could download instructions on how to use all this stuff. Unfortunately, time was short, so I had to pretty much just snatch and grab stuff. But Darnell was able to tell me immediately what items in the lab were also in the field remote units we'd found out about earlier. That was a big help in lightening our load. I actually found some real live ray guns! I snapped one on each side of the tool belt I'd found when we first walked in.

I offered one to Darnell, but he just looked at me and laughed. "You're about the only one here who'll want to use that. Everybody is much more comfortable with their gifts than using those things."

I asked, "What about Sandy?"

"You can take her one, but I kind of doubt she'll want it."

I tied an extra one onto the outside of my book bag. At that point it was time to go. We'd only been down there a little over an hour, but we had quite a haul. We returned to the top floor triumphant. We fully expected to share our delight in what we had found with the group, but they didn't seem to share our enthusiasm about our newfound treasure, although news of the Chapel did get a few "ahhs…"

Before we could even begin to explain, Reggie called out, "Let's roll out people. It's past time to go. We got a lot of miles to cover today."

As I was packing up I approached Sandy as she stood along a bank of see-through pods that ran along the back side of the monitoring station on the far side of the room. We could only guess as to the purpose of these chambers. They were surely large enough for a person or two to comfortably fit inside. Maybe we'd all read too many sci-fi books, but we thought that perhaps they were transportation tubes. You know, from here to back home or maybe out into the plains below. Far out I know, but it wouldn't be the first time that reality has followed science fiction. Anyway, I tossed off my backpack and untied the weapon I'd brought up for Sandy. I handed it to her with a piece of fatherly advice, "Hey, you may need this."

"Really?" She looked puzzled as she took the gun and looked it over. "Did they have plenty of these down below?"

"I wouldn't say a lot, but a good number. Why?"

"Well, it's just that these things didn't seem to do them much good. So, it seems like it might just be something else to carry."

I took the gun as she handed it back to me. "But don't you think…"

She cut me off mid-sentence. "I think I'd rather carry some extra food if I carry anything."

I wanted to argue with her. I knew that I could make water and I figured if I tried hard enough I could make something edible, but her mind was made up. Sandy was like that. That's one reason that I was so afraid to approach her.

I felt like if I got a "No way, Buster!" out of her there would be no second chance nor a chance to win her affections over time. She didn't strike me as the type to reconsider things once she'd made a decision. So, I bided my time.

Having gathered all of our things, we all herded into the external service elevator that had brought us up before. The elevator opened both to the inside and outside, and was roomy enough for all of us to ride down together with our over-packed gear. Descending down we could look through the outward-facing panel to the world from which we'd had a brief respite. The Night Terrors were nowhere to be seen but gargoyles, flying snakes and perhaps most frightening of all, human-looking demons with wings abounded. Monsters that look like us, are always the scariest things. Numerous other horrifying creatures adorned the rooftops of the other buildings as well. Mostly, they fought and sniped at each other. These lofty levels were largely reserved for the winged beasts. Further down, those that climbed ruled, and as we approached the ground we again saw those that crawled and slithered. Kim let out a "Yuck, seems like there are more of them today."

I couldn't help but say, "Yeah."

At last we reached the ground floor lobby. We decided it best to open the interior doors this time. As the doors opened, an alarming sight greeted us. Five men of varying hues and dressed like warriors from a militarized "It's a Small World" reinterpretation stood before us, armed to the teeth. Akina sprang out first, extracting her side daggers from their holsters in mid-air. But before the rest of us could respond in a similar fashion, all five of the men fell to their knees bowing, and called out to her, in English no less, "Queen Nefertiti." On the far left was a Native American in ancient Mayan garb, next to him a man of India. On the far right stood an Asian man with long black hair. Beside him, was a youthful-looking white man.

The one in the middle, a black man, lifted up a gleaming shield and pronounced, "My Queen, your shield."

14. The Call

In truth, awesome deeds are never carried out by us, but rather through us. We are no more than the sand that is blown by a mighty wind, to form the dunes of an endless desert. Once a mortal man understands this, his understanding of the difference between mortality and immortality begins.

Jonah understood this and believed that the path to understanding began with submission and acknowledgement to the higher power of His supremacy. Humility is the first lesson of life. If you can't grasp that simple but important concept, your life is but fodder for those who do, yet ironically you will never know it. Jonah's heart was filled with vengeance. Jonah knew enough to know that vengeance was not his; still he knelt and prayed that God might touch his heart and calm his mind that he might not strike out blindly. At least that's what he knelt down to do. For a minute he felt nothing, then for another. At last he grew impatient and stood up. Energy burned inside of him making him restless. His mind racing with ideas, he couldn't wait any longer. It was morning still, but in his heart he felt like he'd already wasted most of the day. He bolted up and into the front room to join his wife, who was already up and preparing breakfast for the both of them. Typically, they would have been out and on their way to work before dawn, but the previous day had been one of the most grueling either of them had ever known. They'd not arrived back to their hideaway until just before sunrise, so their schedule this morning was adjusted. Besides that, in those few hours Jonah hadn't really been able to sleep much anyway. He was so revved up to do something, anything. His mind had raced all the while. So lost in thought was he that he was almost startled when his wife greeted him with a kiss.

"So what are you thinking about?" she asked him.

"Oh, I had a couple of ideas. But I need to check a few things out first."

"Okay, I see." She went back to stirring the pot as her thoughts stirred. It was a cold dish. She and Jonah both knew that he already knew what he wanted to do, but he just didn't want to tell her yet. So, her task was twofold. First, decide on whether she really needed to know the plans at this point, and second, decide on the best way to get that information out of her husband without causing him to put up the old stone wall. She opted to stop at decision point one. On another day, with fewer things on her own mind, she might have decided to pursue the matter, but not today. Not this day after. She knew that her husband, whatever he was planning, would not likely run off that day and do it. At least that is what she told herself.

The two of them sat there sharing a meal and thoughts of Sara, but little else. Monica ate slowly, while Jonah ate as a man who had somewhere else to be. When done, Jonah rose up, gathering his things in preparation to depart. Still, he knew that there was one bit of information that he had to share with his wife before he left. He knew it would cause issues, but he knew he'd have to breach the subject anyway. From the doorway, he gazed softly at his wife, and just as softly he spoke to her hoping to slip the next words by her. "Hey babe, I might be a little late tonight, so don't wait up for me."

Monica glared at him. "What do you mean a little late?"

"Well, a little late. It's not a big deal. I just don't want you waiting for me," he answered.

"I can't believe you're just going to run out of here, off to pull some stunt, and all you tell me is that you're going to be a little late."

"Well, yeah... I mean no. I'm not planning to pull any stunts. I just need to check something out." He hoped that would suffice.

It didn't. She continued, "Check what out?" Monica was now standing.

He replied, "You know, The Heart of Mystery, the family heirloom at the museum. Karun and I are just going to check it out."

"Just check it out?"

"Yeah, check it out. Okay?" he asked.

"I guess so, but no stupid macho stuff."

"Sure baby." He kissed her and quickly slipped through the crawl space to the world beyond. He couldn't stand the thought of not being totally honest with her. But he was the man after all. And how was he supposed to answer that bit about "stupid macho stuff?" He never did anything stupid on purpose. All of the stupid stuff he'd ever done in his life was by accident... mostly.

Jonah's thoughts turned to the effort ahead. First and foremost he had to inform Karun that today was the day.

Upon arriving at work he quickly pulled Karun aside to fill him in.

A startled Karun replied, "Today??!!"

Manisha popped up from behind the counter where she'd been squatting taking inventory. "Yeah, today! You're gonna get those bastards?"

Jonah turned back to Karun with, "Yeah, today. On top of that I need to get a message to Vicki."

Manisha jumped in again, "Vicky? What do you need her for? You can't trust that girl. She's nothing but trouble."

Jonah answered her, "I can handle Vicki. Once I get the Heart I feel like I can handle a lot of things."

Karun, always one to ask the obvious questions, "So, what is it supposed to do?"

Jonah threw up his hands, "Well, I don't know that yet, not totally." And then displaying a passion seldom seen in him, he pulled Karun away from the counter and Manisha as he spoke, "But it glowed when I came near it. It glowed. Everything within me tells me that once I possess it, a whole new world will open for all of us. I can just feel it."

"Okay, relax, relax, I hear you. Still this all sounds pretty risky. So what's the plan again?" Karun was still asking those basic questions.

Jonah obliged him, "We go there late in the afternoon, right before closing. We'll pay for the self directed tour and then when we are between surveillance cameras I'll flip on the Wave Modulator and really screw up all of their electronics, including the cameras. You and I will slip away into a broom closet and then up into the drop down ceiling. I'll pull back the field and allow their systems to come back on line. But I won't pull it back all the way. I'll keep it around us so that when they do their sweeps afterwards, they won't be able to see us at all. At night we drop down and grab the Heart. Then once we have it, it's back up into the ceiling. We just wait there until the next morning, then cause another blackout, and then scamper out while the lights are out. Pretty simple, right?"

Actually, Karun had lots of questions, but in all the time he'd known this guy he'd never come up with a plan or device that did not simply amaze him. Jonah had earned Karun's respect and trust.

Jonah, on the other hand, was sometimes dumbfounded by the amount of faith Karun placed in his abilities, but in that instant he was glad to have it. Jonah's passion did not completely blind him to the risk. While he knew that Karun was motivated by some measure of revenge, or sense of justice, glancing at his wife, Manisha, made him wary of the cost. But nothing since he'd married Monica had felt so right.

Then too, there was still the issue of Vicki. Manisha might be right, Vicki might just have the hots for him. Then again, when he was single she never gave a hint, at least not that he noticed. But Jonah reasoned that regardless of what she might or might not have on her mind, she could prove quite useful in her role as an underground liaison to those in the Circle. For many living under Blue rule, the Circle was seen as paradise, a land of milk and honey. Who doesn't need that kind of hookup? He needed to send a message to the appropriate contact that he wanted to converse with her. Typically, she would just pop in from time to time, but when he called she usually got back to him quickly, if she was in town.

His co-workers, Deepak and Sridhar, approached him and Karun. Sridhar swung up his hands. "So what's happening, man? What are you going to do?"

Karun cheerfully replied, "We are going to do something tonight. I cannot tell you exactly what for your own protection. But trust me, you will hear about it."

Jonah, having second thoughts about taking Karun with him, responded less enthusiastically. "Well..."

Before Jonah could finish his statement, Karun was back at it. "Yes, read the papers tomorrow evening and you will know all that I cannot tell you now. Just as we struck at Friday's execution and then out at the shore, we will strike again. We will bring this Blue devil to his knees for taking one as kind as Sara. They will pay for the heartache they have caused my Manisha." The men all agreed and patted him on his back.

Jonah just looked at Karun in amazement. All this bravado, did he not understand that he could die tonight? Jo-

nah's faith was such that he never really worried about himself in these situations. In these moments he just responded
as if some divine hand was directing him. But he worried
about Monica; he worried about Manisha and Karun. His
thoughts turned dark when he thought about his siblings
somewhere out there beyond his care and protection. But his
worries about life and death were never about himself. He decided that he would not embarrass his friend here in front of
the others, but later he would make up an excuse why he
couldn't go in with him when he did this deed. At least, that
is what he planned to do.

Manisha, who'd been storing and filing to occupy herself,
noticed the commotion and strolled back over to investigate.
Immediately it was evident who was really in charge here.
"So what's the plan? Tell me." All of the men were silent as
mice. Then, like a grade school instructor, she called out a
name, "Karun." Not so much a question as a statement with a
clear expectation.

To Jonah's surprise he did not crack on the first request.
"We have it covered. You need not worry."

She said again, "Karun."

Jonah looked away, but again Karun stood his ground.
"Look, I told you not to worry. We have it covered."

Manisha continued, "Karun, why won't you tell me the
plan? You know I will come to know every little detail. The
only question will be whether I am happy when I hear it or
upset. You decide."

He looked at her as he handed the store keys to her and
said, "Well, perhaps today you will be upset." He then proceeded to grab Jonah by the arm and they both headed to the
door. His response to Manisha had left her in a state of
shock. She was speechless. But Karun was no fool, he knew
that the both of them had best leave before the volcano Manisha erupted.

Just as they approached the store's front door, it flew open. There to Jonah's surprise was Bruce, one of the guys he'd rescued when he saved Sara Friday night. Bruce, looking like he'd not slept a wink, bathed, eaten or done anything to maintain his appearance, grabbed Jonah's other arm. "Dude, I've been looking for you! You're hard to find. Hey, I need to talk to you. After seeing you in action twice, I am so stoked. Man, I've been talking to people and with your help we can destroy these Blue bastards! Every last one of them!"

Jonah, tongue-tied at how easily he'd been found, was beaten to a reply by Karun. "Sir, do we know you? I don't know you."

Jonah found his tongue, "Karun, this is Bruce, one of the three folks I rescued when I got Sara. Man, how did you find me?"

Bruce replied honestly, "I just asked everyone around here. I gave your description and finally, here I am."

Then it occurred to Jonah that perhaps the Blues had not yet made the connection between him and Sara. Surely they had a description of him, but given that he fought with Matasis at a meeting of Christians from around the entire city, there was no reason for the authorities to suspect that the man they hunted for worked just two doors down from the murdered Sara. Though he also reasoned that if they questioned enough of his brethren they'd find someone that knew that he was not a "Johnny come lately" and that he'd been a part of the group early on and at the time of her death was still good friends with Sara.

It also occurred to Jonah that perhaps Bruce was being watched or followed. If that were the case then it was already too late to do anything about it, although Jonah did instinctively cover his face even more tightly.

Bruce continued on, "Jonah, man I just want to talk to you. I know you're planning something and I just want to help. You gotta let me help!"

Jonah spoke to Bruce in a hushed tone, "This is really not a good time or place to have this conversation."

Bruce grabbed Jonah's arm and exclaimed again. "Man, please let me talk to you!"

Jonah looked at Karun for some expression of objection, but found none. Not wanting to make anymore of a scene, Jonah turned back to Bruce. "Okay, come and walk with us. We can talk along the way."

Bruce smiled, "So where are we going?"

"Does it matter?" Karun answered curtly.

They marched another half a block then Jonah slowed his walk and leaned back toward Bruce. "We really can't tell you. I'd like to, but it would not be in your interest or anyone else's. You just have to trust us on that. As far as involving you when something goes down that you can participate in, I can let you know when something comes up."

"Come on man! What's up with that? Do you want all the glory for yourself?"

Jonah stopped and turned, looking angrily into Bruce's expressionless face. He stood there, not flinching holding back his words. Karun, landing one hand on each shoulder, turned his friend around and they began walking again down the street, one arm wrapped around his shoulder. Bruce followed.

Jonah, still angry, began to mumble, "Glory, glory?" Then turning to Bruce again, "Glory? It's not about glory. How can you say that, you don't even know me?"

They began to walk again. Karun, thinking now of all that had gone on in the previous day, looked over his shoulder to Bruce. "I think it's time we parted ways for now. If we want you, we'll contact you. Where do you go?"

Confounded Bruce asked, "What do you mean?"

Karun restated himself, "Of what congregation are you a part?" Not hearing a reply, Karun went on. "What house do you attend? You're a Christian right? Aren't you a part of one of the houses?" Houses where congregations with no specific meeting place.

Bruce's eyes cleared, "Oh, that. I don't really belong to any group. That has seemed, please excuse me, but a bit dumb given our current situation. Look at what happened at the lighthouse. I think I'll skip that little practice."

Karun looked at him not knowing quite how to respond to that. "Well... obviously you know Heru and crew now. We'll contact you through him. Okay? Either way, we must go now."

"What's up with this guy?" Karun whispered to Jonah.

Jonah shrugged his shoulders.

As Jonah and Karun walked away, Bruce called out, if only to save face, "Alright then, I'll see you guys later."

Two blocks down, Karun and Jonah turned simultaneously to spy if Bruce was still following them. Not seeing him, they set off towards their real destination. Eventually, they would go to the museum, but first they needed to see to the "hook-up man". As in every civilized culture, particularly in more oppressive societies, "hook-up men" exist. The "hook-up man", could be many men, but if you're really in tune with the streets then you know him when you see him. If he doesn't know you, know someone that does, or hasn't seen you around forever, then he's not going to talk to you. You'd be wasting your breath. The "hook-up man" can get you what you need, but it is almost always illicit, or at least stuff that the powers that be don't want you to have. It might be illegal drugs at a high price or legal drugs at an illegal cheap price. It might be whatever. But whatever it was, it was something you weren't supposed to have. In this case it was access. Jonah needed to pass word to Vicki to meet him as soon as possible. Vicki had promised to be back in touch soon to update him on the visa to the Circle, but he didn't know if that would be a day, a week or what. The girl was a spy, and spies tend to keep irregular schedules. However, in the past and it had been some time, he'd dropped her a line and she'd show a day or two later. That was up until she took her little break.

In Karun's basement she claimed it was for a little "R&R" and to debrief the big chiefs of the Circle about what was really going on down in Blue land. As she said, and Jonah believed, there are just some communiqués that you can't do via a third party. However, in his heart he always wondered if it had something to do with his feeling that he was getting a little too close to her and her kind of pulling away because of that. Though they had always had the closest of friendships and he really dug her, he always knew the rules and so did she. But right before she went away the last time, she had said it again, that one thing that hung in his mind like an ancient riddle on a blackboard. "You got married too soon." That one thing kindled an unspoken lust and filled him with possibilities. "You got married too soon." For months during her absence, that one phrase gnawed at him like something wild tearing at his flesh. "You got married too soon." She had said the same thing many years ago, but he paid it no mind. He thought it was just a random comment. Why had she said that, why had she looked the way she did when she said it, why did she touch him the way that she did when she said it? How was he supposed to respond to that? Didn't she know that he was only human, a fragile one at that? Whether he agreed or called her on it, it would still bring into the open that there was this "issue" between them. So he ignored it. And this "issue" was still the same that day as it was then. Was she really hitting on him or just stating an opinion about married life or perhaps making a statement about his wife Monica? Or was it all in his mind? Could it be that she simply wants validation that she's still attractive to him? Does she simply want to rub her own ego? Maybe she's playing a game that she doesn't even admit to herself. She'd said nothing as definitive as that since, but he'd never been quite sure of what she was saying since either. Surely she knew that to say such a thing to a man, one that she knew so well was to plant a seed that would haunt him until the day he dies or until the day he tastes that forbidden fruit.

For her part, Vicki was quite aware of what she was doing. She was a conductor of many things, of which this was just one. Plus, in her own thoughts she had set her mind against Monica. From one piece of information she had built in her own mind an entire persona, one of a woman of deceit and lies. Early on, before their world broke down and Vicki officially became a part of the underground, she'd "run into" Jonah at a game. Actually, she had sweet-talked one of Jonah's boys who owned the season tickets a section over from Jonah's seat to give her his ticket to that night's game. The team lost a lot, so she was able to upgrade her seat to an empty one next to Jonah. She hadn't intended to be so forward that fateful night at the game, but the words had just slipped out. She'd become so frustrated with his obvious fascination for her and his lack of action that she just snapped for a second. For a moment she could not help but comment on how she felt the world should be. How they should be and the kind of life she should be living. It wasn't until she became an intelligence officer that she obtained the one piece of information to which she still clung.

In her role as a field operative in the capitol city she had to provide her superiors with background data for all of her contacts. She'd known Jonah since freshman year, so her review of her file on him was merely cursory. She knew his siblings by name and had several of their birthday dates committed to memory. But Monica was another story. In the

course of her research she came upon Monica's medical records. It was there that she found that during the years that
Monica and Jonah had been out of touch, specifically at age
nineteen, she'd had a very bad miscarriage and her doctor at
the time deemed her as being incapable of bearing any children from that day forward. She was barren. This was her
"Rosetta Stone" from which all future knowledge was derived.
It wasn't long after this discovery that she, as causally as she
knew how, asked Jonah about his and Monica's plan to have a
child. He'd replied, as she suspected to be true, "Yeah, we're
still planning to have one. But now isn't really the best time.
Ya know?"

It was clear to Vicki that Monica had married Jonah under false pretenses. Vicki did not care at all about the circum-
stance surrounding Monica's darkest days. All she knew and
all she cared about was that she had a grain to stand on. To
look much deeper into the whys might dislodge her founda-
tion. This lone fact, frozen in time and context, was all she
needed to justify herself, to herself.

Vicki had never seen herself as one of those "stupid women" who chased after married men. She wasn't one of these
women, she told herself. First of all, Jonah was a good man.
Most of these women involved with married men are just one
in a chain of fools. With her very own eyes she'd seen that
men who cheat don't usually stop with one. She'd seen the
pain in her own mother's face every weekend. But she'd actually, as a part of her job even, watched this man for many
years now and she knew for a fact that there was no one else.
To a fault, she thought, he was faithful. Secondly, she
reasoned that she was different from these other women in
that she knew as a fact, that the wife was, in her mind, a lying heifer. She had to believe this, or how else could she go
forward? Did it not occur to her that these other women had
said similar things to themselves?

But at the time, Vicki's only dilemma was how to make use of this information. She knew that the infertility thing was simply the Coup de Grace, but she felt she needed something else on Monica, something from which the hidden medical condition would simply be the last straw. If she lied about that, certainly she lied about something else. Liars lie after all. She'd hoped that the childhood affiliation with one of the Blue youth groups would bear some fruit, but after years of keeping an eye out for Monica's name in the tons of documents she pilfered every year, she'd found nothing. But her hunt continued even as Jonah hunted for a way out of that seemingly Godforsaken place.

Karun and Jonah rounded the corner and stepped across the street to Heru's barbershop. They weren't there to see Heru. Heru was down with the underground, but this was a totally different part of the underground network that Jonah needed. For fellowship meetings see Heru, but for this type of transaction you need to see one of the guys that hung around outside the shop, drifting between it and the liquor store.

That day the man to see was Rusty. Jonah stepped to him and greeted him. "What's up Rusty?"

Rusty extended his hand and the two men embraced. He then did likewise with Karun. "Karun, you old dog. How's that wife of yours? Still pretty as a peach?"

"You know this. I would not have a wife that was not so," Karun kidded and played along.

Rusty turned and motioned the two men to follow him into the alley between the two stores. "So, what can I do for you gentlemen?"

"Rusty, I just need to drop a word to my girl in the pipes." Now that he was on the street, Jonah was talking the talk as well.

"I hear you my brother," he replied. "What do you want to tell ol' Sombra de Luna?" Sombra de Luna was Vicki's street name, as much as any shade has one. Loosely translated it means Moon Shadow.

"Just tell her to catch me tomorrow. She knows where."

"Will do. Hey, my little boy thinks that light show the other night was Circle work."

Jonah grabbed Rusty's shoulder, "Tell your little boy he thinks too much." Jonah gave him a wink.

Rusty grinned a sly smile. "The Blue heat is all riled up, so watch your step."

Jonah laughed a bit. "You know me, I don't do anything. Karun here is the one to watch." Jonah gave Karun a soft push.

Once they were done with Rusty, Jonah and Karun stopped into Heru's barbershop. They didn't go in for a cut, but just to shoot the breeze with Heru. Karun bought Jonah a sandwich and drink from one of the street vendors that often strolled through the barbershop.

Eventually, Jonah and Karun departed Heru's and headed for the museum. They strode to the point where they faced the museum steps. A December wind swept down the steps and into their faces. Jonah fought not only the cold wind but also the emotion that it brought. This was not a time for fear or dark thoughts, but for focus. Emergencies commanded focus, but this premeditated venture was something different. He'd been thinking of this moment constantly since he first saw the Heart. But in these years of oppression his faith had grown to the point that it was now second nature to steal himself in these situations. So, instantly he lost regard for the cold wind and its sway.

Security was tight in the capitol city, but one advantage Jonah and Karun possessed was that no one was looking for them. All of the face recognition software in the world cannot pierce that defense. Neither of them was on any sort of security alert list. Why would they be? At this point the Blues had no idea that he was the engineer that designed and created the very device that generated the protective field around their most hated enemy. In the great purge, records were kept, but in the scattering and transition of power the whereabouts of fifty percent of the population was lost. It was widely stated that forty of the fifty percent were either dead or living up north inside the Circle. The remainder was thought to be living among the Blues, but no one seemed to know exactly where.

Jonah, however, knew exactly where he was. He was standing on the cusp of the unknown before a building of knowledge. He was taking a chance that he never would have taken back in the days before the change. Not everything about the coup had been bad... at least from a faith development perspective. Sure the sadness would swallow him sometimes, but there was no real fear in him anymore. He knew well by this point that what would be, would be. Whether he lived or died, gained or lost, succeeded or failed, the power did not rest within him. He was not lord of this world.

Karun placed a hand around the back of Jonah's neck and pulled his ear close, "It is time, my friend."

"Yes, I know." Jonah nodded and they crossed the street to the base of the granite steps. Stone lions guarded either side of the path to knowledge. Step by step they climbed. They reached the top to see a sign noting that on that day of the week there was no entrance fee, so in they walked.

The museum itself was quite large. There were the standard things you'd expect to see in a museum. There were the obligatory art works from the masters and the always-popular Egyptian collection. Jonah and Karun passed them all by with appreciation, but their minds did not waver from their goal.

The two of them stepped across a walkway and to the entrance of what was deemed the "Oddity Room". This was a room of "things" that defied description. A couple of the items were potentially mind boggling, like the stone coffins inscribed with detail that would lead you to believe they were the final resting place of two of Christ's Disciples. Carbon dating of some of the contents seemed to suggest that that they were the real deal. Many wondered why would the Blues let such a find still show? The reason was that officially, the Blues were far from atheists. As a matter of fact, they had their own religion. They started with the Hindu belief and then added components from other faiths to suit their needs.

Now many doubted that many of the Blues actually believed in anything, but this custom faith allowed them all to join hands in the belief that they are the highest caste. A revolutionary caste so perfected that they were worthy of praise from the other castes. It was their right. All of these other religions were part of some evolutionary process that served only to confirm their place. So yes, they welcomed artifacts from those beliefs that predated their newfound faith.

But some things in this room confounded even the most elaborate supposition. One such item was The Heart of Mystery. Carbon dating was inconclusive, largely because the data suggested that the Heart's existence predated the commonly accepted beginnings of human history. Scientific analysis suggested that this thing was older than some mountain ranges. Many myths surrounded it, but they all centered around it being some kind of gateway. Still, for years it sat in isolation in back rooms more famous for its defiance to be analyzed than any of those mostly forgotten stories.

Karun and Jonah skimmed along the far wall opposite the Heart. It was as though they were circling it like a predator getting the lay of the land before pouncing. To this date, the Heart had been nothing but a carcass, lifeless and unyielding of its secrets. But today would be different, today would be brilliant. As Jonah and Karun came around the room, inching towards the wayward icon, it began to glow. Karun was not certain just what he was seeing, but Jonah had seen it just days before. He'd not visited these museums, these testaments to Blue power, until just three days before and only then after receiving a message that the Heart of Mystery was coming to his town. (Actually the message stated that the collection was coming to town. But by Jonah's own research he knew the Heart to be a part of this collection.) Jonah's face lit up with glee as he saw his friend try to comprehend just what was happening.

"Jonah, it's glowing!" Karun finally exclaimed, stating the obvious.

"Yeah, man." Jonah grinned.

Part "A" of their plan worked just fine. They were able to slip away from the crowd. There were several security cameras set up in the museum, but by and large the facility relied on sensors rather than human monitoring. Given the development of cloaking technology, the suits that seemingly bent light and the high costs of human attendants, automated electronic sensors were the defense of choice for most government facilities. Since this was just a museum and not considered a sensitive site, a human eye was not actually watching most of the areas. Jonah used this reality to his favor.

Pointing to the supply closet, Jonah reached into his coat and activated one of his devices, the Wave Modulator. It was the same device he used to help save Sara. Once it enveloped him and Karun, they disappeared from all manner of detection except human sight and the optical video cameras. But he emitted a second wave which jammed transmission from every camera in the building (and some adjacent ones too).

The familiar yellow glow of the modulator surrounded Jonah and Karun.

Once they arrived at the maintenance room, they found its door unlocked. They both looked around and then slipped into the small room. Inside they found it full of display-related equipment. There was a workbench in the middle of the room, which the staff used to help them setup up the more complex displays. Still inside of the light yellow glow, they both climbed atop the sturdy black platform. From there they pushed up a section of the drop ceiling and climbed up one at a time. Jonah went first and then Karun. Having carried up with them from the room below a couple of pieces of wood paneling, they were actually able to rest quite comfortably after placing the dislodged ceiling section back into its place. At last, and per their plan, they were able to speak to one another. Seeing that Karun was a bit nervous, Jonah spoke first. "Dude, I think we're going to be okay now. If someone had seen us, we'd be busted by now."

Karun replied with a very unenthusiastic, "I guess so."

"Hey man, this place will close in a couple hours and then we will be able to get down to business," Jonah followed.

As the evening passed and night set in, Karun slept while Jonah, too anxious for sleep, pondered the possibilities. He thought of how he would respond if things went wrong. He thought about what he could do to secure the safety of Karun and himself. He thought about just what the Heart might actually mean to him and Monica. He had no clue as to what specifically it would mean, but it felt familiar to him and it glowed when he came near it. This was like manna from the Heaven. How could he ignore it?

That time of year it grew dark at about 6:00PM. The museum closed at seven and the staff, save two security guards stationed in the lobby, departed shortly thereafter. One of the security guards would make one sweep of the building and be back at his desk by 8:00PM. Jonah would wait until 8:30PM to make his descent. As the time dragged on Jonah realized that the waiting was harder than the doing. Mercifully, 8:29PM arrived and he reached over to shake Karun awake. Still inside the sphere that moved and stretched to protect them no matter how they contorted, the two pulled back the ceiling panel and began to climb down. Karun couldn't help but ask, "So, you are sure this is going to hide us from their sensors?"

Jonah, who in his natural state was perhaps overly honest, answered. "Well, I figure that if Matasis couldn't see through it at the lighthouse, then it ought to work here. But, you never know."

Karun could have done well without hearing that last part. That was the way Jonah spoke in the shop, always underselling things and his ability. Karun put up with it there and learned over time how to read between the lines. But he did not want to hear anything that even remotely sounded like a shadow of doubt. "Come on man, you got to be sure."

Getting to the floor, Jonah attempted to reassure Karun. "Well, I have a couple of back-up plans just in case." Jonah opened the maintenance door just slightly to take a quick peek outside. "Now remember, we don't want to talk once we're outside. I could turn this thing up to block sound as well, but then we wouldn't be able to hear anyone coming."

"Cool," Karun replied back, feeling somewhat better about their mission.

Jonah slowly opened the door such that they both could exit the room single file. The track lighting above was off now, but the lights within each of the displays were still on. Jonah and Karun crept over to the Heart. As brightly as the Heart glowed as they neared it, Jonah's face shown even brighter with genuine glee. As they drew close enough to stand right before the Heart, it glowed so brightly that its shimmer illuminated the entire room. So much so, that Jonah and Karun's long shadows stood in witness along the far wall.

And still Jonah couldn't help but be moved by the fact that he was about to take possession of the remains of, no the heart of, someone from which he had descended. This was someone actually related to him who, in the end, loved all out and held nothing back, not even her own life. His auntie had told him all the stories and shared all the love of this woman, but still this was different. It was life-changing. In the metal bands that encircled the Heart there was a scripture inscribed beginning with the words, "For God..." It was at that moment that the love of that act was fully conveyed unto Jonah and he was changed.

Jonah reached into his coat and extracted a bag of sand. His hope was to place it on the small pedestal on which the Heart sat as he lifted the Heart. He held it in his left hand as he reached out with his right towards the Heart. It burned so brightly now, that he could barely look at it. Jonah steadied his right hand directly above the Heart. Then, with his left hand, he slowly placed the sandbag onto the pedestal as he began to lift the Heart. At least that is what he was trying to do. Things went a little differently however.

As Jonah touched the Heart, not only did it continue to glow, but so did Jonah. The glow started in his hand as he touched it and then spread up his arm and to the rest of his body. He glowed to the point that the light shined even through his clothes. Every opening in his attire exuded light. Every orifice from his body also gave praise to light. So much so, that even when Jonah opened his mouth to gasp, a band of light shown from it so brightly that Karun was forced to cover his eyes. Rolling the bag of sand onto the platform as he lifted the Heart into the air, Jonah's own eyes were wide open and transfixed on the object. But as he released his grip on the sandbag in his left hand the alarm went off. The bag was not the same weight as the Heart and the pressure sensitive podium had screamed its secret and flashed its disapproval.

Karun let out a cry, "Oh my!" as he crouched with his hands covering his face and head as perhaps Adam may have done in the Garden of Eden.

As for Jonah, he was so enamored with the Heart that he only flinched for half a second before reacquiring his gaze upon the glowing icon. Certainly, there was a small part of his brain that was telling him to run back to their hiding place as they had originally planned; to cloak themselves until the search squads passed them by. Surely, that thought was somewhere between the neurons of his brain. But the current between those synapses held no sway. In holding the Heart up in his right hand Jonah began to feel a fluid feeling. Before he touched the Heart he was sure that he had only five senses, but now, moment-by-moment he was becoming aware of so much more. He'd had fleeting glimpses of this several times before, either while in prayer or in a dream. He remembered the emotion he felt when, as a child, that truck was about to hit him. But now, as he stared up and past his outreached hand, the Heavens opened up to him. He saw that there was no ceiling; there was no room, no walls. Yes, they were still there, but there were no barriers. All things were becoming obvious to him. He looked to his right, without looking in the way that we do, and he saw the future. In the same way he looked to his left and saw the past.

Karun, tugging on his sleeve asked him, "What are you looking at?"

From his lips slipped an unsure but certain, "Everything..."

Given that they were only on the second floor, it was no surprise that they began to hear motion from out in the hallway. Karun braced himself against Jonah's arm. In alarm he exclaimed, "Jonah, they are here!"

Jonah still holding the Heart aloft, was not alarmed because he could look, without looking, to his right and see the future. He knew what was to come, but Karun did not. Jonah saw the wall in front of them in dimensions that were previously unknown to him. He tugged on Karun that he might follow him, and out of their predicament. Karun resisted. Jonah spoke to him, "Karun, this is the way out. Follow me."

"But Jonah, that is a wall, the door is over there! Let's run back to the storage room while we still have time!"

"Karun, have faith in me when I tell you I know the way out. It's too late for hiding." Just then two security guards entered the room. The guards froze for just a moment, put off by the bright glow that enveloped the pair of uninvited guests. Jonah spoke again to Karun. "Look, just close your eyes and I will lead us out of here." Jonah knew that there was no way Karun could follow him with his eyes open. He couldn't see what Jonah could.

The puzzled looks on the faces of the guards gave Karun reason to believe that perhaps he had a moment or two to comply with his friend's wishes. He closed his eyes and he felt them moving. He walked with Jonah, holding on to his arm all the way. He could see neither Jonah nor where they were going, but all the way he could still feel Jonah's arm and that they were indeed moving. At long last he felt openness and smelled the scent of fresh air. He opened his eyelids to see that they were now outside and across the street from the museum.

"How, where did, how did..." Karun was at a loss for words.

Jonah, having put down his arm, began to try to explain, when they were startled into silence by hearing the alarm go off across the street. They looked up to a window on the second floor to see a faint, but distinctive yellow glow lighting the entire window frame. They looked at each other as sheer astonishment washed over each of their faces. They were seeing themselves mere moments ago.

Karun covered his eyes again and exclaimed, "Is such a thing for mortal eyes to see?"

The two of them made haste away from there, walking at first and then breaking out into a full run.

15: Queen For an Age

What merits a crown? A lineage? A sword? A word?

Exiting the elevator, Akina and all of us were dumbfounded by what we saw and heard. Here were five oddly dressed men before us claiming to know Akina. And odder still, they called her "Queen Nefertiti".

The five of them were very impressive, but not threatening towards us. Actually, on average they were shorter than us, the lone exception to this being the dark Egyptian out front. He was rather tall. The Mayan was short, but held a steady, intimidating, gaze straight ahead. He dared you to look at him. He wore a traditional priestly Mayan headdress, so you could barely see his dark hair that hid beneath. The Asian guy, whose name was Chin, was nearly as short as the Mayan and stood in a slightly bowed position of respect. He was younger. Whereas the Mayan may have been late thirties, Chin might have been twenty-five. Standing to the immediate left of the Egyptian was a man from India named Sanjay. He was about twenty-five, maybe a little older. His hair was black too, and mostly hidden by the funny-looking hat he wore. He was more adorned with gadgets and maps than clothes. He held a golden tablet in his hands and seemed more concerned with his various holdings than with us. To the right of the Egyptian was the Druid, a white guy with bright, but dirty blonde hair. His name was Martin and he was smiling, a smile that needed no translation. I think he was ecstatic to finally run into some women. He might have been 27 or so. As for the man down in front holding the shield, he was a tall, dark-skinned, bald black man, dressed very much like someone in a Hieroglyphic painting. His skin shined with vigor.

"You speak English?" Akina asked the one out front.

The Egyptian answered, "Of course, my Queen. You taught me."

Reggie stepped up, "Do you know these guys?"

"No!" Akina exclaimed and then slamming her palm into and massaging her forehead, she followed with, "At least I don't think so. I don't know…"

Then Chin spoke up, "Let me assure you, my Queen you do know us. Or at least you will. In fact, it is you who sent us here to protect you."

Akina took a step towards Chin and giving him an incredulous look so cold that it froze his easy smile into an unnatural state. Given that she was slightly taller than him she looked down when she spoke. "I sent you, to protect me?"

The Egyptian stepped closer to them and bowed, getting Akina's attention. "Yes, my Queen, though he is small in stature his heart is the biggest of us all. You handpicked him for this task. We were all handpicked by you, though not all of us are wizards like the Shaman over there," he nodded towards the silent Mayan. This would be a recurring theme with the Mayan Shaman. "We are all very aware of the dark arts of this realm. It is you who warned us of these things."

Akina turned back to him with the same cold stare, so much so that the giant of a man stood up straight and took a step back. She demanded from him, "I sent a team of mystics to rescue me?" He stood there speechless, so she asked again. "Mystics? If you know me, if you really do know me, then you know that I would not do this."

"Look at us," the Asian man said. "Surely you know us, for you have the gift of prophecy a hundred times more than any mortal before. Surely, you know that we are not all mystics. Or are you blind to only your own deeds?" Chin said this already knowing the answer. "How did I know this? It is by your own lips." Now showing compassion, he reached out his hand. "My Queen, we mean you no harm. We are here only to protect you. You sent seven of us here, just for that purpose and none other." While saying this he took the shield from the Egyptian and handed it to Akina. She took it and in an instant it was gone, stored away in her own little temporal cache along with an assortment of other weapons and tools. Only the two daggers she wore on her hips stayed with her at all times. Everything else was in this "forever-land" that only she could access. She could grab any of these objects and bring them to our reality as easily as I might pick up a fork.

"Seven? But there are but five of you," Reggie injected.

The Egyptian replied back, "Yes, we lost two brothers in arms while searching for you."

Then surprisingly, even to me, I spoke up. "Oh, wow, we're sorry to hear that."

The Egyptian, feeling the need to tell me more, followed, "Yes, one of those abominations reached up from below and dragged the first one down. It happened during what you might say passes for night here. The second one was snatched by one of the flying beasts that live in the hills."

Carla added, "Yes, we've seen the Night Terrors. None of them attacked us, but they circled us, viciously."

The Egyptian, speaking for the group, stood at attention and spoke again. "Still, my Queen, we are here to serve you, to protect you on your journey."

Reggie placed his hand on Akina's shoulder, "Your call."

Akina looked to Carla for discernment. "What do you see, Carla?"

Carla replied back, "I'm not at my best right now, but I don't see anything. I think they're telling the truth, or at least as they know it."

"Alright then. Follow us, but don't slow us down because we're in a bit of a rush." Akina said this as she slung her backpack across her shoulder.

Sanjay, the navigator, took out what at first seemed to be a large map rolled onto a scroll. But as he unfolded it, it was more than a map. It was, with some adjustment, a leather seat strung between two wooden polls. Akina's protectors motioned for her to sit as they placed rods on their shoulders and knelt down.

Akina gave them that glare again. "Please... I am not letting you guys carry me. Just keep up."

Sanjay spoke up. "I have a map to where you are going." He reached behind his head to pull that map from the pack on his back.

Akina snapped, "I don't need a map. I know where I'm going." Then seeing the expression on the young Indian's face she caught herself. "Hey, look I don't mean to be short with you, any of you. But it's just that all of this has been a bit much. You know? I've got some things to work out but I shouldn't take that out on all of you. Sorry." She knelt down to help the mapmaker roll and re-pack his scrolls. "Let's just take this one step at a time. I'm going this way. If you want to follow, then do. If you want to return to Egypt, then go. Just tell me, that I sent you home when you get back. I'm sure I'll understand, I guess." Personally, I didn't know how they would have returned home without her help.

At that we set out. Reggie laughed, "This is getting more priceless by the minute. Here I am trekking through some God-forsaken land somewhere between Heaven and Hell with four virgins, five escapees from a King Tut exhibit, a re-formed everybody's girl who's found God, and a hardcore pacifist who can't stay out of therapy." I wasn't sure just who all he was talking about. I knew that Akina, Darnell and I were all virgins but I didn't know that Kim was too. He had to be talking about Kim, since everyone knew that Carla wasn't and neither was Sandy (although it had been against her will, I doubt that made a difference in Reggie's mind). Kim was a bit of a tomboy. To be honest I tend to think of those girls as being a little freer with their bodies or not being into men at all or both. Of course, I learned all of this in locker rooms during my high school days, from a bunch of guys who liked to jump off of things (roofs, tabletops, chairs) and on to other things (other people, tabletops, chairs) like wrestlers on television. I say all of that to say that I wouldn't have expected her to be a virgin. The second thing about his comment was that I hadn't told anyone I was a virgin (at the time it was my secret shame). I wondered how he knew and in any event I didn't appreciate him "outing" me to the group. I don't think he was trying to be mean, but I just think he was being careless with our affairs. Nonetheless, it was a time to move and not to debate.

Darnell picked up his sister and carried her. The men out of time offered to carry her using the roll they'd intended to use to carry Akina, but Darnell declined. As I said before he doesn't really get tired or need sleep, but I'm sure it would have been more comfortable for Carla. However, at that point Darnell didn't know whether to trust these guys or not... and neither did I. Carla needed her rest so that she could watch over us while we slept. I don't know how deep of a sleep she actually got. I couldn't see how anyone could doze at all like that. But with Darnell being her twin brother, I guess she felt a degree of comfort with him that at least allowed her mind to rest. I think in a lot of ways, he was a bit of a father figure for her. Their father died when they were younger. In turn, she was as much a mother to him as anyone. Their mother, my Aunt Deborah, wasn't the most maternal of women.

We reached the edge of the city and paused for a minute before we were to begin our descent. Surveying the horizon, Akina pointed far off into the distance to where we were going. As we began to descend down the slope one by one, the strangest thing happened. The shade of a man appeared before me in the downward path. At first, I thought it was Uncle Paul. But then I could see that it wasn't. The image stretched out his arms wide as though he were trying to catch me. Not watching where I was going, I tripped and stumbled right through him. His image faded in and out, but I could see that he was a black man, about my height. After I passed through him, Sandy turned to catch me and saw the vapor for herself. "Oh, my..." she exclaimed.

Akina, noticing the commotion, stepped back up to get a closer look. "Oh wow, this one is pretty well-formed. Usually these things don't appear as anything more than a shadow, if at all. They are, for lack of a better term, spirits. Mostly all of them are wanderers longing for that place from which we all came. But they cannot find it."

Sandy's voice turned compassionate. "It looks like he's trying to say something, like he wants to talk to us."

Akina discounted it. "You see these guys all the time here. They all want to talk to you, to tell you their story. I don't know if I've seen one quite like this though. But I assure you the story is the same. Come one, let's go." Giving him one last look, Akina smirked and walked right back through him.

Akina led the way with her newfound protectors marching in close order behind her. Behind them, were Reggie, Kim, Sandy, me, Carla and Darnell in that order. Two things were obvious. We did not altogether trust them yet and they were there to protect Akina and no one else. We'd traveled no more than an hour or so when our escorts, Nihil, Dread and Shamus showed up. I'd hoped we'd lost them for good. Dread and Shamus walked side by side with Nihil on a chain between them.

Nihil, dancing, said in a mocking tone, "So, new friends have you now. How special. Wonder how long it will be until you have to kill one of them?" He said this loud enough for both groups to hear. It wasn't until much later that it occurred to me that he might just as well have been speaking to them as us.

The length of Nihil's chains seemed to vary but were long enough to allow him to dance in and between our line while the giants walked behind us. To my surprise he jigged up to my side. He looked like some kind of mange-riddled mutant dog. He leaned his head in towards me before speaking. "You know, Alchemist, you and I have a lot in common, especially from back in the day. But, I digress. I have a question for you. I know you think your little cousin Akina is just about perfect, but have you ever noticed how she has to be right about everything? Even to the point that she will say mean or belittling things to people. Like she knows it all and has to suffer all you fools? It's like she has to be right at all costs. I've heard some pretty spiteful things come out of her mouth, haven't you? Sure she says she's sorry later, sometimes. But if she were all that good, surely she wouldn't talk to anyone that way? Next time she does that, I think you should call her on it, for her own good at least."

The vicious-looking little sprite started to depart, but when he noticed me looking at Kim, he stopped. "She's an odd one, isn't she? Yeah, she's cute, but isn't she just a bit masculine? Not so much the way she looks, but how she acts. I'm not saying that she's this or she's that, but she does seem like she could be. Look at how she dresses, how she hangs with the boys. And have you ever seen her with a boyfriend?"

Drooling, Nihil licked his chops and continued, "Have you ever thought about why you exist? I mean the whole big thing. I know you're atheist now, but do you ever wonder why you're here? I understand your disbelief and all, at least from the view that all of this is pointless. I mean, if there really were a God, why would he create such flawed creatures as you? Why would a perfect being create imperfect beings?

Therefore, how could he be perfect? Yeah, you feel me now, don't you?" Saying this, he danced around in an impish dance better suited for a drunkard before his imaginary audience or a fool before his downfall.

His glee subsided enough for him to still himself to carry on his accusations. "And on the chance there is a God, surely you are the condemned. If there is a God, this much is true; in the battle for Heaven, all of you, all of mankind, would be among the cast out. Most men are much too blind, much too far into their denial of their unrighteousness to see that they were on the losing team. Those souls that are now cast down into an earthly hell of flesh and blood. Your spirits, once divine and immortal, are now completely abandoned and sentenced to death."

Have you ever seen a dog on a pogo stick? That's the best way I can describe Nihil and that really doesn't tell a tenth of how he danced. His cackle was chaotic, like someone laughing backwards. He spoke to himself in a tongue unlike anything I'd ever heard. The more his chains twisted and swirled around him, the more he seemed to love it all the more.

Next he danced up to Sandy walking right in front of me. He began to speak to her, but she put up her hand and shouted, "Get away from me! Don't talk to me, I don't want hear it."

Leaving Sandy, he bounced around the line speaking to pretty much everyone to varying lengths of time. Sometimes he danced, sometimes he didn't. He spoke to Reggie for quite a bit. I had the feeling from their body movements that they were talking about the newcomers to our little party. On the other hand he didn't speak to Carla at all because she was asleep. Most everyone just listened, but the Shaman spoke back to him. I couldn't hear them, but I am certain it was a two-way conversation.

He did say something to Akina, but it was short. She was busy slaying beasts and demons to the left and right. She was on point all day and would not relent to allow any of us to take her place. Not that I offered, but Reggie, Darnell, the Egyptian, Chin, Martin and even Kim all offered, but she declined them all. Sure all of these were minor threats; more like what we saw in the bone yard, than what we faced afterwards on the way to the city on the hill. In some sense I think these creatures were not indigenous to this place, but more like us. They'd either found their way here somehow, or been sent here as some sort of punishment. In either case they found the end of their journey at the end of Akina's blade. Many of them seemed mad with some sort of sickness. I mean, why attack such a large group on your own or even two at a time? Still, she slew them all, as though she was trying to make a point or something. Oddly, Nihil seemed pleased by her work.

Equally odd was that this stretch was the calmest of the entire journey. At least it was from the back of the line. That would all change in an instant on day three of our trek across the valley. We'd agreed to travel for fourteen hours and then camp for what we called night. The Pit was not on our schedule, but we thought it in our best interest to try to maintain one, as to not overtax our bodies. We were approaching the last hour of our day's journey when hell broke loose, literally.

The ground began to tremble. We all looked around and didn't see anything near us or on the horizon. We were walking in the plains but skirting along the side of the mountain range as not to be so open to attack from the winged beasts from the surrounding peaks.

The rumbling grew so intense that I thought it was a landside. I was looking to the slopes above me when the ground beneath me began to crack and elevate. En masse we all began to rise like sprinkles on a soufflé. In the middle of us a

peak arose and from it a terrible head broke free, then a
second, and a third. All three were the heads of a beast. Each
of the heads transfigured or transmuted from one terrible image to another. I'd like to say they looked like this or that, but
nothing in my worst nightmares looked anything like one of
these. This was from a level of hell beneath my nightmares.
What I can tell you is that its teeth were sharp and when one
of the heads opened its mouth, fire spewed out. The breach
was right in front of me.

The Behemoth lifted its first foot out of the hole, and it
was the paw of a dog. As it began to climb out, there was the
second limb, now on the ledge. The second foot was the hoof of
a wild boar. As it raised its three heads to the sky and shook
off the dirt, each of us tumbled from the crest to the ground.
From my back I could see tentacles like those from an octopus
branching from its shoulders, but instead of suction cups,
there were eyes with teeth for eyelashes all along the under-
belly of each wandering arm. In the instant that I looked up
to see the beast for what it was, one of the eyeless heads
locked in on me (I can only guess that the eyes on the
tentacles guided it). With its long neck it extended down towards me and opened its gape. I, still sitting on my hind side,
could only throw up my arms as flames spewed from its
mouth. The fire wrapped all around me and finally I
screamed. The flames nearly blinded me, but when they subsided, although smoke was all around me, not a hair on my
head was singed. I looked to my right and there was Carla on
her hands and knees with her right hand stretched out towards me. She had used her ability to shield me. Got to love
that girl. Then Sandy, once again showing no fear, raced to
my side and literally diving, rolling and reaching under both
my armpits, sprung to her feet, lifting me to my feet as well
and leading me to a place of cover. The beast redirected its
stare to Carla and I leapt from Sandy's arms to pound the

ground in Carla's direction, but Darnell beat me to it. He flew to his sister's aid and met the monster's flames with fire of his own. Carla got to her feet and motioned for her brother to go.

All the others from Kim forward were on the other side of the creature. We had the attention of one of the heads, while they had the other two. Darnell jumped into the air and flew a quick circle around the perimeter of the beast. Dodging the streams of flame, he flew between the two heads facing our compatriots and landed high on the neck on the one that spewed fire at me. The Behemoth was so large, along with the breach it created, that we could not see Reggie, Akina, her guards, nor Kim, that is until Sandy tapped me on my shoulder in excitement pointing, "Look!" There between the other two heads I could see that Kim had also taken to the air. I could see her and her skateboard darting in and out like some very extreme sports star, electricity arching from her hands at every turn. Back on our side I could see that Darnell was trying to sever our attacker's head. The beams from his eyes had begun to cut into the beast. But every time he fired, the beast would jerk so violently, that it threw him off and he had to reattach himself.

I had an idea. I said in a slightly frustrated tone to Sandy, "I think I know how to beat this thing, but I'm afraid to try it."

Sandy, her eyes darting back and forth at all the action, calmly asked me, "What's the problem?"

"Anyone who can't fly needs to back away from that thing before I try this," I breathed to her.

Mind you, to me it was just a thought, a thought that I may have mentioned because I never thought it had a prayer of being tested. But you must also understand, like I told you from the start, Sandy had this unwavering, unjustified faith in me. So much so, that she took my musings as a call to action. She looked over towards Carla and mouthed, "We have an idea." Please understand too that Sandy did this without a word from me as to what the idea was.

Now the distance and roar of the beast was such that Carla couldn't really hear us, and we couldn't hear her either. But something about speaking in her direction got her tuned into Sandy's thoughts and then mine. Moving her lips she spoke back to both of us, her telepathy aiding our understanding, "Sounds good, but the others are so busy that they're not going to hear my mental call out. I'll try but it may take a minute." Basically their minds were too busy to hear much of anything as subtle as a thought, particularly the new guys. Carla had no rapport with them yet.

Sandy looked at me, looked up at Darnell and Kim sweating it out, and then back at me. "Hey, I'll let them know to step off. Just do your thing once you think I'm over there."

"Huh?" I said, befuddled by her statement and too busy avoiding the eye-ribbed, teeth enriched tentacles to focus on what she was saying. Then before I could reach out to stop her, she jumped from behind our rock and in a full sprint raced up and over each embankment that separated us from the others. Tentacles snapped and cracked at her. From what I could see until she was out of sight, she dodged and danced around each grab.

She was out of sight for a good five seconds, but it might have been fifteen seconds. I wasn't sure, and despite my earlier success, I began to doubt not just my sense of timing, but my abilities as well. Then I looked toward Carla and she nodded towards me and I heard something akin to, "Go ahead," in my head.

I pounded my right hand hard on the ground in front of me towards the monster, reaching deeper than I ever had before. I felt the ground beneath the creature, the rock on which it had climbed and now stood. I felt it in my fingers. I felt it changing to my touch. Then, for spite, I laid my left hand on the dirt as well in that same direction, but not as deeply. With my right hand I was turning the ground beneath the beast to gas, and from my left hand a transforming wave of hard crystal spread outward towards the creature. The ground beneath him began to crack, and then it sensed something was amiss. Then with little warning and exponential quickening, everything shattered and the giant beast began to fall back through the hole from which it'd crawled.

But then I saw the most horrible, heartwrenching thing I'd ever seen in my life to that point. As one of the tentacles was receding, it catapulted into the air due to the severity of the angle and pace of its owner's decent. At the end of this arm was Sandy. There she was lifted high in the air. I leapt over the rock from which I hid and ran towards the hole and so did everyone else. As the beast's main body began to cascade down into oblivion, Sandy's descent increased. Darnell and Kim, who were airborne, dove from their respective positions above, down towards the hole. Reaching the hole just as Sandy disappeared from sight beneath the rim of the hole, I, not thinking at all, ran up to the precipice and dove headfirst in after them. To my right I caught a glimpse of Carla diving in after me. To my left I saw Akina running towards us as well, but her men were vainly trying to hold her back. We were all in a freefall after Sandy. I can't say that on the way in that I noticed where Reggie was, but that was soon rectified. It seemed as soon as I jumped in I saw Kim flying back toward and past me, going up the hole's opening and then just as quickly, I saw her dragging Reggie by the hand past me and heading down fast. Carla grabbed my hand as both of us reached out to flailing teeth lined tentacles. We were trying to catch one and hold on tight. Carla caught onto one of the limbs and began to pull me in. We were now in an almost complete freefall, except for what little effect Darnell's efforts had. He had an arm of the monster and was attempting to fly back the other way or maybe hook the arm on something. Below us and closer to the beast's main body, I saw Sandy wrapped up in one of the tentacles. With her were Akina and Kim. Akina, who jumped in after me, must have teleported to Sandy's location once she dove in and could see her. Akina was wailing away with her blades, trying to sever the tentacle, while Kim alternated from trying to pull Sandy free and trying to shock the creature into letting go. Reggie, for his part, was inside of the mouth of the head closest to Sandy. He'd managed to wedge his rod in the corner of the monster's jaw, preventing it from snapping at her or the others working to free her.

The jagged walls on either side of us made it apparent how the beast climbed up to our level from the one below. However, how it got to the hole became a mystery once we dropped through the bottom of the hole. We were now falling in an open space, like asteroids falling to earth. Carla and I were now both hanging on to the end of one of the tentacles. Recognizing our situation, she looked at me and attempted to put a thought into my head. I didn't get it, in part I guess, because I was so zoned in on hanging on for dear life. I can be like that. Then she shouted a clue to me, "Change what's different!"

Carla turned and looking upward, spotted Akina's protectors, except for the Shaman, in a freefall behind us. She released one hand and pointed it skyward. It was clear that she expected me to do as she asked while she worked to bring those lagging behind to the rest of us. For my part, I realized that Carla wanted me to transmute some element that was in this beast, but not in any of us. Since we were all hanging on, that was important. Focusing into my sense of touch I reached out again. I was startled to find that there wasn't a molecule of carbon in this monster. What I did find was silicone and plenty of it. In fact, this life form was silicone-based. Every living thing on earth is carbon-based. But this was something else. Then I made the mistake of looking down. I could see the flames erupt from what was a raging ocean of burning lava. I saw several peaks of rock protruding up- wards, but we weren't headed for any of them. I gulped and my heart began to beat even more intensely as a panic began to set in. When I had first jumped in I had no time to be scared and my thoughts were only of saving Sandy. But now I had begun to think of my own life, even more so as I was con- sumed with the sight of the burning cauldron below. I closed my eyes tight, gripping the beast even tighter. Then Carla tapped, no punched me, giving me a look that needed no tele- pathy or words to be heard. It was a look that said, "Hurry up, already!"

Again I closed my eyes, but this time not in fright. I knew I only had moments left before impact, but I knew just as well that fear was not going to benefit me or any of us. The earlier thought of seeing no way for us to survive even if we survived the landing was gone. I was focused on what I needed to do right then. I reached deep into the beast, pulling at what felt like strings, strings that linked one molecule to another. I felt the tumblers of creation in my hand. I felt and understood the nature of silicone in the putty of creation. I could create noth- ing, but I could change it. I decided that I need not change from silicone to anything else, but instead I could just change its state. Mostly the beast was a mixture of gas, solid and li- quid states of silicone. I wanted everything beneath the top layers of skin to be liquid. I turned the universal atomic code one stroke and the creature bucked wildly. Carla grabbed onto me. I guess on some level she was aware of how lost in thought I was and realized that I could have easily been thrown. I turned the code again and the three-headed beast ceased from struggling. A second later, we impacted.

Of course, I miscalculated. I had envisioned the remains of the beast to be a giant air or gel filled cushion like the stunt-men use to perform falling stunts from high-rises in the movies. Maybe liquid silicone would spew from whatever orifices it possessed, but we'd be bouncing around until he came to rest. But it didn't happen that way. Each of us pierced his skin, which I had made too thin, and entered his body at various points. The liquid silicone was translucent, but only enough to see images and outlines of images, and even then only within a few feet of oneself. The image next to me was Carla. She'd let go of me on impact, but we both swam towards each other. We joined hands and swam a short two meters or so to the outside layer of the carcass. We'd not come up where we went in, but I just reached up and touched the skin liquefying it. I climbed out and pulled Carla up behind me. We both wiped the silicone from our eyes, mouths and nostrils as best we could. Water seemed to flow from my hands as I converted silicon on our faces to water and then took deep breaths. We were the first ones up, but we could see Akina's protectors also exiting around us. Like us, they'd not gone very far in when everything mashed together. But that was not the case for the others.

Carla, realizing in the same instant that I did, that the others were still below, stretched out her hand and swept it back and forth in a sweeping motion. Then she stopped and said, "I've found them."

Their actual location was below the lava line, in the part of the fluid-filled carcass that was below the surface. Silicone has a higher ignition temperature than carbon, but I'm sure they didn't have long to get out before the liquid silicone became even more fluid and dispersed into the lava.

Carla, looking down towards and past her outreached hand, took on a terse appearance as I could see the struggle on her face. Then I saw a red glow beneath the surface from deep within the beast. That glow became white hot as a beam of light broke through the surface about ten feet from us. From this, I saw a flash of lightning and then a streaking Kim, on her skateboard, with Sandy holding on tight. Darnell, the emitter of the initial light I'd seen, came out next. One hand held onto Akina and the other to Reggie. At this point we were all topside and attempting to balance ourselves on the rapidly deteriorating hull of the Behemoth. The general dimension of our sinking raft was maybe forty feet by seventy feet, but shrinking by the second.

Here was the situation in a nutshell. After falling a good 15,000 feet or more, we were sitting on the carcass of some three-headed giant abomination, on a lake of fire, at least 300 yards from the closest shoreline, also in flames, in a place that smelled of brimstone. Oh and we had maybe a minute to do something because the beast was sinking and beginning to burn.

Reggie, trying to stand, gave us his best leading man smile and quipped, "Suggestions?"

Thoughts and words raced around and between us, "One of those guys stayed up there." "Can Michael change this lava to something else?" "No, he'd burn his hand off!" "Akina, can you pop back up there?" "Maybe. I could take somebody, but then there's no way I could pop back here to get everyone." "We need to get to that shore." "But, it's on fire!" "Better to stand on fire than swim in it." We all nodded and then Sandy offered up a request, "Lord, help us." She opened up her eyes and looking upwards, she saw something and realizing what it was shouted, "Lookout!"

A large boulder splashed down fifty to a hundred yards away from us. Thankfully, molten rock does not splash very well; otherwise we'd have all been covered in lava.

Carla looked around, "All these things are just floating."

Kim, catching on, said, "Yes they are, and they've also got a good bit of iron in them."

Reggie added, "Then so should the lava." It was apparent that debris of all sorts was falling from the world above into this fiery pit. It was these chunks of ore that fell that in some part large or small fueled these flames... or so we thought. One thing was clear, as we all began to gather together; we had maybe thirty seconds to do something.

Kim responded to Reggie, "Yeah, but it's too hot to magnetize." Kim's ability was electromagnetic in nature and worked best in the cold. It was blazing hot down there and just being in such a hot place really taxed her gift.

For a split second Kim reached out her hand towards the large, just fallen stone. She couldn't budge it. Then she threw her skateboard down, jumped on it, and zoomed off to the rock. Darnell followed with Sandy. Even though he didn't know precisely what Kim was up to, he wanted to start moving folks off the sinking carcass just in case Kim's plan did work. Akina, for her part, stood still. For some reason her teleporting didn't work well enough in this place to safely teleport anyone but herself such a distance to such a small target. Being off just a bit would put them in lava.

Kim landed on the boulder and hopped off of her board, placing both feet firmly on the ore, in a location where the molten rock amazingly did not reach during impact. And thankfully, the rock was slow to heat up. So, the exposed part of the stone was still relatively cool. As best she could, she began to move the small island towards us. Darnell helped as best he could.

I looked around me and saw that the entire group was now condensed into what couldn't have been more than twenty square feet. Kim was about fifty feet away, but looking down towards the lava line around the stone, I could see the tiniest of wakes beginning to form. She was moving it. Unfortunately, our little dead island's descent was picking up speed. We waited as best we could, but when Kim got within twenty feet, Reggie started tossing people. Right then, I think I would have preferred being tossed, but in hindsight, I am glad that I wasn't standing next to Reggie when he started tossing people.

Finally, Kim's new life barge reached us. She was riding it, as best she could, like a giant skateboard. At that point it was just Reggie, Carla and me on the sinking beast, and we three hopped off almost in one motion as the flames danced around our feet. Carla could have levitated herself off, but I think she called herself protecting Reggie and me. I guess in theory she thought that maybe if she was right there beside us, she could have kept the lava flow away from us via telekinesis. I think we're all glad that it didn't get to that.

At last, we were all on our new home. Still stranded in a sea of flames, we figured it'd be a good hour or so until this chunk burst into flames, not that any of us had any real idea about these things. Heck, we weren't even sure that these were real flames in the sense that we knew.

Looking around as far as the eye could see, all we saw was this ocean of flames. Not good.

Breaking through the entire group, Sandy made her way over to me. And to my surprise and extreme pleasure, she hugged me and said, "Thank you. You saved my life. Thank you so very much." Not that she didn't thank everyone else as well, she did, but she hugged me and I knew that her hug and words were special for me. There I was in the worst place I could have ever imagined, in fact, I hadn't believed such a place could exist, and for a brief, but endearing moment, I had a sense of joy that I'd never known before.

Kim, having made her way to the pinnacle of the rock, surveyed the horizon. This place was darker than the one above. Barely beneath the surface there were things moving around in what we chose to call lava. In the air around us were those shadows we'd seen the night before in the tower. Akina's guards said that it was one of these that snatched their seventh team member and dragged him down below. They darted in and around us, but seemed hesitant to touch us directly. Kim, feeling a bit concerned, stated what we all knew to be true. "You know, I don't think this is such a good place to be."

Reggie, looking off into the distance, yelled, "And it just got worse." There was a massive whirlpool several hundred yards away, and we were drifting towards it. I figured Kim could slow our progress towards the whirlpool, but no way could she keep it up with this rock getting hotter all the time and conjunctively her power over it diminishing.

Then a thought hit me. "Kim, if I, like, super chill this thing, do you think you can fly us out of here?"

Kim looked around thinking for a minute and then shook her head. "I have no idea, but it sounds like it ought to work."

Undaunted and now inspired, I pressed on. "Hey, everybody I'm gonna try to super chill this rock. Then maybe Kim can get us out of here. Once I do this, do not to touch the rock with your bare hand."

I reached down and felt the rock, no felt through it to the point that I could feel the molecules on the bottom rock racing around and then dispersing in the flowing liquid. Reaching in, I held them in my fingertips. I was careful not to affect the molecules right where my hand touched the rock, but everywhere else I attempted to extend the same effect. I gave a nod to Kim.

Kim stretched her hands out again, the strain obvious on her face. Darnell took off, hoping to make the load lighter. Carla began to focus as well doing her best to help, considering that the part of this boulder on which we stood was maybe twelve to fourteen feet in diameter. The top of it, on which we stood, protruded two to three feet above the lava line. So the part of it below the surface was certainly several times that. But before we started we really had no way of knowing. Still, ever so slowly, we began to rise. The iron ore within the rock was nearly super conductive from my efforts, but still it had to be several tons of mass. In fact, a couple of Akina's guards offered to jump off to make the load lighter.

Darnell recognized Kim's struggle, so he circled underneath and began to push upwards. The former quickly dissolving rock was now super chilled. So much so, that Darnell had to remove his shoes and use them as crude gloves to allow him to push from underneath. It quickly became evident that we were picking up speed. I should point out too that while I was helping by cooling the rock, the people in our group who could have saved themselves, willingly threw their fate in with the group. I expected this of Darnell, for I knew him like a brother. But Kim really impressed me. She'd impressed me with her abilities earlier, but she now wowed me with her heart and her character.

Upwards we went. Kim did the majority of the driving in addition to providing a lot of the power, but still Carla did her part and more importantly helped to coordinate Darnell and Kim's efforts.

Sanjay pointed, "There!" He pointed towards the hole in the sky where we had entered. There were a number of orifices visible from where we stood, but ours was quite distinctive by its size.

Kim was looking up and had already spotted the opening. "I see it."

All this time, the shadow beings still twirled around us, sniping at us. We were all huddled together with our backs to each other.

Kim shouted to us, "We're going in."

Once inside the shaft, the heat abated just a bit and the darkness was accented from the glow of Kim's work. The rock actually glowed a light blue hue. Going up, we had one of our questions answered. There was at least 5,000 feet of rock between the world above and where we'd fallen. As we ascended, we could see in the passages and crevices, forms of life that we'd never seen before and hoped we would never see again. It was from this middle ground that our attacker had crawled. Most of these beings were in a way like us, or so we reasoned. But, unlike us, they'd not likely come here voluntarily. I'm sure Kim could have used a rest after the first 10,000 feet or so of free air, but we dared not stop at any of these openings less we face some other challenge from one of the locals, like our just disposed foe below.

At long last we reached the surface and we quickly plopped down just beyond where we'd jumped in. Kim landed us in such a way that we all rolled off harmlessly onto the ground. Upon setting foot on solid ground again, Chin let out a "Hallelujah, thank you God!"

All of us sat up and stared at each other. Reggie asked the obvious, "What did you say?"

He restated himself, "I said Hallelujah. Surely, you understand this."

Akina started to ask him where'd he gotten that from, but only "Where..." made it past her lips as he stared back at her. She realized that he'd gotten it from her future self.

The Egyptian spoke up, "Certainly, my queen, you know that everyone in your personal guard must be a believer. You would not have it any other way."

Akina stood up and paced around mumbling to herself. Speaking out loud and pushing her hair back in exasperation, "Oh, what a weird chick I must have grown up to be." A couple of folks rolled their eyes, like they were thinking, "Well, you're halfway there already." But no one said anything. Mostly, I guess that was Reggie and me doing the eye rolling.

She followed with, "I think I need to go and have a talk with myself."

We all wallowed about a bit more, climbing to our feet one by one. Each of us was totally exhausted. Our clothes were still soaking wet with the silicone slime from the beast.

Reggie, wobbling to his feet, trying to wipe the slime from his face, laughed, "And it just keeps getting better." Reggie flung his rod at a four-foot worm, with razor sharp teeth. It and several of its brethren had caught a hold of and clung onto the rock that we rode up. Out of their element and on dry land, they were squirming about like fish out of water and they were snapping blindly trying to devour anything their teeth might snag. These were the smaller of the creatures we saw swimming about beneath the surface of the molten flow. Reggie's spear drove through one of the creatures and pinned it to the ground like a butterfly to a display case. Pulling his weapon from the now still killer, his laugh dissipated as he sighed, "So, now what? You know what, don't even answer that."

Kim, after shocking another of the squirming ill-behaved biters, gave Reggie a look that seemed to ask, "Why are you giving all of this attitude?"

Reggie called out to a pacing Akina, "Akina, are you sure you know where we're going?" It was clear that Reggie was having some severe doubts about Akina's competency. The rest of us may have been having similar thoughts, but we were still on the team emotionally.

Reggie, ignoring Kim, looked around, panning the horizon. It was darker now, than when we'd all dove in after Sandy. "You know we are in a very bad place here. Maybe we need to rethink this whole thing." We all shrugged our shoulders, looking to each other for direction. Reggie said to us en masse, "Has it occurred to any of you that if you're following someone who knows the future, that that person might be inclined to simply follow the dotted lines just to make sure things happen the way she's seen them? Maybe she feels compelled to see her vision of the future come to be, good or bad. But what if she is wrong? Maybe there is not just one future. We follow her through this place like she's God. But she is not. You don't need Carla's gift to see that she's confused. Wake up guys, we should all be dead right now. Do you know where we just were? Where we are?" Reggie took an uppercut golf-like swing at the last worm with his rod, which happened to stick its head up. He sent its head flying a good fifty feet.

Reggie moved towards Akina, to press his accusations, but Akina's bodyguards stepped between them. Reggie laughed again, "And who are these fools? Akina, what's up with this?" Now angry, he stated to the four remaining protectors, "If any of you ever steps in front of me like this again as though you think you're gonna do something to me, I will do to you what I just did to those worms. Do you understand me?" The bodyguards didn't flinch or blink, but we did.

Darnell, trying to mediate things a bit, offered, "Well, maybe since she knows the future, she knows that we'll all make it through all of this."

We all looked at Akina expecting her to confirm Darnell's conclusion, but she was silent.

Reggie raised his voice a bit and asked out loud. "So, do we all make it through this alive?"

Akina looked down and away, but still said nothing.

Reggie, now looking away from her, said more softly, "Do any of us make it home alive?"

Akina, stepped through her guards and looking at the group of us, answered with a soft, "Yes."

We all stood silent for a moment amidst the scattered bones, distant howling, plumes of smoke and fire. In our own silence we could hear the creatures cry to each other. Most of the growls were from beasts we'd not even seen as yet. Danger all around us, but we were all silent. None of us wanted to ask the question, the question that most hearing those words would have asked. We were silent.

In hindsight it occurred to me that each of us realized to some degree that it didn't matter. None of us wanted to know. If we knew we were one of the one's to die, would we fight any less hard? Or if it were not us, would we give up or fight any less for those who were destined to die here? Our futures were bound together, as we always knew, and this little piece of information wasn't going to change that.

Amazingly, our little tag-a-long trio of Nihil, Shamus and Dread were nowhere to be seen. This would have seemed the perfect time for them to fan the flames between us.

Finally Akina offered, "I guess you're asking yourselves why I would bring us here if I knew that not all of us would make it home? But you don't understand this place, here is there. I don't know that I can explain in a way that you can understand it now. If you cannot understand space and time, how can you truly know Heaven or Hell? Understanding God's will is something that cannot be understood by one's head, but rather by one's heart and soul. Even the language of Heaven is so far removed from what we now understand language to be, that I cannot hope to explain these things to you."

Of course, Sandy was ready to offer words of encouragement. "Well, we just have to look..." She stopped mid-sentence. Raising her left hand and pointing out beyond Akina, she spoke loudly, "Look!"

Behind Akina, in the distance, there was a relatively small plateau. But from the top of it came a glow that shone like nothing else in this place. Its glow was different, and it had taken the darkness descending for us to see it. Somehow each of us knew that this was the place we were looking for in our journey. We weren't supposed to reach this place for days, but nonetheless, there we were. Somehow our most recent peril had brought us closer to our goal. With hardly another thought, each of us ran to grab his or her backpack and joined up again before scurrying off as fast as we could, collectively, towards the glow.

As we got closer, we could make out more and more detail. It became clear that the glow was emanating from two sources atop the plateau. Within a hundred yards we could see a tall, upright figure. The second glow was lower and broader behind the glowing figure in the foreground. As we got closer still, one by one we began to run. Sandy and I pretty much brought up the rear. When we reached the foot of the plateau, we stopped and pressed through our kin folks and Akina's guard to get a better look.

It was the most glorious thing I'd ever seen. Standing in front was an enormous angel. His bronze skin radiated like the sun low in the sky, and his wings were so bright that I could barely look at them. The wings themselves shone like the sun at midday. He held a sword in his right hand, the tip of which stabbed the ground just beyond his left foot. He had to be thirty or forty feet tall. In the glory behind him I could see three persons seated on the ground, campfire style. I moved to the right just a bit to get a better view. There behind the angel they sat, Aunt Deborah, Aunt Ruth, and my mother, Sarah.

I fell to my knees, "Oh my, oh my.." I kept repeating, as I began to weep. My cousins began to climb up the plateau. Darnell reached down and grabbed me beneath my armpit to lift me up. All this time a part of me had the feeling that my mother was dead. I couldn't remember a funeral, wake or any specific grieving, but yet I had been grieving all this time. How long, I couldn't say.

As we approached the top of the slope, the angel smiled, stretched out his arms and spoke in a baritone that reverberated as though we were in the halls of Heaven, "Welcome."

16: I Stand Accused (Accusation)

Rest. To some it's a reality, for others a myth or worse still, a delusion.

Karun and Jonah stopped running about half a mile from the museum, but their hearts and minds raced on beyond them. Their bodies seemed ready to give up their respective spirits. The coldness of the air documented each time their spirit appeared ready to depart their fleshly host, but each breath in was a new covenant with life. It was a covenant to carry on with life until the last breath.

It was around 9:00PM, so their doings, while not unnoticed, were hardly responded to by the locals. As in many big cities, even Blue cities, most of the populace preferred not to get involved. Besides, the violence sensors would have gone off if their running and now heavy panting had any nefarious connotation.

Blocks away from the scene of their first-ever breaking and entering, Karun and Jonah were oblivious to the handful of individuals milling about. Both of them, hands on knees, glanced back in the general direction of the museum. Seeing nothing, they both smiled. The alarms of the museum didn't sound loud enough to really be heard past its grounds. The purpose of the alarm was not to alarm the residents living in close proximity to the facilities, but rather to ensure that all of the onsite security staff, regardless of their preoccupation, was rallied to the cause of said alarm.

In that moment Jonah looked up to Karun and grinned, "Thank you, my friend."

"It was my pleasure, my friend," Karun laughed back.

Jonah took Karun by the shoulder and led the two of them into an archway of one of the restaurants that lined the street. It was one of those places where they keep a copy of the menu behind a glass case. Facing the case they pulled their newfound prize from inside Jonah's coat. Shielding it with their backs, the two of them gazed upon that challis again. It began to glow again in Jonah's hands, but not as brightly as before. Still it was bright enough to draw attention on a dark night. Jonah had begun to slip it back into his large inside pocket, when Karun asked to see it. "Here, let me hold it," Karun whispered.

But in his hands the Heart did not glow and remained dark. He frowned at this a bit. Jonah tried to comfort him, "I guess it knows that I'm family."

"How does it know? Maybe we are missing something. Let me hold it like you did."

Jonah passed the object back to Karun. He turned and gripped the Heart every kind of way but it would not respond to him. Jonah put both hands together with his palms up for Karun to return the heirloom back to him. Karun gently placed the newfound toy into Jonah's outstretched hands, and again it glowed. "See?" Jonah said with as much compassion as he could. Thankfully, in that age many personal devices were illuminated, so their glowing treasure brought no more attention than anyone else's.

Karun then went on to the obvious, "So what does it do?"

Jonah took a deep breath before stumbling out an answer. "Well, we know it's a great way to get out of a jam. Besides that, I don't know. I feel with all my heart that this is the key to something big."

Karun laughed, "Oh, I can believe that."

Jonah, tucking the Heart into his inner pocket of his black trench coat, agreed. "But we need to get back to my workshop in your basement before we do anything else with it."

The truth of the matter was that the Heart represented to Jonah hope of a better day, a better day somewhere else.

The two of them returned to the shop just a hair after ten to see the lights still on inside. Karun turned his head in puzzlement. Jonah asked, "Is Manisha doing inventory tonight?"

"No, not tonight," Karun replied as he reached for his key to unlock the door.

Karun inserted the key and turned the knob allowing the door to swing open. There in the glow of the evening were Manisha and Monica sitting at a small table next to the register. Their faces were flushed and their eyes teary, but their smiles were uncontainable. The two of them stood up holding hands and holding each other closely. As the door swung closed behind the guys, Monica announced, "Manisha gave her life to Christ tonight!"

"Oh, wow... that's great," a stunned and almost speechless Jonah replied as he made his way over to the women, shifting his body to the side to reach down to hug the much shorter Manisha. He glanced back at Karun, "Are you okay with this dude?"

Karun dropping his bag, laughed, "How can I not be? My wife has chosen a path for her life. She was Hindu in name only. All the talk in this shop about what the Blue's are doing to our religion and I am the only one who goes to temple. Now, my wife cares about something. I say hooray."

The four of them wrapped their arms around each other and shared a group hug. They spoke about the things they would do together in this new life of hers. They speculated on how her parents would react back in India. Manisha made a little inside joke that only she, Karun and Monica, being half Indian, understood (the three of them spoke the same dialect). Monica told Jonah, that she'd explain it to him later.

After their laughter had died down, Jonah looked at Karun, and Karun nodded back. Then Jonah addressed the two ladies "Hey, we have some news too. We found that family heirloom that I've been talking about."

Monica replied, puzzled, "You already told me you found it. It's down at the museum. Right?"

"Let me rephrase that," Jonah started again, "We have it."

Manisha jumped in, "You have it, as in you have it here?"

Jonah gave a slight nod. But before he could open his mouth, Monica barked out quickly, "You mean, you stole it! Oh Lord, my husband is a thief!"

Karun tried to defend his friend "Stole is such a strong word. Can't we find a better word?"

The two women just looked at him. Karun took a step back. Then Monica continued, "So, do you even know what it is supposed to do?"

"Well, no not yet. Not everything," Jonah confessed.

"So, you broke into the museum to steal this thing and you don't even know what it's supposed to do? And now that you have it, you still don't know?" Monica asked.

Jonah tried to recompose himself. "Well, I think I kind of know one thing it does, but I intend to stay up tonight and find out more about it."

Karun dared to open his mouth again. "Me too..." he eked out before the stares froze him again.

Monica returned her gaze to Jonah. "I can't believe this! So, why do you need to stay up tonight to see what it does? Are you planning on returning it in the morning?"

Without thinking, Jonah blurted out, "Well, I sent a message to Vicki to stop by and I wanted to be ready just in case she comes tomorrow."

"Vicki!" the two women said in chorus.

Monica put one hand on her hip and motioned towards her friend with the other, "Girl, I got this."

Manisha quipped back, "Well, just let me know."

Karun took another step back.

With her free hand Monica began pointing at Jonah, "Why are you calling Vicki out here? You don't even know what

that thing does, if anything. Plus, Vicki would be the last person I'd call if I'd just stole something, considering she's likely
got the Blues on her tail too. And..."

Jonah interrupted, "Can we go back to that first point you
made? You were going kind of fast. I do know one thing it will
do." He reached into his coat pocket and pulled out the object.
Immediately, it began to glow.

Still cynical, Monica sniped, "So, it glows. Is that it?"

Then before she could say anything else, a second Jonah
stood beside her, just to the left of the first Jonah. Then the
first Jonah focused in on the Heart and faded from sight.

Manisha said in an almost rhetorical manner, "What just
happened here?"

The second, new Jonah spoke. "See, it does seem to allow
for some degree of time travel. When I hold it I cannot only
move forwards and backwards across this floor, but I can also
see through time and walk through it just as easily as I can
walk through this room."

At last the ladies were silent. All four of them stood there
in silence for a good five seconds. Then Monica said quietly,
"Do that again."

It wasn't long after that that Karun and Jonah headed
downstairs to do some more scientific tests. They worked
through the night. The ladies for the most part stayed upstairs. They took turns checking in on the guys, offering and
bringing them coffee when requested.

Jonah and Karun documented and theorized about how
the device worked, while the women talked about and theorized about just what these men of theirs intended to do with
their new toy.

As the morning approached, all four were still awake.
Monica called her job to let them know that she wouldn't be
in today. Her employers were non-believers, so her many
"church activities" put her in regular conflict with them. On

more than one occasion they'd threatened to find someone else who was more appreciative of the job and willing to work late four days out of five. Now the way Monica figured, she already did that. It's just that the days she had to leave on time, didn't always jive with what her employers would have liked, although it could have been worse for both sides. Monica was introduced to her employers (an older couple) through their son, the "hook-up man", Rusty. This was the same Rusty that Karun and Jonah had met to pass word to Vicki to meet them. The couple knew that Rusty was involved in some not so legal things. And perhaps more importantly, they knew that Monica knew it too. That gave Monica a leeway that she never asked for and never knowingly took advantage of. In fact, what Monica's employers didn't know was that she would never turn them in like that... even if they fired her. However, they weren't the most trusting pair so their mind-sets were frozen in that way. As for Monica's religious activities, the old couple was hardly in favor of it. Their biggest concern was what would happen to the two of them if someone found out. But then again, when your son is the "hook-up man", what can you do, especially when your home and office have profited so much from that fact?

This morning, Monica's thoughts were far from her grumpy taskmasters. While she talked the night away with her friend Manisha, she thought about how being here gave her life meaning. While Karun and her husband worked the night away in the lab, she thought about how happy she was with her life. She was married to a good man who loved her. Sure, he wanted to be in a good place to raise children, but beyond that there was no real reason to leave. Plus, she remembered what the doctors had told her about her having children although she'd never really accepted what they'd said. On the one hand, leaving made sense, but her heart was divided. She couldn't see how moving to the Circle could make their lives any better where it counted.

At 6:50am sharp, ten minutes before opening, a knock came from the front door. Both Manisha and Monica had dozed off a bit, and were a little startled by the sound. Manisha got up and sauntered over to the locked doors. Looking through the blinds, she dropped her head and then gave a knowing look back to Monica before she turned the lock. Pulling the door open she gave as cheerful a "Good morning," as she could muster for Vicki.

Vicki, for her part and to her credit, replied likewise. Stepping past Manisha, Vicki unwrapped her scarf and ruffled her hair. "Good morning, Monica."

The three of them were clearly and absolutely aware of how they felt about each other, but did not speak it. Each longed to tell the thoughts of her mind and heart, but said nothing. From the first crack of the door each of them had realized that this would not be the day. Today was a day of civility they all agreed in silence.

Vicki took two more steps toward Monica. She gave out a polite, "So, how have you been?"

It was after she took those two steps that Monica noticed to her amazement that Vicki had on makeup. Additionally, as Vicki slid her coat off, gone were the jeans she always wore. In their place was a nice skirt and blouse. The only thing about her outfit that seemed in place were the high water boots. Stunned for a second, Monica failed to reply right away to Vicki's question. So Vicki bent down just a bit to regain eye contact with Monica. "Monica?" Vicki called, with a slight smile.

Monica stood back, placing her hands on her hips. "So, this is undercover wear today?" She flashed a glance at her girl Manisha, who was just as incredulous over the attire.

As Vicki rolled up her scarf to put it in her coat pocket, she answered back, "You'd be surprised."

As Monica was about to answer, Karun and Jonah burst into the room from downstairs.

"Hi, Vicki! You made it," Jonah nearly shouted. "Have we got something to show you!"

Karun added, "Yeah, this will blow you away!"

Both of the gentlemen caught up in the moment but not completely insane, acknowledged their wives and gave Vicki a quick hug. Karun grabbed Vicki's arm and pulled her towards the stairwell. "Come, let us show you." The three of them disappeared down the steps.

Monica and Manisha gave each other another look. Monica could be quiet no longer. "Did you see that?"

Manisha called back, "Dressed like she's going on a date."

Monica, still reliving the moment, asked again, "Did you see the makeup she had on?"

Manisha snapped back, "How could I not? She had enough of it on. Lipstick yes, and even eyeliner. Vicki never wears eyeliner."

Monica had begun to walk to the stairs, when Manisha took her arm. "Hey, hold up. Let's freshen up a bit."

Monica stopped a second to look at her reflection in the storefront window. To herself she looked every bit of someone who had stayed up all night. She wanted to cry, which made her eyes all the puffier.

Manisha grabbed her friend by the hand and led her to the ladies room. "Come, I have some things here that you can try."

Monica released a "Thanks," to Manisha as the two of them walked off.

Down below in the workroom, Karun and Jonah went through a series of demonstrations for Vicki. Always the skeptic, except when it came to Jonah, Vicki found all of this almost too fantastic to believe... even coming from Jonah. It wasn't so much that she didn't trust her own eyes, it was more a case that there had to be some other explanation for what she was seeing. Then Jonah went on to explain how essentially it also allowed him to walk through walls. It also afforded him the ability to hide objects like his Wave Modulator and the Excavator, slightly out of phase with the reality we all see. But he could see them and retrieve them as easily as any of us might pick them up off of a kitchen counter. Vicki was aghast at the thought on top of what she'd already seen and been told. It also crossed her mind that this was so fantastic, that no matter how she spun her story about Monica being a security risk, the elders were likely to ignore it to get this prize. Of course she didn't want Jonah to know this. Her plan was still to get him to come north leaving Monica behind. She had every confidence that if she could get him alone, away from Monica, that she could turn him to seeing things her way. Vicki reached out for the Heart asking, "Let me try."

Jonah handed it over to her. Like Karun before her, Vicki turned the Heart every kind of way but she saw and felt nothing.

Jonah informed her, "It only seems to work for me. Sorry. I'm sure there may be others, but I would think that maybe they'd have to be family members. I don't know."

All three of them turned to see Manisha and Monica coming down the stairs and into the room. Manisha was smiling at how well and rapidly she'd applied her skill of makeup application to her newfound canvas. Monica for her part, smiled brightly as she entered the room. She strolled across the room, stepping softly, to take her husband's hand. She was sure to sneak a look at Vicki.

Vicki returned Monica's glare with a smile. In an instant she knew how she was going to handle this situation. Handling situations is what Vicki did for a living. She was good at it. But apparently Monica was unaware of this. She'd learn. Vicki shifted her weight and pointed to Jonah and asked, "Hey, can you show me how you walk through stuff?"

"Sure," Jonah said as he uncoupled himself from Monica and stepped back behind his work area partition. Jonah held the Heart aloft before speaking to the group. "I hold this and I can see so much more than what you see. It's like I can see added dimensions." At that, Jonah took a step towards the half wall. Right before he walked into the barrier, his image began to fade, but while he was still visible he reappeared on the other side. "See, what I think happens is that on a molecular level I am out of phase with this reality and somehow that is allowing me to pass between the molecules."

Karun stepped forward, placing his hand on the wall, "Or this wall does not really exist."

The girls laughed before Jonah supported his friend's theory. "Karun is right. It could very well be that we are limited by our own perceptions. What we see, what we can touch, what the very atoms from which we are formed can sense. Remember, atoms are but drops of energy bound arm in arm to form what we see as solid matter. In many ways, all matter really is, is condensed light. Therefore, we in essence and in being are derived from light."

Manisha injected, "Therefore, we are children of light."

Jonah responded, "Yes, countless generation, upon countless generation, but yes we are."

The turn in the conversation offered Vicki an opportunity. She was an engineer by training and for every answer Jonah and Karun gave, Vicki posed another question. She did this to restrict the conversation to just the three of them. They launched into a theoretical debate that was far beyond the two women who'd been up all night. Manisha had a bachelor's degree in Business, but Monica never finished college. It was Vicki's intention to remind her of that.

Manisha managed to get in a witty comment that gave four of the five a chuckle. It was obvious that Monica didn't get it. Moment by moment it was obvious to Jonah that his wife was feeling more and more left out. Seeing this, Jonah attempted to conclude the line of discussion with, "Let's move on. Bottom line, time is relative and we see it here, just as Einstein said."

Monica replied to this with a question, "Was he one of your professors at school?"

Vicki was quick to respond in a patronizing tone that sounded sympathetic, but was really condemning. "I guess you'd say he's a scientist from back in the day." She said this as though she was going to explain, but to do so was pointless.

Despite Monica's limited Blue education, Karun was astonished that she did not know who Einstein was. He couldn't contain himself. "You've never heard of Einstein?"

Monica shook her head, paused for a moment and then turned to walk out of the room. Manisha defended her friend, "You know they don't teach about Einstein in the Blue schools." Manisha took off after her friend.

Concerned about his wife, Jonah started to follow them, when Vicki grabbed a hold of his arm. "Hey, just one more thing and I'll let you go. If I'm going to show this to the Circle elders, I am going to need you to demonstrate it on me. Do me like you did Karun. Take me through a wall. Not this partition, but a wall."

Jonah thought for a moment and then agreed. "Yes, I will, but I need to go upstairs for a second." As he reached the stairs, something hit him. It was a sense of loss. It was as if he already knew he'd lost something. He began to leap up the stairs. Reaching the top, he threw open the door to an empty showroom.   Jonah stood there for a moment then walked softly towards the ladies room. Before he reached it, the front door of the store flew open and in walked Manisha. A confused Jonah asked, "Where's Monica?"

"She left. Went to work," Manisha stated curtly.

"I thought she called in sick today?" a stupefied Jonah replied.

"She did." The frustration was now obvious in Manisha's voice.

"I messed up, didn't I?" Jonah conceded.

Manisha just looked at him, but said nothing.

Jonah adjusted himself and stumbled back down the stairs.

Back downstairs Karun greeted him with a questioning look. "Where's Monica?"

Jonah answered concisely and without elaboration, "She went to work?"

Karun offered a, "But..."

"I know." Jonah cut him off with a look that said, "We'll talk about it later."

Vicki fought back a smile, and tilted her head in faux puzzlement. Then, letting the moment go to get on with her agenda, she grabbed her overcoat. "Jonah, I need you to perform one more test for me before I go. If you can do this, I'm sure it will win you points with the elders of the Circle. I want you to teleport us through these walls to the sewers on the other side." Now Vicki wasn't crazy about going into the sewers with her new outfit on. Even with her waterproof knee high boots and matching trench coat, the smell was still going to soak through her protection. However, that was one of the advantages of being a "Secret Agent"; you never have to worry about anyone questioning your expense account. And given the prize she had found this day, she could have purchased a thousand suits and no one would have questioned her. Plus, when you consider her main objective to get into the mix between Jonah and Monica was accomplished without flaw, it was certainly an investment well spent... in her eyes.

Jonah slipped on his goulashes as Vicki slid on her boots. Rising up, Jonah helped Vicki put on her coat as Karun began straightening up the foyer where items needing repair were left for Jonah and where he placed them once they were fixed. Jonah and Vicki stepped past him into the hallway. At the end of the hall was the large steel door that led to the sewer. Behind them were the stairwell, the shop room entrance and the basement restroom. Jonah took Vicki's hand, "Now you have to hold my hand and close your eyes for this to work. I don't know why, but it seems as though we have to be on one accord for this to work, and when the transported person, you in this case, has his or her eyes open I can't move them."

Vicki gave a "huh?" like she didn't understand, then laughed, "I know. Let's just go. All this theorizing is making my head hurt."

Facing the door and holding aloft the Heart in one hand and Vicki in the other, Jonah stared straight ahead as he saw the heavens open up again. He pulled at Vicki but began to see her fade. "Vicki, close your eyes."

When she did, she felt them moving. She didn't dare open her eyes given that she knew that Jonah hadn't done this enough to say definitively what would happen if she opened them while they were "going through."

Approximately seven seconds later, she heard the comfort of Jonah saying, "You can open your eyes now." But even before that she'd sensed the slow moving water around her feet.

There they were, the two of them standing in the sewer just outside the huge metal door. Vicki nodded her head like she was at a jazz concert and vibing on the flow. "Fantastic!" she said in all honesty, "Very cool." Working in technology she'd seen many wonderful things, but never anything like this. Then, catching herself in the middle of her excitement, she reminded herself to stay on point, to remain on message. She reached out both hands grabbing both of Jonah's arms. "This is great, and I will contact my handler right away so that he can contact the elders. But I have to be real with you about getting both you and your wife out of here. For the elders to react this way about her there must be something else about Monica that the two of us don't know, or at least not me. Is there anything you can think of?"

Jonah shook his head.

Noting that, Vicki continued on, "Well, maybe you should ask her. I know she went to a Blue school and joined that paramilitary group."

"That was like the Girl Scouts," Jonah injected.

"I know that, but all the folks up in the Circle know is that these organizations are breeding grounds for their army and politicos. Still, with all that you bring to the table, even before this, you should have been issued a visa, no questions asked. Something is up, but no one is telling me, so you need to check it out. Maybe it's an issue that I can help with."

Jonah gave a defeated, "Okay." It nearly broke Vicki's heart to hear him so sad and to dash the exhilaration he'd felt just moments before. But she felt she had to do it for his own good.

She pulled him close and squeezed him tight. "It's going to be okay. I promise. I have to go now, but just hang in there." As he realized that she was departing, Jonah hugged and squeezed her back. Then in the moment that they were clinched she gave him a lingering kiss on the cheek before whispering "bye..." into his ear.

Vicki turned to walk away, glancing back only once. She knew he'd still be looking. And he was. But after that one look she marched on. She could hardly believe she'd managed to pull off such a coup. Jonah would in effect, snoop out any other secrets in Monica's past and pass that information onto her. She'd played them both perfectly. She should have been ecstatic, and on a certain level, she was. But doubts, which can be deadly in her line of work, haunted her in regards to her plan. She'd not thought about the sadness this whole process might cause her beloved Jonah. Nor was she particularly happy about causing Monica pain. Sure she was a liar, who'd roped her best friend into marriage under false pretenses but the thing about her being a Blue sympathizer was pretty much a crock and Vicki knew it. Perhaps in her mind, Vicki was like an arresting officer who feels that she has to plant evidence to ensure a conviction. Vicki was convinced that Monica was unworthy, and it was her job to show that to Jonah. She reasoned to herself that sometimes the truth can be painful and this was just one of those cases.

17: All Things Considered...

"...Mama." Alone this word stood. I didn't say it so much as breathed it. Again that primal thing within me pushed past my conscious thought and called out "Mama!" a second time.

It was then that I noticed a hand on my shoulder. It was not Darnell this time, but the angel. At first, I was startled but then he opened his mouth to reveal a tongue of flame. It burned red in his mouth. "They cannot hear you. Your mother is deep in spiritual warfare."

At his words, I stood straight up and tried to take in just what was going on. There behind the angel, on the ground, sat my mother, my Aunt Deborah and Aunt Ruth in a circle. My mother, Sarah, glowed with such a golden shine that she shone like the sun. But Aunt Deborah, Carla and Darnell's mother, sat in shadow. Her continence was so much of darkness that she actually seemed to soak up light from her sisters. Aunt Ruth glowed as well, but her light flickered like a candle in a breeze.

One by one, within two seconds of each other, we all turned back to the angel as though we all knew that he was about to speak. "As you can see, your Aunt Deborah is the one who has fallen. Your aunts, Sarah and Ruth, have risked their own lives to save her. After your Aunt Cil died, Deborah gave into the temptations that Cil had always steered her away from. Cil ruled her with the firm hand she needed. Now there is no one that can tell her what to do. That's too bad. The gift she was given, like all power given to mortals, attracts wicked spirits. Who can practice witchcraft without being a witch? Her sisters are willing to give their all to save her, but she is like a black hole, literally sucking the life out of them. Still, Sarah is strong. The light flows from her, but the well within her is deep and it provides. The faith within her is stronger than Deborah's weaknesses. Behold your Aunt Ruth and how her light faints. She has grown weary and is now herself in danger of succumbing to evil. You have come at a most interesting time."

Before my very eyes I saw my mother open her eyes and turn her head towards Aunt Ruth. Her mouth began to move as she spoke towards Aunt Ruth. We could not hear the words, but we could tell that she said, "Ruth." A second later Aunt Ruth opened her eyes and the two of them conversed. We didn't know all of what was said, but it didn't take long before, to our amazement, Aunt Ruth stood up! Her eyes locked onto my mother's eyes. Standing there, with her chin up and illuminated by the light coming from my mother and the angel, we could see the tears streaming down her face. Aunt Ruth was a tenderhearted woman, so seeing her cry was not unusual, but it was always heartbreaking. These circumstances made it even worse. She never had children of her own, but she loved and accepted all of us. Each of us standing there could remember some kindness she'd shown us. She was always foolish in love and her sisters decried her lack of discernment. Every man she ever loved broke her heart, but not once did she pick up her hand in vengeance, as she could have. In this way she was a lot like Sandy, but in other, meaningful ways she was not. For example, a telemarketer might call Sandy and she might listen and be polite, but in the final analysis, she'd say goodbye and that would be the end of it. However, Aunt Ruth was a pigeon for everyone. She never quite grasped why anyone would lie to her. Her biggest weakness was infomercials.

We watched as she spoke and my mother smiled back at her. She glanced once at Aunt Deborah. Then she seemed to take a breath, before turning and slowly walking away.

The angel spoke again. "Your Aunt Ruth feels like she has failed, but she has not. Perhaps she cannot see where she has helped Deborah and feels like she has abandoned Sarah. But the truth is that Deborah will in days to come remember Ruth's presence and kindness. And Ruth fails to see the comfort she gave to Sarah. The light she shared gave strength not only to Deborah but also to Sarah. The well of light in Sarah overflows, in part, because of the love that Ruth has for her. Everyday Sarah sees Ruth as God sees her, and that blesses Sarah as well."

Reggie, who was the child of our recently departed Aunt Cil, asked, "Where did Aunt Ruth go?"

"Your question is difficult to answer in a way that you might understand due to the fact that you are still bound by space and time. What I will say is this. As you see the world she has moved on emotionally, meaning that she has let this thing go. What you do not know is that Ruth, in trying to win her sister back, began to attend the coven to which Deborah belonged. In fact, in one discussion she tried to persuade Sarah to attend with her so that she too could better understand Deborah. It was then that Sarah realized that Ruth needed to back away. Ruth's willingness to do that which she shouldn't to gain Deborah's favor was not out of love, but weakness and dependency. Ruth was willing to do anything for her sister's love, but Sarah would give everything to save her sister. In fact, Sarah believes there is no greater service than to give one's life for those you love. And do not be fooled. Those with whom Deborah now affiliates want this consequence very much." The angel stretched out his hand to the darkness around. Following his hand we could see the creatures of the night prowling in every direction. For the first time I noticed that while Akina walked around the circle, her protectors from history were huddled together just on the edge of the plateau. Puzzled, I looked at the angel and he smiled as though he knew something that I did not.

Sandy, on the verge of tears, cleared her throat and began to speak, "Is she..."

The angel cut her off, "No, you do not understand. Sarah is alive and as you would see it, up and doing things. But you see her here as one in quiet meditation, because she is in a constant state of prayer. Her soul is continually bowed in humble prayer." I was a bit perplexed as to why Sandy would be asking that about my mother Sarah, rather than Aunt Deborah. Deborah was the one cloaked in darkness. And what little we could make out of her features were ghastly. Her flesh appeared and faded, showing her skeleton beneath. But beyond and worse than that, we got glimpses of something else within her. It had the face of a demon. I could see that this infection was like blight or mildew on a rose bush. The dark patches of the demon would show themselves at various places on her body and face but in the next instant they'd be gone again.

In spite of this, Sandy, pleased and now more relaxed and clearly focusing on my mother, looked again at the angel. And he, knowing the question in her mind, replied, "My name is Caleb."

Aunt Deborah was a scary figure to me. Even before all of this, I was always a little leery of her. Up until then I thought it was because I found her shrill or loud or something like that. But was it because I'd always known that this was in her or would be someday? Carla knelt down beside her mother and Darnell joined her on the ground on the other side of their mother. Carla looked up to Heaven and began to pray. "Lord, show me what I must do." Carla looked at her mother and began to weep. In a moment her weeping turned to wailing as she prayed on, "There can be no happiness for me, no good outcome, to see my mother like this. Lord, is there something that I have done? Did I drive her away? Was I not there when she needed me? Was I selfish? I know that I was. Was I blind? I know that I am. How can this be? How can I help my mother? Just tell me and I will do it. Just tell me how, Lord?" In her despair, she reached out for her mother. But the image we saw was just a shade and Carla fell through the image to lay prone in the dirt below. There she wallowed in the dust crying, "Mama, mama." Darnell scampered over to her side and pulled her up into his arms. Together they sat on the ground. She continued to cry and whimper as Darnell tried to rock her to peace. I noticed tears on my own face, which had abated, flowing anew, though slowly like melting snow in March.

Kim, who had actually attempted to follow Aunt Ruth when she departed (she faded into the mist), turned to the angel. He gave a look of compassion to her, "I'm sorry I can't answer that for you. Your time to know this will come. But I can relay this one message today. Look beyond. Look down there where you traveled. See those wisps and flutters of light. They are your brothers and sisters. You surmised correctly when you concluded that many of those chained down and slowly being dragged below are those who suffer addiction who are not in recovery. Many of their spirits are already tied and bound for Hell. Although they are living, their spirits are of the dead. They feel they have no hope. But now, look over there. Your spiritual siblings circle around a central spirit. I will tell you that the spirit in the middle belongs to someone with Down syndrome. Can you see that where they are is brighter than that which surrounds them? I cannot answer your question or quell your anger; I can only show you this. I am not the One."

Looking into the distance again, I began to see things that I had not before. I could see three or four winged lights in the distance. I focused again on the foreground and saw that there was a small light present right behind Akina's guardians. It was as if seeing Caleb had opened my eyes. I looked back to Caleb and he smiled, "That is a little prevenient grace." He actually seemed to chuckle.

He allowed me to complete my question, I guess for the benefit of the group at large. "So, why don't we see more of you and why am I seeing you now?"

The angel spread his wings appearing to take in a breath, "If you could see the angels all around you, you would worship them. All these things are true because you cannot comprehend the Master, therefore you cannot perceive Him fully. But He has provided a way for you to feel His presence. As for us, in your waking life you may only hear us, and then only at the Master's direction. If you do see us you are typically unaware that you do. As to why you see me now? He granted it to be. Now, you all have missed something else here. You have seen someone that is just as out of place here as yourselves, but you did not recognize his passing. There are spirits all around you and you see them as wisps. But there was one that you passed through that was not like the rest. He is a traveler like you. Actually, it is ironic; he is searching for you even as you search for your aunts. And no, don't ask who he is. You will know when the time comes."

Finally, Reggie spoke up. "We came here to get our aunts, to take them back. We need them back home. We need their help."

Caleb's brow furrowed. "And you believe they can solve your problem?"

Reggie, looking perplexed, which was unusual for him, scratched his head before answering. "Well, I thought, I think they can help."

"How?" That one word in isolation from Caleb's mouth was deafening.

Reggie became agitated, "How? Surely, you know their gifts. How can they not help? Aunt Deborah, you know what she can do. Aunt Ruth cannot be harmed physically. And Aunt Sarah, oh my, you know how she can bring it! How can you not see this?"

Curtly, Caleb roared back, "How can you not see what is right in front of you? What do you see? Do you not see the importance of this battle? Have you considered what will happen if your Aunt Deborah is not saved? Given what you see, how can they really help you now? Have you considered the value of one soul? What is its worth? What would Heaven do for one soul? Do you know how many demons you have released? How much difference do you think your aunts can make? Have you thought about how your cousin Avis was led astray? Besides her own mother, who cultivated the spirit of mysticism within her, who else played a role in her fall?" The angel's gaze fell on Aunt Deborah. "But, I will tell you this. All three of your aunts now know that you are looking for them. That is a gift unto many mothers, not the least of which, yours."

Reggie rubbed his eyes and asked, "So what you're saying is that we really didn't need to come here. They sensed that we needed them."

"Yes," the angel replied.

Sensing Reggie's eyes and thoughts upon her, Akina asked the angel, "Then it was in the searching, not the finding, that we accomplished our goal?"

"Yes," the angel replied again.

"Will we see them when we get home?" Sandy asked.

"Yes," the angel said a third time.

Sandy walked over to Darnell and Carla. She stretched out her hand to Carla and pulled her up into an embrace. Darnell got up on his own and after dusting himself off, also hugged both his sister and Sandy. Afterwards, the three of them walked over to the rest of us near the angel. Akina's bodyguards were still in a corner of the plateau a ways behind us, almost crouched with the exception of Chin. He was standing from them looking at us.

Walking past Caleb towards us, Carla stopped to inquire one more time. "So, when you say they will be home, does that include my mother?"

Caleb seemed to sigh, "Yes."

Darnell followed, "Will she be healed?"

Caleb said nothing, but just looked straight ahead towards the horizon.

We all gathered around in a circle. Reggie's face had turned hard and so had his voice. "We need to talk," he said to the group.

Akina nodded in agreement. "Yes, we do."

Then, almost startling me again, I heard the angel say, "Down there. Have your discussion down there. You will be safe as long as you remain at the foot of this mound... at least from any physical harm." I don't know if he wanted us to leave the hilltop for our benefit, our aunties', or his own but no one questioned him. We all stepped down the hillside. In plain sight, fifty to a hundred yards out, we could see Nihil, Dread and Shamus sitting on a large rock. And from where we stood, I could just make out the Shaman standing to the left of them. Nihil, in chains, danced upon the top of the rock. I noticed that the chains now not only linked Dread, Nihil and Shamus, but now also the Shaman. All three chains ran to Nihil, the smallest of the three. Seeing this, we all gave a collective grunt and rolling of eyes. Since the Shaman had bailed on us, none of us felt compelled to be too concerned that he was now linked up with these creatures. Whether it was willingly or by force, we didn't much care. His boys glared at him even more fiercely than we did.

Reaching the bottom, Reggie could contain himself no longer. He snapped at Akina, "Just what the... what are we doing here?" Amazingly, being in the presence of a divine being had at least the temporary effect of curing Reggie's tendency to flavor his speech with expletives.

"What?" Akina hollered back.

"You heard the angel. He said we didn't have to come here," Reggie reminded her, not that she needed it.

"And he also said that it was the searching for them that made them aware," Akina shouted back.

Sandy jumped in to make some kind of peace. "Yes, but I think he was saying that we could have sought them in another way and we would still have accomplished our goal."

Reggie, stunned for a second that he and Sandy seemed to be on the same side of an issue, recollected himself to add, "Yeah, that's what I mean."

Then Sandy butted in, "... but all of this is hindsight. None of us was wise enough to know beforehand that we didn't need to come here; that our very searching would have been enough. Given her gift you would have made the same choice."

Kim turned her head, "So, Akina, basically you're just trying to connect the dots. I mean by your jumping around in time you get these snapshots, and you have to fill in the rest."

Akina, now back in her normal tone, answered her. "Yes, that's basically it. See, if you think about it, even when I time travel I still only have one life to live. Even though according to the calendar I'm eighteen, physically I am certain that I am past my nineteenth birthday and then some. So, I may leave the current time and come back a second later, but if I spend a day somewhere else, I've still aged a day. Therefore it would be impossible for me to live through each possible moment to come to get every detail of our lives to come. And it's not like our actions are published in the newspaper either.

Mostly, in short order, I have to piece together clues. In coming here, I knew that we did come here and that the Aunties did subsequently appear. But no, I didn't know all these details. I certainly didn't know that we didn't have to come here to get their attention."

Suddenly, a light went off in Carla's head. "So, you know if my mother will survive what she's going through."

Akina hesitated, "Yes, but I'm not sure if I should tell you."

Carla decried, "Not sure if you should tell? What are you talking about? Tell us!"

"Okay..." Akina began to yield.

"No!" shouted Sandy. "If an angel of the Lord will not say then how can you? And not to be cold, but what difference will it make today, right now? You know that today she is alive and you know that someday she will die. If God says that it is better that we not know now, then who are we to argue? Perhaps there is something to be learned in not knowing everything."

Carla huffed and looked to her brother, but he said nothing. Oddly, Reggie chimed in on Sandy's and the angel's side... I guess. "The way things are going, she'll probably get it wrong. Y'all know I'm not as religious as some, but I just saw something out of my children's Bible telling me it's best that we not know right now. Given where we are and our situation, I'm willing to go with his take on things. Besides, as Sandy said, I don't see how knowing who will be there to greet us when we get back is pertinent to us getting out of here. Do any of you?"

Caleb flapped his wings and we felt a breeze, the first cool one I think we'd felt since being in there. Until then, we'd only felt waves of oppressing heat. It prompted me to ask of the group, "So what now?"

Akina thought for a second and then looking around the group said matter-of-factly, "I think we go home. But we can't go the same way we came. That was a way in. No, that was our way in. For reasons I'm just now beginning to understand, I can't take us all back together. Apparently, an older version of me did, at the very least bring Uncle Paul here, but he had others to call on to take him back. Or maybe it was the fact that he was immortal when he was here. But somehow traveling with others throws my gift off when trying to return from this place. It's like I can't make my walk, their walk. And if I do leave with one of you, there's no telling how much time would pass here before I returned. It might be hours, days or even years. But there is another way. On the far end of the basin there is a portal through which we all can return to our lives as we knew them."

"So, you know the way there?" Reggie asked.

"Yes, it's not hard to find. Not like here. The way out is what provides what little light you see in the dome of the sky."

Kim jumped in again, "But why do I get the feeling that's the easy part?"

"You're right, we'll have to fight every foot of the way," Akina confirmed. "I say we rest up here for the days to come. We'll need it. As Caleb said, we'll be safe here. In the meantime, I need to make a quick trip."

Carla cried out, "A trip to where? You're going to leave us here? Have you lost your mind? Who are you going to see that can't wait until we get back?"

"Myself," Akina answered softly. "As Chin alluded to, I'm good at seeing other people's future, but not so much with my own. And actually, in case you were wondering, I can't just go visit myself in the future. I've tried and I just can't do it. Maybe that's one reason I'm having so much trouble here.

You know, with it being outside of our time stream. I don't know.

But I do know that I can visit myself in the past all day long. And I think seeing my bodyguards here has shown me a loophole in the whole visiting my future self problem. I can't visit myself in the future, but I can visit my future self in the past. And maybe I can get some answers from that older me. I need to go back in time and meet my future self. Myself, Queen of Egypt, that felt the need to send these men here to protect me. Since she is my future self, she will know the answers to the questions I have. In fact, it is to our mutual benefit that I go. She can help me prepare us for our trip."

Even Reggie couldn't argue with that logic. And since Akina knew that she would survive this adventure, it was pretty safe for her to go anywhere she pleased. As she mentioned to me later, you never know what kind of pain you might encounter in life, but you pretty much know your destination. That's how it was with her.

I looked towards the angel Caleb. Generally speaking, he faced the darkness with his back to the far off glow. But right then, his right arm was raised as he pointed in the direction of the light. That was his answer to the question in all of our minds.

Chin walked away from the others and over to me, "That was amazing!"

But then the other three bodyguards stepped over and almost sheepishly asked, "Can you explain what just happened here?" The tall dark Egyptian asked me, "We saw a light that stood among you, and we heard your voices, but we could not hear anyone speaking back to you. But still you conversed as if there were another person there with you. How is this?" It dawned on me that three of the four remaining protectors of Akina had not seen or heard anything the angel did or said, and likewise regarding our aunts. But before I could inquire further, Akina tapped the Egyptian on his arm. She motioned for him to follow her.

Akina gathered the others and began to speak softly with them, gathering information for her trip, I surmised. Halfway into her conversation Reggie stepped over, interrupting them, "So, if we're supposed to be resting, how is it that you're going to accomplish that while jaunting literally through space and time? You're not Darnell, you do need sleep."

"Cousin," she started, "I understand your concern. But realize that while I am gone days and nights will pass for me, but you will be the same. I will sleep. Besides, I will, if I get it right, be back merely a minute after I leave you, as you see it anyway. And since I know where this place is now and I'm traveling alone, I won't have near the trouble finding my way as before.

Actually, I'd love to take some of these guys from the old world back to where they belong. But they won't go. They say if I bring back my future self's ring of Ra, then they'll know that the me, that is Queen of Egypt, stated that they may return. Plus, it is pretty near impossible to take someone against their will, if they're conscious." She then returned to her conversation with the mini-United Nations. When she finished, she lifted her head to all of us and in a low shout called out, "I'll see y'all in a few minutes." With that, she began to walk off into the distance. With each step her image became a little fainter until within seven steps she was gone. Time is an uncaring and cold master to every mortal save one, Akina. For her it is no more than the shade of a great tree, which she can choose to stand in or step out of.

Reggie leaned over and said into my left ear, "I tell you, being able see the future really can make you cocky. See how she just walked off like she was walking into the store for a carton of milk? But I tell you, she doesn't know as much as she'd like us to believe. It's like she said, she only gets snapshots when she goes back in time. She can tell you the big picture, but she's weak on the details. That's why she's going to see her future self. She doesn't know exactly how things are going to play out here. She's here taking a test she hasn't studied for, so now she wants to go back and look at the study guide. But who's to say that older Akina won't be any less arrogant and uptight with young Akina, as young Akina is with us?"

I didn't really want to hear most of that, but that last part did raise an interesting question. Would Akina, Queen of Egypt, be willing to share anything of value? Or perhaps a greater question still, who is to say that this future Akina is benevolent? How do we know that she still has love for us? If Uncle Paul and Aunt Deborah went bad, why not Akina? Okay, maybe Aunt Deborah had issues from day one, but what about Uncle Paul? He was some kind of hero that fell like Icarus from the sky. If the day can set Uncle Paul ablaze, what hope do any of us have?

Looking at my cousins, my thoughts began to drift back about a year and a half before. It was the reception right after Aunt Cil's funeral. We'd all convened at Aunt Cil's house for dinner. Black-draped and solemn, member after member of our family stepped over to Reggie to offer their condolences. He bore it all quite well, all things considered. It was hard on Kim too. For her, Aunt Cil was the only mother of which she had any clear memory.

Funerals, besides being a time to grieve, can also sometimes be a time of discovery. The passing of a family member seems to free lips frozen by a confederacy of the unwilling and now suddenly and supposedly repentant. There were so many hushed words and glances in my family that even then I knew something was up. Nothing like this of course. No one sane could have imagined something like this. Between older family members coming outside to where we young folks had gathered to share our own pain and laughter, Reggie, Carla, Akina, Sandy, Darnell, Kim and I summed up the bits and pieces of our lives. I knew then that Reggie knew much more than any of the rest of us, and I hoped he would enlighten us, especially one as ignorant as me. But given the conspiracy to keep me totally in the dark about our family, it's obvious why neither Reggie nor anyone else would give up that information.

However, besides not really getting any kind of answers, I found an undercurrent of bitterness brewing between the branches of the family tree.

Carla took this as an opportunity to ask Kim about her sexuality. Carla's gift is very good about seeing one's intent and active desire. But those things that are latent within our subconscious are less clear to her. Actually, it started as a backhanded compliment. Kim had worn a dress in our presence for the first time any of us could remember since maybe the fifth grade. Typically, Kim was skater-girl down. Baggy jeans and a five dollar t-shirt was her outfit of choice. Dressing up was a pair of better fitting jeans and a t-shirt without words on it. Carla made a comment of how nice she looked and asked why she didn't do it more often.

Kim, picking up on the undercurrent of her question, replied "Why don't I do it more often? So, what are you really trying to ask?"

Akina stepped in front of Carla between them. "I think what Carla is trying to say is that the skirt looks really nice on you. I know it's a sad day, but you look so cute."

Carla cut back in front of Akina, "Well no, since she's going to bow up at me and all, let's keep it real. What's the deal with you?"

Keep in mind that all of this was before Carla got "saved", or more correctly "rededicated". She was very much like her mother, Deborah, but seldom so mean-spirited as in that moment. This was also during the time I mentioned earlier as being a period where Darnell felt like he'd lost his sister, "though she still walked the earth," as he'd say. I guess something in Kim's demeanor threatened her position of alpha female in our little group.

Kim shook her head and then glared at Carla. "The deal?"

Carla continued, "Yeah, what's up with the way you dress? You're 16 years old and you're still on this tomboy kick. You're like the only girl in your little posse, but I never see you with a guy, like on a date. You don't roll with the girls. I'm just concerned about you and where you might be headed. You do like boys, don't you?"

Darnell, who had been sitting quietly on the steps jumped up to grab Carla's arm.

Kim, half laughing, half crying, raked back, "You bitch! You God awful bitch." Kim turned and walked away.

But it was too late to still Reggie's ire. He'd been standing slightly apart from us while he puffed on a cigarette and spoke in whispers to Sandy. He stamped out the cigarette and stormed over in Carla's direction. "What is wrong with you? Today you bring this BS into my home?" Normally, Reggie cussed like a sailor, but I guess the weight of the day gave him pause. He looked at Darnell and then at Carla, "You need to worry about your own house. I don't care if your brother is the What Would Jesus Do freak of the week, it ain't natural for an eighteen, nineteen year old man being a virgin and not even trying to do something about it."

Carla shook loose of Darnell and stepped forward pointing back at her brother. "At least he dates. In fact, he has a girlfriend. I don't know what they do. But whatever he does or doesn't do with her, I know it's with a girl. And hey, if Kim's into chicks, cool. Just be upfront about it."

Reggie moved in close towards Carla. Akina and Sandy, one on each bicep, tugged on him in an attempt to restrain him, not that either of them could hold Reggie if he decided to go at Carla. For Carla's part, her brother stepped in front of her, though I know their relationship was very strained at that point. He wouldn't have raised a hand to Reggie, but he wasn't going to just let him take a swing at his sister. Reggie looked towards the house and then at me, before leaning in close. His chin and face peered over and around Darnell's shoulder putting him eye to eye with Carla. He spoke without a hint of doubt in a hushed but strong tongue. "Just because a girl knows how to keep her legs closed, doesn't mean a damn thing's wrong with her. In fact, at 16 it means there's something very right about her. See, I know my life is foul. And so is yours. But instead of looking yourself in the mirror, you'd rather try to drag everyone else down to your level. Even your brother here." Darnell stood between them like the gate to a walled city. Reggie continued, "But if you ever step to Kimberly like that again, I'll make sure you're sorry. I don't care who's around." He stared at Darnell as he straightened up and stepped back.

The event was also odd in that Reggie actually acknowledged some concern for Darnell. I think Reggie loved Darnell, but it was hard to tell sometimes back then. In a way, Reggie was like the bad angel of my teenage years, taking me to clubs and places I wouldn't have ever known about, much less gotten into. Darnell was always trying to get me to go to youth retreats. While I didn't seem to fit into one world, I couldn't see myself in the other one either. Up to that point, Reggie had belittled Darnell's pursuits and made an example of him of what not to be in front of me. But in the struggle over my life, Darnell never spoke ill of Reggie. And I think it was this day, when Darnell stood between him and Carla, that Reggie gained respect for Darnell. Carla's brother was willing to take any blow, suffer any consequence, to spare his sister, even though at that time she was totally out of control and not very loving or loveable. Maybe it was burying his mother that gave Reggie cause to reflect on the properties of Darnell.

Now here, in this unfathomable place called the Pit, Carla sat on a rock braiding Kim's hair. Of all the things I'd seen in this place, perhaps that was the strangest considering the scene at Aunt Cil's funeral almost two years ago. Still, all of us were far from perfect. Issues abounded within and between each of us. Speaking to Kim and Sandy, I heard Carla say "Sometimes it's not what you attract, but what you let in."

Sandy replied, "True, but once you've given your heart, what can you do?"

Then, out of the blue, Carla, the most talented songstress of our group, broke out into an "acapella" version of "Love Changes". And while Akina possessed a very angelic soprano voice, Carla's alto touched something deep inside. Her earthly tones could pluck even the most worn heartstring. And the song she sang took on new meaning for me that day when I thought about love being more than romantic love. I thought about the changes that agape, unconditional love can bring.

Sometime later, Carla, Darnell, Kim and Sandy walked over to us. Reggie asked the group at large, "So, what do y'all think? I mean about our fearless leader?"

Carla glanced over at her brother before answering, which led me to believe they already had this discussion. "Well, I'm not crazy about her taking off like this."

"Me neither," Kim said softly. "It's like she's trying to work out her own demons on our dime. I mean, we all got issues, you know? We all just want to get out of here now. I don't see where her going back in time to find herself, literally, is going to benefit the team one way or the other."

Darnell tried to defend her and mediate a bit. "Well, actually, relative to us, she'll be back soon. But yes, I do get your point. She has been a bit distracted since we got here."

Reggie added, "Yeah, if it was anyone else besides Akina, I would be amazed if they didn't freak out. But something else is going on. I know that she's been seeing that shrink, Dr. Sitgraves. So perhaps she's losing it this time. Maybe all that cool she's always had is about to boil over. I mean the way she was slashing those critters in the open field was almost maniacal."

All of us, except for Sandy, nodded our heads in reluctant agreement. Reggie continued on, "Let's do this then. Let's see how she acts when she gets back from wherever she is now. If she's okay, we'll know just to keep an eye on her. I just wanted to see if y'all saw the same thing I did. Also, we'll need to keep an eye on the old foreign legion over there too. Remember, their charge is to protect Akina, not us. We're expendable as far as they're concerned."

Then, without warning, a bright blaze erupted about twenty feet from us. I cringed, but the others realized that it was just Akina returning. The effect differs sometimes, depending on how far she's traveled. When the glow diminished, Akina forced a smile to us. But there was a distant look of loss in her eyes that her smile could not hide. The mist in her eyes held the tears of centuries gone by. Had there been a breeze it would have blown my dear cousin away. The thoughts in her head and the gifts in her hands would seem a blessing to anyone, but to her they were a curse. I expected her to return to us brimming with accounts of her older self. I hoped she'd tell us about how she got the gold earrings that now dangled from each ear. I thought that maybe she'd tell us some happy news about our fate, even if she made it up. And although she would later share all these things with us, right then our thirst for knowledge was left unquenched. Instead, she composed herself to say loudly to all of us, "It's time. We need to go, now."

As we gathered up our things to head towards the light just over the horizon, I heard cackling, hissing and snorting from just beyond the rocks. It was Nihil and the others in his lot.

18: Rabbits in a Snare

Surely the simplest lies are the slipperiest and perhaps the most perilous. Even in silence and thoughtless moments, lies can cause entire lives to be lost. Even holding one's tongue can be a lie.

Wide-eyed most of the way home, Jonah ran through his mind a dozen times just how he would approach Monica. Surely, he thought, the folks in the Circle had misinterpreted some minute piece of Monica's life. They'd sit down together and figure it out. Jonah could believe nothing else.

He'd left work early and arrived home hoping to hear Monica's standard "Hey, darling." But today he heard nothing. He searched the main room and the hidden room behind the wall and still he heard nothing. He plopped down into a chair at the dining table and thought some more. Jonah's first thought was that his wife had stopped over to Marta's place for a chat. He'd always known that she confided in Manisha, but maybe the events of the afternoon had driven her to seek a second counselor. His main thoughts were on how they were going to get out of this place, but he knew that he'd have to appease and reassure her regarding Vicki's visit. Although something didn't sit right in his own heart, there was no logical reason not to accept Vicki's help. And that tick in his heart regarding Vicki was no different than the temptation most every man felt from time to time. Maybe it was a little different. But surely, every man that has battled lust has said the same thing. No one is free of these feelings, and surely they do not stop the world from turning. Certainly getting Monica to somewhere safer was beyond any neurotic thought of his. Sitting there alone, his thoughts turned to Sara again and the words she said. She'd told him there were sheep to feed here, implying that his longing to be somewhere else may not be a part of God's plan. But again, wasn't it his first responsibility to care for his wife, even at the cost of his own life? But then it occurred to him also, that he was the one wanting to leave this place. His wife went along with his plan to leave, but she'd implied more than once that staying would be acceptable to her. It seemed to him sometimes that she had a bit of a martyr complex.

Jonah sat staring at the worn blue and green dishrags. Their color faded, they seemed less than clean, filthy even, so how might they clean anything he wondered. The kitchen was in order, but still it was a dirty mess to him. And then there was the ever-present smell. He'd run a line into the same drains that supported the road above them, but still the kitchen had a stench to him that he'd grown so very weary of over the years. There had to be more to life than living in what amounted to a hole. A fancy hole, mind you, but still at the end of the day it was a hole. It would be so easy to run away from all of this. He had the means, so what had he been waiting on all these years? Monica's argument had always been, run to where? But he had a "where" now at his fingertips. For a moment, and just a moment, he thought, "You know one way or another, with or without her, I could blow this place." Jonah's eyes focused in on the drapes that hung from the faux window above the sink. Then his eyes and his heart fell to the drawing behind the drapes. It was a rendition of the sun that he and Monica had drawn together to brighten up their kitchen. And in the windowsill was an anniversary card Monica had given him. Jonah stood to pick up the card. Like always, the card opened with the date in the upper left corner. Monica dated all the cards she'd given him. Reading the card gave him pause to consider the blessing Monica was to him and how all he had, his wife, his skills, his very life were all a gift and not truly his at all.

An hour passed and still he sat, contemplating life, the state of dishrags and how every one of us is soiled just like these rags and yet we can still be used to remove the stains of this world, if we allow ourselves to be used to do so. Jonah also thought about Sara and how she'd admonished him about running from the work to be done right here among the Blue. It was a nice theory he thought. In the Bible, Paul and Silas had witnessed to the very guards that held them captive, while they awaited their own deaths. But Jonah thought the Blues were not just ignorant. They know the Truth and they've rejected it. And Jonah reasoned that if his own life was like anyone's in the Bible, it was Job. Although he knew he'd not lost nearly as much, certainly he'd made a good start in that direction. One brother was most certainly dead. The other made his way for the Circle, but none of Jonah's sources had any knowledge of him there. And his sister, who'd moved to China right when things got shaky, was now a member of the Chinese space program. As a doctor on one of their Star Liners, supporting the creation of "Jump Points" in far and distant worlds, she spent most of her days traveling at near the speed of light. Jonah's life lasted little more than the time it would take his sister to eat dinner. By the time she returned to earth, if she ever did, Jonah's bones would be dust. And not that Jonah was big on material things, but he'd lost his home, his savings, his transportation, his job, his career, his security and at times it seemed his hope for ever having any of these things again. All that remained from before were Monica, Vicki and Heru.

He thought about the prisoners he'd freed with Sara. There was quiet Pam, joyous Jared, and nervous Bruce. And quite honestly, Bruce made him nervous too. He'd shown up at his job for Heaven's sake.

And then there was Dave, the son of a high Blue official. He'd just joined the group at large. He was full of fire, but also seemed to be the last person the group should trust. But few things in Jonah's life had occurred without reason. And his spirit told him that meeting Dave would be important to one or both of them.

Jonah also briefly thought about his battle with Matasis and his henchman, Demon. He knew that having done such a thing he should be afraid, but he was not. Perhaps he was too numb. Besides, death, or the thought of being dead did not scare him. In fact, he'd thought often to do the job himself. He didn't want the Blues to take his life, but the losing of life was not the issue; it was the how with which he concerned himself when he did think about it.

Then he thought about the Artifact, the heart-shaped joy that he knew would rid them of this place. It was the key and he knew it. He just needed time to figure out how to use it. He reasoned that he could use it as a chip to get safe passage for himself and Monica to the Circle. But it troubled him that each time he used the Heart, it glowed a little dimmer. Was the glow tied to his emotion, as Karun suggested, or was it something else?

Jonah's mind began to troll through the underlying contentions within his marriage to Monica. So often her eyes asked that he let her in, and just as often his hands would reply in a gesture that he didn't know how. She wanted something, something finite, but the hole within him was bottomless and could never be fully defined, much less expressed to someone else.

∞

Another twenty-nine minutes passed and still no Monica. Jonah began to worry. She'd stormed out of Karun's apparently in quite a huff. Was she that upset to do something crazy? No, he knew her better than that. But if she was upset, maybe she got careless. Jonah stood with the intent to walk over to Marta's house to see if Monica was there or had at least been there. But as his hand landed upon his coat, his wife, bundled from head to toe, came sliding beneath the opening into the living room area.

Her eyes froze on him. "Just getting in?" she said with pitch.

"Oh, no. I was just about to go back out and look for you." Jonah secured his coat back on its hook. "See, I have a cup of tea." What was this? He wasn't used to having such an interaction with his wife. Trying to change the tone, Jonah asked as softly and lovingly as he knew how, "Where were you? I was worried."

Monica lowered her head and peered at him between the slim slits remaining in her eyes. The squinting would have been enough of an answer, but she added a huff for emphasis.

It was obvious to Jonah that his rough day at sea was nowhere near being over. He hoped to weather the storm without losing too much of what remained in his life. A thought popped into his head, one that neither he nor any other man in a similar position would be able to resist throwing out there. "So, you don't want to talk? We can talk lat..."

"Oh, I want to talk! I'm just so disgusted that I'm afraid of what might come out of my mouth. If it weren't for Karun and Manisha being able to confirm your late nights at work and that I know how long it takes you to get home, I'd think you were having an affair with what's-her-face." Monica hung her outer garments on the hook next to Jonah's.

Jonah thought to provide Vicki's name, but thankfully knew better of it.

Monica, after a bit of venting, finally asked a substantive question. "Why do you still associate with that woman? What good can come from it? Haven't we had this discussion before? She's a spy. Spies only serve their masters. Befriending them benefits nothing and only puts you at risk. Tell me, how is this good for us?"

Jonah was caught a bit off guard in that finality. Maybe it was a rhetorical question. He hesitated for a second, thinking that Monica might again cut him off with another question, for which she really didn't want an answer. Sensing that this was a real opportunity to get a word in, Jonah ventured a response. Actually, he had two things to say. The first was, "Well, you know ordinarily, I would agree a hundred percent with you. Really, I would. But you know we're in a bit of a bind here. We're living here beneath a bridge in a country very hostile to our well-being. In fact, they kill folks like us. On top of that they seem be upset with the fact that someone, that would be me, set off a nuke in their capitol city and that someone, again me, put their Blue god, Matasis, on temporary lock down. They're executing Christians left and right, and my latest actions aren't going to help our chances. And..." Jonah was about to mention Sara, but he knew there was no need.

Monica, sensing the same thing, conceded an "I know."

Jonah continued since she now seemed open to his major rebuttal to her argument. "Given all of this, I don't see where associating with a spy really adds that much more risk to our lives. It's a gamble, yes. But at this point it's the best play we have."

Monica seemed to be digesting that when Jonah's human nature got the best of him. "And just to clarify, I am not befriending a spy. Vic..., she and I have known each other since we were seventeen."

"What?!!" Monica yelled.

"I'm just saying that you made it sound like I was seeking her out."

Monica, not believing what she was hearing held her mouth agape for an instant. "What difference does that make? I know how long you've known her. But we both know that it's an inappropriate relationship. I don't consort with ex-boyfriends, so why are you still talking to her?"

Having breached this line of questioning, Jonah was now obligated to defend his point. "I knew her before we were married, just like you knew Karun. But I don't freak out every time you mention his name. Plus, you know that Vicki and I have never dated. She thinks of me like a brother."

Monica replied in a doubtful tone. "Mmm... Maybe she did. I don't know about now. And don't compare her to Karun. He is a married shopkeeper. Vicki is a single spy. And I've known Karun since I was thirteen, and with my being an only child, he really is like a brother to me. I trust him and there is nothing between us like that."

"But you and Karun did date in high school. And like I said, Vicki and I never did." Jonah's ego still had the best of him. He knew there was nothing there between them there in the present. Plus, he trusted Karun, but this double standard bugged him to the point that he couldn't keep his mouth shut.

Monica looked at him almost laughing, "You know good and well about that. Everybody knows about that. We still kid him in the shop about it. You know it's not the same for Indians. We went out a few times, mostly supervised, so that our families could see if we were a match." While Monica was basically half Black and half Indian, since her father left the country well before hostilities broke, Monica was raised mostly Indian. Her mother refused to leave, like so many others that moved to the Circle and other destinations. Monica continued, "We went to the movies together a few times when we were fourteen or fifteen. We never even kissed. Manisha was with us too. In fact, we double dated with Manisha and her boyfriend at the time. For Indian women it's all about getting married. We don't date in the same sense that you do here in this country. And yes, before you say it, I know that even Heru, who went to school with the both of you, says you never dated. I get all of that. But hear what I'm saying. Women change. What they want in a man can change. I don't know if that's what's up with Vicki or not. But it's clear to me that she's working you. And whatever her real goal is, it's equally clear to me that she's up to something. I don't understand why you can't see this?"

Jonah threw up his hands. He understood Monica's point. But two things occurred to him that he knew better than to say. First, he knew Vicki well enough that spy or no spy she would never do anything to hurt him. But now was not the time to play up how well he knew Vicki. Secondly, he knew that if Karun sought Monica as a youth, he still felt some kind of attraction to her still. That's just how men are. Karun is a good man and he'd never breach the trust between himself, his wife, Monica or Jonah. Still in an objective sense, Jonah felt that he had far more reason to be jealous. Why should he be penalized for being more secure than his wife? Monica sees Karun at least three times a week and speaks to him twice that much, whereas Jonah saw Vicki only sporadically.

Monica was then struck with a question. "So just what did she say to you when you showed her the Heart?"

Jonah's demeanor changed because he was happy to see the discussion go this way. "Oh, she was impressed! She said that such a device would prove very useful to the Circle in their fight against the Blue Lords."

Monica followed, "So that's it? We're going?"

Then Jonah remembered what else Vicki said. "Well, she's going to see. They still seem to have an issue with us. But we're thinking that this thing will be so hot that they'll take us anyway."

Like a laser, Monica homed in on what Jonah didn't want to talk about. "What issue?"

"Well, Vicki mentioned that Circle security seemed to have some issue with you."

"Did she say what it was?"

"No, apparently they won't tell her. She was hoping that I knew what it was. I told her I didn't know of any issue. Baby, there isn't anything in your past that might raise a red flag is there?"

Monica paused to think for a minute and then replied confidently. "No. You already know all the really important things about me."

Jonah let out a sigh of relief. "Good. Then we'll just have to wait to see what they say once they find out what we have and what it can do. I think it's going to be a no-brainer."

Monica answered back, "I hope so. Hey, there's a memorial service for Sara this evening. Do you want to go?"

Shocked, Jonah answered back, "A memorial service? Doesn't anyone remember what just happened? Who decided this? Shouldn't we wait for the Blues to calm down just a bit?" Then Jonah thought for a bit. If the meeting was already scheduled then it was too late to stop it or reason with anyone about having it. Monica's attendance would not change that, so arguing that point had no real merit. It was obvious to Jonah that he should go to at least provide some kind of protection for the group. "Okay, yeah, I'll go. What time do we need to leave and where is it?"

"We're going to meet in an old abandoned hotel outside of town. Actually, it's just one exit down from where you used to work. If we leave now, we can get there before it gets too late. Oh, and in case you were wondering what I've been doing since I left town, I went over to Marta's to help her prepare some food to take over with us." Monica stepped from the kitchen to the bathing area and began to disrobe.

As his wife removed her clothing, Jonah asked himself the reason for this war between them. It would be so easy to cave in to her desire, but what kind of man let's his wife tell him with whom he can and cannot be friends. He never tried to tell her with whom she could associate. And he'd never do that. Maybe that was just a basic difference between men and women. Men seldom try to change a woman and women always try to change a man. Could the problem here be broken down so simply? He didn't even think that this was a marriage threatening issue. It was just a bump in the road, and yet he felt the need to say something else. But everything he tried to say only seemed to make things worse. To him, at that moment the peril of words outweighed the security of silence.

They washed and changed quickly enough to be on their way within twenty minutes. Jonah packed his bag full of all the things he thought he might need. The weight of his backpack slowed him in keeping up with Monica. Although he suspected that she was pushing the pace so that she wouldn't have to converse with him, he didn't really want to talk either. A part of him still felt like they should. Thankfully, they caught up to Marta and Jorge. The food Marta and Jorge carried was split between the four of them to share the load.

Eventually, they reached the old hotel. From the outside it appeared to be deserted. The only sign that one was in the right place was a small cross drawn in the sand just off the roadway. Each time the group had gotten together, the particular organizers would try to outdo each other with how creatively they displayed the symbol of the cross marking the spot.

Tonight however, given the somber nature of their convening, a cross drawn simply in the sand was most fitting.

Wandering through the hotel, the four of them eventually found the boiler room in the basement. They gave the knock to the door and waited. There had to be a lookout in the hallway leading up to the door even though they could not see him or her. But there was always a lookout watching the door. The lookout always had some means to communicate with those behind the door. Wherever this person was, and how he communicated, remained a mystery to Jonah that night. Slowly the door swung open to a room of candles and grievers. There were the usual folks you'd expect, like Heru. Some of the folks who came up from Atlanta were still in town and present. Surprisingly, Ashok was there as well. It was thought that since his wife's role had been revealed, he'd go deep undercover, but there he was. Monica and Jonah both broke into wide smiles when they saw Karun and Manisha. Jonah reintroduced Jorge and Marta to Karun and Manisha. Jonah knew that the women knew of each other through Monica, but he wasn't sure if one knew the other by face. It turned out that they met a number of times at various gatherings, but Jonah didn't know this going into the room. What Jonah did do was to reach into his backpack and pull a simple wave broadcast beacon. The energy wave it sent out was invisible to the crowd and blocked out any electronic prying eyes. Of course, the major flaw in what he was doing was that if the Blues were tracking any particular individual that person would disappear from their screen once they crossed the radius of his broadcast. Generally, that would not be good but when you're tracking people electronically, they tend to pop in and out all the time due to physical barriers or electronic interference. Jonah set his broadcast as wide as he could such that if the Blues did become suspicious they wouldn't be able to pinpoint just where in the perimeter the group was hidden.

Jonah reasoned that the benefits of masking their location did not outweigh the risk, nor did he ask anyone there if he should be doing this.

After making their way over to console Ashok and pitching in to help with the food service, the six of them tried to blend into the background, as one often does at memorials. The aromatic scent of the burning candles and the flicker of their flames filled and accompanied the spirit of love in the room. The boiler room had many nooks and crannies, so it was difficult to know just how many people were there. As people continued to come in, Heru took center stage. He spoke to the group at large. "Hello, friends. First let me just say thank you to each and every one of you for being here tonight. Your being here to celebrate Sara's life, despite what's gone on the last several days, is a powerful testimony to the kind of life she lived. In a few minutes we are going to open up the floor to anyone who wishes to speak of Sara, who she was and the impact she may have had on your life. I know personally that I was blessed that God allowed me to know someone like her in my lifetime. I know that the Kingdom of Heaven I see here on earth would not be as bright without her having lived. Like I said, in just a moment we are going to open this up, but please don't feel forced to say anything. Just being here, even in silence, we are lending comfort to each other and building up the body of Christ. So please mingle a few minutes more and we'll get started. Thank you."

Several people walked up to Jonah, Monica and their friends, each with a recollection of Sara to share. All parties smiled at the moments brought to mind.

Then, as Jonah's face continued to survey the room and the people around him, his eyes came back to his wife. Monica's face had gone pale and lifeless. Her unblinking gaze had fallen upon a young man making his way over to the group. The man reached out his hand to greet Jonah. It was Dave from the bus and the last gathering. Dave was one of the Blues who could turn his blue hue on and off. He seldom chose to be Blue. But it occurred to Jonah that Dave's being a Blue was not what was troubling Monica. As Jonah made the introductions around the circle he came to Monica. "And this is my wife Monica." Jonah hesitated for a second, waiting for them to make some acknowledgement of having previously met. Hearing none, he continued, "Do you two know each other?"

Dave spoke up, "Oh, I thought we did, but I must have been mistaken."

Then before Monica could reply, a look of recognition swept over Manisha's face too.

Monica spoke only loud enough to be heard, "Yes, it must be a mistake." Monica did not look up as she said this. She was not skilled in hiding her emotions and that day was no different.

Dave, sensing her uneasiness, sought to extract himself from the group and thereby somehow spare Monica. "Well, it was nice meeting you all. I'm so sorry it had to be like this. It's such a sad day. And though I know we all rejoice in the life Sara led, it's a hard day for all of us." His gaze fell on Monica, as though the group should accept this as the reason for the sudden darkness of her continence.

As Dave walked away, Monica and Manisha gave a look towards each other of which only they knew the meaning. Then Monica grabbed Jonah's arm. Speaking softly but firmly, she sighed, "Jonah, we need to talk." With that she led him out of the boiler room to another empty basement room with a small window at the very top for ventilation. A lone sliver of moonlight shone through it.

Once in the room, Monica closed the door behind them. "Listen Love, there is something that I think I need to tell you."

For Jonah the moment was unreal. He could not believe what his wife was about to tell him. Really, he could not even think of her with another man. He could not fathom her breaking their marriage vows. Thoughts of how could he have failed his wife so totally that she may have done this also rushed through his mind. Still the utterance fled from his mouth. "Dave? You and Dave?"

She shook her head, "Dave? No." Monica started to turn away, but then thought that saying such things with one's back turned was not the right way. She turned towards her husband and took hold of both of his hands. "No, not Dave, his father, Marcus, Chairman of Capitol City's Blue Lords. When I was young and struggling, before I met you, I was Marcus's mistress."

"His mistress? Like you were having an affair with him?"

"Yes, but it was more than that. Initially, I was hired as a nanny for his son, David. Over time, I became a part of the family and in addition to my pay, he paid the rent for my mother and me. Sometime in between he approached me." Now, Monica did look away.

Jonah followed her, "Why didn't you tell me this before? I mean I knew you weren't a virgin when we married."

Monica turned back, "Yeah, right! You really wanted to hear about how I was the kept woman of a Blue Lord."

Jonah conceded, "Okay, I see your point there. But surely with all that's gone on, seems you would have told me by now."

"So, there is a good time to share such things?" she smirked, though her eyes began to water.

"Well, you could have told me earlier tonight when I asked you if there was anything in your life that might be a red flag to the Circle," Jonah explained.

Monica cringed and began to shout, "The Circle? You're worried about the damn Circle? They're a bunch of stupid people hiding beneath an ice cap praying that the Blue Lords are going to implode or something someday. What have they got to do with our lives? Should anything I say or don't say to my husband have a darn thing to do with them? I could care less about them. You're worried about our lives here; I'm worried about our lives there. I don't call hiding forever beneath a sheet of ice living!"

Jonah, who never screamed at his wife, yelled back only to garner her attention, "It's not about the Circle for me either. It's about us. I was just asking that if you couldn't tell me then, then when? I mean Circle or no Circle, shouldn't I be able to ask you a question and have you tell me the truth! It's obvious that Manisha knows. What about Karun? And how many others? I just want to know why you couldn't tell me the truth!"

"The truth?" Monica asked. "You want the truth?" Still upset she complied, "Okay then. You're going to find all this out soon enough. Do you know why Sara could be so bold and flaunt her faith so freely? It's because of me. Because of me, Marcus let it be known that Sara was not to be touched. In fact, neither she nor her husband's business was to be targeted. The problem was that Sara was converting too many Christians, even Marcus's son David. Maybe David was the last straw, I don't know. I do know that he asked her many times to stop. He told her that if she continued, that he'd no longer be able to protect her. And that is why we are here today."

Jonah removed his cap and scratched his head. "This is a lot. Is that why you don't want to go?"

No, it's not why. But it has crossed my mind that if we ever get hauled in, I don't think Marcus will let them kill us." Monica stretched out her arms wide.

Jonah stumbled around lost in thought. "This is just hard. That you were his mistress, I can live with, but that he's somehow protecting us. That, that makes me sick inside. Like I'm not a man."

Monica followed him and spoke as he was turned away. "I understand if you want to go."

The silence between them hung heavy in the darkness.

Jonah turned to her, "No, it's not that. I don't know. I'm confused right now. How I feel, how I think I should feel... I don't know."

Jonah walked around a bit more breathing deeply and sighing. Facing her, he told her the main thing on his heart. "It's just that I tell you everything."

"No, you don't tell me everything." She paused for a moment and then continued, "Some of the biggest lies are hidden in the things we don't say." Monica gave him a knowing look. Then her eyes widened and startled, she yelled pointing behind Jonah, "Oh my God!"

Over Jonah's shoulder in the narrow window, two blue faces were pressed against the pane staring back at the two of them. Jonah let out a quiet, "They've found us."

19: The Trouble with Demons

We gathered up our things and set out after a tight-lipped Akina. Dread and Shamus pulled close with Nihil between them. The doglike Nihil extended his head in a very unnatural way towards Akina and smirked as he asked her, "What's the matter Boo? Did you not enjoy your trip? Odd isn't it? All the things you've seen and the one thing that freaks you out the most is yourself. You got issues."

Reggie injected himself into the conversation. "What's he talking about Akina? What happened back there?"

She answered him as she continued walking, "Nothing that concerns you, any of you. It's personal."

Reggie and I exchanged looks that said, "How can these things not matter to us?"

Reggie insisted, "So, what did you find out? Tell us."

Akina glanced back in frustration, "I found out that we need to go this way." She pointed generally in the direction that she was already walking.

Nihil took that opportunity to stir the pot. "Someone looked in the mirror and what that someone doesn't want to say is that perhaps she has lost faith in herself? What will you lose faith in next? Your God, perhaps?"

With that comment, Akina took a swing at Nihil, but he darted out of the way. "Get away from us!"

Nihil said in a slither, "Oh child you know I can't do that. This is your lot in this life."

Then, from deep within, Akina spoke firmly to Nihil, "Thee, get thee behind me."

At that command, Nihil began to float towards the rear of our procession away from the front and Akina but he ran his mouth all the way. "All of you belong to me, just like the Shaman here!" Nihil rattled the Shaman's chain.

Then, in an instant it became clear to me, what had been hidden. I had assumed that Nihil had been a prisoner held between Dread and Shamus. But no, Nihil was their master to call on them as he pleased. And now so was the Shaman. This beast would have us all so. My heart sank. And somehow Nihil seemed to know this. He veered into the line towards me bearing his teeth and barking. I started to bolt from him when Sandy, stepped between us and yelled, "Stand down, demon root!"

Nihil curled back and continued his trek towards the end of the line, the rattle of his chains becoming fainter as he proceeded.

Sandy spoke softly to me. "It is as it always has been for men. It's only that you see him clearly now. Nothing else has changed. He'll be back and I may not be here, so you need to buck up. Okay?"

I rolled my eyes at her. Half disbelieving, half astonished that she spoke that way to me. Perhaps the biggest epiphany of the entire experience was that Sandy was not the shrinking violet that I thought she was.

Nihil continued his rant as he scurried around. "Demon? Child, I'm an angel. I'm just going through a bad stretch here. But so are you, aren't you? Don't you want to know why you're here? Who you are? And what you used to be?"

No one said a word, but Nihil laughed, "Okay, you forced it out of me. All of you were angels too, rebel angels dancing to my tune. Cast down from Heaven, you're no better than I am. Convicted before the day you were born, each of you. Look around you, this is your world stripped of the guise and beauty of space and time. I ask you, is this Heaven or Hell?"

Looking back and stumbling as I tried to keep up, I heard Akina cry out, "Check it out!" Right in front of her was the

shade of a brown-skinned Black man. His essence seemed to
fade in and out like the last vestige of an early morning
dream. It was the same man that we passed through as we
descended from the city on the hill into the valley. This was
the shade that Caleb the angel mentioned. But this time
there was something different. Hanging from his neck was a
small board fastened by what looked to be shoelaces. Unlike
the last time, he smiled. It was as though our stopping and
seeing him brought him some sort of relief. The letters carved
into the board said "Jonah". His lips mouthed, "I am Jonah."
He pointed to himself in a very obvious motion. Having our
attention, he lifted a second broken board to right below his
chin. It read, "I am your descendant." Our collective mouths
fell open.

Reggie moved slightly to the side, looking at Jonah more
closely. Jonah dropped that board and took another from his
left hand, raising it with his right. It read, "I need your help."
He turned slowly so that everyone could see his words. Finally, he dropped the plank and raised the last one to his
chin. On it was an address and beneath that a date. Akina
read it aloud, "Washington, DC, December twentieth," and
then her mouth dropped open. The year was a figure that astonished all of us.

Darnell stepped forward and asked, "Is that right?"

Akina whispered, "I guess it could be." Then a look of realization crossed Akina's face as she viewed the date and location again. She looked at the image of a man again and
stroked her brow. "No, couldn't be." She mumbled to herself
as she discounted the thought.

Sandy surmised, "I guess since he's here on his own, he
must be some kin?"

Akina pointed out, "But he's having trouble. He has some
of my gift but not all of it. He has the look of a man that's
been searching for a long time. I hope we are worth the time."

Darnell asked, "So, when you say he's having trouble, do you mean because he's shady and all?"

"Yeah, he's not fully here. See, I've run across some folks that are kind of like me, but they can't really navigate. They can just move through time, randomly. Occasionally, they make it back home, but most just wander for ages until they grow old and die. Unfortunately, some of them wind up here, outside of time, but never on purpose. Jonah is different. First, he is just a shade and not fully formed. Second, he sought us out, and better yet found us. Given the nature of time and space there is no way this is random. It's as though physically, he can't quite make it work, but some part of him can. To be honest, I've never known anyone who could even do close to what I can."

Carla chirped in, "Well, apparently Uncle Paul can too. Or at least he could."

"Yeah, either that or he was with someone that could," Akina acknowledged.

A thought occurred to me and I spoke it out loud, "So I guess this confirms that at least one of us makes it out of here alive. I mean, none of us has had any kids yet." Hearing nothing, and seeing no response, I uttered, "Right?" All eyes fell, but each eye avoided Reggie.

Reggie spoke to everyone but no one at all. "It's not like I know for sure." I knew Reggie was sexually active, but apparently I only knew the half of it, and little of the how of it. The how of it was that it was far too often unprotected.

Carla replied, "Hey, Akina already told us that some of us make it out of here."

And with that, we were back to the same emotional point, the pain of knowing that one or more of us was not going to make it home. As Jonah forced a smile and began to fade, Kim burst out in tears to Akina. "Why can't you just tell us?" Tears came swiftly to Akina's eyes, which told me that this whole time she'd been on the verge herself. It was clear, that even though she hid it well, Akina too was just as stressed as any of us. Kim realized immediately her error and rushed to Akina's side. Hugging her, she said tenderly, "Hey, I'm sorry cousin. You love us and I know you'd tell us if you could. I'm so sorry. Really, I don't want to know either. Come on, let's get going."

Akina lifted her head. "Thanks, but it's not just you. It's me and the person I am to be. Y'all don't know this, but I spent a month there pleading with my future self. She's set herself up as a god, she and her husband, Akhenaten. I pleaded for our lives here. I wanted to know what is to come for us here, and she wouldn't tell me." Akina continued to weep. "She wouldn't tell me. I asked her why, and all she'd say is that what must be, will be. How can that woman, that cold woman be me? How? Has she forgotten the pain I feel right now?" On her knees, Akina lowered her face to the ground. Sobbing softly she rocked back and forth. "I wouldn't doubt that it is my future self that brought Uncle Paul here in the first place. I wouldn't put it past her, me, whatever."

Reggie flashed a look at Darnell and me that said, "Hey, I told you she was freaking out."

Sandy knelt down in front of her and brushed her hand back across Akina's head. She spoke at her bent head. "I know you're going through a lot, but it's going to be okay, really it is. All of us are mortal. No one here expects to live forever. For you it must be very hard knowing what is to become of each of us. But try as best as you can to not to let that knowledge rob us of what life we still have together."

Akina sat there for another half a minute and then stood, trying to dry her eyes. I think she was a little embarrassed to have broken down like that. As she walked between us she touched us all. She reached to touch her guards but they drew back. They'd be been instructed on penalty of death to never touch the Queen. To this she just grunted and looked around out to the distance. My eyes followed hers. All around us was every vision of Hell imaginable. Fire, ash, the stench of brimstone, shackled souls fluttering like flags in a storm and heckling demons on our heels. And still, the worse hell was in our hearts. Akina retied the cloth across her nose and mouth and turned into the wind coming from the horizon. She called out as she began to march, "We'll have to get out of here, recapture all of those demons and then deal with Jonah's problem, whatever it is." Her words were upbeat now, but her body language betrayed her. She moved as one already weary, who finds out she is not near the completion of her journey. But still, she walked on as we all did.

As we trekked along I made my way up the line into the middle of Akina's guards. As I said before, Akina lead our procession with team multi-national close behind. The rest of us followed with Darnell traveling last in our pack. I walked between Martin and Sanjay. I felt a certain comfort with them in part I guess because of the guards, these two joked the most. The Egyptian was stoic and even a bit menacing in his protective posturing around Akina. The Asian guy, Chin, was humble and very focused on doing a good job. Unlike the Egyptian he seemed to realize that we, her family, were not a threat. He was rightly more concerned with the environment around us. But he was still all business. However, Martin was jovial and teased Sanjay, but never in a hurtful way. They both spoke to the back of Chin's head telling him to lighten up. I figured their humor was more of a defense mechanism than bravado, but still some of it was funny... fatalistic though it was.

Sanjay called out to Chin, "Hey man, it's only Hell. We're as low as we can go. It's all uphill from here."

The Druid chimed in, "You know my south Asian brother, I'm going to need to rethink my whole life because of this little excursion. No more of this harlot of the month thing for me."

Sanjay questioned, "Of the month?"

"Okay, the week," the Druid conceded.

"The week?" the Indian asked, again skeptically.

"Alright, alright, whatever, you're missing the point. Maybe I should consider being a priest? Hmm, but those guys have to marry their sisters, don't they? Mine's a nice girl, but I don't think I want to do that."

Sanjay said with a straight face, "I've seen your sister, and I don't want to marry her either."

Not missing a beat, the Druid continued as though muttering to himself. "Of course Mom and Dad might be a bit upset. But then again, maybe I'm adopted."

Again, Sanjay replied, "Trust me, you are not adopted. Cast out maybe, abandoned possibly, but adopted, I can assure you, you were not." Spoken again to apparently deaf ears. I couldn't help but smile.

Martin took several steps and then reflected, "You know, maybe this whole purity thing is not gonna work for me." Several eyes fell on him in silence at this comment, including Chin. Undeterred, the Druid followed, "What I need is a wood nymph."

"Won't you get splinters when you kiss her?" Sanjay responded in a deadpan tone.

"No, you don't get it. They can change their appearance such that you have a different woman every night. Just imagine the possibilities!" Martin let out a little growl from his medium build.

By this time it was very clear that Chin had purposely ignored them. His eyes had glanced all about except towards the two of them but he could be silent no more. "So, if you cannot escape this fate, better to wallow in it? I ask this not to cause you trouble, but to cause you to examine your own thoughts."

While Martin was left speechless at the premise, the gaze of the Indian focused. "So, the choices of this life are to be a saint or a demon?   Is there no room for something in between?"

Chin replied, "None are perfect, but look around you. Here you see the truth of the peril that awaits the stiff-necked man."

Given that I was and am a recovering stutterer, I had to think of exactly what I wanted to say before I entered the conversation. "So, what is it that you believe? You sound like a Bible thumper."

Chin turned towards me, "We have no Bible, only the words of Queen Nefertiti or Akina as you call her."

I couldn't help but ask, "So, are you guys Christians?"

The three of them looked at each other and then back to Chin. "We believe in the God of Akina, but to say we are Christians would not be correct. We, or maybe I should say, I believe in His coming. I believe that the Messiah will come to mankind. Queen Nefertiti has traveled time and beyond, and she has told us that these things are to be. She has seen them with her own eyes. Some among us doubt; some outright disbelieve." His sight fell on the Shaman in the distance. "Queen Nefertiti has tried to spread her teachings to all of Egypt, that there is One God. The biggest problem she's had is with the priests of Ra. She's trained and tried to weave in some of her own priests into the order, but there's a lot of resistance. Actually, that's mostly what we do, protect her from those priests who want her dead."

$$\infty$$

We had been marching for about four hours when we came upon what appeared to be a mist-covered riverbed. The mist was so thick that we could not see through it. The four hours had been relatively uneventful. Although we did encounter the more mindless of the creatures here, apparently our kill count had resonated with the higher thinking predators there. The Pit was no different than the world above in that regard. The truly evil know whom they can mess with, and whom they cannot. Akina stopped and we all gathered around her to see what she was looking at and why she stopped.

In front of her on the river bank was another stone inscribed like the one we saw at the foot of the city on the hill. Where the previous one was tall, this one was broad and mostly covered in dust. It stretched maybe twenty feet across, with only the top line of writing visible.

The Egyptian asked Akina, "My Queen, why are we stopping? Our goal glows ever brighter."

She turned to him, "We saw one of these before you found us. It's some sort of prophecy. Our Uncle Paul was here in his youth. Apparently, he had visions of the future and inscribed these stones for his descendents to find one day. Somehow he knew we'd be here. We'll need to dig a bit if we want to read all of this."

The Egyptian drove his staff into the ground and motioned for the other guards to join him in doing the Queen's bidding. Reggie cleared his throat, "Hey, it's our stone and our prophecy. We'll uncover it." It was clear that Reggie had been waiting for an opportunity to put these guys in check. The Egyptian was a tall, sculpted man, with an attitude to match. He and Reggie were Alpha males, although in different ways. The Egyptian had the air of an officer. But one could imagine that his current position had bred a degree of arrogance within him. Anyone that had eyes could see his pride and vanity. This made him a perfect mismatch for Reggie. Reggie was an

Alpha male in that he refused to let anyone control him or tell him what to do. He didn't mind working to elect a leader. In fact, in those cases he was cool with authority and leadership but he despised those who just assumed themselves to be in charge, like the Egyptian. It was amazing that they'd made it that far without coming to blows.

Reggie motioned for me to step forward and instantly I knew what to do. As before, the words we could see above the surface were in Latin. The words read

ECCE DAMNATORUM AMNEM!

I moved to the stone, as Sandy translated the Latin aloud. "Behold the river of the damned!"

And just as before there was a recess into which a human hand could fit. I placed my palm upon it and for a moment a memory not my own flashed across my mind's eye. It was interrupted by a sense of movement as I felt as the stone began to rise from the earth. My mind raced back to what the previous stone document said.

> One will live and die by the sword, while another shall die and live by the Word. One shall find life. One shall lose her heart and be swept away. One shall perish this very day. One shall reach the end and begin again.

It was our collective hope to see something a little more optimistic this time around.

The monolith rose to a height of about fifteen feet. As it climbed, the words hidden by the dirt became visible as they shifted from Latin to English. I deduced that somehow in touching the stone it, in return, touched my mind and translated its inscription into words that I, and thus all of us, could understand.

The remainder of the etched inscription read,

> Children, you have not heeded my warning. But upon grievous consequence do not ignore me now. Beware this river of the damned. The toll is heavy here. If you go forward, gird your loins for what lay beyond. The one who shall die by the sword, shall not die this day. The one who lives by the Word, shall watch His flock. The one who finds his life, will avenge his mother. The one who shall lose their heart, need not this journey take. The one who shall die, knows it already. And the one who will begin again, is but one step in 10,000 to come.

My cousins and I stood around the stone transfixed by its words. Akina spoke first, "I guess it's pretty clear that one who loses their heart is me. Does that mean there's like some big love affair in my life?"

Kim reminded her, "But you do marry the Pharaoh, right?"

Akina, hesitated, but then continued, "Yes, I do, but he is the most hideous man to look at. I don't know if it's all the inbreeding or what. Still, my future self claims this undying love for him. I had my doubts. I have my doubts still. I can't imagine being with... that man. Maybe I met someone else, and then I ran back to ancient Egypt to get away from the guy and married the Pharaoh on the rebound?"

Carla, in her husky voice, laughed, "Yeah, right. Switching focus here a second, but y'all do notice that we're one person short in this prophecy?"

I added, "Maybe the ..." I was lost for words.

Sandy filled in, "the Prophet? That would be Uncle Paul."

"Maybe he couldn't see the future clearly. I think Uncle Paul is a lot older than any of us knows. I mean surely, given when this was written and the time that has passed, he has more descendants than us?'"

Sandy corrected me, "But he knew which ones would be here. If I had to guess, I'm the one who's not listed."

Akina suggested, "But your father is cousin to the Aunties?

Sandy smiled, "Or so we're told and choose to believe. Even if my dad really is related to you all, everyone here knows that I don't look anything like my daddy. Akina, you of all people are most in denial. You could check it out, but you carefully avoid knowing this."

Akina replied, "I could find out, I guess. But like I said, this time travel is not as easy as y'all make it out to be. I could go back in the day and stalk your momma to see who she was hanging out with besides your daddy, but first, I don't have that kind of time, and secondly, even if I were to see them in the act, that don't make whoever, your daddy. Despite all my gifts, I can't do better than a DNA test when it comes to something like that."

Sandy deferred a bit, "Okay, I see your point. But, y'all look at me?" She moved her hands in unison as though displaying a showcase. "Look at me. Look at these freckles. Carla's yellow, but neither she, nor Aunt Sarah or anyone else, to anyone's memory has got freckles like me. They're all over my body. Both my mama and daddy are from the same small town as your aunties and both our families go back in that town for generations. So, there is a good chance that we're related some kind of way, if only on my momma's side. But still, Uncle Paul's blood may not be rolling though my veins. I mean if any one of us is the one not mentioned on these tablets, it would be me. You guys think that anyone who can actually see you doing your gifts is one of you. But that's not true and I would not be the first exception to that rule."

Reggie conceded, "I think she's got a point." We'd all been playing blood cousins for years ignoring the elephant in the room. But this was the end of that charade. Still, as a giggling Kim grabbed and hugged the arm flailing Sandy, it was clear that being family was so much more than just being related by blood. On the other hand, Darnell nudged me and gave me a "Here's your chance dude," kind of look. I looked at Sandy and seeing how she was so embarrassed, I could imagine taking care of her for a lifetime. She was so terribly sweet.

I read the tablet over again, "The one who shall die by the sword, shall not die this day. The one who lives by the Word, shall watch His flock. The one who finds his life, will avenge his mother. The one who shall lose their heart, need not this journey take. The one who shall die, knows it already. And the one who will begin again, is but one step in 10,000 to come." You could pretty much plug and play the rest of us into any of those slots. Reggie's mom, Aunt Cil, died of natural causes, so I didn't see him avenging anyone. Given that a masculine pronoun was used I assumed that to be Darnell or me. The one, who lived by the Word, could be any of the three guys. Reggie traveled the world and spoke many languages. He has a real thirst for knowledge and was an avid reader. Darnell didn't read much, and could never pass for an English scholar, but still he read his Bible regularly. I on the other hand didn't do much Bible reading, but was the obvious bookworm of the group. Living by the sword could be any of us. Kim and Reggie were mercenaries. Darnell and Carla battled evildoers on a regular basis. But all of us had slain our share that day. It also sounded like one of us was going to be around for some time to come, while another, as we'd heard before, was going to die today. So, in the open possibilities of our minds, with the exception of Akina, each of us was fair game for any of the prophecies.

We knew that Akina would survive this, which we knew from the beginning. And we knew that one of the guys survived to avenge his mother. That meant that at least Darnell or I would survive, according to this prophecy anyway.

Next our thoughts shifted to the riverbank before us. Akina walked to the side of the monolith and squatted, looking left and right for some sort of clue. Reggie called out, "It looks harmless now."

Akina said back to him, "Yeah, it does. But I think we're missing something here. Uncle Paul left this right here for a reason." She remained close to the ground as Nihil approached the Egyptian who had moved up beside me.

Nihil spoke quietly into his ear. "In their hesitation, they show their fear. Now is the time for you demonstrate to the Queen your bravery. Secure your place among the Hall of Heroes. Secure your place among the fearless. If there be creatures in the mist, surely your mighty staff shall slay them. Your staff is more powerful than any club that brute might carry." The brute Nihil was referring to was Reggie. The Egyptian's staff was decorated with ornate rubies, emeralds and sapphires. Reggie's was more like a club that was built for whacking things. The Egyptian's staff could morph into different objects or beings, or so I was told. Sounded like a parlor trick, but I would think these guys traveling with him, having the inside scoop, would not follow him unless they too believed what he could do with that thing. I did see some kind of beam of energy flash from it against some of the lesser critters we faced, but nothing compared to the fire that erupted from Darnell's eyes or Kim's fingers. I think he was a little insecure about his staff having met us. Nihil was preying on this.

The Egyptian held out his staff over the bank. It began to glow and his eyes began to flicker and roll to the back of his head as though he was dreaming. When his eyes opened something inside of me felt a darkness about it all. His jaundice yellow eyes were those of a cat. Then he made a pronouncement to Akina, "My Queen, I have searched and there is no danger here. But should there be, in your service, I will strike it down!" Reggie and I looked at each other like, "What is this fool talking about?"

Carla, who was kneeling with Akina, looked up to release a "Huh?" before shaking her head.

The Egyptian's staff glowed brightly as he stepped over the bank and downward. But with his first step, a cascade of movement rippled across the riverbed and what was hidden, was now revealed. The bed was not empty but full of ghastly, ghostly bodies floating downstream from our left to our right. Each of them struggled against the other to rise above. Several decaying hands reached up to take hold of the Egyptian's leg. Before we could reach him, he was pulled beyond our grip by a torrent of lost souls. Darnell began to take flight, but Carla frantically grabbed a hold of his arm. "No!" she shouted. "I have reached out to lift him but their hold is too tight. He is beyond hope. He is lost."

Chin commented, "He was lost before he ever came here." The other two seemed to be in shock, but Chin expected this.

It seems a rude comment now, but not in the full context of what I believe he meant. His face was full of regret and sorrow. His statement somehow prompted Sandy to ask him, "You saw the angel back there didn't you, while the others could not?"

Chin nodded his head in the affirmative, as he told me before.

On the far side of the river of the damned we could see masses of people as far as the eye could see. Each of them was struggling not to be the next one to fall into the streaming current of anguish.

Carla cried out, "My God, is that what we have to go through?"

Akina acknowledged, "Yes, we do. I've been to this place several times, but I've never been this far. I pop in and out of this side, but that area over there is something else. Hey, look upstream."

Now visible was a bridge, maybe a hundred yards upstream, spanning the river. Atop it in the middle stood another angel.

Reggie, always the tactician, instructed, "Come on, let's get to that bridge while we can see it."

Nihil and his posse, on the other hand, waded into the river and walked upon the lost souls. Nihil let out a laugh as he shouted, "This is all your God's doing, you know? This is the fate of the damned. It is my fate, it is your fate for following me in the time before time." This is what he said. The Shaman who had thrown his lot in with Nihil was reluctant to step into the river of lost souls. He struggled against his chains. An impatient Nihil shouted at him, "What's your problem? Oh, I get it, you're one of those. Everybody wants to be a bad boy, but nobody wants to pay the price. Remember, you sought me out." With a yank of his chain from Nihil, the Shaman fell into the river and was quickly consumed, his chain to Nihil breaking as he was swept along. Nihil mocked the struggling man, "Oh, don't worry, I'll save you a lakefront view down below."

Sandy scoffed as we walked, "Liar. He won't be running anything in that day. That's the trouble with demons. They lie. And even when they tell a grain of truth, they lie because their larger intent is to deceive. There is no truth in him."

Reaching the bridge, we walked up to the angel, expecting him to say something, but he did not. He stood there in silence. There were other angels further down the bridge towards the far side. Each of them looked to be just as silent. I guess in that place the time for talking was over for anyone that could have listened. We stopped just short of the other side to speak among ourselves. In the far distance we could see the Light, the way home. But between us was a sea of lost souls on their way to damnation. The crying and screaming was sickening. Seeing us on the bridge they somehow sensed that we were not among the damned but just passing through. The arms and faces of those near the bridge stretched out towards us. They pleaded, each one like the howling wind. I wanted to cover my ears and close my eyes. I didn't dare look below at the ones already in the river. Where the ones still on shore appeared human to me, those below were misshapen and grotesque. Akina turned towards the masses and let out a sigh that we all shared. My respect for her leaped ahead of where it had already been. She didn't have to go through any of this. She had a free pass home, but she chose to go through this with us. With Reggie and Carla by her side, she said loudly, "As Uncle Paul said, gird yourselves."

20: Other gods

Seeing the troopers through the cloudy glass and now hearing their personnel transports and tanks, Jonah grabbed his backpack and rushed into the hallway with Monica. Once there, the commotion made it plain that they were not the only ones to notice the soldiers. One of the two lookouts came rambling down the stairs towards the boiler room. Jonah yelled to her, "Here take my wife and tell everyone to stay put. You'll know when it's safe."

Jonah, not knowing exactly what he was going to do, turned to leave, trusting that none of his friends would get in his way. But before he could take a step, he caught a glimpse of his wife, still teary-eyed and not going into the boiler room. Instead, she was walking backwards, slowly into the shadows. Jonah called to her, "Monica! Monica, where are you going? Go into the boiler room!"

"I can't be with the others right now," she called back to him.

"Monica, get in the room, I don't have time right now!" Perhaps if he had known... if he had known that the moment was at hand, he would have replied differently. Perhaps, even in the chaos, when there was no time, Jonah would have taken time. Maybe then his next words would have said something less exacerbated than, "Monica! Monica!"

Jonah's mind, sharp, and always in motion, reasoned that really there was little difference in defending the boiler room and the hallway outside it. He loved his wife, but in his anger he did not say "goodbye." Instead, he just gave her a fed up look as he scurried up the stairs swinging his bag around to his front as he galloped. The upstairs entry to this stairway was somewhat concealed, but Jonah reasoned that the troop-

ers may have found it already, so he slowed as he approached
the door to listen. Through the door he could hear the soldiers
interrogating two of his brethren assigned to this entrance.
With his hand on his Excavator, Jonah thought to burst
through the door, but reasoned that he had a second or two to
set up something that would be far more effective and a lot
safer for all concerned. Jonah peeped through the spy hole
just to check on his comrades. He could use his Wave Modulator to entrap every soldier and tank. He could then constrict
the circle and crush them all or just allow them to suffocate.
But as he'd often thought before, those who serve the Blue
Lords were people too, with families and all that goes with
that. He didn't really want to kill anyone. Then Jonah had a
second idea. He could use his Excavator in a way he'd not
thought of before.

Behind the door, but not beyond the rising voices, he
keyed in his parameters and listened for the response. The
first thing he heard was a scattering of gunfire and he
thought, "Why are they shooting?" The next thing he heard
was one of the interrogators exclaim, "What the…?"

Jonah again, looked through the spy hole. He could see the
soldiers drifting towards the doorway. One of them cried out,
"They're sinking! The whole yard, all the way out to the main
road, just turned to quicksand."

Then one of the other soldiers, there were three of them,
turned to his captives and asked, "Is this the doing of your
God?"

The two believers turned one to another, but gave no answer. Jonah watched them and beyond as best as he could
from his hiding place. Through the open door to the outside
he could see men struggling frantically in the mire. Jonah
knew that the mud was only one and a half meters deep, but
the terrified men did not. As the men wailed about, Jonah
could see what he was really looking for. The tracks of the

heavy armor were halfway submerged. It was then that he implemented part two of his plan. With a couple of taps to his device, the ground solidified and the men and their machines were stuck.

One of the believers spoke up to the spellbound men. "I suggest you let us go. I'm sure that the angel that did this will be coming for you next!"

The soldiers threw their weapons outside as the doorkeepers motioned and then parted like the Red Sea. However, the two sentries did not head for the exit, but once the soldiers left, instead headed towards the camouflaged door from which Jonah did his work. Jonah quickly put his gadgets away. Thankfully, he'd already set up an electronic shield like he'd done before so that the aircrafts could not image anyone on the ground. Plus, the shield served the purpose of cutting off all communication to and from the troops to anyone outside of the bubble.

The door swung open with the two guards a bit startled to see Jonah standing there. Then a look of recognition swept over the female of the pair. "Hey, you're that guy."

All three of them gave a glance over to the door to make sure they were alone. Then Jonah replied, "Yeah, I guess I am."

The male guard said with a laugh, "You've been busy."

Jonah lifted his eyebrows, "Yeah, I guess so. Hey I'll run down and tell the others they can get out of here now."

"You do that, we'll watch the door." Then he whispered to Jonah, "It's so clear that God has a call on your life. You know this, right?"

Jonah nodded, and then bounced down the stairway. Reaching the boiler room door, he gave the knock, which he'd thought he'd forgotten from years ago when he was so active in the body. Of course it was Heru, ever the shepherd, that opened the door. His generous smile ignited immediately at seeing his old friend. His smile was only in part for whatever his friend had done; it was foremost for the fact that Jonah was alive and well. And he smiled at what God had done, not that he knew any details, but yet he knew. Jonah said, "Let's go. Get everyone and let's go."

Heru waved his arm back towards the crowd and they began moving towards him. The group numbered between sixty and seventy believers, but as they gathered to the doorway, Jonah became increasingly anxious, for he did not see his wife. He asked Heru, "Where is Monica?"

Heru took a moment and shook his head and said, "Man, I've not seen her since you both left the boiler room."

Jonah worked his way into the crowd towards Karun and Manisha. Reaching them he asked them the same question. Manisha answered him, "She's not been back. We thought you were together."

Jonah's heart sank, and for the first time in this whole trial he began to despair. He looked down the hallway, away from the stairwell, into the darkness and called for his wife. "Monica! Monica!"

His change in mood struck his friends hard. Karun spoke, "Manisha, you go with everyone else I will help Jonah find her."

Of course Manisha paid him no attention. She called out as well, "Monica! Please come out. We can talk about this. Jonah loves you more than anything. Please, let us talk about it."

While everyone else headed upstairs, the three of them proceeded down the hall. There was no lighting to speak of in this section of the basement. All the doors were closed and even if you entered one, these rooms did not have slivers of window as the rooms closer to the stairs possessed. Reaching the end of the darkened hall, they found a door. In the warm glow of his tools Jonah fumbled for the doorknob. The door opened to a landing with short stairs on either side up to the ground above.

"She must have come this way," Karun stated. Slowly they walked up the stairs to the right. Raising their heads above ground they could see the shoulders and heads of a hundred men, planted like strange cabbages. Thankfully, most of them had their guns at their sides and not about their heads when the ground froze solid. The men called to them as they walked between them. They called for help, but the three friends were oblivious to their cries, not because they were dispassionate, but because each of them knew that Jonah would free them soon and that their discomfort was only temporary and not life threatening.

Catching up to the departing body of worshipers, Jonah again searched the crowd. And again, every one he stopped confirmed with a grimace that they had not seen Monica. He knew this each time before he asked, but still he did. The crowd was hard to take in, given that it was dark and each party was headed in a different direction. Their thinking was that the metal birds hovering above would not be able to cover the 360 degrees of possibilities for leaving this place. Without ground support, the Blues would never be able to corral a group such as this dispersing in that manner at night. But this very same movement made it all the more difficult for Jonah to find his wife. He stood in the middle of the yard before the road, amongst these strange human cabbages. His friend, Karun, came over and spoke quietly to Jonah. "Come my friend let us go and see if we can pick up her trail. It is clear that she is gone from this place."

Jonah was looking down when a hand landed on his shoulder. He turned to see that the hand belonged to Pam, the other woman he saved when he rescued Sara. With her were Jared, David and Bruce. She spoke to him, "Your wife is missing?"

"Yes, she left right as we were trying to stabilize the situation. I don't know where she is."

Pam brushed his shoulder and tenderly said, "I'm sorry. Can I help? I want to help you find her."

Jared, whom Jonah also rescued, touched his other shoulder, "I am with you, brother. Just tell me what you want me to do."

Bruce, who Jonah had found before a little too eager to do battle with the Blues, made his presence known. "I'll help you too, but what is he doing here?" Bruce motioned to Dave, son of Marcus, Chairman of Capitol City's Blue Lords.

Dave held his head down saying nothing, but Jonah spoke for him. "He's here to help." Somehow thinking of Dave's needs lightened Jonah's own mood and immediately his mind began to race thinking of possible approaches to finding his wife.

Before Jonah could speak his thoughts, a man in one of the armored vehicles stuck his head out the top of it to call to them. "Are you looking for the woman that came out of the basement exit before you?"

"Yes!" Jonah shouted.

The soldier, a captain, replied, "If I tell you which way she went, will you let my men go?"

Jonah considered for just a second weighing the safety of his friends versus the need to find his wife, then he answered, "Yes, I will, but only after we're at least thirty minutes on foot from here... and you must come with us." In replying so Jonah also noted that the officer's side arm remained in his holster and that he showed more concern for his men than himself.

The captain spoke as he climbed down, "I expected as much. That's a deal I can live with, so to speak."

Jonah felt compelled to answer back, "Captain, if we wanted to hurt anyone, we would have done so already."

He smiled and nodded, "Yes, I know that. In fact, your wife said as much when she came out. Contrary to the propaganda, I have found most Christians trustworthy and kind. But I guess you want to know about your wife, don't you?"

Jonah looked at the man, now regretting that he'd not been more selective in his words. Not only could this man and several others planted around deduce that he was the culprit in these deeds, but that the woman who preceded him from the building had been his wife. Not good. He looked for some hint as to whether he could trust this man. Jonah's features and skin color gave away that he was certainly not a Blue, not even a color shifting one. Few Blue families would choose a hue of brown for their child's alternate skin color.

The Captain continued, "She really didn't speak to me besides to ask me where the Major was. Naturally, I pointed her towards the rear of our formation. She took off running. Once she got there she said a few words to the Major and then they took off up the road. His vehicle was on the pavement beyond all this goop, so he wasn't stuck like us. I don't know for certain that she left with him, but I would assume that she did."

Jonah nodded in acceptance of what the captain told him of his wife.

The seven believers and the Captain began to walk in the direction of the main road. Most everyone else avoided the main road with good reason. Karun shook his head at some of the Indian mercenaries stuck in the dirt along with their employers. Unlike Monica's mother, most Indians refused to work in the service of the Blue government, especially the military. That was viewed as the height of betrayal to the cause.

The Captain offered, "I tried to call out earlier, but all of our communications are jammed." He paused for a moment as if to allow Jonah to say something. But Jonah said nothing. Then the captain went on to ask, "You're the one aren't you? The one that's got all the suits riled up. Right?"

Jonah didn't want to lie and he didn't want to acknowledge anything, so he simply said nothing.

Jared helped him out, "People rile themselves up mostly, no input needed."

In the dark, the group fanned out as much as they could while still maintaining contact with one another as they walked to the main road. Each of them took turns calling out to Monica, except Bruce. He was too busy watching the Captain and Dave. He gave Dave a hard look as Dave crossed his path to approach Jonah.

Dave walked beside Jonah, silent in his loss for words. But Jonah, sensing his discomfort, reached out to him, "Hey, it's okay. I know about Monica and your dad. All of that has nothing to do with you."

Dave breathed a sigh, "Man, I am so sorry. My dad's a piece of work. I was just a kid when all that was happening. I might have been nine or ten years old. I was almost thirteen when I finally figured out what was really going on. But by that time they were over. I don't know if it means anything to you, but he was with Monica longer than any of the others. In Blue society, women can't really say much and this kind of thing is expected. But I really think my mom was the one who put an end to it."

Jonah lifted an eyebrow to Dave, "It's ended? I'm not saying that my wife is still having an affair with him. By no means am I saying that. But I know that they still communicate. Right?"

Dave nodded his head, "Yes, that is true. But to my knowledge it is very rare and even more seldom direct. On more than one occasion she has pleaded for the life and liberty of our brothers and sisters."

Jonah stepped over a fallen tree and looked back to Dave. "I know. Apparently, she'd gotten Sara out of hot water more than once."

Dave peered into the darkness, straining to make out Jonah's face. "Yes, she did. Make no mistake, Monica is a good woman. None of us is perfect, but I tell you the truth, Monica is one in a million."

"I know." Jonah spoke into the darkness. Jonah thought about the Artifact and whether he should try to make it across town to get it and try to use it to trace back through time or whether he should continue on with the group looking for clues or some kind of trail. He'd not been able to travel more than five minutes back in time. He wasn't sure how he'd manage the three to four hours he'd need to retrace by the time he got to the lab in Karun's store. But mostly his thoughts were those of regret. He regretted how things had ended with Monica. That is what broke his heart the most and left him with a sense of helplessness. She was all he had in this world and maybe she didn't love him? He thought about every doubt of their relationship he'd ever had. Maybe he'd hurt her so bad that she'd run off and wouldn't be coming back even if they did find her? But he had to try. He had to see her again. Nothing else meant more than that. Jonah had never been insecure about their relationship, but something was different this time. His spirit told him so.

Manisha shouted out, "Do you think that she might have gone home?"

Jonah answered her, "I don't know."

Dave followed, speaking softly to Jonah. "She's your wife, you know where she's gone."

Jonah said nothing.

Dave replied to his silence, "My Dad."

Monica was a true believer in Christ, but also a pretty devoted believer in the "we can talk this out" view of the world.

For her it seemed, at times, that the root of all evil was not the love of money, but the failure to communicate. Monica was going to go to the source, her friend in the Blue hierarchy to try to negotiate an end to all of this. She knew that her husband, whom she happened to be very upset with anyway, would not approve, so she took off on her own. The fact that this friend happened to be her former paramour was not relevant in her mind given what was at stake. Monica didn't think like other people, and Jonah saw that as a sign of purity about her. Others weren't so kind in their estimation of her. Some of these others had their own motivations for thinking the way they did... known or unknown even to themselves. But that night only the truths in the hearts of Jonah and Monica were in question. As for Monica, she didn't return to the boiler room in part because she did feel some degree of shame and wanted to set out on her own to make things right. Jonah, for his part, pondered the whereabouts and condition of his wife almost to the point of despair. But something within him fought against it, as that same something had fought with and for him all the days of his life. To that point the Spirit within him had always triumphed over the psychosis of any given moment. Also afflicting him was the sense of disbelief that his wife had once been the mistress of a Blue Lord. The thought boggled his mind. He grasped it, so he sought to put it aside, but it was a consistent second thought that battled back to the forefront of his conscious mind alongside the ever-present sense of despair. Wrapped around all of this was a deep feeling of guilt, as Jonah replayed every conversation, every word said or not said. Had he done or not done something? Had she read through him to see something he had missed? She had not been honest with him, but in her last words to him, she claimed that neither had he. Had his friendship with Vicki hurt her so that she felt that there was nothing here for her? Hurt her so, that she would put more faith in some old Blue lover than in him? He'd not laid a hand on Vicki, had never tasted her lips and yet his wife felt betrayed? And truth be told, he had been tempted, but isn't every man tempted? If these are the rules, then how can any man pass? But still, she was gone and he was left with the feeling of guilt. The spirit of shame spun around him, and with each swoop snapped pieces of his psyche.

If to be tempted is not sin, but to lust is sin, then where is the line between them? Can mortal man know these things or is this the province of God alone?

High above them aircraft hovered. They could see the vehicles aloft, but the pilots could not see them due to the protective shield. Previously, it was clear that the crafts were searching, but now they hovered separated by a measured distance between them. Jonah sensed that perhaps that they might be broadcasting a message. Knowing that sound waves can kill, Jonah tweaked his settings to allow only a narrow range of safe sound waves. As the bandwidth opened, the words of the loudspeakers blared into the ears of the group. "I repeat; lower this barrier immediately. There is no escape. Jonah, we have your wife, she is in custody. Give up now for everyone's benefit. Lower this barrier immediately!"

Jonah then came to himself again, and having certainty of the situation, embarked on a new plan. "Everyone come here." After everyone had gathered around, Jonah continued, "They have Monica. It doesn't sound like she ever made it to Chairman Marcus. So I have to deal with this, but I want all of you to go home. I, and I alone, have to go and get my wife."

Bruce moved towards the Captain, "So, what do we do with him? We can't just let him go? He'll tell them all about you." Bruce had raised this question, but this was not the real reason for his asking. Vengeance was in his heart.

Jonah answered him, "He might tell them something, but they already know who I am. And in the end, either way, what can I do about it? I'm not going to kill or hurt him... and neither are you. Let him go."

"But..." Bruce protested.

Pam rebuked him, "That is not our way. You know that."

Jared stepped between the Captain and Bruce, as Bruce grumbled, "Do you guys not understand that we're in a war?"

"Oh, we do, but not as you think," Manisha pronounced.

Once the Captain had departed, Karun approached his friend, placing a comforting hand upon his shoulder. "So where will you go? Monica could be hidden in a hundred different places around town."

Jonah smiled at Karun, "I don't know where she is, but I do know where to go to get her back."

"And where is that?" Karun asked.

Without blinking an eye Jonah whispered, "The Blue Parthenon."

Karun blinked rapidly, "Home of the Blue gods? You're joking, right? You think they have your wife there?"

"Actually, no I don't, but that is the very reason I should go there. Since I don't know where Monica is being held, the best thing to do is to start at the top and work my way down."

Karun bowed a bit. "Surely God is upon you for even thinking of doing such a thing. It seems impossible, but so has the last week. Why should things change now? Do you need my help?"

"Thanks Karun, but I need to go alone. I'll see you at work tomorrow. I might be a little late though." Both men laughed just a bit.

Manisha walked towards them in the dark; while everyone else stood off a bit. "Come pray with us before you go," she offered.

After a group prayer and quickly devising their exit plan, each group departed.

Jonah had been led by the Holy Spirit to take off immediately but in the minutes since that vision, Jonah reasoned that it would only make sense to take the Heart with him. He was desperate to get his wife back, but he reasoned that the only way to get his wife back was to give these guys a quick punch in the mouth. Unlike Bruce, Jonah did not believe that all Blues were bad, but at the highest level, he knew in his heart and with all his being that the Blue Illuminati was pure evil. And that kind of evil only understood one thing, force.

Although he had been a reluctant actor in this play, Jonah did realize that he had made quite an impression on the powers that be. A whole legion of men and armor, along with supporting air power, had been sent to bring him in. But unlike what Bruce hoped for, Jonah had no intention of starting a revolution. Nor like Sara had inferred, was he content to remain in this place as a witness. Maybe if it was just him, things would be different, but what man doesn't try to do something to better his family? Surely God would understand that he had responsibility to his wife to get her out of there. And to that end he saw no better route than the Heart. He hadn't yet been able go back in time and change events, but was becoming quite good at shifting back a minute or two, or sliding through this reality from one location to another. Jonah was certain that such a gift was intended for him to use to get himself and Monica out of this place.

But there was something else too, and this had been in the back of his mind since he found the Heart. Jonah wondered if he could use the powers of the Heart to go back in time and find his ancestors. Specifically, the generation his Auntie had often mentioned. Now that was a group to be reckoned with! All he'd have to do is find them. He knew of their time traveling adventures, so why couldn't coming to Jonah's current time be one of those adventures? He could certainly use their help. But the vision he'd glimpsed came to him again and he was filled with a sense of urgency. It was a sense that told him that he did not have time to retrieve the Heart.

With the tools at Jonah's disposal, getting past the Blue dragnet was slightly more than child's play. He managed, as planned, to create some diversions that assisted his friends in their escape. And as promised, he released the mud-bound soldiers.

Jonah made his way to the transit station. He kept his face hidden as much as possible. Being winter, his manner would not raise suspicion. Besides, he knew that no sketch of him could be drawn in much less than half an hour, given that the Captain had a twenty minute walk facing him. It only took Jonah about twenty to twenty-five minutes to reach the station. The station was elevated and one stop past the nearest checkpoint. He sought the most vacant car and boarded it. It was odd to Jonah how the Blues had so many men manning the perimeter of where he'd been, but no one at the transit station. Were they so arrogant that they could not conceive that a commoner such as himself could pass through their snare? It was clear that the Blues just really didn't get the technological path he'd taken over ten years ago. It had to be a case of group-think in their labs. The other thing was that the Blues firmly believed these acts had been the work of a Blue working with the Christians. No Christian, outside of the Circle, had access to this type of technology. Still, Jonah took it as a blessing. That time of night only service people rode the trains.

Sitting there, Jonah began to think about his wife and all the things he would say to her if he could just see her one more time. His anger with himself had been held in check by the series of tasks involved in getting away from the soldiers, out of the woods and to the train. Sitting alone, stop after stop, Jonah had nothing to do but to contemplate his life and the events of the past week. Jonah wasn't sure that he could articulate his crime, but he was certain of his punishment. Not seeing his wife and having things end like they did was something worse to him than death. Hurting Monica was the last thing in the whole world that he ever wanted to do, and somehow he'd done it. And still he wasn't certain what he'd done. He wanted to cry, but again, as before, the tears would not come. Jonah closed his eyes and reasoned again that there was indeed, something very wrong with him. And maybe someday, Lord willing, he'd find out what it was.

As Jonah road further, he became increasingly certain that there was indeed something amiss with him. There was the issue of his recent dream life. Jonah understood that most people dream in metaphors, but for many of his dreams lately nothing less than madness could explain them. He dreamt of such godforsaken places the inhabitants of which sought his very soul. Horrible demons would chase him. But in every instance when he'd been cornered and all seemed lost, he would begin to pray and never had he not been delivered. Often times the dreams would begin with Jonah, encountering his long lost ancestors and then deteriorate from there. But just as often Jonah would have dreams of Sara and an almond-faced girl. In that dream he saw the girl standing amongst a herd of goats on a grass-covered hill. The stalks of the brown wheat-like grass were just about as tall as the little girl so the goats were hard to see. But you knew they were all around because of the way the grass moved. His heart went out to the little lost girl. Pushing through the goats, he reached to comfort her, but before he could, Sara appeared in front of him. She stretched her hand out directing his vision to the valley below. In the valley of equally long brown grass stood other children of every hue among many other goats. In the dream Sara turns back to Jonah and says, "Without you this harvest will die in the field and be tossed into the fire."

In the dream Jonah wants to ask what is he to do, but the words will not come. Sara places her index finger to her lips and speaks again to Jonah, "Be quiet and listen. Are you, or are you not a child of God? If you listen, you will hear the answer."

In the rail car, Jonah suddenly realized that he'd been day dreaming since the last stop. But even in his altered state, a part of Jonah kept a careful eye on those around him. There were two older women sitting near to him. They'd worked well past the age anyone plans to work. So according to Blue logic, they'd not planned and therefore planned to fail. Ergo, they received no assistance from the government. Contrary to most other cultures, and even to how they treated their own, Blues placed a higher value on commoners in their more productive years than those who'd passed their prime. Support programs for commoners in their formative childbearing years were common, but aid programs for the elderly and chronically ill did not exist. Common folks had to take care of their own. That was the deal. The Blues found the elderly and sick a poor investment.

Standing, or better yet, dancing and swinging between poles, was a teenager. No music was playing, but it was clear that he heard a melody in his head. This kid lived in the street. He might or might not have had a real mental illness. Typically, a youth of his age would be strongly encouraged to check into a youth center. But many kids, and some adults, faked mental illness and substance abuse problems so that the Blues would leave them alone. Actually, a lot of folks used this reality as an excuse for getting high. Jonah couldn't accept that reasoning. Sure times were hard in Jonah's day, but how was that any different in any age?

Again, Jonah's mind rambled through every misplaced word he'd spoken to Monica. Like the young man swinging back and forth, his thoughts took one turn after another. And as with the young man's behavior, Jonah could not discern if his own thoughts were rational or not. He would have preferred his mind to be more like the two old ladies. He needed to steel himself, but instead his mind raced with questions.

At last, he began to pray, and even there he chastised himself for not doing so sooner. Jonah prayed for peace mostly. He prayed about the task at hand, but it was almost an afterthought. Once he'd had his second vision, he had little doubt that God had this firmly under control. He didn't really know the details, but he wasn't afraid, not about that anyway. He was very much afraid that he'd hurt Monica forever, the one person he cared most about in this life.

At the end of the line, only he remained in his car. The trip to the Parthenon from the church meeting site had not required a transfer. He passed right through the heart of the city unmolested.

The doors of his railcar opened and Jonah stepped out onto the cold and empty platform. These trains were fully automated and did not typically carry an operator. Jonah walked to the end of the elevated platform and peered over the side towards where he thought the Parthenon should be. And there, on a not too far away hill, he could see the glow. That far outside of the city, the lights of the Parthenon made it easy to find.

Once he saw it, Jonah's duplicity of mind vanished like last night's nightmare. From a distance the Blue Parthenon looked very much like the original. But that was where the similarities ended. Unlike the one in Greece, this one did not serve as the treasury for a league of nations, but instead served as the earthly home of the Blue Illuminati, also known as The Blue Lords. The Blue Parthenon sat upon a hill, surrounded by rugged landscaping, except in the front. Going in the front entrance of the grounds one could proceed directly up a set of stairs to the Blue Parthenon itself. The main structure was lined with granite pillars. Inside were statues of the four principal Blue Lords, sitting in a semi-circle as though they were holding court. From left to right sat lords War, Pestilence, Chaos and Death. There were also a plethora of lesser Blue gods, like Matasis.

Matasis's statue was much smaller and lined the perimeter along with the other lesser gods. But the stone depiction of him was still much larger than any mortal.

Blue Pilgrims made this pilgrimage during the holy season. The whole event was a bit hedonistic. The sacrificing of non-Blues was a daily, if not hourly event. It was really a pillar of Blue culture and society that they were the chosen people, not the Jews, Christians, Hindus or Muslims. And as the chosen, they had every right to walk upon the backs of non-Blues. In their doctrine they likened non-Blues to any other animal on the planet. And like any other animal, the Blue man had dominion over them. In fact, to illustrate this point, the Blue Pilgrims would tear apart the bodies of the sacrificed and consume pieces of their flesh. Many mainstream Blues didn't really have any desire to do this. But since it was the law and a fiercely protected one by the more extreme among Blue society, the "feast" as it was called, carried on through the years as a "high" point of these pilgrimages. Jonah smirked, thinking that he too was a pilgrim, but not the sort they'd ever planned on. Turning towards the exit stairs, Jonah spotted an officer headed his way. Jonah bowed a bit and did not look the officer in the eye.

The officer, who was much younger than Jonah, spoke to him. "Get along now. No loitering."

Jonah nodded again, and scurried down the stairwell. It sickened him. When downtown among the masses it's easy to let these little gestures slide, but the last thing Jonah wanted or needed right then was to get into a battle of egos with the neophyte cop.

Out on the street Jonah made his way towards the Blue Acropolis. The Blue Parthenon sat atop the Acropolis, like the original in Greece, but around the base of the hill was a twenty-foot concrete wall. About 60 percent of the site was also lined by what used to be known as the Potomac River. Jonah knew this fact, and so did a good bit of the free world, but not the locals. Most of the citizens born under Blue rule knew nothing other than the Blue reality and the Blue version of history.

The temple and surrounding area took up quite a bit of space. The wall bordering the street where Jonah stood ran for more than half a mile. The depth of the bordering cross street ran even further. The wall, which bordered all street access, was about twenty feet thick and housed a passageway for sentries to pass back and forth. Every hundred meters or so, there were doorways for the guards to enter and exit. But for everyone else, the pilgrims mostly, there were only three points of entry. There was the main gate and the two smaller gates. The main gate was to Jonah's right and faced the intersection of the two streets that boarded the complex. The smaller gates were split between the two border streets and stood flush to their respective avenues. Jonah stood between the main gate and the smaller gate to its left.

Jonah had strapped his Wave Modulator to his left wrist and his Excavator, which could change any material from and to solid, liquid and gas, to his right wrist. He prepared to make his assault.   At first he thought to just knock everything down. His wave device could tumble the wall and the temple beyond, all from a safe distance. But there were people in the walls, and Jonah had no desire to take anyone's life. Jonah was hopeful that just getting to the top of the wall would provide the right angle for him to finish his task. If not, then he'd either have to climb the rugged terrain leading to the pinnacle or he'd have to take the front stairs. The choice would be obvious to most, and for Jonah too, but just not in the same way. Pilgrims longed to walk and spoke often of climbing the Blue Stairway to Heaven. The thought of walking up those stairs was untenable to Jonah.

Above the front gate was an arch and on it was written, "Point of no return". No Christian, since the construction of the Acropolis had ever returned, having passed through these gates. That was the claim. Some folks doubted this, but if ever a Christian had made a round trip alive, there was never word of it. As for Jonah, this was the reason he'd not mentioned the details of his plan to his friends earlier. He reasoned that they might consider this a suicide mission, and it might well have been. But again, Jonah wasn't really afraid. For him it was living that was frightening at times and not dying. And more specifically, at that moment, Jonah's most prevailing fear, the fear of failure, was nicely tucked away.

Craning his neck around to read the inscription on the archway of the main gate gave Jonah pause. Each door was inscribed with Blue scripture; the most striking one to Jonah that night read "Abandon all hope, all who pass here." The text was meant for Christians designated for sacrifice. Many from Jonah's own congregation had passed through these gates of Hell never to return. Jonah wondered if one of his brothers passed through a similar gate during the slaughter that took place in the destruction of Atlanta.

At reading these words a righteous anger swelled in Jonah and he cried out, pleading to God, "Lord, do not let this stand!" With barely a second thought, using his Wave Modulator like a bullhorn, he called out to his potential combatants, "Move away from the main gate, now!" Jonah waited a few seconds as all eyes fell on him. Then with barely a third thought, he punched in the data needed to create a force beam from his wrist that rammed into the center of the gate. The beam was twenty feet wide by twenty feet tall by the time it hit the impressive solid metal doors. Each door must have weighed at least a ton or two, but both of them flew off their hinges and into the Acropolis like cardboard in a strong wind.

Knowing this would draw a crowd, Jonah headed off towards the gate to his far left. He quickly and effortlessly pressed a couple more instructions into his device and a dimly lit ramp appeared before him that he ran up to reach the top of the wall. Most of the lighting in the area originated from the top of the wall, but very little lighting actually illuminated the wall itself. All the lights pointed downwards, leaving Jonah very much concealed unless one was looking right at him, and that suited him just fine. Jonah could have encircled himself in a protective shield, but while that would have made him invisible to the electronic eye, its glow would have made him the star on a very oddly placed Christmas tree. As the sentries scurried from their hiding places to the front gate, Jonah took stock of his situation. From atop the wall, he could see the top third of the Parthenon. Either tool strapped to his arms could do a good bit of damage from where he stood, but the anger coursing through his veins was such that merely knocking off the top half of the structure was not good enough. He would have to get higher to really clear off the entire site. Looking up towards the structure he spotted a lighting tower with scaffolding built up around it on the river side of the central mound. It was high enough for him to get a good shot. In theory it was possible that Jonah could take off the whole hilltop, but that again would be a bit reckless. Not that Jonah thought any of those Blue soldiers would give a second thought if it was him that might be hurt by such a broad action. But he was not them and could only do as he was bound to do.

Unless it's a holy day, no mortal can actually step foot into the Blue Parthenon. So as long as there was no one standing directly behind it, his action of knocking it down would not be a problem, in the life-taking sense.

Giving no mind to the footmen on his lower right, Jonah configured his toy to provide a bridge from his wall top location to the base of the light tower. Using the Wave Modulator, Jonah created a wall between him and the soldiers.

Backpack strapped across his shoulders, Jonah ran from his hiding place and onto the glowing pathway, passing in and out of beams of light in his course. The men, having clustered in and around the fallen gate, fired in his direction to no avail. Reaching the lighting tower's base, Jonah jumped from his bridge and immediately began climbing rungs of scaffolding. Huffing and puffing, but still very much focused on the task at hand, Jonah reached the top platform. He glanced over to the Blue Parthenon where the statues of the Blue gods were seated. But as he stood up, peering between the columns, Jonah caught sight of the Blue god, Death turning towards him. The shock of it was enough to cause Jonah to stumble backwards. Balancing on the edge of the plank, Jonah's anger rose again, even as the giant granite statue

began to stand. Jonah punched in a command to form a ram-
ming wave to knock the building down. The light colored
beam instantaneously plowed into the Blue temple and it
began to tumble. Jonah saw the Blue gods Pestilence (the female form of the group and the antithesis of "mother earth" in
other religions), Chaos and Death, but he realized that he did
not see War. The moment he realized that fact, War's mighty
battle axe slammed into the light tower. His weapon cut clear
through the underpinnings and sent the entire structure tilt-
ing backwards away from the temple and towards the slope
that led to the river. As everything fell to the ground, Jonah
jumped clear of the wood and metal, rolling as he hit the
ground. He looked up to see War regaining his balance and
glancing back to Death, their head god. Death and the others
were shaking off the debris from the fallen temple and gathering themselves. In the sky beyond them and on the ground
around them Jonah could see a number of lesser gods in various states. It appeared that his act had really devastated
some of the smaller gods; in fact more than a few of them
were now counted among the debris. But his old foe Matasis
was not one of the fallen; in fact he was aloft and hovering
right above Death's shoulder.

Jonah quickly put up a wall between himself and all of
them. He instinctively shuttled backwards down the hill a bit
to create some space between himself and his cast of foes. Jonah's heart was racing, but his mind was still clear. He saw
some of the lesser gods and Heralds bump into the wall of
light and fall back. But his heart sank when he saw Death
and the other major gods step through his barrier. War
swung his hatchet at Jonah, and instinctively he shifted, but
not as we know it. Rather than just moving through space, he
also moved through time. He jumped through the axe coming
down at him to War's right side. The Blue god of War pointed

in Jonah's direction as the other gods looked on. Even through their stone faces, astonishment was evident. As War raised his axe a third time Jonah lifted his right hand and sent up a bolt from his Excavator that, to Jonah's surprise, liquefied War's tool of destruction.

Death stepped to the forefront and reached out his hand. Even before his grip touched him, Jonah could feel the coldness, and he drew back. Jonah rolled and attempted to vaporize the darkness, but his Excavator's state-changing energy just passed through the abomination Death. Chaos laughed at Jonah's failed attempt. However, Jonah noticed that Pestilence moved to avoid the matter-altering beam and made note of this as he fell into the water. He regained his footing in the shallows of the riverbank and stood unblinking at each of them.

Death stepped into the water towards Jonah, as the other gods surrounded him. Jonah cried out, "Oh Lord…". However, he was not speaking to the beasts of this world. Death grinned and stretched out his hand. But at that very moment the Heavens opened up and a pillar of fire dropped from the sky between Jonah and Death. War and Chaos strode to press Jonah from their angles, but two more pillars of eternal fire spun down from up above. The granite oppressors, confounded, still tried to press on, although Pestilence remained in hiding behind the others. The pillars danced to meet every challenge. Now totally in the water, Jonah struggled to stay afloat. He struggled not so much to breath, but to witness what his God was doing. Then something bumped into him. It was one of the planks from the scaffolding. Jonah grabbed a hold of it and began to float downstream. Pestilence hissed and beseeched Death and the others, "Are you going to let him just sail away?" But Death raised the back of his hand to her and she grew silent.

As he continued to float away, Jonah looked back at the flames, the Behemoths and the ruined Blue Parthenon, and for the first time in a long time, Jonah smiled. He couldn't stop smiling and even laughing. He laughed at even how it was clear to him that he'd never really needed the Heart of Mystery. It was clear that God had instilled this gift within him and sadly it had taken an old family legacy to grant him the faith to claim what was already his. He laughed too at the fact that it reminded him of an old movie he'd seen as a child.

Jonah continued to smile and revel in the moment. Victory was all so near now. Certainly, when he made his pronouncement tomorrow, demanding Monica's release, the Blues would have no choice but to release her. But then he thought about Moses and all the iterations he went through to get Pharaoh to set the Israelites free, and he stopped smiling. He thought about it a while and reasoned that he, in his demand, would simply cut to the chase. "Release my wife or perish."

21: Damn, Damn, Damn

Hopeless.

As far as the eye could see, there was nothing but wave upon wave of tormented flesh, wave upon wave of eternal loss. Up until the moment we set foot on that bridge between the living and the dead, I guess all we'd seen hadn't really touched me. It had frightened the crap out of me yes, but touched me, no. With each step from the apex of the bridge and proceeding to the other landing, I descended into another level of personal abyss. Seeing what lay in front of me, every molecule within me wanted to run away. But to where would I run? Below me, in the riverbed, was an even worse scene, if such a thing was possible. Back over my shoulder the land of monsters and nightmares looked like the Promised Land. I froze suddenly in my tracks about twenty feet short of the bridge's end, causing Sandy to bump into me.

Sandy asked as quietly as one could, given all the soul wrenching wailing piercing our ears, "Mike, what's wrong? Is it the screaming?"

I looked at her and then around to the others in complete bewilderment. "Un-unh, we're not going down there are we?" The question burst out as though it had a life of its own. Everything within me screamed, "No, don't go down there!" It was simply a much more horrific sight than I could have ever imagined. And down below us Nihil, who had crossed the river by walking on the heads of the damned, reached the far shore. He reached up and grabbed the hand of a woman teetering on the edge and yanked hard as he pulled himself up. The woman tumbled head over heels down the embankment. Right before she hit the river of bodies, the chain that tied Nihil to Dread, caught her around her neck. Dread gave the chain a jerk and the woman was flung up eight feet into the air. She landed in a clump. Shamus stepped over and put his heel to the back of her neck, pushing her down into the muck of damnation. The woman screamed horrifically and did so until her face was planted and the back of her head stepped upon. I'm certain that she is still screaming into the darkness.

Darnell was on the verge of jumping down there when his sister grabbed his arm to restrain him. Not that she was by her physical body strong enough to hold Darnell, but it was his love and respect for her that held him fast.

We all stood there for a minute watching the river of damned souls passing beneath us. Not one of these would ever see what lies above the clouds. Not one of these would ever come to fully know the mysteries of this life and the one beyond that could be had, a future for which no bill was due. The void had a claim on them now, and hollow Nihil grinned in the delight that they had become like him, without hope.

Beyond the river and as far as we could see were legion upon legion of damned souls. Each of them sightless and groping at torturers they could not see. All manner of demons plagued them. Most troubling to our task was the apparently higher concentration of winged demons here, than on the other side of the river.

Akina called our collective attention, "We've got to go. We can't help anyone down there." I glanced down again at the woman who'd been tossed as she rolled over and I could see the emptiness in her eyes. The light had indeed gone out in her long before we arrived.

Nihil jumped up onto the top of the far right pillar at the end of the bridge we were crossing. With his arms wailing he gave out a loud howl. Then he looked straight at us, "See, this is the work of your loving Father. Damnation. It was by

His word that all these were damned. And what was their sin? They failed to confess Him?

Then the demon Nihil stared directly at me. "You, boy, clearly you see the futility of life? Don't you think that many of these heard His call and tried to serve Him? With your gifts why not serve yourself? Enjoy your life to the fullest while you can, for when it's done, it's done. Given that your fate lies here, there really is no point to your life. Only death awaits you. There is no place in Heaven for a loser like you."

Sandy stepped in front of me and drove him back with her words. "We will not hear your lies today, demon. Our Father chooses whom he will. Your comments have no bearing of what is to be and what is not to be. You only speak to deceive."

Sandy grabbed me by the arm and attempted to move me forward to rejoin the group, but I protested. "But I'm afraid." I could not believe that those words had come out of my mouth. I'd been scared the whole time pretty much, but I'd managed to keep that fact under wraps. But something deep inside of me, something instinctual, told me not to go any further. It was like looking over the edge of a cliff. I knew not to take another step.

Still on the bridge, I looked to my left to see Martin and Sanjay on their knees before Ho Chin. He'd pulled a bottle of water from his waist and wetted his fingers with it. He was reciting scripture to them as he made the sign of the cross on their foreheads.

Sandy gained my attention again. "So are you ready?" she asked me.

I replied, "I don't know..."

She gave me a look and said, "Oh you know; you just wish that you didn't."

Ho Chin finished and hugged Martin and then Sanjay. Martin arose and stated to Ho Chin, "You know I'm still going to harass you?"

Ho Chin smiled and laughed, "I expect nothing less."

Sanjay wiped his brow, "That is a relief. Martin can feel free to continue to impale himself upon my sharp wit, while he attempts to bludgeon me with his."

As Ho Chin walked towards me, the two newly confirmed converts continued on. A seemingly offended Martin questioned, "I'm not sure I like what you've implied."

Sanjay quickly quipped back, "Implied? Did I not state my position clearly?"

Ho Chin placed his hand on my shoulder and spoke to Sandy as he rubbed my shoulder. "Do not worry. One thing about this place is that it is very clear who has the hand of God upon them." Then moving closer, he spoke these words to me. "God has a claim on your life, Mike. Already His grace is upon you."

I didn't want to hear it and in my pride I pulled away from him. My addiction to myself, my own thoughts and my own logic was proving a heavy load to bear in this place of chaos. I had no anchor for things beyond me and everything here was beyond me.

Sandy leaned in, "He's right, Mike. God knew this day would come, and he knew you would not be ready yet, so He has made provisions for you. Even before you gave your life to Him at ten years old, His prevenient grace was upon you. And also now, in this time of your life when you're unsure and you doubt Him and have turned away, His Grace watches over you. So, do not fear. God is with you, even now."

I looked up to see that everyone was gathered around me. I was so caught up in my fear that I hadn't noticed. I was so embarrassed that I tried to quickly wipe away my tears to somehow hide my shame. But my cousin Akina walked over and pulled my frantic hands down away from my eyes and hugged me, kissed me on my cheek and held me until I stopped heaving. On the bridge between life and death, she held me still. Removed from all sense of order and facing death I found a peace beyond all understanding there on that bridge. My other cousins reached in to touch me as Ho Chin had. No one said anything, at least not in words. Each touch told me all I needed to know.

Then Reggie called to us, "Come on, let's go."

Nihil sneered, "Fools, all of you." In his anger, Nihil reached down into the masses and grabbed one of the lost souls by the head. "I have a sea of fools to choose from." As he placed both hands on the man's head, the man began to wail, even moreso than any of the others. The man screamed and convulsed. His body twisted and jerked and still he could not break Nihil's grip. I knew instantly that he'd taken possession of this man.

Darnell let loose a burst of ethereal fire that caused Nihil to release the man and scamper away. Carla gave him a look of satisfaction. Darnell grunted and commented, "Without filling that man with a good spirit, some other demon will come and take up residence. But for a moment he has only his own burdens to deal with."

Reggie called me to the front near the lowered swords of the angels guarding the bridge. "It's time. Stay close to me." He didn't have to say it twice.

As the silent angels allowed us to pass and enter into the masses, Akina took the lead.

The hands of every damned soul reached out for her, but as is her gift, Akina was able to allow their hands to pass right through her. For the rest of us, it was no so. Hands groped and teeth snapped with our every step. About five steps in, one of these lost souls bit my arm. "Ow!" I cried, as I instinctively drew back. No sooner had I cried, than Reggie's staff swung back to punish my attacker.

Reggie commanded me, "I know you feel sorry for these guys, but you're gonna have to fight back. They're hungry and don't care about anyone but themselves."

It occurred to me that I could use my gift to do something very nasty to the next hungry soul that tried to take a bite out of me. But something within me really didn't want to do that. And then I remembered the shield that Akina had given me. I took it off my shoulder and began to use it. At first I used it to just push them back, but when that failed to deter them, I began to swing the shield back and forth in an arc. That seemed to get their attention, but then something got mine.

After swinging to my left, and just as I was about to swing back to my right, I caught sight of a face. It was a face that I recognized from high school. It was the face of a friend of mine. His name was Charles, but we called him Chuck. In eighth, ninth and tenth grade he was part of the little group I hung out with, as much as I was a part of any group. But by the eleventh grade he had begun to change. We were no longer cool enough to hang out with anymore. He started showing up for class stoned and not really caring that he was. By the time the rest of us were heading off to college, he was dealing. I, and all his friends, knew that he was out of his league. It was to little surprise that by our sophomore year of college we heard that someone had broken into his apartment and killed him. Actually, the way I heard it, he'd been executed. I can't help but think that there was something that I could have done. But the truth of the matter is that at that age, I was pretty much a mess myself.

But there he was. Caught in the moment, I froze. Again, Reggie caught sight of me and intervened. "Dude!" he called, "You're gonna have to get with it."

In that moment I pulled myself together on the outside. But within, having seen Chuck, I was forever changed. There in the field of the damned, each of us pushed through as best we could. And some of us didn't push at all. I looked back to see that Sandy had broken down crying. She was crying for each hand that reached out to her, even though that hand meant her harm. Darnell picked her up and carried her in his arms. And while Darnell was pretty hard to really damage, he was not impervious to pain. He felt their clawing and bites, but he did not retaliate. He simply pushed through as lovingly as anyone possibly could. Carla erected a telekinetic barrier that shielded not only herself, but the remaining three time-traveling guards as well. Carla's face was wet with tears also, but her focus was unbroken. Kim, who brought up the rear, had no tears. Her countenance was more of anger, but I wasn't so sure to whom it was directed. Her protective measure was similar to Carla's. She simply allowed the current that was within her to run free across her skin. Every time a lost one touched her, they got a shock. Even the damned weren't so impaired as to touch her twice. In fact, if they knew anything at all, it was pain.

Walking through, rather than fighting the damned, Akina was so far in front of us that we lost sight of her. Reggie called out, "Akina?" but heard nothing back. Still despite the chaos, we could see the light marking our destination in the distance.

The demon Nihil jumped up on the shoulders of two of the damned and threw a strap around their necks steering them through the populace. Both of his minions followed, trampling blind groping souls with each step. Nihil laughed, "Fools! Do you know why the Bible says that God knew you before you were born? It's because He did. You were all His, before you were mine. When I was cast out of Heaven, I wasn't alone. You're all just as damned as I am. You just don't know it yet."

Then in an instant it was clear to me that Nihil had begun his assault on us in earnest. He leapt from the shoulders of his drones and onto Darnell's back. Dread and Shamus each took an arm of Darnell's while Nihil tore at him. They dragged him off from us. At once we all tried to come to his aid, but the multitude of damned corpses, swinging and flailing about in their blind panic were too much to pass through quickly enough to match Nihil's pace. Within seconds it grew difficult to see them at all. But I could see with each swing down Nihil made another accusation. "And do any of you really know what Heaven is like? This prize that you're fighting for, do you really understand it? Then why do you fight for it? It is a place of the spirit and not of the flesh. But is it not those things of the flesh that you enjoy the most? Those things of the flesh are in your nature and your seeking after the light is really pointless, isn't it? Look at all of these and you are no better. Bound by the flesh you were born, and bound by the flesh you shall die."

I pushed as hard as I could, but the masses of people were so overwhelming that in truth I was being carried along with the crowd away from Darnell and back towards the river. Reggie had left me and was fighting desperately towards Darnell. Blind wandering body upon blind body impaired his journey. But then to my left I caught sight of Kim on her board rising into the air. Bodies clung to her and her board left and right, but next I realized that Carla was standing on the board too. Together they struggled to free themselves from the masses. And then as they headed off towards Darnell, still with one tenacious, unwanted, and apparently shockproof passenger, two winged beasts like the ones we'd seen on the other side of the river swooped down to attack them. And as they fought these demons an even more fierce panic broke out among the damned as the ground around

Darnell and his persecutors began to open. Nihil meant to drag Darnell down below this first level of Hell for what purposes I couldn't even imagine.

Carla and Kim worked together to fight the winged demons off, but when Carla saw the ground begin to open she yelled something to Kim and she let out an electrical shockwave to allow Carla the room to jump. From about thirty or forty feet in the air, Carla dove down into the quickly sinking floor below. I couldn't see what happened next, but according to Kim, Carla surprised the fallen angel Nihil. Apparently, he was expecting something fancy, but she just reeled back and popped him in the mouth. Free of having Nihil on his back, Darnell swung one hand and then the other, freeing himself from Dread and Shamus too.

Carla, using her gift, slung large stones at Nihil as she shouted, "Stay away from my brother!" In that moment, Akina finally made it back to them. Akina took Carla and disappeared, while Darnell took to the air to assist Kim.

However, it was in his rising to the air that I first realized that Sandy was no longer in his care. I tried to call to the others over the den of wailing souls and our own emotions, with little success. I got low and began to scamper between the feet of those falling towards eternal midnight. My destination was the original point of Nihil's attack on Darnell. I reasoned that she shouldn't be far from there. Working my way against the grain, at last I managed catch a glimpse of her curled body on the ground. She was being trampled by the damned. As I pulled close to her I could hear the others calling out to her. I shouted, "Over here!"

I wrapped my arms around her and used my talents as best I could to keep them off of her. She was crying, but I couldn't begin to tell you how many of those tears were from being stepped on and how many came from the pain she felt from seeing and feeling all of these lost souls. Lying there and trying to cover her, I also couldn't help but notice some of the bruises she'd already endured. Almost immediately, a deep sorrow came over me as I thought about when she was raped by those guys back in high school. Lying there I knew that I'd give any price, forsake any mercy destined my way, for her well-being.

One of the walking dead lay on top of us for a moment because I'd grown weary of fending them off. Then all of a sudden, to his surprise and ours, he flew off of us. As he rose into the air I could see Reggie holding him aloft, before he flung him back into the crowd. Then Akina came walking, literally, through the crowd. She knelt down and took Sandy into her arms. I released her to Akina's loving embrace. Then, in an instant, they were gone. Reggie took up position between the oncoming crowd and me. Then Akina reappeared. Wrapping her arms around me, we disappeared from the midst of the madness only to reappear on a hilltop overlooking the scene. Here we were pretty much out of the way or at least as much as anyone could be in such a place.

When she'd brought back the last of her guardians, Akina disappeared one last time to retrieve Reggie. After she returned with him, Akina apologized for leaving us and explained that she was looking for a refuge such as the one we stood upon. It was in clear view to her and she knew that could allow her to safely teleport us there one by one. This perch she found was much closer to our goal and from there we could devise a plan. Akina stated, "Here's the deal. In the distance you see that circle of light. That is where we need to go. So, we need to figure out a strategy to get there." Of course, in the back of my mind I was thinking of reasons why it would be best to stay where we were.

For me, at that point, I felt like the fear was coming in waves. I'd be fine for a few seconds and then boom, right back into shallow breathing and a racing heart. I wondered why did these panic attacks start just then? There were many other opportunities to wig out before that one. I reasoned that maybe it was all the lost souls that finally threw me over the top. Anyway, I was standing there attempting to focus on my breathing and calm myself when the strangest thing happened, mid-heave. Our shadow friend appeared again, the wisp we'd seen twice before. The first time he was a shadow. The second time he came bearing barely legible flashcards. But this time his mouth opened and words did flow.

"Hi, my name is Jonah."

22: Return to Nineveh

It was nearly an hour later before Jonah decided to extract himself from the river. He saw a lot of commotion ashore, but he reasoned it was just the Blues looking for him. However, it wasn't fear that delayed his exit from the water but his desire to linger in the glow of the miracle he'd just witnessed before he rejoined the battle. Hugging the planks of wood that fell into the water with him as he drifted down the slow-moving Potomac River, Jonah mused on the mind of God. He thought the pillars of fire were very old school of Him, but Jonah supposed that God wanted it to be clear to all that this was the hand of God. Jonah was one to thank God for each breath and saw God's hand in all things. But Jonah also realized that there were those who didn't. Jonah had not yet recovered his wife, but he was filled with an abiding hope that consumed his doubts.

Jonah kicked his way towards an upcoming marina. He maneuvered towards a floating pier and climbed out slowly. Dripping wet, he stood up. Somehow he'd managed to keep both shoes attached to his feet. As he began to walk towards the heart of the marina he passed a maintenance worker just beginning his shift. The man, with broom in hand, gawked at Jonah as he passed by. It was obvious that the man had witnessed Jonah's exit from the Potomac. Jonah gave him a smile and raised a brow, but kept walking.

It was about three in the morning and Karun's store wouldn't be open just yet. In his tattered attire it was very apparent that Jonah had been in a fight. His condition would certainly have drawn attention and that's one thing he didn't want in that Blue world, especially not that night. He would go to Karun's as quickly as possible and would simply ring

Karun to buzz him into the apartment that he and his wife Manisha kept above the store. Thirty minutes later, a water-logged Jonah arrived at Karun's shop. On the side of the shop entrance was a door leading to a stairwell. Jonah pushed the button to ring Karun's apartment. He rang it with some urgency. It took a while, but eventually a sleep weary Karun asked, "Who is it?"

Jonah answered, "It's me, Jonah. Can you let me in?"

Before Jonah heard a reply, he heard the door unlock and he pushed in as Karun called, "Come on in, dude."

As Karun unlatched the front door, a robed Manisha had entered the front room. "Is it Jonah? Does he have Monica?"

When Karun opened the door, Jonah burst into the room with an uncontainable excitement. "Quick, turn on the news!" None of them had the audio transmission implants that most folks born into Blue society got shortly after birth. "The most outstanding and incredible thing just happened! It was truly amazing! I wish you had been there! My God, my God!"

Jonah began to relate to them what had taken place as each of them listened intently to the airwaves. The more Jonah told them, the more that Manisha began to scream and shout. Karun cried, "Oh my God!" and "I don't believe it!" and, "You're kidding me!" with each twist and turn. As their excitement grew, so did their puzzlement that nothing about the incident had yet been broadcasted.

Karun surmised that perhaps the Blues wanted to keep this quiet, so he suggested, "Let's see what our favorite station has to say." He searched the airwaves to find just what frequency the Christian pirate radio was transmitting that day. The authorities always tried to jam it, so they had to change frequencies a lot. Tuning in, they all got quiet as Karun turned the radio down to a mere whisper. They didn't want the neighbors to hear.

There in the last darkness of a new morning soon to be born, they heard, "...again as we've been saying since we've been on the air, the Parthenon has been destroyed and the reports of what actually happened can only be described as Biblical... We're talking Old Testament, fire from the sky, Biblical."

The three of them jumped up and down circling around, hands held like first graders. Their joy was in that these ungodly beings had gotten "theirs", but also in the hope that Monica might soon be free. Surely, such an awesome display would prompt the powers that be in the Blue world to figure out quickly that she was not worth the wrath of God.

They were wrong.

Soon after that pronouncement the Christian radio station went silent. The Blue stations still gave no hint that anything was amiss. The quiet airwaves made the three of them just a bit nervous. They decided that it was not safe for them to be with Jonah or for him to stay there. Jonah decided to go to a safe house, at least until they got some sense of just what was going on. Jonah suggested, "Let's all get a couple more hours of sleep. Then you guys go down and open the store. A little later I'll slip out and make my way across the park to the safe house."

Manisha and Karun went back to bed and Jonah curled up on the couch. In that brief time, Jonah slept but his dreams were restless. He dreamt of Monica first and then of Sara. Again Sara said to him, "A day of decision is coming soon when you will have to decide if you will serve the Lord totally."

In his dream, Jonah replied, "But am I not doing that now?"

Sara replied, "Faith is the substance of things hoped for and the evidence of things unseen. You must let go of the world and trust Him totally. You must step beyond that which you can see and feel. You must have faith."

In the morning the loving couple arose and Manisha made a quick breakfast for the three of them, although with Monica still missing, Jonah had no appetite.

Karun and Manisha left for the day. Then about twenty minutes later Jonah left. As carefully as he could, Jonah went down the back stairwell and across a small parking lot located right behind the building. A long alley extended to the left of the lot that exited into the park. On the other end of this park was a safe house, one of only two that he knew of that were downtown. In the early and still eerie light of morning, Jonah entered the alley. He could make out that a crowd had gathered on the edge of the park. At first he could not see the reason for their gathering but then, about halfway down the path, he could tell that there was something going on in the park that apparently warranted some attention.

Reaching the end of the alley and pushing his way through the masses gathered there, he could see clearly the source of their astonishment. There in the trees hung many bodies. It was a new and terrorizing scene to everyone there. Jonah, a student of history, knew this scene. He had studied and thought on such things. That knowledge and those thoughts had both empowered him and bound him over the years. It came quickly to him that the Blues knew that the irony here would not be lost on him. From every oak hung at least one dangling body secured at the neck by a noose. In what remained of the darkness Jonah had difficulty making out the faces, but he knew who they were and he knew what this was. This was the Blue answer to his encroachment last night. And these were his people, fellow Christians of every shade.

Pushing through the last of the crowd, Jonah entered the park alone. No one else in the crowd dared to breach the imaginary line of what is and what should never be. There was a stillness that defied Jonah's understanding. Typically, this time of morning there'd be a light breeze announcing the coming of the new day. But the air was stale that day, fouled by the evil of men.

For all the horrible things that man has done, all the weapons of greater destruction that he seeks, nothing stings like evil with a personal touch such as this. Jonah stumbled not just physically, but on every level of his being, into that bizarre garden. Reaching the first victim, Jonah looked up to see his swollen disfigured head and fell to his knees. He did not recognize the man in flesh, only spirit. He was a believer like him, but now dead and it pained Jonah so to see and feel this horror. Ribbons were wrapped around each of their wrists, identifying them as "Christian traitors". Thinking then, Jonah began searching through the shadows cast by the other trees for faces that he might recognize. Not seeing anyone he knew, he rose up to his feet and began an almost frantic hunt through that vineyard of suffering. Left and then right he went. Two steps forward and then one back he went. Almost halfway though the park, he saw her. It was Pam, the woman he'd rescued when he freed Sara. Again he fell to his knees, and while there, his eyes focused on a body hanging just behind Pam; it was Heru. Heru, who served beside him in their church choir back in the days before these awful times. Heru, who had encouraged him to marry Monica when he'd told him of his plans. Heru, who'd provided safe haven for so many in this current age. Jonah fell prostrate, his face buried in the dirt, his hands grasping at what grass remained from the night's activity. Heru had died trying to save others; even in that first moment Jonah already knew that. As Jonah thought back about what a good man Heru was, an anger began to swell up in him and he let out a yell into the ground like he'd never screamed before. Jonah decided he would bring the wrath of God down upon these devils. He would wipe the entire city out like the Sodom it was. Then he thought why stop with the city, why not the whole nation. These fools had no idea what he could do.

But then he thought about his wife, Monica. They would not kill their bargaining chip until they had him in custody. This Jonah knew from the moment he learned they'd captured her. And while broadcasting a message to the Christian community would be an effective means to have them evacuate the city, it would do little to free Monica. He would have to play along just long enough to verify that Monica was safe.

Finally, Jonah noticed that others had entered the park after him, and by Jonah's reaction it was clear that he was a grieving Christian or friend of Christians. A couple of officers approached him. As Jonah raised his head he could see the look of recognition in their eyes that told Jonah that they knew who he was. But in that same instant Jonah slipped back in time the seven seconds it took him to step behind the large oak behind them. From where the officers stood, Jonah seemed to disappear into thin air. No, he'd just walked around the corner, bypassing the illusion of time to leapfrog his away from the park to the safe house.

Jonah made his way around back to a door between the two garbage dumpsters and collapsed there on the ground. Although his body was curled and still, his emotions were ricocheting from sadness, to anger, to regret and despair. So much so that he could not muster the focus to walk through that door. Mostly he felt grief, especially at the loss of Heru. He felt anguish that he'd never be able to again share the knowing silence between two men on the same page about life and the world. Heru could have easily been a blood brother to

Jonah. And then there was guilt. So many were dead and he, Jonah, was the cause.

It was then that the door above him opened and Dan, the owner of that safe house, stepped into the alley and reached down to a stunned Jonah. Dan called, "Hey Jonah, get up! Quickly now." Jonah, understanding the risk Dan was taking, immediately rumbled to his feet and followed Dan through the door.

Dan led Jonah through the hall and past the stairwell to an apparent dead end. Dan reached into his pocket and pulled out a keypad. He quickly punched in an access code. But nothing happened. Dan tried again and still nothing happened. Dan lowered his head and said in a firm voice into the keypad, "Bruce, unlock the door." Dan murmured to Jonah, "At times like this I wish I'd never allowed that room to be locked from the inside. You know, just in case the keypad ever fell into the wrong hands, you still can't open the door if the people inside don't want you to." Again Dan called out, "Bruce!"

An invisible voice came over an unseen intercom speaker, "Who is that with you?"

A joyless, but still tearless Jonah fully removed his hood revealing his ebony crown. Whether it was from recognition that Jonah was indeed a good man or that he could with a couple of movements melt the whole wall away, Bruce unlocked the door and it swung open.

Dan gave Bruce a look as both men entered the room. There were two others, two women, huddled in the darkest corner of the room. Jonah noticed right away that everyone in the room, with the exception of Bruce, looked like they'd been in a fight.

Bruce reached out to Jonah to touch his arm. "You're alive? You're alive? How did you get here in broad daylight without being caught? Even an electronic cloak cannot stand the test of sunlight."

Bruce continued asking unanswered questions as Dan led Jonah to a chair on the far side of the room. As Jonah sat, Dan offered, "Would you like a drink of water?"

Jonah nodded and Dan filled a plastic cup for him. Jonah took a sip and then leaned forward, covering his face with his free hand. Jonah's mind was still reeling from the sight of his friends hanging in the park like grotesque ornaments. Not even eight hours ago everything was going better than he could have hoped. Not even eight hours ago, he'd been a part of something comparable to things he had read in the Old Testament. Not even eight hours ago he thought it a certainty that the Blues would release his wife. And now? Everything had spun horribly out of control. One of his best friends was dead, so many of those he loved were taken from this world as though they were murderers, and his wife seemed further away from him than ever before. The responsibility for all of it, he felt, was at his feet. It was his actions that had led to all of these things. "No, no, no..." he wailed, as he stood up and pounded his fist into the wall. He wanted to cry, but on the verge of tears each time he would pull back and the anger would come. The anger at his Blue tormentors would push back his tears and bring him a degree of earthly clarity and resolve. All the while, a dread-filled Bruce rattled on like an incessant demon. And all the while, a spirit of shame sought to have Jonah curled and huddled on the cold concrete flooring.

In the meantime, a silent Dan stood by. Dan watched Jonah, and when he'd slowed enough to sit and breath, Dan refilled his cup with water.

Still it should be noted that, while those all around him, even the Blues at the park, were steeped in fear, the Lord had made Jonah so that he would not be. Perhaps Sara was cor-

rect when she said that Monica and Jonah were "dysfunctional, but in a very fearful and wonderful way." Sure, Jonah had
his anxieties, but his fears were about the well-being of his
wife and friends and about failure, seldom about his own life,
at least whether he lived or died. No sane person wants pain,
but there are those who don't mind leaving this world, even
though they happily leave the date of departure up to the
Lord.

Dan, always watchful of his monitors, noticed that
someone else was seeking refuge at his backdoor. Dan acknowledged, "There is another one." So he departed to address the matter with the potential tenant.

However, as soon as Dan left, the ladies joined Bruce's
chorus, crying for retribution. "Failure to respond in kind
would be complicit with their act," one of the women said.

Bruce admonished him, "How can you set all these things
in motion and not finish them? What of the sacrifices already
made? How cruel would that be to all of us? How cruel would
that be to those hanging in the park, not a hundred yards
from here?" And then Bruce's voice got very low as he leaned
into Jonah. "Then there is the matter of your wife..."

Bruce stood erect and walked across Jonah's line of sight.
Jonah's eyes followed him with an unblinking gaze. It was a
glare that told Bruce to be careful here. But the die was cast,
and Bruce was not one to retreat. "Do you still believe her to
be alive?"

"Yes, yes I do," Jonah said quickly and then slowly.

"Even though a hundred hang in the park? Why would
they kill all of them and spare her?" Bruce accused.

Jonah retorted, "Do you really want to know? Do you think
you can handle it?"

"Try me," Bruce said.

The answer came as even a surprise to Jonah, "If she were
already dead, the Lord would have told me. I would know."

Bruce was incredulous, "Oh, you've got to be kidding me? We're talking about the real world here. I'm sorry to say, but your wife is dead, move on. I believe in God and I believe we see His will in what He does. If He blesses you with fortune then you have found favor in His eyes and you are a good man. If He curses you with misfortune then obviously there is sin in your life. And, as in your case, if He blesses you with a hammer, then you're supposed to use it to defend His people. You have been blessed with a hammer between your ears and in your hands. How dare you sit here in the dark while those who have slaughtered God's people walk the earth? If you had acted more strongly and sooner against these opponents of God, your wife would be alive. By the very fact that you have these tools in your hands, it is clear that you should have and still should go out and smite these fools! Are you deaf man? How many times must God tell you this? How many more must die before you do what God has called you to do?"

The two women in the room chimed in with their agreement to Bruce's call to arms.

Jonah stood up filled with anger, "How dare any of you say these things to me? Don't you know that I have lost my entire family to the Blues? The few who haven't left this world in spirit through death have left it in body and will not return in my lifetime. I am a hollow man in this regard. And now they have my wife, and still you speak to me as if I am deaf, dumb and blind to these things? Be certain, nothing would satisfy my flesh more than to see this beastly nation brought low. But God said, vengeance is the Mine, not yours or anyone's here." Jonah stopped and looked around the room for a second.

He continued, "At this point, I am dead to this world; and I have no hope of happiness in this life, but I have a hope in Heaven to give what's left of my life to that great cause, to serve my Master and to do His will. And if God allows, I will find my wife."

One of the women in the room that was lit mostly in black light, arose from the corner where she'd been cowering. She walked over to Jonah as she pulled her hair back to reveal a slash across her forehead. "Look at this!" she said. "I got this when they invaded our home. They dragged me, my husband and our child into the street. One of the men in the mob hit me with something hard and I blacked out. When I awoke, he was on top of me. I screamed for my family as I tried to fight him off, but he and the others with him just laughed. So now I am here and I don't know if my family is alive or dead. But in my heart I know the answer. Have you seen the park?"

Jonah nodded.

"Then you know," she continued. "Who will hold them accountable for this, if not us? It is not a matter of vengeance but of justice. They must pay for this."

Jonah thought for a moment and opened his mouth, "What exactly would you have me do?"

The woman responded, "They have to pay. If what I've heard is true, then I know that you have the means. Lay this city low or even this nation if that's what you have to do, but they must be stopped."

Jonah answered her back, "So, let's be clear, I should kill them, kill them all."

"If that's what it takes. They are a murderous people. Any penalty brought against them will be well earned and past due," she said.

Jonah nodded his head and then asked the woman a question, "So, how did you escape?"

The woman answered, "There was a gang of them and they all intended to take turns with me, but when it was the third man's turn, he held back the others long enough for me to get away."

"So, if I lay this city low, should this man die too?" Jonah asked her.

She hesitated for a second before answering, "Yes. Sometimes the few have to pay for the sins of the many. That's what God did in the Old Testament. Some of the Blues may be decent people, but by and large they are an evil people. So, do what you have to do to protect us today and let God sift them out on that day."

The room went silent with these words as everyone looked to Jonah. He said nothing. Jonah thought about a number of things, but said nothing. He thought about his friend Sara and he thought about his wife. But he also thought about the bodies of Heru and Pam hanging in the park just yards away. He thought about how much each of them had sacrificed their lives here on Earth. And he thought about how to honor that gift. Like his namesake, he too had been a prisoner of wanting to serve God as he, Jonah, thought he should. For the last ten years he had quietly waited on the Lord to punish these people. He waited on the Lord to execute His vengeance. And now, although he felt the woman's pain and certainly understood her complaint, something deep in Jonah's soul held him back. True, they were his enemy and he hated what they stood for and the things that they did, but he realized that he didn't really "hate" them. The people in that room had unwittingly served to make that distinction very clear to him. While Jonah far from loved the Blues, he didn't hate all of them, not like he now understood hate. Jonah would later reason that it was not his place, as a servant of the most-high God, to take vengeance. If one believes himself to be a Christian and hates someone to that degree, one must be so consumed with hate that he or she does not care what God has to say about the matter.

Dan returned to the door with the new guest in hand and buzzed to be let in. He entered the room, leaving the door open. With him was a young girl of about ten. Her hair was matted with blood and her blouse was drenched in it. Dan explained, "She was attacked and left for dead. When she awoke she made her way here." This was the child from Jonah's dreams. Jonah's mouth fell open at the sight of her. This was Jonah's burning bush. She was the living confirmation of all that was on his heart.

The young girl was shaking and in need of medical attention. Jonah kneeled and wrapped his arms around her, trying to warm and comfort her. Bruce veered around them to step outside the room, but for the most part Jonah paid him no mind, as he was focused on the child. "You're okay now. You're safe here."

The almond-eyed girl didn't respond, so one of the women in the room also kneeled beside Jonah. She took the girl's moist hand and spoke to her in a motherly tone, "My name is Elizabeth. What's your name?"

The child at last opened her mouth and engaged the living again, if only for a moment, "My name is Amy."

Dan whispered grimly into Jonah's ear, "Word is that they plan to hang 1,000 tomorrow, if you don't give up. And that doesn't include those who'll die before they ever make it to a hangman's noose." Dan's gaze then fell on Amy.

"Amy," Jonah said softly, "We won't let them hurt you anymore." In that moment Jonah knew with absolute certainty what he must do. For if he answered the question, "Are you, or are you not a servant of the most high God?" then the choice was simple. If he was truly a believer, then by doing what was right, doing what God called him to do, he would be performing an act of faith. And if he was faithful unto death, God would surely make things right beyond anything that his own hands could ever accomplish. Faith in God required trust beyond that which is seen.

Bruce stepped back into the room and jumped back in the conversation, "So, you're going to take these punks out now, before tonight, right?"

Still kneeling and staring at Amy, Jonah answered him, "I am going to take care of it."

"What does that mean?" The other woman, the one with the gash in her own head, stepped forward from the shadows.

"It means I'll handle it," Jonah said more strongly than before.

"How?" she asked.

Jonah replied, "I am going to make them a deal to end all of this." Jonah rose to wet a cloth and handed it to Elizabeth who was still kneeling next to the girl.

"A deal? Man this doesn't end until they're all dead. That's the only deal. What don't you understand about that?" the standing woman demanded of Jonah.

Bruce backed her, "Amen Sister! See, I knew you were going to wimp out. That's why I just made provisions to make sure you don't chicken out again."

"Provisions?" Jonah asked.

Bruce said nothing, but gave a sly you-wait-and-see smile.

Within two minutes they heard a pounding at the outside door. They could hear it because Dan had left the door to the safe room open when he entered. They could also hear the aircraft overhead even though they were in the basement.

Dan knew instantly and cried, "Bruce, what have you done?"

Bruce smiled again, "They pulled me out of my bed last night too, but I sweet-talked them into a deal. I told them that on occasion that I do come across the one that they're looking for and if they would agree to spare me, I would in turn contact them the next time I ran into Jonah. So, when you brought in the little girl, I stepped out and turned on this little tracking device they gave me. In hindsight, I think it was a doubly clever move, given your passive nature. Now you will have to fight!"

Elizabeth sprang to her feet and shouted, "Man, are you insane?"

Dan moved to close the safe room door, but Bruce said to him, "At this point, closing that door now will just make this a hostile, ugly situation."

Dan conceded the moment and stepped away from the switch, but he yelled at Bruce. "Man, what is wrong with you? Do you understand what you've done to all of us?"

Bruce began to smile again as the back door came off its hinges, but before he could fully break a grin, the other woman in the room, his former ally, began to swing on him. He didn't have any scars when he came into that room, but he certainly did when she was through with him.

Seeing the spirit in Bruce, Jonah was reminded of a verse from a poem he once read that began, "I see nothing when I look at you. My eyes are filled with what's not there. I hear nothing when you speak. My ears are filled with volumes of meaningless noise. When I try to touch you, you cannot be touched. And for once my fingers are happy that they are blind and deaf."

As Jonah saw the mechanical battering ram pull away and the soldiers begin to enter, he reached to his wrist and began to key into his Wave Modulator. It had been hidden all that time from his current roommates using his newfound powers of space and time, however modest they may have been. Immediately, a glowing yellow light bathed all of them.

Again the wave barrier was set such that certain ranges of sound waves could pass through. So Jonah heard the Major proclaim, "Come on out now, we have you surrounded."

Jonah called back down the hallway to him, "I'd like to speak with someone regarding the terms of my surrender."

Bruce cried, "Surrender? You're kidding right?" Jonah ignored him.

The Major replied back almost laughing, "Sir, we don't negotiate with criminals, especially non-Blue criminals."

Jonah raised his arm and then keyed some additional commands that caused the wall of energy to move out slowly towards the soldiers. The moving wall began to push some of the soldiers back. The Major ordered them to open fire. None of their weapons could penetrate the barrier. The men were forced to retreat outside the doorway. But Jonah did not stop there. His wall continued to expand to the point that it met and pushed out the wall surrounding the doorway. Bricks and wood tumbled into the alley and still Jonah continued to expand his territory. He stopped the expansion once the wave barrier extended at least seven yards beyond the building and into the alley. Jonah stepped out into the alley within the glowing protective rectangle he'd created. At the nod of the Major, the men opened fire again, but again to no avail. They began to back off so that the aircraft circling above could have a shot. They fired both missiles and particle beams at Jonah only to see the sum of their effect was to blow out some of the brick walls and all of the windows in the alley. When the smoke cleared and the reverberations had subsided, Jonah cleared his throat and spoke loudly again. "Could you please call your Commander so that I can negotiate my surrender?" This time the Major got on the horn. Certainly it was a redundant call, for the Major knew and so did Jonah, that the Major's superiors were already very much tuned into the happenings in that alley.

The others still stood within the building, but once the bombing stopped, that didn't stop them from offering their opinions. Of course Bruce was the most vocal in the sense that he was doing the most talking. He was still trying to play both sides and did not want the soldiers to hear him. "Why are you going to give up without a fight? Don't you know that they will kill you?"

Jonah replied, "Oh, I suspect there's a good chance they might. But the truth is that I will die when it's my time to die. The Blues have nothing to do with that and neither do you."

Bruce pleaded, "Then if you won't fight them for yourself, then do it for us. Think about Dan, the women and the little girl."

"And yourself?" Jonah asked.

"Well, yes, there is me. But I figure after what I've done, you're not likely to do anything for me," Bruce confessed.

Jonah glanced back at him, and just smiled.

Finally, the Major returned. Grudgingly he spoke, "My superiors will hear your terms, but only once you're confined."

"Fine, if you will swear not to harm any of these people that are with me," Jonah requested.

The Major made one last concession, "Sure."

With that, Jonah lowered his protective shield to only cover himself. The Major asked him to remove that too so that they could cuff him, but Jonah refused saying, "I'll do that later, once I've come to some agreement with your leaders."

The Major nodded his head and turned to lead Jonah to the paddy wagon. Although they heard Jonah's request on their behalf, the others, with the exception of Bruce were visibly upset that he was going into custody. Jonah looked back towards them and gave a reassuring smile. Seeing this they smiled back. Something within his spirit conveyed the hope inside of him to their spirits and they were then well with his departure.

The wagon closed its doors and proceeded to carry Jonah away for his date with the Sapphire Illuminati.

23: A Man Who Gave Back the World

"Are you, or are you not?" I asked the image of man.

"I am," he replied with a smile as the others gathered around.

I stuttered to the brown skin, thirty-something looking man, "And... and... you're...?"

"Jonah, or given that you are of the flesh, you might prefer to see me as Jonah's spirit. But who my flesh is to you, is your descendant. You are my ancestors in body."

Reggie asked suspiciously, "Is this guy for real?"

Akina stepped forward and reached out her hand towards Jonah. She moved her hand back and forth a couple of inches from him, as though her hand were a scanner. "So, you are the one who's been, excuse me, shadowing us? Why?"

Jonah turned, and while looking down, began to pace along the ridge. "In the weakness of my flesh, in the subconscious of my earthly being, I chase after you pleading for your help. In essence I am here now, due to a longing within my flesh to find you. To make it plain, I manifest clearly before you only when my body sleeps."

Carla then asked, "So, you're not real? You're a dream?"

Jonah answered, "Oh, I'm very real, but to Jonah I am a dream, only the gist of which he will remember. What you see in me is the same that is in each of you. I am what was and what remains beyond each of you in your own lives."

Reggie retorted, "You speak in riddles, man."

Jonah smiled again, "The truth is always a riddle to those who do not understand it. I speak as clearly as I can. Those things beyond the flesh are always a mystery to the flesh, which in part is why you should not be here. Although I will confess, it is good for me that you are."

Sandy spoke up, "All things work together for good for those who love the Lord... even when we mess up."

"Yes," Jonah confirmed. "Simply put, I am here on behalf of my flesh. My own fleshly anxieties have sent me wandering night after sleepless night, in search of you. Now many an earthly spirit does wander here in the wee hours of the night, but what makes me special is that my earthly vessel has a portion of your gift that allows me to actually find you here and to have coherent conversation with you. Of course on a divine level, it is not that simple. For His own reasons God has allowed this exception to the rule to exist, my meeting you here. It seems that God loves my fleshly counterpart. That's not to say that God loves him any more than any of His other sheep, but it's just that my counterpart, as you say in your day, gets it. In a similar manner as the way in which he understands creation, such that he has created technologies well beyond his age, so too does he understand our Creator's mind more than most. For God's own purposes, he is the advent of a new age of Judges. Surely you see that in the flesh, I am just a shadow of Akina. You will do far greater things than I even dare to dream of in my time after you, so to speak. Therefore, also be aware, that you are not long for your current age. Consider, you were made and allowed to parse time and space for a reason."

Kim, who was standing towards the back of the group, spoke up with a question. "So, if you want us to help you, where do we find you?"

Upon seeing Kim, Jonah released his biggest smile yet. "Right now, my flesh is sleeping in a cell in the basement of the Capital City jail three days before Christmas. My flesh wants you to come right away so that you may help me find my wife, but I know more fully, that tonight is not the night. If and when you do travel to my time, you will know the time and place; that is, Akina will know. Here, absent of my flesh,

I have faith that my Father will work it out and I do not worry. He has spared me so many times before and I know that no harm will come to me until that day that He calls me home. And that hour will be at His discretion and no one else's. My whole being is okay with this and always has been. But there is a conflict within me regarding my wife, who is missing. In spirit I trust God to deliver her. But in the flesh I am very anxious about her safety. So anxious in fact, that I, Jonah's spirit, have come across time and space to find you in an attempt to reconcile body and soul. But like you, at the end of the day, this was a trip that I need not take. For as with most dreams, I am, as Freud has said, simply an expression of Jonah's attempt to resolve conflict in his life. But what my flesh does not fully grasp, is that this battle is not his. It is not in his control and yet he cannot let go. Therefore, here I am. I am hopeful that meeting you here will help to bring peace to the mind of my flesh."

Reggie, looking a bit puzzled, tried to cut to the chase, "So, do you want us to rescue you or not?"

Jonah stared directly at Reggie, "Brother, I want you to follow where the Holy Spirit leads you in my regard. If you will do that, then it will be well with me, come what may."

We all, including Akina's guards, stood in silence trying to digest what he was really telling us. Finally, Jonah spoke again, "I know that's a lot to take in right now, but when the time comes you will know what to do. Let me say this before I go. I know that I do not have your gifts, but one gift I do have is understanding. So let me share this one thought that may help you down the road.

Time is an illusion created by the Infinite, so that we, the finite, might have relevance.

Remember that, and you may save yourself some steps in this walk."

Jonah was done, and as he began to fade into a whisper, he smiled one last time before he completely disappeared. After he departed, we all looked at each other with raised brows. Finally, Reggie turned away and faced the distant light, squinting just a bit. "We need to get going," he said matter-of-factly. "But before we go, I'd like to try something." Reggie reached across his back and took out the small bazooka-looking object he'd found in the armory back in the city on the hill.

Akina asked him, "You don't have any shells for that do you?"

"No," Reggie replied, "but it's not that kind of toy. It's a laser cannon. It's in disrepair, but I have an idea. Mike, you can create a combination of Xeon and other gases within this cylinder, right?"

I answered, "Ah huh, yeah I can do that."

Reggie went on, "See, I used to build lasers in school, and it's really not that hard to create a basic one. While you guys were sleeping in the command center, I found this. I didn't find any gas tanks for it, and it looks like the charging source is dead. I think Kim can charge it up. I'll want you to create a gaseous mix in the ratios I give you. Then we'll see what happens. It won't be the most efficient laser, but it ought to work."

Amazingly, after only a couple of false starts, we had ignition. It was then that I realized that I had vastly underestimated Reggie's intellect. Whereas I knew a lot of theory, in less than ten minutes he made it clear that he was my superior in the applied sciences. Reggie called to Sanjay and Martin, "Hey guys, I'm going to show you how to use this. Do you think you can you handle it?"

They both nodded in confirmation that they could; so Reggie went on. "We'll need this once we reach the battle lines. I don't want to use it on these poor souls." He looked out over the masses. Even stony Reggie was moved by the vastness of loss below us. It was as if they stretched out forever and the banks of the river behind us were some sort of event horizon to a point of singularity that none could escape. But even those that were far from the banks and closer to the light were equally doomed; they just didn't know it. Blind to the realities of their predicament, they moved in a sort of organized chaos towards an unhappy end.

Finally, Reggie called the group around to give us our marching orders. "When we leave here we're going to form something like a triangle with Kim on the point. We saw back there that these guys really don't like to be shocked. She should be able to carve a path for us, but to be on the safe side I'll be just behind her on her right and Darnell will be opposite me on her left. Sandy and Mike, y'all follow side by side tight in behind Kim between Darnell and me. Chin, you line up behind me and Akina you follow Darnell. You other three get behind Sandy and Mike with Carla in the middle. Carla's gift should give us some notice of anyone coming up from the rear. Keep in mind that these are non-combatants. Once we reach the front line where we'll have to fight our way through the demons, we'll reconfigure. Hopefully, we'll be able to use the laser cannon to clear a path. If things get tight, it'll be hard to use the cannon, but when we do, these guys will holler "fire," before they fire, at which point we all hit the dirt. We don't want any friendly fire taking anyone out. Questions?"

Sandy raised her hand, "Can we join hands for a word of prayer first?" We glanced at one another as we joined hands and formed a circle. As Sandy began to pray I peeked around the circle at my loved ones. All of us standing there, in that place, holding hands, heads bowed, bound in love and prayer. I was nearly overwhelmed with emotion, and if I had truly known what would come next, I'm sure that I would have been. But still, something within me knew, even then, that this was a precious moment. Akina twitched a bit and then wiggled her nose. Darnell held her hand and offered up a timely "Amen," here and there. Carla held Darnell's other hand; but she was looking at Kim, whose hand she also held, and smiling. It was a loving gaze that she held for her young cousin. Kim, for her part, was bowed in silence as her head bobbed back and forth. Her hair fell over her eyes and swept back when she lifted her head. To her right was Reggie. The difference in their heights caused Kim's right hand to be held aloft by his. You could say what you like about Reggie and the life he led, but you could say nothing about his love and dedication to his family. Much like Aunt Cil looked after our mothers, so too did Reggie tend to this generation. I imagined that he took on so many assignments around the world so that we would not have to. It was as though he really didn't want us to soil our lives and souls with such things. I stood between him and Sandy. Sandy was all aglow as she prayed. She prayed for everyone, except herself. She even prayed for Akina's honor guards who were joined hand to hand between her and Akina.

Finally, I heard Sandy say, "... in Jesus name we pray, Amen." At that, my focus returned to what was before us. I must say that even though we were literally at the gates of Hell, I wished that I could go back to that moment in that circle and hold hands again. If we could have stood there a hundred years, what a blessing that would have been. Looking back now, I realize that the gates of Hell could not prevail against the love in that circle.

As we released our hands and went into the formation that Reggie requested, Chin reached over and grabbed my arm. "Man, how are you doing?"

"I'm good. I think I'm ready. How about you?" I asked him.

"Brother, I try to stay ready. I mean if this is to be my day, then it will be. So why worry about it? I plan to live my life out loud, until the day I leave this world."

"Amen," I heard Darnell say to his words.

We were loose in our formation as we descended the hill. But as we approached the throngs in the plains, we tightened our lines. Kim raised both of her hands to let out the first arc of current into the crowd. You could see that it pained Kim to do this. As they cringed, so did she. Reggie encouraged her saying, "Good job. I know it's not easy to do this, but it's better than the alternative." In other words, it was better than turning the laser cannon on them. As we moved out into the sea of people it seemed to be working. Also, I think the fact that these folks, while desperate and trying to latch onto anything that might offer them some security, were in no way as panicked as the ones closer to the river.

About forty yards out, I noticed that Sandy was crying again; so I reached over and put my arm around her shoulder. "Hang in there Sandy; we're on our way home now."

At first she gave me a look that said that I really didn't understand, and then her face softened a bit and she forced a smile to allow me to believe that I had comforted her in some way. But I knew even then, that I had not. Sandy wasn't crying about being there; she was crying for the seemingly countless lost souls wandering around us, and our leaving or staying wasn't going to change that. I could see Nihil and his group in the distance, cackling euphorically at the pain of those lost souls to the left and the right that seemed to stretch out forever.

Kim could hear Sandy's sobbing and it was clearly apparent that she wanted to reach back her hand, but Reggie cautioned her, "Stay focused Kim. She'll be okay."

∞

For the most part, the first leg of our journey towards the light went as well as could be expected. But it was when we reached the line of demons herding the Lost that things began to fall apart. We had drawn within fifty yards of the demon line when Reggie instructed Martin, Sanjay and me to prepare the cannon. Kim had given it a charge right before we departed the hill; so we were ready to go. At about thirty yards we stopped our progress to set up. Being stationary required a more active style of managing the throngs surrounding us; so we wanted to move quickly. The three of us moved to the front while Kim still provided a barrier of sorts. I looked at her and saw that she'd been crying too. None of us wanted to hurt these folks; be they damned or not, they were not ours to judge. I laid my hands on the laser cannon and felt the molecules inside of it. Turning them by that point had become second nature to me. The only real effort was in remembering where to take them to get the desired effect. But the actual energy, weight and state was little work for me by then. "Go!" I hollered.

Martin held the barrel of the cannon on his right shoulder, while Sanjay, being the navigator, aimed it and then yelled "fire!" as he pulled the trigger. He aimed high because we did not want to hit any civilians and, by and large, most of the demons towered over their victims. The Bluish-white beam burned through the air. Martin and Sanjay panned the beam from left to right. The burn only lasted four or five seconds; so they had only swung the beam thirty to forty degrees when it burned out. But it was more than enough to garner the attention of our adversaries. The first creature it hit fell backwards and as we panned left to right others lost limbs or were in some other way maimed or disfigured.

I laid my hands on the cannon again. In about five seconds we were ready to fire again, so we did. This time we took down even more of them. At this point we, meaning Reggie, decided that we should try to breach the demon line; so we moved up into their midst.

The hoard of demons descended on us from the left and right. To my left Darnell caught the first long-eared demon with a right cross that floored the beast. And then turning, he somehow sensed a second larger scoundrel swinging a large grungy sword at him, and he jumped above it into the air. Holding there in mid-air, fire erupted from Darnell's eyes and burned directly into the eyes of his overly-muscled opponent, causing him to drop his sword and fall to his knees. Darnell picked up his sword and drove it into the midsection of the next charging combatant.

To my right Reggie was holding court and dispatching demons to some unknown fate at a furious pace. A hand reached up from the ground below and grabbed a hold of his right leg. But Reggie was no ordinary treat for those down below either. He lifted up his left leg and stomped down breaking and severing the arm that held him. He pulled the hand and forearm from his ankle and kept moving.

Kim had a little more difficulty. A simple shock did not have the same effect on these monstrosities as it did on the masses. She had to crank up the voltage a couple of notches to get the desired results.

Carla was to Kim's right on our perimeter. As we had entered their line, some of the beasts were now at our rear. Large parts of Carla's gifts were of little use in the Pit. The whole reading minds thing didn't work very well on these mostly mindless abominations. But through her telekinetic abilities and her ability to feel and sense things around her, she did her share and then some. Plus, she had Akina next to her, helping out as best she could.

I'd never seen Akina like this. She was lights out and silent as she took on her foes. When I caught glimpses of her face, her eyes and face were totally drained of any emotion. Even her Angela Davis afro seemed unfazed by the events around us. Akina's hair was poised and symmetrical, as were her movements. Demons swung again and again into nothingness. Again and again, she reappeared with daggers imbedded in their shoulders, necks and arms.

Sandy was squatting right behind me, trying to stay out of the way as best she could.

Chin stood right on the other side of Sandy from me. He watched our backs and took on any demons that made it past our front line. I could see instantly why he was a part of Akina's future personal guard. The size of the foe seemed to be immaterial. Every demon that made it to him was humbled by the encounter. I had offered him the shield Akina gave me, but he just smiled when he told me to keep it.

I laid my hands on the cannon a third time, even as our enemies bore down upon us. The three of us, Sanjay, Martin and I were in the middle of our pack at this point, but now Sanjay was sitting on Martin's shoulders with the cannon. He could do this since the laser cannon had little to no recoil. He could also lower it for me to refill its chamber with excitable gases.

Plan "A" had been for us to continue firing forward to clear a path for all of us to follow. But it was clear by this point that was going to be a hard line to hold. "To the right!" Sanjay yelled to Martin. Kim was on the ground with some cat-like, enraged predator bearing down on her. Sanjay pulled and released the trigger for a short burst aimed at Kim's opponent. The beam cut him in half. But it was when we turned back to the front to spend the remainder of that round toward our original path that things went wrong.

The first thing I heard was the scream and it cut me to my core. In that place screams abounded, but I knew instantly the origin of this one. I turned to our rear to see the most horrible thing I'd ever seen. There was Carla lifted high in the air on the horn of a rhino, the white rhino we'd seen twice before. His horn had pierced through her back and protruded through her stomach as though she were some kind of trophy on the end of a spear. Instinctively we all closed in towards Carla.

Darnell turned to yell out, "Carla!" He'd not even taken two steps towards her when he was tackled by an opportunistic foe twice his size as he turned his back. Even from his belly Darnell was able to get off a blast that seared into the rhino's neck which caused his head to fall so quickly that Carla fell off of his horn. He attempted to gourde her again, but Akina popped in front of him and separated the beast from his weapon with one stroke of her blade. The rhino, bleeding, and now sensing his loss, stumbled off several feet away and fell.

But no sooner did the rhino hit the dirt, Nihil, Dread and Shamus appeared right behind Carla's fallen body. Nihil announced, "Feeding time, fellas!"

Barely were the words out of his mouth before Dread and Shamus lunged towards Carla to consume her. Their mouths, then open, revealed them to be the true beasts that they were. But before they could take the first bite, Sandy, who had made her way to Carla's side, sprang up grabbing the chains that tied them to Nihil. As soon as Sandy touched their chains she began to glow. Then she pulled on their chains, pulling them back and away from Carla.

In the next moment, while Sandy was holding Dread and Shamus at bay, Akina reached out her hand and said, "Mama." Suddenly, Avis appeared holding her hand. I thought in my own mind, "What the heck?" Crazy Avis was not who I wanted to see at that moment.

Then I saw her face as she kneeled beside Carla. She looked totally at peace. It stirred a memory in me of when we were little children and Avis had us all in a circle while she read Bible stories to us. And when she laid her hands on Carla, it came to me what her gift actually was. In all the time since this adventure began, I'd never stopped to ask anyone just what Avis's gift was? I was certain that God would have no part of witchcraft, but I never thought to ask the question. But the moment she touched Carla, I knew, and I knew that I'd once known this before. Avis's primary gift was the gift of healing. She had given her life to Christ when she was a child and received her gifts shortly thereafter. It was only later that her mother was recruited into a coven, although she dabbled in such things well before she ever met Uncle Paul and effectively offered up her own daughter as a living sacrifice to Nihil's flock.

Nihil chided Dread and Shamus, "Have you lost your power over these, these who you drove from the garden so long ago? Have your lashes lost their sting?" They struggled against Sandy's hold, but to no avail. In each hand Sandy held a chain. She held one chain to each of her unwilling captives. Nihil was behind Sandy running his mouth constantly. An odd and welcome outcome of these events was that the demons seemed just as perplexed as we were. They continued to attack us, but many of them were clearly in awe of Sandy's ability to restrain Dread and Shamus.

Given what was going on, I had an idea to even the odds a bit. I yelled, "I'm going to ice everything down!" I squatted down laying my hands on the ground.

Meanwhile, Avis continued to minister to Carla. Her right hand covered Carla's wound, while her left hand rested on Carla's forehead. But so entranced was I with what was going on with Carla, Avis and Sandy, that I didn't see the next thing coming. I felt a swooshing of air and a commotion behind me. I turned quickly to see a large winged beast rising into the air with Reggie tightly gripped in its talons. Kim was trying vainly to rise into the air to his defense, but she was being held down by a number of creatures clinging to her. I sprang towards her, trying my best to pull them off of her. Every beastly arm I touched I froze to the breaking point and still there were more. Finally, I reached a tender arm. It was Kim and I pulled on her with all my might. All the while she was screaming "Reggie, Reggie!"

And just as I felt like I was pulling her free, one of the demons bit into my ankle and I too screamed. This seemed to excite them, as the one on my ankle bit down harder while a second one bit into my shoulder. I screamed again, but even louder as I felt my shoulder crack and I saw my own blood squirt into the air. As I was being pulled down I could see to my left a very bloody Chin on the back of a beast that had Martin in a strangle hold. I did not see Sanjay at all.

Just as I was hitting the dirt, a third beast approached me and I felt the ground beneath me begin to open. Through the narrowest sliver of light, I saw Sandy fall to her knees and cry out, "My God!"

It was at that very moment that I felt a movement, a charge, an energy, a presence, life moving through the crowd. It hit me and ran through me filling my bones with fire, and yet I was alive, more than I had ever been before.

The beasts that surrounded me became, in an instant, charred, still figures, and a moment later their ashes were caught up in the current and streamed away. I rolled to my knees, their ashes all around me. There was ash everywhere, so much so, that I could hardly see two feet in front of me. But I could hear, and what I heard was unlike anything I'd ever heard before. It was music that no earthly words could describe. And in that same instance I knew, for a knowing had come upon me. I looked to my right into Kim's eyes and saw my own reflection and I knew that she knew the same as I.

A host of individuals stood before us that we could not make out for the swirling ash. And still, I could see that there was a light moving between them towards us.

Finally, one last gust spirited the remaining ash away. Then I saw His face and my whole being cried out "Lord!"

24. Goats

Jonah's cell was the center cell of three, adjoined on the left and right by empty cells. He was in the basement so the hard concrete floor was very cold, even though the air temperature was in the mid-sixties. The cell was one of three for high risk prisoners. Each was designed for one inmate only. There was a single bed, toilet and sink. However, since these prisoners were deemed too dangerous to move, the setup allowed for visitation without the detainee leaving the cell. The front of the cell was made of a see-through plastic with a gap in the middle. This gap had a plastic door for the inmate to enter and exit from, but on the cell side of that door there was a second wrought iron door. This internal door could remain shut while the outer door stood open, allowing the prisoner to speak with counsel. Outside of each of the four cells was a simple desk with one chair. Since all the chairs were moveable, any visiting attorney could easily pull an extra chair up for his associate or assistant.

Jonah arrived in his cell at 1:30PM in the afternoon, on December 22. He sat alone. At 6:00PM that evening he had a visitor. He was expecting a Blue official, but instead, in through the door walked Dave, the Blue attorney for the leading Christian-friendly legal firm in town. A startled Jonah stood up, "Dave! Oh, wow you're here. I wasn't expecting you or I guess anyone I knew to come down here. Thanks."

Dave smiled, "Don't sweat it. It's hardly the first time I've been in this basement. I can only hope that this room is clean of bugs."

Jonah answered, "You mean the electronic kind?"

"Yeah," Dave replied. "If they bugged down here regularly folks in the legal community would know about it. Half the defense lawyers used to work for the state. But, just in case, I got this bug sweeper from the friend of yours that came to my office as soon as he got word you'd been picked up."

"Who was that?" Jonah asked quietly.

"The same one from the boiler room, Karun. He offered to pay all your legal fees, but I don't think it will come to that."

Jonah was touched by Karun's loyalty and friendship. "Yeah, Karun is a great guy. But I don't think you need that, I've got the room electronically sealed and I've got a charge going out that won't let recording devices save much of anything."

Dave asked. "So, how are you doing, really?"

Jonah smiled, "I'm fine. I have no idea how things will work out, but I know that they will and I'm at peace about everything. I want to see my wife more than anything in this world. When I saw Heru and Pam hanging in the park I was filled with so much anger that I made up my mind to level this entire city. And by that I mean I intended to kill them all. In my own eyes they were an abomination. In my own eyes, I said damn them all. My only hesitation was how I would notify all of the non-Blues to get out of town. When I left the park, I realized that I was not going to get my wife back, not from people who could do that. My mind was made up to kill them. But God said 'No.'"

Dave, who was sitting on the front of the table closest to Jonah's cell, leaned forwards, "How did God speak to you?"

Jonah took a breath. "When I was in the safe house I heard my own arguments said back to me, and they all rang hollow. The factual content of each argument was correct, and still it was all a lie. God said to me, who am I to cast judgment on these people? Freeing my wife was one thing, but my mind had gone way beyond that to vengeance. And vengeance does not belong to me."

Dave stood up, "Wow, you're a better man than me. After today, who could fault you for wanting to destroy this place?"

"Surely that was my plan, and after the Parthenon, I thought it was God's plan too. But God wants to save these people. The blood shed by the saints up to today was for this purpose, right here, right now. And he has called me to deliver a message of repentance to them. And still it is difficult. Every time I think of Heru, I am filled with a rage that I can barely control.

And yet... and yet, I have seen behind the veil of time; I have known the workings of creation. After all the wonders I have seen, how can I utter a word against God? There are things that I have felt in my spirit that I cannot convey in words. Words don't exist for the glory I have felt and the grace I have known. It's so very hard to explain. Down there in that safe room, hearing them cheer me on to kill all the Blues, I saw clearly the devil's snare. Sara, Pam and Heru's lives and sacrifice were not about vengeance, nor is my wife's captivity. Each of them offered their lives as a living sacrifice, and to shed blood to honor them would go against everything they gave their lives for, everything they lived their lives for."

Dave adjusted himself on the table's edge before asking, "So, why did you give yourself up? I mean I guess I understand, as a Christian, being led not to kill, but why did you allow them to bring you in? Surely, with the tools at your disposal you could have fled the city. I'm sure we could have gotten Monica released eventually."

Jonah tilted his head in puzzlement, "Did you not see what they did in the park? And that was just the beginning. The majority of the Blue Illuminati couldn't care less how many die, Christian, Blue or otherwise. My running away would have only emboldened them to kill more of us. There was no happy ending apparent in this path, but we will all have one now."

"What do you mean?" Dave asked.

"I need to speak with whoever is calling the shots these days. We have some demands," Jonah replied.

Puzzled, Dave asked, "Demands?"

"Yes," Jonah confirmed. "I have it on good authority that they need to hear this. And I'm sure that they want to talk to me too."

Dave replied, "Oh, yeah they do. The DA called me to say that they are formalizing charges against you. But I think they're having a difficult time figuring out what to charge you with. I mean to them, and forgive me for saying this, you're a non-person. So, if they charge you with destroying the temple and the surrounding compound, they'd have to acknowledge that a non-Blue has done such a thing. They don't want to do that. In fact, they'd rather not acknowledge any of your es-capades. Also, at this point, since they've not charged you with anything, it's difficult, though not impossible, to form a defense for you. But I get the sense that you're not much wor-ried about a defense or bail, are you?"

Jonah answered him honestly, "No, I'm not. But for every-one's benefit, let's move forward like I am. I don't want to play my hand too soon."

Dave stood up gathering his things, "So, I guess that's it for tonight, huh? I or one of our aides will be back in the morning just to check on you. Once I hear what they intend to charge you with or they schedule an arraignment, I'll be back for sure."

Jonah replied, "Well, let's see how things go."

Dave left and Jonah curled up into the corner and slept. As his flesh laid down, his spirit stepped forward in his dreams. His spirit conversed with the Lord and the Lord told him of things to come and things to be. Jonah's spirit listened intently and was at peace with everything God told him.

Jonah slept until nearly midnight when he was awakened by the sound of the desk chair sliding back outside his cell. Jonah rubbed his eyes and tried to focus on the well-dressed man sitting behind the desk. He appeared to be about thirty years old, but Jonah had learned how to spot the older Blues, and this one was certainly older. Some of the clues were visual, but it was more of an air that one picked up with the older ones. His short cut black hair contained a few silver strands and even sitting down it was clear that he was a rather tall man. A second later, recognition swept over Jonah. It was the Blue Lord, Chairman Marcus. He opened his mouth, "Jonah."

Jonah replied, "Chairman."

Chairman Marcus uncoupled his hands, "So you know who I am. Good, we thought as much. Therefore you know that I speak with authority on behalf of the Council. I take it you also understand who I am to you by now."

Jonah answered him, "Largely, I do, but I'm sure I don't know the half of it."

"No, you don't." Chairman Marcus gave a wry smile out of the side of his mouth as he undid his cufflinks. He didn't bother to hide his regal blue undertones. To Jonah this meant that he either lacked respect for Jonah or he planned to be totally transparent. "But still, of all the members of the council, why did they send me? Well, to be honest, most of them are afraid of you, and yet they are even more afraid of sending an underling to speak with you. They don't understand why you surrendered, and most of them think that all of this is a part of some grand scheme of yours or the Circle to lure them out of hiding and into your presence so that you can kill them all. I told them that I doubted that was the case, so of course then they all said, 'Why don't you go?' They gave me a listening device, but I'm sure they can no more hear this conversation than any other you've had. Still, I made a big fuss about being wired and how that might set you off.

But of course I wanted to be the one selected to see you. As you may have also surmised, my loyalties are a bit divided. You know that my son, your attorney, is a member of your faith and your wife is a dear friend of mine. In fact, she may be the only person in this world that I actually trust. She's pathologically honest, to a fault. I'm amazed that she hasn't spilled her guts to you before now."

Jonah spoke up in his wife's defense, "What woman will admit to her husband that she was some other man's mistress? I don't know if that was something material for me to know."

Chairman Marcus answered him, "I'm sure you would have wanted to know if that man happened to be a Blue lord? But I waste my breath, don't I? Love is blind after all. But let's get down to business here. First the formalities, the council requests that you lower your defenses immediately and submit to judgment. Obviously you will not do that, but my question to you is, given all that you've done, why did you turn yourself in now?"

Jonah answered him quickly, "So that I could have this conversation with you."

Chairman Marcus sat upright in his seat, "Oh?"

"Yes," Jonah continued, "I knew that if I turned myself in, I would see you. And seeing you now in the flesh, I know why I was led this way. There is more between us than anyone in the council knows, isn't there?"

The Chairman's eyes widened. "How do you know this? I've never told anyone, not my family, and not even Monica."

The Chairman could sense with certainty within his own spirit that Jonah understood.

Jonah smiled a bit, "I always know family when I see them."

The Chairman leaned in, "Who has told you this?"

"I could tell you, but you wouldn't understand unless you were a man of faith," Jonah replied, already knowing the answer to that as well.

"Okay." Chairman Marcus sat back. "We are from the same family tree, you and I. In fact, against our own laws, I have a registry of every legal birth in this nation. I know who begot whom and how related who is to whom."

"And..." Jonah led him on.

"And, I did this for a number of reasons, but in part to keep track of which families were of the true line and which were added via a test tube. In other words, this supposedly endless lifespan we Blues now enjoy did not come from our own thoughts, but from a mutation that the Creator did allow." Chairman Marcus raised his eyebrow to match Jonah's risen brow. Then Marcus continued, "We took the eggs from pure line ageless women and fertilized them with pure line sperm to create templates. From these pure line templates we collect seeds to this day so that when a couple applies for a legal birth, we take some of their DNA and add it to a template egg. And since we Blues are not the most fertile people anymore, a consequence of bypassing the natural process, couples seldom stray outside of the process because who doesn't want a child with an 'infinite' lifespan? And as you know, several firms had access to these original eggs, but the one that caught on to essentially brand the kids so that they came out blue won the day. And here we are. You do know that your father was a part of the true line?"

Jonah said softly, "Yes, I figured that, given that he was also from the side of the family with my aunt who'd been around as long as anyone could remember."

The Chairman, now back in control of at least his demeanor, laced his fingers again before speaking. "And although I am sorry about the loss of your father, clearly we can both agree that the term 'infinite' is a bit of a misnomer. If you live long enough, something's going to happen to you. The failure to age does not protect you from most diseases, as you know in your family. And I must say it's not looking good for you now. I mean this revelation doesn't really change much about your situation does it? I have tried to help in the past with other prisoners and situations, but I don't know what I can do in such a high profile case as this. I'll be lucky if I can maneuver enough council members to spare your wife's head. As it was, they had planned to kill a thousand overnight if you did not honor their demand to give yourself up."

Jonah stuck his arms through the bars in the opening where the plastic was swung open leaning on them as he spoke, "Well, see that's the thing. I have some demands of my own before fully surrendering. Those demands are that you will allow religious freedom, you will not rebuild the temple to your gods, you may no longer make human sacrifices to them, and you will release my wife, never to harm her again. In return, in addition to surrendering, I will remain silent about the things that I have done."

Chairman Marcus leaned in again, "Jonah, you know we can't do any of that, not officially. Maybe I can get Monica's life spared and maybe we can have a period in which we unofficially turn a blind eye to Christians practicing their faith for some period of time, but that's it. Plus, not to disparage my Blue brothers, there's no way you can control anything once you give up."

Jonah took a step back and closed his eyes, "You are right about one thing: all of these things even now are beyond my control. But it is not me that you need to heed." At that moment, Jonah slipped out of time and space. As he did, he stepped through the cell door and, picking up the Chairman's pen, twirled it before him before continuing, "The Lord God says that unless you agree to these terms, all of your temples will be destroyed tonight."

Not only did Marcus see this, he also saw a transfigured hand upon Jonah's shoulder and a glimpse of a host of beings behind him. The Chairman sprang up, knocking over his chair and cried, "What manner of man are you?"

Still filled with the Spirit, Jonah answered him, "And still you ask the wrong question. Like you, I am just a man. What you should be asking is, "What manner of God stands with me?" Now go and tell the others what you have seen and heard. They will not believe you. God knows this, but that is the order of things." With this said, Jonah returned to his cell.

Chairman Marcus gathered up his fallen possessions, staggered, only half believing what he'd just seen from the quiet man now sitting in his cell.

Jonah spoke to him again, man to man. "So, how long have you been a believer?"

Puzzled by Jonah's outreach, Marcus froze in his tracks.

Jonah, spoke again, "You work for my enemy, but you are not my enemy. So, when did you confess your faith?"

Marcus blinked and then regained himself to take a deep breath before answering. "I confessed to no one, save God Himself. And it pains me each day to know the truth, but to continue living the lie. Have mercy on me, a man who knows our ways are wicked, and simply stands by. I am a man who values his own life above making a stand. On occasion, I take actions to save those in The Way, but I never push too far as to put my own life on the line."

Jonah stood up again, "So, how did you come to know Christ?"

"Your wife," Marcus answered. "How she stepped away from me and the things I could provide. How she lived out her faith. She is a good woman; I hope you know that."

"I do," Jonah knowingly said.

Marcus continued, "She asked me one day why I never ate any of the sacrificed meat? I told her that since I was a child I knew it was wrong to eat the flesh of another human being. She told me that was the Spirit of the Lord upon me. She told me that the Spirit of God has been with men of many faiths since man was created and that the Bible was basically an account or diary of man's walk with God.

Jonah said, "She told you well."

Marcus nodded.

"You must hurry now and tell the council what I have told you. By the way, what are they charging me with?" Jonah asked.

"Heresy. Rich, isn't it?"

Jonah, let out a, "Ha, yes it is."

Chairman Marcus departed and as he traveled home, he spoke with the other Chairs. To his own amazement, Marcus told them most everything. He was in constant fear that they might someday see through his words and into his heart regarding his faith, but that night he spoke plainly without fear.

As expected, after much discussion, the council of the Blue Sapphire Illuminati rejected Jonah's demands.

Promptly at 2:00am on the morning of December 23, storm clouds that began to gather when the Blue Lords rejected God's terms, unleashed their fury on the Blue capital city. At 3:00am sharp, the first firestorm unfurled its pillar of fire on a suburban Blue Temple. But unlike the pillar that protected Jonah previously, this tornado of fire, spewed 200-mile-an-hour winds of flames. The storms spread across the capital, spreading fire to the city's temples as well as their fertility and longevity research centers. What precipitation they gave, were droplets of burning coal. The storms ravaged the city until 3:00PM that day.

In the interim, some citizens, once they realized the storms were targeted in their assault, stood on their rooftops where they could watch the spectacle. The whole sky was ablaze. There were over one hundred fires across the capital that day, but God's wrath was very exacting. Although the fire and military crews worked frantically to contain the flames to their original targets, it was clear that God had been merciful, at least to any who had an inkling of the ways of God. For those still clinging to the Blue faith, it was a wholly different experience. Their whole world was coming apart and they wanted answers from their leadership.

During all of this, Jonah sat quietly in his cell. Most everyone in the courthouse building was in the basement, but they were lined up and down the hallway outside of the holding area for high risk prisoners like him. Jonah could see plenty of action on the other side of the cell block door through the door's windowpane. He didn't need to be a mind reader to know that the people on the other side were terrified. In his time alone, Jonah began to see some of the wisdom of God in this matter. Where he had, in his anger and grief, wanted to slay them all, God, as is His right, chose who was to live and who was to die. All that was beyond Jonah's understanding, but the one thing that became clear to him was that at or near the root of the problem with the Blues was their belief in and pursuit of immortality on Earth. Being mortal and believing themselves to be immortal made many of them inhuman. Such beings, by and large, do not listen to God. Like Satan, they believe themselves to be God. Feeling themselves to be immortal, they gladly took up with evil spirits and more and more depraved acts to keep themselves excited about their own empty lives.

Conditions in the hallway outside of the high risk holding area returned to normal by 4:30PM. At 5:00PM, Jonah had a visitor. It was Dave.

"Jonah, you could have told me that was going to go down!" Dave exclaimed.

Jonah answered him, "Where's the fun in that? Hey, I didn't know myself, not exactly anyway. I had a dream the other night that I couldn't quite make sense of totally. But I knew what to say to the Chairman. I assume you know that he was here?"

Dave sat his briefcase down on the table, "Yes, how could I not know that? Actually, my dad called me a couple of times today, asking a thousand questions. What a role reversal that is for us. But yeah, he told me what you told him. I told him that I didn't know anymore about your intentions than he did. So don't tell me anything that you don't want him to know. My dad may be saved, but I can't guarantee what he might do when it gets hot for him. Plus, I don't want to be in a position to have to lie to my Dad. I've done it before, for the cause, but I've hated it each time. Honor your mother and father, right? Oh, suffice it to say, no one held court today, so there hasn't been any movement in your case, not that you're worried about any of that."

Jonah smiled at him, "No, I'm not. But thanks. I don't have all the answers by any means, and I'm struggling myself to understand it all. But I know that you should be representing me.

Dave sat on the edge of the table facing Jonah, "Well, I'm glad you have so much confidence in me. I hope you feel that way later. Hey, to that end, I've got to run upstairs and see if

I can find anyone around here that can actually sign something. But while I'm gone, I have one of our employees with me that wants to see you alone. To be honest, I was doubtful about allowing this, but she made such a case that I had to bring her."

Jonah stood in quiet wonder as Dave walked to the holding room door. He swung it open and in stepped one of the last persons Jonah expected to see.

Before closing the door, Dave said, "I'll leave you two alone. She knows her way back."

The door closed to moments of silence as the woman walked slowly to the table. "Hi Jonah" she said in relief of the silence.

Jonah's mouth fell open, "Vicki..."

25. Grace

Often you may wonder what God thinks of you, and what He would say to you if you ran into Him in the parking lot. Would He be pleased with you? Not that any of us is perfect, but what if day after day with willful intent, you failed to pick up your cross, like me?

That moment was upon me, but instead of in the parking lot I'd always imagined, this meeting was to take place at the very gates of Hell. On my knees, my eyes were transfixed on my Lord, surrounded by a heavenly host, and more. There were also mortals with Him. A small band of soldiers, men and women, from the City on the Hill stood to the right of Him. I recognized the emblem on their vestments from the city. I guess I should have found that a bit more odd than I did initially, but given the circumstances, I think anyone can understand why I didn't give them a second look.

The Lord walked over towards a prone Carla. Avis was kneeling next to Carla while Akina stood to the right of Avis. As He approached, Akina knelt down next to Carla's head.

Then I saw what, at the time, I found to be the strangest thing. The Lord knelt down as well and laid His hand on the forehead of a lifeless Carla. As He did so, and even though His back was mostly turned towards me, I could see that He smiled at Avis, Akina and Sandy standing several feet behind them. Each of them returned His smile. Then He called to Carla, "Awake Carla, child of mine."

Carla's eyes flickered and opened, to which I heard Kim to my own right exclaim, "Lord Almighty, Creator and Giver of life..."

He knelt there speaking to each of them softly. I heard some of what was said, but I was too far away to hear it all.

They would tell me later in detail what He said to them, but it's not the same as hearing for yourself. In the days and years to follow, each would tell the story in his or her own way, each version slightly different than the other's. And yet I have a clear understanding of what was conveyed to each of them. We all experienced God differently, and yet the same God was experienced by each of us.

He spoke to Carla first, "Yes, Carla you are HIV positive, but do not feel that you have turned your life around in vain despite what others may say to you. I still have much for you to do in this life and that mission will make use of this thorn. And forgive yourself. For none of you are without sin, but I have forgiven you and you are free of these burdens. Your passion has overwhelmed your gift of discernment in the past, and at times, it will again. But have faith that I am with you and will cover you even when you fall." I know that He said more to her and I know that during the course of His talk with her He motioned in my direction. Still to this date, I don't know all of what He said, but many years later I learned that one thing He told her was that she should allow me to love her during her illness. Doing so would minister to my soul and help me deal with what she was going through. And it was true.

The Lord told Carla that although a part of her would remain here, she would continue to fight against evil and having been here she, as well as the rest of us, would see evil more clearly in our waking lives. But He told her that she was never to return to this place in the flesh ever again. Carla would live until the day of her thirty-second birthday and I would be at her side on that day. Even though Carla would physically join us in a number of our battles against the darkness, we would rely mostly on her prayers.

The Lord lifted His head towards Akina and she immediately burst out in tears. "Father, Mother, Lord, please tell me it's not true. Please tell me that I will not betray you!" Akina had seen her future self and was not pleased at all by what she saw; in fact she was heart sick over it. She felt an apprehension since the moment we arrived, and her trip back to ancient Egypt, and other stops along her life's journey had confirmed it.

The Lord answered her so, "Akina, this cup you shall not pass. But my grace is sufficient. As you know, due to your gift you will live a very long time, much longer than even ten Methuselahs. Still, you are mortal and over time you will sin and pull away from Me, but I will never abandon you and in the end you will return to Me. It is already written." He said this last part referring to the Book of Life.

Akina bowed her head and wept. Akina would someday lay down her life in an incident about which I only know in part. The end result of it was that Akina would travel back in time and that Aunt Cil would rip her beating heart from her chest. Like her son Reggie, she had the strength to do such a thing. I'm a little sketchy on how or why Akina's heart was preserved. But what I do know is that on three separate occasions Akina, knowing her future, tried to kill herself. And on each occasion one of God's angels had stepped in to save her. Their names were Amber, Eva and Karen. And each time they wore the guise of a girlfriend of hers. She didn't find out exactly how her life would ultimately end until many, many years after our encounter with the Lord, but oddly it gave her a sense of peace, like a fulfillment of what she learned that day. He told her other things as well, but I could not hear them all.

Akina and the Lord both stood and He embraced her, her tears dripping on His shoulder.

The Lord then moved on to Avis. He reached out his hand to her and assisted in pulling her to her feet. She stood before the Lord with her head bowed. He said to her, "Avis, I know the abuse you suffered as a child in the absence of you earthly father, Paul. I know of the evil that was in your mother, and I know everything that she did to you and allowed to be done to you. I know how your father, Paul, the greatest exorcist of his day over the years became too familiar with some of the demons he encountered regularly. I know how he fell for your mother, an openly unrepentant wicked woman, and married her. I know how your earthly father, Paul deluded himself into believing that allowing you to be bathed in darkness served some greater cause, when in fact it served only his own desire to be great. And I know how you were raped by a demon-filled man and bore a child from it. I know in part you are a product of the witchcraft you were taught since child-hood by your own mother, even as your father took you to church on Sundays. I know that because you were blessed with both the gift of healing and miracles, Satan has pursued you from your birth. I know all these things. But I also know about the blood on your own hands. And sane or not, you have hurt a lot of people. But I have a plan for you.

I cannot allow you to remain in the world as you are, so you will remain here. You will shepherd Carla's spirit, that part of her that remains here in this place. When her night-mares come, she will think of Me, but she shall also see your face and the person you were in your youth, and the person that she dreams you will become. You will also work with these." The Lord motioned towards the men and women in uniform from the City on the Hill. "You will use the gift of healing that I gave you to minister to their injured and sick. And you will do so for generation upon generation. You will remain here until such time that I decide to return you to the world as you know it. But be you mindful that none of this re-deems you. It is only by My grace that you are saved."

"Yes, my Savior," answered Avis softly, not lifting her head. "Lord, I am so sorry. I've hurt so many; how can you forgive me?"

He reminded her, "Have you not read your Bible? Did you not teach these to fear me? Do you not know that I am the Good Shepherd?" He reached down to pull her chin up so that He looked into her face.

Crying, she answered Him, "Yes, God of my fathers. You will search without ceasing for any lost sheep, and celebrate its return. But Lord, I am not a sheep, but a goat." Her chin fell back to her chest.

He lifted her head again, "I tell you the truth, I do not give up on any of my sheep. Why do you think I stepped down from Heaven if it was not to search out my lost ones and to bring them safely home? Are you not my child?"

"Yes, Lord."

"Then have faith, even in the darkest of days. For the light within, is greater than the world. I have placed this light in you, and it shall not fail. Your mind was twisted to the point that you thought you were the sixth angel described in the book of Revelation. But you are not; you're a sick little girl who needs some help. You've been ill for some time now, and there are many things that you still need to work through in counseling. I've provided a couple of people here to work with you. And remember, I am with you always." He gave her a warm hug and handed her off into the arms of her daughter, Akina.

Then the Lord stepped around them to Sandy. On her knees she looked up and smiled. I couldn't see His face from where I knelt, but I could see that he opened his arms and exclaimed, "Sandy, my good and faithful servant, well done."

She rose to her feet and moved quickly to His embrace. At first she didn't say a word, but basked in the moment, smiling broadly and shedding tears of joy "Through you Lord, I have overcome fear and shame and the nothingness in between them."

The Lord spoke to her softly, "Yes, you have. You can rest now. You are with me. You're home."

Then it hit me and I let out a question that was only loud enough for Kim to hear, "Sandy?" I wanted to jump up and shout and beg Him not to take her. I wanted to say that she was mine and that I could not imagine life without her. I wanted...

Then I heard the Lord in my head telling me to let go, to let her go. I said softly again, "Sandy..." as I too began to weep. In hindsight I realize that she was gone the moment she took hold of Nihil's chain and began to glow.

The Lord released her and moved clockwise to Chin, Sanjay and Martin, speaking to each of them and telling them of His plans for each of them. I don't remember much of what He said to them. He was saying things about their lives for which I had no reference. But I do remember the big grin and sigh of relief on Martin's face. From the others I learned that one thing He told them was that each of them would be returned to his own age.

Next, He moved on to Darnell. The Lord motioned for him to rise. Darnell pronounced, "Christ, Jesus, my Redeemer."

And the Lord said to him, "We talk every morning, every night and throughout the day, so we know each other well. That is how it should be. I commend you to keep doing what you're doing. Keep your heart and spirit open to me so that you might hear me when I speak to you."

"Yes, Lord," Darnell replied.

"My call for you and your life is different from the others here. Of these who came with you, you are the one that will fight evil both here and in the waking life you know. Like your Uncle Paul and your aunties, you will exorcise demons. You will cast out demons in My name from the world seen and the world unseen. Demons hide in this unseen world, but they will not be able to hide from you."

Admittedly, all of this would have seemed quite strange and out of place just weeks before. But now every word made perfect sense and would all the more so when my turn came around.

Then the Lord continued on past where Reggie would have been. Reggie had been taken up by the winged beast and we had not seen him since before the Lord arrived. He stepped towards Kim, who was on her knees next to me. And the words from her mouth shocked even me. As soon as He came to rest in front of us, Kim cried in anger, "Why?" She paused for a moment and then continued on pleading. "Holy Spirit, why?" I looked at her again and for the first time began to see the kind of pain she was in.

Again, the Lord knelt down and spoke to her as she stared into His face. "Kimberly, why do you let others define you so? I made you and you are wonderfully and fearfully made. They chase after false gods of form and fashion, while you chase after what is pure and good. They chase the world, while you chase Me. People judge you and do not realize or even understand the love you have in your heart. If they do not truly understand what love is, how can they know me and how can they love you?

And Reggie, Reggie is fine and back home already. This is not his day. What you have seen, he will need to accept on faith as most others do. And although I have a plan for Reggie too, he has chosen to live by the sword, and he will someday die by it too. He knows this and so do you. But My call to you is to walk with him until that day, even as you have done already. He loves you with all his heart, and protecting you is the joy of his life, so let him. And someday, before I call him home, he will see my love in you and the things that you do."

"Yes, Holy Spirit." Kim nodded in acceptance. "But one more thing…"

But before Kim could complete her question, the Lord spoke again. "People suffer, because they are mortal. And what you may not see is that in being mortal you are not perfect; you cannot be. And not being perfect, without pain, you will quickly abandon your humanity and your God. In order to teach you about love, I must first, in your flesh and the flesh of others, teach you about loss and allow you to learn about darkness. Quite soon, you will visit a society that has become quite good at avoiding loss and closing their eyes to the darkness in their own lives. In their minds they no longer have pain, sickness or death. When you see them, ask yourself, what do they lift up? What do they worship? What do they love? Ask yourself how they might be healed?

Consider my servant the Apostle Paul who encountered me on the Damascus road. How much more human did his thorn make him? But greater still, how much more human do his struggles make all of you by his witness? Think about for whose benefit did your cousin Sandy's suffering serve? Even in death, you will never forget her, and she has lit a torch in your own heart that will never go out.

I am teaching you love. I am love. And again, how can you understand love without loss? How can any mortal see the light, without the darkness?"

Kim nodded again, "Yes, Lord."

The Lord spoke again, "We will talk more later but for now I have work for you to do. You too will fight evil in the world. But you shall do so for many years more than most of these. In fact, the number of your days will extend until the year of your birth. You do remember your mother, Monica? You will see her today and not die until the age in which you see her again."

At this, Kim smiled and the Lord placed His hand on her shoulder and pronounced, "Walk in My Spirit, always."

And although she remained on her knees, I could see her soul doing back-flips.

And naturally, seeing Kim smile, I continued to smile when the Lord looked over to me. But when He looked at me, He wasn't smiling anymore. He wasn't frowning either. Instead, He raised a questioning brow and asked me to take a seat on a large stone, which up until that moment I had not noticed. He took a seat on the one opposing it. "Michael, why have you kicked against Me so? Why do you deny Me so? Are you so afraid of what others will think that you would deny Me and who you are? Sure, you claimed Me back on the bridge and you see Me now, but will you claim Me when you're back in school philosophizing with your friends? Will you see and acknowledge Me in each wonder of this world? If your own intellect is your god, then let's be honest about it."

I was basically speechless, although I somehow let out a puzzled "Lord?"

He spoke again to me, "Are you, or are you not, a Christian?"

"Yes, I am," I replied.

"Then if you are a Christian, why do you deny Me when you are asked? Are you ashamed of Me, Michael? Do not answer Me now, because I do not want to hear any lies today. You lie to yourself, if you like, but I know the truth. In time, I will ask you again."

"Yes, Lord," I replied.

He went on, "Let's talk about some other things. First, knowledge is a gift from me to you, but it is not to be worshiped, no gift is. Secondly, though you see Me now, as I allow you to see Me and as you are capable of seeing Me, ultimately I am unknowable to you in the flesh. So, while I commend any who strive to know Me better, do not let that thirst for under-standing of the unseen supplant your faith in Me, as many of the Gnostics and Mystics do. That is a foolish thing to do. No mortal can know God any more than a flower can know its gardener. That is why I am here, to bridge the gap back to you. For in this person you can relate and thereby instill a part of Me within you. And by that Grace, I offer you the Kingdom of Heaven even now. Not tomorrow, but now. Thirdly, talk less, listen more, not just when you speak with Me, but to anyone. Fourth, the path to peace is not secure; it wasn't for the saints before you, and it will not be so for you either, but My Grace is sufficient. You must learn to live by faith. Fifth, Religion without humility is no faith at all. Re-member that. Sixth, I am more concerned about the sheep than the shed in which they live, be it a nation, a city, a building or the flesh. Seventh, remember as you walk with Me, we are having a conversation, not a negotiation.

Now I tell you all these things, not just for your own bene-fit, but for the benefit of those you will serve in the calling I have for you. I am calling you to start churches in My name, to be an apostle, not just on earth, but to the stars beyond. The gift I have given you will allow you to walk on other worlds without air or water. Your cousin Akina and you will sojourn through the physical realm spreading the good news and My love. Through Akina, you will be able to return to earth on many occasions. Also through your gift your body will regenerate more than most mortals, and your life will be longer than most. I have made you and Akina this way to serve this ministry."

Even in that moment I knew that I would not live out all the days that my body would allow. I knew that a sacrifice lay in store for me. But in the next moment I looked over at Kim who was still sitting next to me and was struck by the realiz-ation that she was a descendant of mine. Of mine and ...

In mid-thought, the Lord interrupted me, "A descendant of yours and a descendent of Akina will marry one day, many years from now, and from that line Kimberly will be born. And to your next question, yes I will provide a wife for you. Lastly, when you see Me again, I will not appear the same, because you will not be the same."

The Lord stood and looked around, giving each of us one last knowing smile and then said aloud to all of us and to each of us specifically, "Go in Peace and may my love be with you always." And with that He touched His hand to my forehead.

When His hand touched me between my eyes, there was no more me. I ceased to be and there was only God. Yielded and being completely of God, there were no fleshly senses of any use, not eyes, hands, nose or ears. And still, the presence of the most Holy was upon me and was me. My sins forgiven, I was one with the Holy One. But then I felt the presence of the Lord departing from my spirit. As my senses came back online, seven waves fell over me. They descended one at a time and fell like filters on a lens. The first five the flesh could not comprehend and only my consciousness knew. How can words describe that which existed before and outside of creation? Truly, my God, you are unsearchable. The sixth level was the hand of God which spawned creation. The seventh veil was space and time as we know it. At this point it would be easy for me to discuss the veils of existence that I experienced as I left that place. However, it would not be good to convey such knowledge, which some label as mysticism, lest any of us should think ourselves to be like God and fall again.

The next thing I knew, I was underwater, floating. No, not quite, I was being held and something was covering my nose and mouth. Then I was being lifted out of the water by two pairs of arms. On one side of me was Reverend Orman and on the other Reverend Summerhill. Where I had been warm, I began to feel a chill. The simple white gown covering me clung to my body and felt heavy against my skin. When my ears drained and my eyes cleared, I could see the congregation standing on the shore praising God. The Pastors looked at me and then released me once I was steady on my feet. I saw Reverend Massey standing in the water to my right to receive female baptism candidates. But to my left was Reverend Brown, standing on the side, motioning for me to walk towards him. My eyes still blurry and my mind twirling, I waded across the water towards the shore. I reached Reverend Brown and he passed me on. But as I passed him I looked up and saw Darnell holding a large white robe towards me. My squinting eyes then flew open and I could see Akina, Kim, Reggie and Carla standing around him. They were cheering and seeing them I began to run splashing through the water. I was about a yard away from them, when I leaped into them. Collectively, they caught me in the air. The six of us bounced on and off of each other so much that we fell to the ground like we'd done so many times in pre-school days. Then I saw my mother moving through the crowd and I sprung to my feet and ran to hug her. I wondered if she knew the number of her days like we knew ours. I wondered if she knew that some day, according to what Uncle Paul had written, I'd some day slay the one who would take her life. But in the moment of our embrace, none of that really mattered. I said into her hearing, words that I don't know if I'd ever, as an adult, said before to her, "I love you so much, Mama."

She whispered back to me, "I know. And I love you more than you'll ever know. If I could take every knock and every fall for you I would. If God allowed, I would without a moment's hesitation."

My mother pulled away from me and sent me back to my cousins as she headed home to cook up a feast for us.

∞

About an hour later, after most of the congregation had departed, we sat in the grass on the hillside overlooking the waters. Memories flooded my mind. In the flesh, I realized that Sandy had been killed several weeks ago in the mission field. The van she had been riding in went off the side of a mountain, one dark, rainy night in South Africa. But in my spirit I could still see Sandy smiling when she greeted the Lord and I knew that she was okay with how things worked out. She had overcome the fear and shame of being a gang rape victim and like a butterfly, had left her cocoon of empty security. Survival may be about security, but life isn't, not if you're living it fully.

What had been days in the Pit, was months in the flesh, six months actually. We'd begun our journey in the fall, and it was now past Easter. Anyone who had not traveled with us could argue that it had all been a dream or some kind of group psychosis. But for the six of us and our family, we realized that if anything, life here trapped by the guise of time measured by light, was an illusion or at most only a glimmer of the full story.

Again, to be breathing in the glorious air of the plane of existence into which I was born, I sighed deeply. Looking down the hill and over the water and the people therein, I thought about how many search for a God of tomorrow or some secret knowledge, when God is right here, right now. Sandy knew this and maybe if I had, I could have been a better friend for her when she was going through her challenges.

Sensing my thoughts, perhaps because they were her own too, Akina reached over to me. "Brother Mike, we all miss Sandy. We all loved her."

Carla, sitting on the other side of Akina from me, leaned forward to catch my eye. Smiling she said, "And she felt the same way about you, that you did about her."

I thought for a second and then asked Akina, "But didn't you know that she would die soon?"

Akina thought for a moment and answered lovingly, "Yes, but I wanted her to be happy, even if only for a little while, and she was. You made her happy. But one of her biggest joys in the end was seeing that you'd returned to the flock. Having grown up with you she refused to believe that you no longer believed. I know for a fact that she prayed for you every night. I'm sure she was looking forward to picking things up with you when she got back home."

I took comfort in their words, but it also made me mindful of the time I'd wasted. I could see that Sandy's hesitation with me wasn't about her own fears, but was a reaction to my spiritual uncertainty. She was looking for me to get right with God before she pursued any kind of romantic relationship with me. I'm sure that in her prayers she was more concerned about my salvation than having me for a husband someday.

Darnell, sitting a bit to my left, added, "Yeah, it was a blessing seeing Sandy all lit up like we did there before we came back. God gave us a clear view of what others must see through the filters of their flesh. Yes, in the end she was happy." Darnell had returned with a second sight. It was a sight that allowed him to see spirits as clearly as he saw flesh. As the one chosen by God to continue this family's history of exorcists in His service, not only in this world but also the world unseen, Darnell was very accepting of his call. Darnell was a modest man who understood at an early age that his strength came from the Lord. We all fought demons, but Darnell was designed and created specifically for that glorious purpose.

Reggie, sitting on my far right and down a bit, was happy
to be home, but couldn't help thinking about Avis. Being only
three years younger than Avis, he knew something about
what happened to her, but he never realized fully how it af-
fected her. Like so many younger relatives of those in abusive
situations, Reggie felt guilty that he hadn't done more, even
though he too was just a child at the time. We told him as
much, but still he sat there with a twig between his teeth
pondering. He also wondered why God's Holy Spirit had not
been upon him there in the Pit? Why had not God conversed
with him?

Kim stretched her right arm across as much of his
shoulder as she could reach and said to him, "You just have to
trust that whatever God has done, in the long run it is for
your benefit. Perhaps God wants you to step towards Him?"

I totally agreed with this first part but wondered about the
latter. After all, the Lord had come to me and yanked me by
the collar. But then again, maybe Reggie was closer to the
right path than I was. Perhaps our Heavenly Shepherd knows
that just a call to Reggie would bring him back to the flock,
whereas with me, He had grabbed me by the ear and dragged
me back. I would have a chance to talk to Reggie about this,
but this wasn't the moment.

Carla leaned in again saying to Akina and me, "I can't believe that the two of you will be traveling the stars spreading
the Gospel. That just blows my mind!"

"How do you think we feel?" I half laughed back to her. I
think a part of Carla wished that her call had been like ours.
But she certainly wasn't envious beyond a passing thought.

Akina added, "Yeah, space boy and I have a lot of things to
figure out before our first mission trip. God is so awesome,
you know. We'll take a practice run to the moon or
something."

I started to correct her, to tell her how the moon might be outside of our physical tolerance, but she interrupted me, "Alright, science boy, I know that's not an earth-like environment. But you know what I mean." This was the beginning of a little habit she would develop of assigning these crazy names to me, all in love of course.

I took a sip of my Coke and burped loudly in response to her chastisement.

Reggie turned around and asked of the group, "So, when are we going over to Mike's house for dinner?"

I perked up, "I imagine we can head over now and just kick it until dinner is ready. Hopefully Uncle Paul will be there." Uncle Paul, as he was want to do from time to time, hadn't been around much in the past few months. His being gone was a matter of concern, but not worry. And although his days of being an exorcist were pretty much over, he still from time to time would get calls to consult around the world. Uncle Paul had forgotten more than most of us would ever know regarding these matters, but he was still a very good resource in the fight against darkness.

Akina interjected, "Yeah, we can do that, but we do have another stop to make first."

We all nodded; so she continued, "We'll be gone for a while, but be back in plenty of time for dinner. We have a promise to keep."

Six months ago, we would have said to a person, "Let's eat first." But we were not the same people anymore. Together we all stood up and joined hands, forming a circle. I think each of us was struck by the absence of Sandy, but each of us knew that this circle was and would remain unbroken, regardless of what the years would bring.

After giving praises and thanks, Akina smiled at Kim and at everyone. Then Akina asked all of us, "Okay, close your eyes please. We'll be there in a second."

26: Sweet Sorrow

Why do we do the things we do? Why do we yield ourselves to those things that torment us? Why do we forsake happiness for a path of destruction? Why do we trade joy for woe? Why do we do that, which we would not do?

After Vicki turned on a small jamming device on her person, which really wasn't needed since Jonah wasn't allowing any electronic signals in or out of that room, she allowed her coat to fall from her shoulders to the floor. Initially, she had stepped slowly towards Jonah, then she broke form and dashed to him. Reaching their arms through the bars they embraced as much as the barrier would allow. Bewildered, Jonah spoke a single word, "How?"

"Working for this firm as a paralegal is my cover. Amazing, isn't it? Of all the law firms in the city," she said into his ear. For a second she thought about providence and their shared belief that there are no coincidences.

Jonah replied, "Does Dave know?"

"No, but I'm sure he suspects. Of course, half the staff at firms that take the cases we do, are subversives," she said offering her own opinion.

The cold bars could not diminish the heat Jonah felt from Vicki's face next to his. A little awkwardly they pulled apart. Vicki, whose very life relied on her being composed at all times, surprised herself with the show of emotion streaming down her face. Still holding his hands she asked almost pleading, "Jonah, what have you done?"

Jonah tried to smile, but trembled a bit at the realization of what he was doing. "Vicki, it's not that big of a deal, really. I just, just had to do it. So many people dying, it really wasn't much of a decision. What choice did I have? Kill them all? I can't do that. I mean I could, but I can't. This is the moment, right? This is the moment that I stand on my faith. This is the moment when I stand before the Lord?" Jonah's eyes pleaded with Vicki to understand.

Vicki, understood him, but she didn't want to. Surely there had to be another way and she told him so, "I hear you Jonah, but what good is it going to do? Whatever deal you've made with the Blues or plan to make, do you really think they'll honor it when you're gone? Can you see far enough into the future to know that they will do what you've asked them to do?"

Jonah answered as best he could, "No, I can't, but I will know. The fire storms of last night were not my doing, but our Father in Heaven."

Vicki asked him, "How do you know this?"

"I had a dream that it would happen, and it did," Jonah said before going on. "Vicki, after all that I have seen how can I doubt?"

Gripping his forearms even tighter, Vicki leaned back and down to where she could catch Jonah's downward looking eyes. Looking directly into his eyes she spoke convincingly, "I get that, but why do you have to turn yourself in? Why do you have to die? What good will that do? Huh? Who will that save?"

Jonah looked directly back at her and said matter-of-factly, "I, and what I know, could destroy the world, and in their minds they can't let me live. I'm sure their own spies have told them that those of the Circle only have the one device to protect them and wouldn't dare turn it off and open it to see how it works for fear of breaking it. So the Blues know that I'm the key and they will not rest until either they have the knowledge or I'm dead. So even if I walk out of here, it's only a matter of time. And as I've seen firsthand, time isn't real. It's an illusion, created by the Infinite so that we, the finite, might have relevance. Tomorrow is today and today is tomorrow."

Vicki pulled back in close again to him, pleading face to face with him, "Jonah, I understand all of that, but now is all we have and the time you spend here matters! Do weighty thoughts stir your heart? Do signs and wonders keep you warm at night? Is your faith such that scripture smiles back and shares a laugh with you? Does the hereafter hold you like this, when you're in pain and afraid? Flesh and blood people need other flesh and blood people. Do you understand?" Vicki wiped her sleeve across her cheeks soaking up her own tears in the fabric.

Gulping down air, she removed the last veil to her soul. "Don't you know that you're all I really have in this world? You're the only person left that I can trust. You're my best friend and I can't...." At this point Vicki was heaving in tears, "I can't bear even the thought of you dying. What, what about Monica? Huh? If you'll leave this place, I'll help you find her and I'll get the two of you out of here. You can run away and start over anywhere you want." This was a confession to herself that she would rather he live without her than to die in her arms.

Seeing that Jonah was still not swayed by her pleadings, Vicki changed tactics. She thought perhaps to outsmart him. "Could it be that all this time travel, even a couple of minutes forwards or back at a time, has made you a little mad? No one has ever done this before. The Chinese travel to the future in their space program, but they don't ever come back. Have you thought about that? And what if you're not sane? What if you're imagining all of this, or at least important parts of it?"

Feigning anger, she tried to speak harshly to him. "Doesn't the Bible speak against committing suicide?"

Jonah spoke to calm her, "First, this is the only reality I know; so what choice do I have? Secondly, this isn't suicide. I'm just choosing not to fight. And it's more that I'm trusting in God. In the middle of my anger and my own murderous rage, He held up a mirror and I saw myself. What God allowed me to do to rescue Sara, that was good. And destroying that temple where they've sacrificed so many, that was good too. But to take up the providence of only God and in a blink of an eye kill an entire city of a people, that's not right. I thought it was, but I was wrong. The line between righteousness and vengeance can be very blurry, especially when you're filled with anger. Those of us living here are not struggling everyday for vengeance, are we? Sara, Heru and all the others didn't give their lives for me to spill blood did they? That's not what this is all about is it? I mean if we're really who we say we are, vengeance is not justice."

Allowing her inner thoughts to inspire her, Vicki questioned, "Justice? Justice? What about this is just? Huh, tell me that? Hundreds killed yesterday, thousands upon thousands sacrificed over the years. A whole people who only love God and seek to love others driven underground under penalty of death. And here am I, being who I am, in the belly of the whale with the only man I've ever loved in a way that a woman should love a man. That 'love him no matter what type of love', you know what I mean? But he's married to this other woman that he loves. See, but I know she lies to him. I know that she was raised in the Blue way. I know that she was, for years, the mistress of a Blue Lord. I know he thinks she can have children, but I know that she can't. I know how he cherishes me the way a woman should be. I know how time and time again this man put my interest ahead of his own. I know how this man has risked his life for mine, time and time again.

But what can I do? I know my friend is married. I know we are both Christians and so is she. It seems so unfair, so unjust when I know that you're in love with me. I look back at our lives, and at every turn it's as though God has stepped in so that we couldn't be together. I can't understand, and I don't have the faith to accept it. It tears me up inside like nothing else in my life ever has."

Jonah answered her, "Vicki, yes, I do have feelings for you, feelings that a man should not have for anyone other than his wife. I blame myself for that. Perhaps it was my own negative self image that blinded me to what was really going on between us. And I do love you, you know I do. But do not be confused; that's it, it can go no further. I have a wife whom I love and strive with my whole heart to honor as my wife for the woman that she is. And while what you say about her may or may not be true, what difference does it make? If there is an issue between my wife and me, it is an issue for us to work out and not our friends, no matter who they are. Yes, you were the girl of my youth that I ached for most. My flesh was weak then and is still in regards to you. But I struggle against that sin, as I wrestle against every darkness in my life. If you really love me, like you say you do, then you will help me in my struggle even if it serves you not. You stood with my wife as a bride's maid on our wedding day and pledged before the Lord to support our marriage. If you love me like you say you do, then you'll love those who I love. So if you love me like you say you do, then you must love Monica. And if you don't feel it in your heart for her, you must act as though you do on behalf of the love you have for me. You must see about her as I would. That is, if you love me like you say you do?" Jonah asked her.

Vicki fell to her knees in front of Jonah's cell weeping bitterly and tearing at her own clothes. "Oh, what have I done? It is my own fault that you are here behind these bars. It is my fault that Monica lays in captivity somewhere. It was with my own hands a week ago that I set these terrible things in motion!" Vicki stared into her open, tear-soaked palms.

Jonah fell to his knees in front of her and using his gift, he reached through the impediment to embrace his dear friend of half his life. "Given how I feel, how I have felt, and how I have allowed those feelings to fester, I could be kneeling where you are right now and you could be here. It is only by God's grace that it is not so.

Jonah grabbed his friend by her shoulders and moved her to arms length, so that he could look into her face. "You know that I love you and would never want to do or say anything that would hurt you. Heaven help me, there isn't anything that you could ask of me that I wouldn't do for you, even if it meant my own life."

Vicki leaned in to wrap her arms around him again. This time she rested her chin on his right shoulder, rather than burying her face in his chest as she'd done before. Looking out past him into the back of the cell, she thought about a thousand things, one of which was the sacrifice that she herself was making besides just being there. Yes, Vicki risked breaking her cover by coming there, even if their conversation was protected. But she was also disobeying instructions by the Circle leadership to kill Jonah immediately, should she be unable to extract him from imprisonment. By not doing so, she was effectively saying that she, herself, would never go home. By not following orders, she was now a traitor. Given that her handlers knew that she'd gone to see Jonah, going back to the Circle would mean certain conviction and execution for her. But she had a new life here now. In that moment, in that embrace, she committed the rest of her life to loving those who Jonah loved and that meant Monica and the other Christians working behind the walls of that modern day Nineveh. She would never again see life within the Circle. Gone was her condo, from which she could see the northern lights. Gone was her bank account and a retirement of leisure. Gone were easy mornings in the café in the bottom of her building where she would casually read the papers of the world. But could any of those empty things compare to this fullness she now felt? Could they compare to the call she now heard? She would see to it that once Monica was released, the Blues would never touch her again. Vicki pledged her very life on it.

Vicki pulled away and stood as did Jonah returning to his cell. Vicki asked him, "Do you know if they'll torture you, once they bring you out on stage?"

"It depends on where the wheel falls. Certainly, I could use my gift and extract myself, but part of the deal is that I don't reveal my gift in front of the cameras." Jonah grimaced a little at the thought.

Vicki offered, "I could make it quick for you if you like. You know, if the wheel falls on something really gruesome, I'll be in the audience." Vicki began to weep again just thinking about it.

Jonah, still thinking about his friend, "No, I don't want that on your hands. I'll be okay. Although my flesh is weak at times about this, I know that it's going to be alright."

"I know," Vicki replied. "So what's next?"

"Well, as you know I made some demands yesterday, and they chose to ignore them. But, I have another message for them tonight. I'm surprised they haven't already come by. It's dark again already."

Vicki laughed a bit, "Maybe all that fire from the sky has gotten them a bit off schedule?"

Jonah looked at her and raised a brow, "Hey, that might be true, but given that what comes next will be even worse, they might want to make their way over here. Actually, you probably need to get out of here. I'm sure Chairman Marcus will be by shortly."

Vicki reached out to Jonah, acknowledging that the time had come to part. Her arms extended through the bars and as his came back to embrace her, their foreheads touched ever so slightly between the bars. Vicki confessed, as tears again dripped from her eyes, "This is the worst day of my life." With arms still entwined and faces looking mostly down, Vicki went on, "You know I try to have faith. I try to have faith like I see in other people, but I don't understand this. How can this be happening?"

Jonah answered her, "Vicki, I don't have all the answers. All I know is that each of us must have faith enough to do what we've been called to each day. Today is all we have. All we have is this moment and each of us must trust God for the next one. What I can tell you is that God has a plan for your life and all of this is not in vain. He has his reasons and you have to trust in that, whether you ever see the answer in this life or not. And don't worry about me, I'm not afraid to die. They cannot take my life, but I give it freely. I don't fully understand it all, but the Lord has told me that if I do this thing, if I trust in Him, He will do a wonderful thing, well beyond what these hands could ever do." Jonah tried to find a dry patch of fabric on his tear and sweat-soaked shirt with which to wipe Vicki's tears. Jonah continued, "Please tell my wife that I love her more than anything in this world."

"I know," Vicki answered, both of them noting the stark truth and the irony, but saying nothing.

Jonah took charge of the situation, "Come on Vicki, it's time to go."

"I know," she answered again. "I just can't believe this is it."

Trying to soothe and speed her departure, Jonah offered some encouragement, "Hey, who knows how long this dance will play out? I'm sure that we'll see each other again."

Vicki held up her hand motioning for Jonah to stop. She knew the deal and didn't want to hear him trying to placate her. She picked up her coat and pulled out snacks and water for Jonah. "Here, I brought you something to eat. They don't screen for food. Manisha sent the slice of cake. She and Karun said it was your favorite. And I added in some of my nutrition bars." After passing the items through the bars to Jonah, who was clearly taken aback by the thoughtfulness of his friends, she placed her jamming device in one of the now empty pockets. Then she walked over to Jonah again and tenderly kissed him on his forehead. "Let us never say goodbye, but only see you later. That is, if we are who we say we are."

"Yes, we are," Jonah affirmed. "So I will see you later."

Vicki, holding her coat in her folded arms, backpedaled for several feet, keeping her eyes trained on Jonah, before she turned and walked slowly towards the door. She placed her left hand on the handle of the soundproof door and paused. Looking back at him and fighting back the tears she called out to him, "Hey tech boy, I'll catch you later!"

"Later, girl without a shadow!" Jonah called back to her.

As Vicki began to pull on the door, she mouthed silently, "I love you."

Jonah replied in kind, mouthing, "I love you too."

And that was it as she pulled open the door and swung her body through it. The guards gave her a couple of odd glances upon her exit, but she made mention to them that death penalty cases were always hard on her. For the most part they accepted her explanation, but did talk about her once she was gone. They questioned if she was really cut out for this kind of work, and dismissed her as a "silly girl". But Vicki was anything but a silly girl.

It was about 5:30PM when Vicki left and Jonah was alone in his cell trying hard to slip past his regrets, but his recriminations were diligent. If he'd been stronger he could have

saved both Monica and Vicki so much grief. He truly regretted that. But then philosophically he reasoned that he, Jonah,
was not the first married person trying to figure out how to
integrate friends of the opposite sex into their married lives.
Jonah thought about how for years he'd kept his thoughts
about Vicki in a box. She was the one woman he refused to allow himself to think about in that way, because if he did, he
couldn't in good conscious see her again. But like Prometheus,
he failed. The thing he least wanted to think about, haunted
him the most. How much worse must it be for those who have
actually been intimate with these individuals? Why had he
tried to fight this on his own? The simple truth was that you
can't, regardless of who's right or who's wrong, place a third
person in a position to jeopardize your marriage. That's just
the way it is.

Jonah couldn't say that he was looking for opportunities to
see Vicki, but perhaps he could have been more real with
himself and her and put a halt to things way before all this
happened. And still, she was his friend and had real need of
assistance in their collective struggle against evil. Jonah,
thought maybe sometimes God intends for us to struggle
through these things, and that some greater good may arise
in overcoming a situation, rather than simply being removed
from it? And yet, could it be that some situations are not even
to be overcome, but serve merely to refine our souls, so that
things not of God might be sifted out or burned away?

At 6:00PM sharp, Jonah was startled by the flinging open of
the hallway door. Six masked men stormed into the room.
They tossed gas and explosive grenades into his cell. The mu-
nitions exploded all around him, only to be followed by the

men lifting their own weapons and firing into his cell through the opening.

To Jonah's immediate relief his personal field held up. The only gases he allowed to pass were nitrogen and oxygen, so he was unaffected by all their efforts. Once they were done, Jonah could tell, even through their masks, that they were bewildered by their lack of effect. They glanced back and forth and then one of them pulled the pen on a red grenade, that once activated released a cleansing gas to inactivate the gas emitted by the others they'd thrown. When the little emblem on their vests changed from red to blue, they filed out of the room without a word to Jonah. Jonah told them "Bye, don't stay gone too long!" Although Jonah had been surprised, he'd figured that they'd try something. That was the main reason he wanted Vicki to vacate.

Next, at 6:35PM, the door opened again and in strode Chairman Marcus but before he'd taken three steps into the room, Jonah shouted, "Where's my wife?"

"For security reasons, only a couple of Blue Lords know where she's being held. But don't worry, she's safe, and if I have anything to say about it, she will remain so," the Chairman replied.

Jonah, not totally satisfied with the answer, said, "Maybe if you guys spent a little less time trying to figure out ways to kill me and focused on the question at hand, we could be done with all this already."

"Sorry about that. They're a little on edge because you're not letting any signals pass in or out of here. I told them the deal, that this really wasn't about you, but the board felt that they had to try. And while I didn't tell them everything we discussed yesterday, I did tell them about you walking through the wall of your cell."

Jonah answered him, "I'm just glad no one got hurt."

The Chairman stared at him, "You're glad no one got hurt? These guys tried to kill you! I'll have to report back that not only are you dangerous but mad as well."

The Chairman undid the buttons of his black overcoat and sat down behind the table, lacing his long fingers in front of him on the desk top. "So, let me ask you something. Why are you here? I've heard a hundred different things in the last couple of days. Some say that you're here just to secure what you asked for, that is to save the Christians and other faiths from persecution. But most think it is something else. A good number of board members believe that you are a Christian mystic bent on training up other Christians in your arts so that they can fight the Blue Lords. That is what Matasis believes, or at least what he says he believes. But can you teach this secret knowledge to whomever you like? Can you teach any believer to be a mystic like you?"

Jonah bowed his head for a moment or two, and then looked up at the Chairman. "How can you ask these things? First, there are mystics as the world knows them and then there are, for lack of a better term, Christian Mystics. But in all your years, I see that you are still new in the Way. So let me break it down for you.

The kind of mystic you speak of is one who seeks knowledge of God for his or her own purpose.

The kind of Mystic I speak of is one who has had an encounter with God. This kind of Mystic is one who has experienced a special encounter with God and has learned some deeper understanding of God through that experience. And while he or she may be able to convey some essence of what they have learned, they cannot pass along the experience. The experiences are initiated by God; we can only stand at the ready in a state of worship. This is what the Apostle Paul experienced on the road to Damascus and it is what many

Saints and everyday believers have experienced throughout the ages. But for each it is a personal experience, a personal relationship with God. And no two may see God the same, but trust me, God is the same God. And as long as you seek the gift, rather than the Giver of the gift, you will never have that which you seek today. Seek God first, and if God decides to bless you with His presence, then He will. If not, then God will not. Be mindful that this experience grants you what God gives to you, and is not something that can be manipulated by any person.

Regarding whether I am here to train up an army of mystics, my previous answer should address that, but let me say explicitly, no. In fact, I have no agenda, save that I listen. I have no agenda, save that I serve. I have no agenda, save that I love."

The Chairman thought about what Jonah said, and while he wasn't quite sure about any of it, at that time a seed was planted that would bear fruit in the months and years to come. However, the Chairman's original question still hung in his head, "But, why? Why are you willing to just give up? What's in it for you?"

Jonah stirred a bit, "Well, as you see it, I am making a deal, my life for the release of all religious prisoners, including my wife. And in part, that is why I do this, but God allowed me to see that in Truth I do this for you, meaning your people, those that worship the darkness. As with Sodom, in the next few days God will offer you a choice. You can choose life or death. Tonight the Lord says that those things you love will be swallowed up."

A bit perplexed, Chairman Marcus asked for clarification. "What do you mean by those things we love and swallowed up?"

Jonah answered him as best as he could. "It came in a dream to me and I, myself, am unclear on some of the details.

But I do know this much, that you do not want any of this. I beg you, speak with your council. Convince them to give up this fight or a terrible thing will fall upon your nation tonight."

Chairman Marcus knew that Jonah did not lie and he was afraid. But he also knew that the Sapphire Illuminati would post no warnings to any of the Blue masses, much less non-Blues. So he made up his mind that he would quickly pass this information to those in the press who he'd trusted in the past whenever he wanted to leak information. He knew that they would get the word out. Although the warning would be vague, given the events of the previous night, many would be appreciative of any warning, even one as nonspecific as this one. Chairman Marcus stood, picking up his black hat, "Still, I don't understand. Is this worth your life?"

"People are being tortured and killed and there is something that I can do to stop it. How can I not do this, if it means the lives of thousands upon thousands?"

Chairman Marcus shook his head, "You're a better man than I. I can't imagine doing such a thing."

"No, not today you can't," Jonah answered him in a leading way, alluding again to what would be one day. Jonah paused and then continued, "But you must be on your way now. Tell the Illuminati what I have told you, quickly. I already know how they will respond, but it is God's will that they have a choice."

The Chairman positioned his hat on his head, "So there is no change in your terms?"

Jonah affirmed, "No, but again, I'm just the messenger. I would ask one thing though, please tell my wife that I love her very much and that she has been the one joy that I have found in this life. Please tell her that."

Chairman Marcus bowed, "I will, when I see her." And with that he was gone into the night. It was almost 6:50PM when he left.

At 7:00PM, Jonah knelt down to pray. After giving thanks and confessing his own sins, Jonah prayed first for his wife and her safety. He prayed that she would someday forgive him for the fool which he had been. He prayed for the Blues, and he prayed for his fellow brothers and sisters in Christ and their shared struggle. He prayed for his family, living and departed. He thanked God for friends like Sara, Heru, Karun, Manisha and Vicki, and then he prayed a special prayer for each of them. He also prayed for Bruce who had betrayed him.

After Jonah finished praying he exercised a little. He figured it may have been a little obsessive to do so, given his current state of affairs, but it was his workout day, and he reasoned while alive, he should go on living.

Next, he sat down on the single bunk in the cell and enjoyed the meal that Vicki had brought him, more than just about any meal he could ever remember. Besides Manisha's huge slice of cake, there was an Indian mango from Karun's private stock. He was always claiming how Indian mangos were the best in the world. At his first bite, Jonah agreed with him. And Vicky had supplied him with a number of the snack and protein bars she was so fond of. Anyone not living on the run as she did, might turn their nose up at such fare, but that night, Jonah found them splendid. Jonah laughed a bit when he pulled them from the bag. That was his girl Vicki and her minor obsession of finding the perfect energy bar.

When Jonah was done eating he laid back on the cot and fell into a deep sleep. By this time it was after 9:00PM.

Jonah slept well, better than he had in a long time. Around midnight he was awakened by a tug on his shoulder, or so it seemed to him. When he opened his eyes he felt the earth shake. Then he looked at his watch and knew that it was beginning. Where he had not known clearly what was going to happen the night before, on this night he had a better understanding of the dream given to him. The ground beneath those things that the Blues loved was opening up and swallowing those things whole. All around town the earth swallowed up their temples, their banks and their longevity centers. These things Jonah knew, but he didn't know about the indoctrination schools and the shops that sold sacrificed flesh. The trembling of the ground came like thunder, some distant, some close by. Jonah was on his knees praying, but he shook with each tremor he felt. Jonah prayed fervently for his enemies, that they might be spared and that they might repent. Jonah prayed deep into the morning. He prayed and prayed until he fell asleep on his knees. Then he was awakened by a second touch, but this time when he opened his eyes, he saw not one, not two, but three angels of the Lord standing before him. Each of them had wings as bright as the stars. Their shimmer lit up not only his cell, but the entire room. The center one spoke first, "Do not be afraid, we are angels of the Lord. I am Robert. With me are Lauryn." She nodded. "And Natalie." She smiled. "Do not despair, God has heard your prayers and God will spare the lives of many tonight. Also the Lord has seen your faith, and has decided to show favor unto you."

The angel Natalie spoke next, "Our Father in Heaven, by Grace alone, grants you the knowledge that not only is your sister still alive, but so are both of your brothers. And although they are both in hiding far apart, the Lord will make it so that they are reunited."

Then the angel Lauryn knelt down beside Jonah, taking his hand, "Your wife, Monica is pregnant with your child. Even now another angel of the Lord is speaking with her, confirming the dreams that the Lord has given her the last three nights."

"Oh, my God!" Jonah cried out.

"Stand up and give Natalie your other hand," the angel Robert instructed. "We are going to take you to meet your wife six months from now, before the birth of your child. This child will be the fulfillment of God's covenant with you, that if you remained faithful, He would bless you and your family. Now let us go and see what God has done." And with that they took him up into the sky and beyond to a time that would not be his own, to show him the fruition of God's promises.

Jonah was, in a word, speechless.

27: A Future Past

Faith is the substance of things hoped for, the evidence of things unseen. This much is true, but sometimes, yes sometimes, God allows us to see beyond the veil.

Before we ever arrived to this future age, God had laid out the path for us to follow. Before we arrived He'd given Monica three nights of dreams like He'd done before her husband's execution. Before we arrived He'd already aligned each star on that cloudless night. He hung each star for our gain, even as He set each step we took for their benefit as well. He set all these things in motion before the creation of the Earth.

Monica arrived to the emergency location first. This was the reconvening spot she and Jonah had picked out when they first moved to the area years ago. If the location of their home under the bridge was ever compromised, this was the place they were to reconnect. In the dreams that Monica experienced, she was led to come here to this location to have her child. It was a good location in that it was well off the road and heavily wooded, with the exception of one large clearing.

Since she'd been set free from Blue captivity, Monica along with Vicki, Manisha, Karun and others remained in the countryside in hiding, relying totally on the blessings of God and each other for survival. Most of the Blue populace had, according to God's plan, turned away from their wicked ways. Open Sunday church services were now an accepted practice, but some demons like Matasis still roamed the streets. And even though they kept themselves to the shadows so as not to be detected by the masses or the authorities, they still sought to carry out their own agendas. Matasis for his part, still sought the death of Monica. Having access to her "file" he knew that supposedly she was barren, but he hadn't survived all those centuries by leaving anything to chance. He wanted to kill any possible seed of Jonah's.

It was evening time when we blinked in. Landing in an open field just beyond where Monica and the others were encamped, our arrival interrupted their dinner. Even in the twilight we could see their collective heads turn in our direction. Akina stepped forward and called out to them, "Hello, we come in peace."

A call came back, "Who are you?"

And then a second call from someone else, "And why do you not know the password?"

We all looked at each other wondering what to say, but then Akina called out again, "Monica! Has not the Lord of Hosts told you we were coming?"

Half a minute of silence passed, but I noticed that Carla, who was standing next to me at that point, began to smile. Moments later the entire group, all of whom were sitting on the ground, stood up and most of them began walking our way. There were fifteen to twenty of them marching out of the darkness. A couple of adults stayed back with the children. As they got closer, a woman in the middle of the front line of the group announced to Akina, "Hi, I'm Monica." I was standing close enough to get a good look even as the sun fell. I was astounded by what I saw. Here was a woman who was the spitting image of my cousin Kim. She was a dead on, though slightly taller, slightly older and pregnant, version of Kim.

Akina reached out her hand, "Hi, I'm Akina and we're..." but before Akina could finish her statement, Kim broke through everyone and cried out, "Mama? Mama..."

Everyone in Monica's group took on a puzzled look before Karun spoke up, "Ma'am, I'm sorry but this is her first...," but before he could finish Manisha reached out and grabbed his arm stopping him.

"Can you not see?" Manisha asked her husband. "Look at her; she is the spitting image of Monica."

Monica looking for confirmation asked, "Who are you?"

Kim, trying not to cry while catching her breath, "My name is Kim, and I believe I am your daughter."

Monica's right hand went immediately to her mouth. "Oh my, that is the name I was given in my dreams to name my child. It all makes sense now. Come here." Monica reached out her arms to receive Kim.

Kim was smiling so hard it hurt, "The last time I left here, you said I'd see you again, but I'd given up on that day. But here we are." Kim pulled back a bit to see Monica's belly. "That's me in there, huh? Hi, little Kimberly. Or should I say hi, me." Everyone laughed.

Dan, the safehouse owner, who was with them, smiled and reached out to shake my hand, "Are you with the Chinese?" He asked this because it had been rumored for years that the Chinese had found a way to travel through time. Some people reasoned that they must have found a way to travel through time since they were building space portals to other star systems and galaxies. Well, the truth was that at that time, the Chinese did indeed know how to effectively travel into the future via their starships and portals. They understood that as you approach the speed of light, time slows for you, while it speeds along for everyone else, thus you travel to the future. Lay people reasoned then, why not just travel to the future to a time when they already know how to travel back in time? It's a largely circular argument, but suffice it to say, we were not Chinese.

I reached out my hand to Dan. "Dan, my name is Michael and no, we are not Chinese." In Dan's day many Chinese were people of our hue, so it was not an odd question to be asked.

Besides, our English from centuries gone by sounded a bit odd to them.

Collectively, we all began walking back towards the camp-site. Kim walked arm in arm with her mother, while Monica began, at last telling her all the things a mother would tell a daughter who is now a woman. Reggie nudged me, "Kim first left here as an infant, for her own safety. But Akina brought her back a time or two after that for very short visits. The last time she was here she'd just turned five years old. After that last visit Akina brought her home to our house and we raised her from that point on. I think I was fifteen when Kim moved in. We got along right from the beginning. She's part little sister and part daughter to me as well, you know?"

"Yes, I believe I understand." I said to Reggie, in this rare tender moment for him.

Once back at the campsite everyone gathered around for introductions. It was then that I formally met Jorge and Marta. Lastly, an old woman came out of the children's tent and hugged each of us tightly. She looked into our eyes and held our cheeks in her hands as her eyes welled with tears. We found that a bit odd, but on the scale of things we'd seen it didn't mean much at the time.

Missing from the group was Vicki. Vicki had left that morning before sunrise, after having a revelation during her morning devotion that "today would be the day," which was apparently her only explanation for leaving camp. This was the first time since Monica's release that Vicki had not been there. She made use of the time to visit Dave at his law office. At this point Dave was still fighting the good fight from within the system. And with the law more firmly on the side of religious freedom, Dave's days were full trying to right past injustices.

When we were done introducing ourselves, Akina began to tell them who we were. She mentioned that most of us were blessed with the gift of miracles among other equally valuable gifts to the kingdom of God. All of this they understood. What was harder to explain was just why we were there.

There at the very gates of Hell, the Lord spoke to us and instructed Akina to bring us to this time and place. He told Akina it was to fulfill a promise and that was all that we knew. We assumed that promise was the one that I heard Him mention to Kim there, that she would see her mother today. But none of us knew the extent to which God's mercy would shine on us that day.

As we were in the midst of trying to explain what we'd experienced in the world unseen, making sleeping arrangements and clearing away plates there in the darkness, a light appeared in the southern sky. At the same time during the course of this discussion it became clear to me just how differently some things appeared to each of us while we were there. Some in the group were afraid at first, for they thought that it might be Matasis and one of his minions or some other demon. But one of the properties that we took from our encounter with God was the ability to discern evil from that which is of God. Right off I and each of my cousins recognized that these were angels approaching. As they descended, the tree line shimmered with their heavenly exuberance. Once they were about forty yards away, each of us, one by one called out "Jonah."

The angels deposited Jonah at the feet of Monica and Kimberly. The angel Robert spoke first, "Monica, this is your husband Jonah from last Christmas Eve. Jonah, this is your wife six months after her release. And this is your daughter Kimberly."

But before he'd even finished his introductions, Jonah was hugging both of them as tightly as anything he'd ever held before in his life. I could hear him whispering in Monica's ear, "I'm sorry baby."

I heard her say back to him, "No baby, it was me."

As the angels stepped back, everyone else rushed forward towards the reunited family. Marta grabbed Jonah by the waist from behind and pressed her head into his back. "Jonah, you're alive!" she cried out with a sense of relief that was tangible to anyone that heard her.

As the angels departed from view and people began to pull away from the mass of humanity that formed this group hug, they began to ask questions which illuminated to Jonah both their misunderstanding as well as his final fate here on earth. "Listen, listen everyone, you don't quite understand. Yes, I am Jonah. But..." and he was so sad to add, "I am Jonah from last Christmas Eve brought here today. I still have a date with what awaits me. And I'm okay with that. Really, I am. But praise God that He allowed His servants to bring me to this future day that I might see my wife again, free and looking radiant. And He's also allowed me to see this most precious gift." Jonah wrapped his arm around Kim as she buried her head into his shoulder. "So, praise God and thank Him for this most blessed of days. I am a most blessed man to see beyond his own death to the promises of God fulfilled. I don't know how long I will be here, but every moment here is a miracle and I will cherish each of them as such."

Monica bowed her head, placing her hand upon her protruding belly and the child within, before glancing over to Jonah.

Jonah smiled back at her concerned look, "I know this is a lot to consider, but I am so pleased and thankful to be here for the birth of my child and doubly to see her here as a grown woman.

While most of the group was focused on Jonah, it was apparent to some that Monica was biting her tongue as she looked away. Then Jonah's eyes fell on me and my cousins and it was clear that he didn't quite recognize us. Kim, realizing this, jumped in, "Daddy, these are my cousins." Before she could even begin to introduce us, the word "Daddy" coming from her mouth had left us all undone, especially Reggie. By the time he extended his hand to Jonah, his eyes were full of tears. He loved Kim so much, and to see her reunited with her dad like this filled him totally.

As Jonah was shaking Darnell's hand, Carla asked him, "Do you remember meeting us?"

Jonah replied, after holding her hand, "Yes and no. I feel like I've met all of you before, but I can't remember where."

Carla assured him, "We'll explain it to you later."

After shaking my hand, Jonah reached to shake Akina's hand, but she moved past his hand to hug him. She said to him as she was hugging him, "That's not how you greet your great, great, whatever grandmother."

Jonah smiled and said, "Thank you." Then he began to look around a bit with a slightly puzzled expression.

Seeing this, Monica helped him out a bit. "Vicki is not here, but she's fine. She went to town early this morning to run some errands. I think somehow she knew you'd be coming today and she wanted to give us some space." I didn't know what she meant at the time, but now knowing the whole story, it made sense.

Besides telling my own story, I am also the scribe that has documented Jonah's story as well. In fact, it was on this particular visit that I began to document our family's walk with God. To do so was also my calling.

In the sixty days that we would stay with Jonah, Monica and the remainder of their group, I would spend time each day documenting what they told me. Sometimes they would share their stories collectively and other times individually. And although we would return to this time and space on a number of other occasions, never again would I have access to this many of the participants in this grand play at one time, except in my dreams. Over the years I have found that the better I know someone, the better sense I can make of their dream.

The grassy meadow beyond the camp had been Jonah's favorite place to go on Sundays or anytime he and Monica could get away. It was also the place where he and Monica had agreed to meet in case they ever got separated or the location of their home was ever compromised. And although things had not turned out as they had hoped, Monica was still led to camp in this location. And so Vicki was also led to camp there. Neither knew exactly why, but they knew that if they were obedient to God's call, a blessing awaited them here, even though they had no idea what it might be. However, the night prior to the day we arrived, Vicki had been given a dream, like Monica had. But the message that Vicki had been given was that this was the day that Jonah would arrive. And though it was more than she could comprehend, Vicki took it as truth. She did not want to be a distraction to the happy couple. Although she'd confessed everything to Monica and Monica had forgiven her, Vicki still, six months later, thought about those past events everyday and those thoughts grieved her so.

Monica took Jonah's hand, and the two of them started off towards Monica's tent. She asked him, "Are you hungry, baby?"

Jonah smiled and said, "No," to his very pregnant wife as he followed behind her.

Kim, who had let go of her parent's hands, was literally dancing for joy. She could not stand still. The light inside of her simply had to come out.

As we were being herded off towards the common tent used for visitors and other miscellaneous items, Marta and Dan began to fill us in on the events of last December. "Wow!" was all that any of us could say.

The tent we entered was sparse, and surprisingly well lit. It was not bright by any means but the central area was illuminated much like it would have been were there a camp fire there instead. Cut logs served as table tops, on which sat various items ranging from towels to pitchers of water.

My cousins and I sat there in a circle with a select number of our hosts talking for hours. Karun, Marta, Jorge and Dan were all present. Manisha was in and out until she'd seen to getting all the younger ones ready for bed; then she joined us an hour or two into our discussion. It was about 2:20am when we heard voices outside our door. A couple of the guards were speaking excitedly to a female voice that I didn't recognize. After hearing more movement, the drapes of the doorway into the tent parted and there stood a statuesque black woman with a wide smile, in the process of undoing her head scarf to reveal the most royal glory to ever sit upon a woman's head. She opened her mouth and said to us all, "Hello everyone and welcome to our humble home. My name is Vicki." Something within me told me that very moment that this would be the woman I would marry someday.

She dropped her bags in the corner, poured herself a mug of water and then sat down in the open place next to me. I smiled and introduced myself. "Hi, my name is Michael. And this is my cousin Carla."

Carla reached across me, "Hi, good to meet you." As she said this she gave me a glance that let me know that she knew what I thought - that this girl was all that and then some. According to the others, it didn't take a mind reader to know that I was instantly smitten. Even through my brown skin it was evident that I was blushing. Vicki saw that my cup was empty; so she grabbed the pitcher of water to her right and reached over to her left to refill my cup. Then she smiled at me and I smiled back.

I should point out how sometimes it can be divine providence not to know the whole story. Or as some would say, ignorance is bliss. I never really believed that, but in this case it was true. First off, when she smiled at me, I thought she was feeling the same connection that I was. But what I didn't know was that Vicki smiled at everyone. Secondly, I was 21 years old; I assumed she was something like 25 or 26 years old. I came to find out later that she was 33 years old! Who knew? You couldn't tell it by looking at her at all. But by the time I found this out, I was already hers, whether she knew it or not.

I proceeded to introduce her to the others. When I got to Kim, Vicki responded strangely. She twisted her face and leaned forward to speak across the circle's center to Kim, "Kim, that must be a family name?"

We each shook our heads and Carla said "No, not that we know of."

Vicki shrugged her shoulders and let it drop.

Then Marta asked Vicki if she'd gone in to see Jonah yet. Vicki shook her head and replied, "Oh no, they need their time right now." As she finished saying this, Manisha, who was sitting on Vicki's right, reached over and squeezed Vicki's hand, giving her an affirming nod as well.

There was so much to talk about. It was almost 3:00am when Darnell asked Vicki, "So, what do you do here? What's your role?"

Vicki, after swallowing a sip of water and clearing her throat told him, "I'm head of security here and Monica's personal bodyguard. I may not look like much, but I can handle myself."

"Oh, I can believe that," Reggie quipped. His trained eye had noticed right off that Vicki was "packing".

Vicki touched her sidearm, "Oh, these things. Yes, I guess they are a bit of a giveaway. Most of the residents here aren't armed and if I had my way I wouldn't be either. But it is what it is, today anyway. Even though we have the law on our side now, this one particular demon and his goons are still after us."

Akina paused to place her cup back down before asking, "And which one is that?"

After taking a deep breath, Vicki breathed out to us, "He calls himself Matasis."

The conversation stopped right then and there as my cousins and I looked at each other. It was such heartbreak for us to be reminded that this fool was still around in this day and age. Even at that time, we already had some inkling of the family members he would kill over the years. This included my own mother, which sickened me. The weight of our part in his release was almost too much for us to bear. For me personally, I remembered what the Lord told me that one day, that I would be the one to bring this demon down. But to be reminded that he would still be around hurting people until that day tested my faith in a way that it had not been since we left the Pit.

Dan reading our faces correctly, "So, you know of him too?"

Before any of us could answer we heard a noise outside. Akina's eyes opened wide and then narrowed as she announced without a blink or stutter, "Matasis is here. Remember, keep away from him. One touch from him is death to most."

Although, Matasis had a number of weapons and abilities at his disposal, he hung his hat on his ability to disfigure all he touched.

We all stood up, but Akina motioned that she should step out first. The mouths of our hosts were agape when she exited out the side where there was no opening.

Two seconds later a thought appeared in my head from Akina via Carla that Matasis was hovering just out the front side of the tent apparently waiting for us to come to the aid of the fallen guards. Matasis had obviously noticed our voices through the tent's lining. His stealth attack at three in the morning on a sleeping camp was about to blow up if he didn't handle whoever was in the tent.

Kim slowly removed her board that was already extending out of the top of her backpack. She then lifted her index finger, looked at Darnell and then to the ceiling. Next, she held up a second finger and then to Reggie and the front entrance. In one nod the plan was agreed upon. In the next nod it was executed. As Carla motioned for everyone to get down, Darnell looked to the heavens and invisible fire burst forth from his eyes, cutting a large hole in the top of the tent. Kim immediately flew through it. I could see that as soon as she was through the top she had turned her body to fire an electric bolt at Matasis who was waiting on weaker prey to slaughter.

Then just as quickly, Reggie raced through the drapes at the front of the tent and into the darkness. Darnell was close behind him. The rest of us rushed out after them. Outside, Reggie had tackled Matasis and was holding one of his arms fast behind him. Darnell had his arms wrapped around his feet holding them together. The demon laughed, "Fools! None can live that touch my being." But at that moment he did not realize that the two men holding him were immune to his touch. Reggie was impenetrable and Darnell's recuperative ability constantly corrected any cellular imperfections as soon as Matasis' touch caused them.

A killing beam emitted from Matasis' eyes but dispersed around his own head. This was Carla's doing. She had enveloped his head in a protective shield. It was no easy task, but since we were so close to him and she was well rested, it worked.

Akina, holding a torch she'd just lit, stepped into Matasis' line of sight. She held the light to her face and leaned over enough for Matasis to have a good look before announcing her salutation. "Hello, daddy."

The Blue giant, at last realizing whom he had stumbled upon, began to struggle in earnest. "Damn you!" he cursed. "What are you doing here; you're all dead, save the old lady. And she's afraid of me."

Out of the then quickly gathering crowd came an old woman yelling, "Stop telling tales, demon! I am not afraid of you."

The old woman drew close. "I've never been afraid of you, since we freed you from your prison in New Orleans."

Vicki tried to get the old woman to keep her distance, "Alright, Aunt Kim. Save your strength, I think they have him."

"Aunt Kim?" I thought, and then we all realized that this was indeed Kim as an old woman. Somehow, she had reconnected with Monica in the months since that past December. Kim indeed had lived through all the centuries fighting the good fight.

Matasis, replying to Vicki's request to old lady Kim, laughed, "They have me? They have nothing!" With that the shape-shifting demon became a very large serpent. This freed him from Reggie since he no longer had arms to bind. But Darnell still had a hold of his tail, which had been his feet. Matasis coiled to snap at Darnell, who was quicker, and the demon missed him. Matasis tried a second time but by then Carla was telekinetically restraining his head movements, as best she could anyway. The convulsing serpent was hard to keep a grip of, and, in fact, during the brawl a few killing beams did get past her guard, but thankfully they didn't hit anyone.

Actually, as we came to find out later, this was a rare occasion in that Matasis had sought conflict without his minions. His last Herald had been killed by Jonah when he destroyed the temple. We suspect that he moved alone that night to avoid detection by the camp sentries or law enforcement, not that any of these forces could have stopped him on their own. The sentries had in the past been very adept at warning the others before he'd actually located Monica. The Blue army could stop him, but they didn't patrol the streets. It was obvious that Matasis expected to find a lightly armed camp of pacifists and one pregnant woman by the name of Monica. And in a very old school villain way, he sought to kill the child of his enemy in the womb.

My cousins continued to struggle to subdue the beast when he shifted shapes again. This time he took on the form of a minotaur. Bucking wildly, he slipped from Darnell's grip even as Reggie tried to reach his neck.

Matasis regained his footing and began darting back and forth, trying his best to avoid Kim's electric bolts and Darnell's righteous fire. Clearly, he was attempting to make his way back into the woods. Akina appeared in his path, but he scampered right through her. She did not dare to solidify that he might touch her. Matasis managed to get about seventy-five feet across the north end of the field when he abruptly ran into something and crumpled to the ground. I imagine he figured this invisible wall had been Carla's work. It had not been.

Matasis turned back and began to gallop towards us. He sought to intimidate us into parting and allowing him clear access through the camp and into the woods beyond. In the darkness he could take on many different shapes or even depart his host body for some unprotected creature of the forest.

Once he got past the tree line he would be lost to us forever. But we stood firm. As he lurched into the body of us, Darnell hopped onto his back. Reggie, finally, got a hold of his neck. Matasis continued to fight desperately until he got a glimpse of the creator of that invisible wall that now confined him. It was Jonah. The sight of Jonah, alive and in the flesh, stunned Matasis so, that he reverted to his original host body, the one we saw when we first freed him, which was that of a five-foot-ten gray-haired man of average build.

It was in that moment of transition that I saw my chance to "lay hands" on Matasis. As I worked through the crowd and reached for Matasis, my cousin Reggie, who along with Darnell, now held the demon tight, said, "No, don't touch him!"

I said calmly, "No, it's okay." Trusting in what God had told me, I placed my hand on the forehead of Matasis. Certainly, his flesh was different, but still it was flesh. It was physical, and God had granted me dominion over these things. One moment his red, hate-filled eyes glared at me, and the next he was a pile of ash blowing in the wind. The irony of this and the other events leading to his destruction were not lost on any of us, that being how he had disintegrated many of his enemies.

Jonah walked over to me, and grabbing my hand said, "Thank you, he's hurt so many."

"I know," I told him, but it stuck in my throat that this demon that I had slain that day would one day kill my mother. Surely there had to be another way. Surely, when we returned to our own time there should be something we could do to change these events. This was on all of our hearts, with the exception of Akina. She had been riding the waves of time quite a while even at that point in our young lives, and she already knew that there was only one time line, and it already takes all things into account. Also she would add, which was harder for me to grasp, that "...in an infinite universe, why would you need multiple time lines?" These thoughts were hard for me to understand.

We would have the next fifty-nine days to figure out and talk about all these things. Much would transpire in those days in the forest and only in hindsight do I see what a special time it was for all of us.

Kimberly was born on day five of our being there. Kim the eldest served as mid-wife to deliver Kim the minor. Kim in between, cleaned the newborn child and handed her to her mother Monica. Seeing the three of them gathered around their mother was both sublime and wonderfully beautiful in every way.

Of course we spent plenty of time with Jonah, Monica and Vicki, although perhaps the most entertaining time we spent was with Kim the elder. Apparently, over the centuries Kim the elder had become quite the storyteller. Being experienced in the ways of time travel, she was careful not to tell us too much about our lives to come. I'm sure she wanted to, but she and Akina were on the same page in that regard.

We also had many discussions with the group at large. When we told them about the ministries that God had called each of us to, the question arose, "Would God really provide ministers in purgatory, limbo, the world unseen, or whatever you might want to call it?" The second pivotal question was like the first, "Would God seek out other life forms as He did man?" Of course, my cousins and I knew the answer to this question. The Lord, Himself, had met us on our own Damascus road and told us so. But each of us understood their doubt and hesitation. It was during those sixty days that I came to the understanding, as the Apostle Paul had, that it is often best to keep the message of God's love simple. Not everyone is ready to understand all the things of God. And that's not to look down on anyone. I know that there are others who've experienced things that are beyond me and my walk, and for them to attempt to share those experiences with me would serve only to confuse me.

It was also during this time that I got to know my future wife and truly fell in love with her. Through my interviews with her, I saw her heart. And through her dreams I saw and admired her repentant spirit. Monica led the camp, but Vicki was her stalwart support, speaking up when needed, but more than happy to serve in the background.

For her part, Vicki, at first, did not take me seriously. She liked me as a friend, and she saw great potential in me and my gifts, but I was just too young for her. Plus the group was very much in survival mode, and romance was literally the last thing on her mind. Now of course, at the time, since she paid me no mind, she didn't realize that she too would be an ancestor to Jonah. Years later, she would come to appreciate how God had always thrown obstacles between her and Jonah to keep them apart. As I said before, over the years we made a number of trips to this place and time. In the course of these visits I grew up, even though not that much time had passed for them. When we visited right before my twenty-ninth birthday, Vicki told me that she had begun to see me in a different light. She was thirty-four at the time of that visit, so for her, little more than a year had passed, whereas for me it had been nearly eight years since I first met her. After we married, Vicki and I would muse that my courting her had been some real Old Testament Jacob-type stuff for me, in that I had to wait so long to marry her.

But I must say that for the first half of our marriage I didn't see that much of my wife. This was because of Vicki's pledge to look after Monica and the fact that we were trying to maintain a relationship across different centuries. For instance, Monica could go to sleep at 10:00PM on a Friday night then Akina would arrive to pick Vicki up to bring her to wherever or whenever I might be. Once her visit with me was done, she'd return Vicki to that same exact instance in Monica's time. Per Vicki's request and Akina's suggestion, they arranged it so that wherever I was, more time passed for me than did for Vicki between visits. That was to help me to keep my wife's aging gradual for to me. This meant that if five years passed for me on planet "X", then they'd be sure that the elapsed time for Vicki would be more like three months. We had to do this to some degree also because a lot of the worlds I evangelized on where not places where Vicki could survive.

Now, all of this worked much better when I visited Vicki. Given my retarded aging, there was little need to play mind games with the timelines. From Vicki's perspective I could leave in the morning and be back that afternoon, even though for me it may have been months or even years. Early on it was seldom years because that would have been disconcerting for both of us. As I got older, I learned better how not to bring the time away home.

I am happy to say that I was able to take Vicki back in time to meet my mother before she died, even though I didn't marry Vicki until after Matasis killed my mother. It did require that my mother keep the secret of having met my wife from me the remainder of her life. But I'm sure, given the options, she was glad to have that opportunity.

During the sixty days it also became apparent why Monica sent baby Kim away with Akina back to our time for Aunt Cil and Reggie to raise. While Matasis was no longer, his followers and other demons that had survived their temple's destruction still sought the life of Jonah's child, which was Kim. Sending Kim to another time would put her out of their reach. Those that were of the darkness could not surf the waves of time, only the Light controls the veil of time.

And whereas hostilities abated over the years for most of the rank and file of the resistance, they didn't for Monica. Actually, the pain and suffering borne in her defense led Monica to a decision similar in many ways to the one that Jonah reached.

Monica decided to leave the Washington, D.C./Northern Virginia area for lands further west. During this particular point in history, which happened to be a point in time between the age I was born and the years in which men learned to travel to the Pit on their own, the Blues controlled most of what is known today as the Continental U.S., Mexico and most of Canada. But they actually only inhabited what we know as the Northeastern United States, the upper Midwest, the west coast of Mexico and Belize. There were two main reasons for this. First, there weren't enough of them to populate such a vast land. And secondly, because of their affinity for urban areas, you couldn't find many Blues south of North Carolina or west of Missouri. Ironically, the fact that they bought into the idea that they could live forever, made them more neurotic about being near good health care and avoiding risks like the deserts, tornados, hurricanes, and earthquakes.

Interestingly, but not surprisingly, those who wanted Monica dead claimed victory, but Monica claimed nothing but thanks to God that the bloodshed had subsided.

Of course, Vicki went with her and together they traveled through those largely empty lands until Monica's passing years later.

One thing I can tell you is that the Chinese did in fact leave the planet over about a ten year period. Not so many years later, relatively speaking, they returned in full force to confront the Blues. Together with India they made a show of force that caused the Blues to blink. The Blues surrendered unconditionally. Most of the world was happy about this. By the time of this confrontation, the Blues had long since stopped the practice of sacrificing non-Blues for the fun of it. However, they were still very much an aggressive and imperialist country. By developing star portals, the Chinese had been able to leap into the future, and somewhere along the way they figured out how to jump back in time. Not to any time before the day they left, but close enough to mete out some justice. The Chinese reestablished North America, Europe and Africa as republics. Not many of the locals in this story lived to see this play out to the political eventuality just mentioned, but a good number lived long enough to see the winds changing to the point that they could see a new day coming.

On the afternoon of day fifty-nine, Akina, Monica and Jonah discussed the possibility of sending baby Kimberly back with us. Akina, already knowing the outcome of this conversation, suggested a plan to protect Kim until she grew to an age to protect herself. Monica and Jonah agreed. The couple spent the remainder of the day holding their newborn daughter and looking to our Kim and older Kim as confirmation of their decision.

Day sixty was totally different.

One of the angels that brought Jonah, visited him in a dream the night of day fifty-nine to let him know that they'd be coming for him the following day. The next morning before devotions, Jonah told Monica of his dream and she cried out so loudly that every tent in the camp could hear her. Jonah didn't want to argue with her, especially around the baby, so he stepped outside, but Monica followed him. She yelled at him, "How can you go back?"

Jonah spoke calmly but forcibly back to her, "I can't change history. It doesn't work that way baby."

Monica cried again as she grabbed a hold of her husband's arm, "We could leave today, run away from all of this. God will work out the past."

Jonah shook his head, "I've come too far to do that. I ran from God most of my life and I don't want to do that anymore. This is what He has called me to do and you know it too." He hugged and tried to console his wife, but she fell into a heap at his feet, holding on to his leg.

I happened to be interviewing Vicki over breakfast at the time this drama broke out. Beyond them in the mist I could see the three angels we'd seen before when Jonah arrived in camp. I could tell that seeing the emotion in Monica brought a similar feeling in Vicki as well. She held back as long as she could, but when she saw Monica fall to her knees in tears she could hold back no longer. She rushed to the couple's side. Her own tears beginning to stream down her face, Vicki said softly to Monica, "You have to let him go. These two months have been a gift that few, if any, have ever known. But you were there with me. You know what happened. Yes, you do. We prepared him and buried him together, out there in that field, the field that he loved. You and I, we know this. It's his time now, same as it will be ours someday. But you will see him again, even as you've seen him today."

Monica relaxed her grip ever so slightly, which allowed Jonah to pull her to her feet. Vicki nodded to Jonah, indicating to him that she thought Monica would be alright now. Jonah then pulled off both of his devices, the Excavator and Wave Modulator, one from each forearm, and handed them to Vicki.

Leaving Vicki behind, the married couple walked arm in arm towards the waiting angels. Then Monica had a thought, "Can you wait just a second before you take him?"

The angels nodded, and Monica ran off to their tent and returned just as quickly with their child in her arms and a card. It was a Father's Day card that Vicki had picked up at

Monica's request. It was a bit late to be giving it, but it certainly meant the world to Jonah. He read the card and smiled. Jonah leaned down and kissed the baby on the forehead. Then he kissed his wife and they prayed. Once they'd finished, Jonah kissed them both again and then began walking towards the angels. By this time the whole camp was outside. They were lined up on Jonah's right and his left, forming a corridor in the direction of his destination. As he proceeded, a number of residents smiled and asked God's blessings upon him, while others, like Marta, rushed forward to give him one last hug. My cousins and I, who were originally seated behind where Jonah and Monica argued, moved to the end of the line next to the angels on the edge of the mist. Proceeding down the line, Jonah said goodbye to each of us.

Reaching the end of the line, Jonah turned and took the final step into the arms of the angels gathered to take him home.

The angels, glowing still, took Jonah into the air and as they ascended into the clouds and the sky beyond, there was not a dry eye or unbroken heart to be found below. And so the Potter's wheel spun that day that we might be sculpted even more, broken and remolded closer to His image.

Day sixty was also our departure day. First, that afternoon Akina took baby Kim as planned. And even though her mother Monica knew that Kim would be okay, it took her until late afternoon to prepare for baby Kim's departure. Seeing our Kim helped, but still it was hard for her.

The highlight of that day may have been the two-hour afternoon walk we took as a group with old lady Kim. You could tell that she was just so happy to see us again. As always, she had to be careful with her words, being sure not to say something out of time with where we were in our lives. The walk ended with us running into a returning Akina on a dusty road not too far from camp. Akina said to us "It is time."

As the sun set we returned to camp to say goodbye to everyone. We were so totally changed by our visit that we could not wait to visit again. In fact, we told them that we'd be back in a month to check on them. That was like a year later for us, but just a month for them.

The six of us walked off into the woods to find a patch of ground where we could all sit and join hands. As we sat down amidst the foliage, I, like Jonah before me, was struck by how much had changed in our lives, while the world around us stayed the same. Those plants could care less about my worries and our lives. It comforted me to know, that even if we humans mess it all up, the world would still go on, and God's creation and creative process will survive us.

Akina asked us to close our eyes, and then in an instant we were gone. We arrived back in our own time on that same hill from which we departed, not a second later than when we had left, although our seating order was a bit different than how we were seated when we first left. If anyone saw us depart, they'd shake their heads something fierce upon our return.

After dusting ourselves off, we immediately made a beeline to my house where my mother had prepared a feast. There was chicken of course, but also turkey legs, stuffing, cornbread, sweet potatoes, collard greens, squash casserole and her famous lemon pound cake.

When we were done eating, my cousins and I all piled into Reggie's car to visit Sandy's grave. When we got there the sun was still up, but a cool evening breeze was blowing, that ruffled the dandelions and the long wheat grass. Darnell placed the flowers we'd brought at the foot of her headstone. I knelt down to tend to the plot. I've never been neat, but

Sandy was and she'd want her plot tended to. I touched her headstone and sighed before getting up.

It seemed that she left us far too soon in the course of things. And although she was gone, I still dreamed of her. One particular dream that was shared by my cousins and I was of Sandy riding on a chariot with wheels of fire. She was adorned in a flowing white gown that glowed burnt orange and red. With great joy she announced gladly God's grand plan for the stars. Wherever God's creatures are downtrodden, there God will be to lift them up. Wherever they are hungry, God will prepare a table before them. Where they are naked, God will shelter them. We shall take God's Love with us, and by us risking all to minister unto others they will see God's love and share it among themselves, that they too might have a hope for tomorrow.

Some will argue that these creatures are better off not knowing God and His call to rise to a level of existence beyond that to which they were born. And having been an atheist, I understand this point of view. In fact, it's what I once preached to all that would listen. But if your own life, your own walk is not evidence enough, no amount of words from me will change your mind. Likewise, if God's message, that it's not about you - that you should consider for a moment to care for others more than yourself - does not ring true to you; if you believe we would be better off serving our own needs, then this call is not for you today. But let's say that you do agree with the message, but not the delivery (the thought of an all-powerful, all-knowing creator that is beyond our comprehension), please reconsider the message. What I am saying is that for me Christ has been the gateway through which I have begun my journey to know God. I will not complete this journey in this lifetime; in fact, far from it. I'm claiming no great knowledge, none that is specifically applicable to your own life, but if you will walk with God, His Spirit will guide you to your own personal discovery of your purpose in this life on earth and beyond.

And now I write you from a world not my own, breathing air not my own and drinking waters of another world that would be toxic to most humans. For this world these are the final paragraphs of the last chapter. The other priests in this mission are doing their best to sum up the existence of their people and world so that we may hide these writings in a capsule that will survive us all. Akina is not scheduled to return before things come to an end here. She asked me to leave with her on her last visit, but I wanted to be here with these people on this day.

It is in these last days that I've taken my own notes and formed them into the story you've just read. If it be God's will, I will, as time allows, tell you more of my walk with God and that of those who have walked with me. But to finish the first leg of this journey, we must complete Jonah's story.

28: A Past Future

Jonah awoke early Christmas morning, to find the holding area flushed with Blue Lords. Through his sleep-filled eyes he saw Chairman Marcus standing in front calling through the bars to him, "Jonah, Jonah." Standing behind Marcus were about fifteen other Blue Lords of various shapes and sizes, including Matasis who had shifted shape into a stature that would fit in the room.

Jonah rubbed his eyes likely thinking of his last memories of ascending in the arms of angels. He shook his head and opened his eyes wide, trying to adjust to this new reality. Everything was coming so fast, but he was trying to adjust as quickly as he could. Jonah stood up and instantly he could tell by their collective change in body posture that they, with the exception of Marcus still feared him. Even though they could certainly tell that he was no longer blocking electronic transmissions in or out of the holding area, they still believed him to be dangerous. The fact of the matter is that he'd left both his Wave Modulator and Excavator at the camp before returning to his cell. But his captors didn't know this, since he typically kept these devices hidden. Jonah stretched a bit and asked, "So?"

Chairman Marcus looked to his left and to his right, and then spoke, "We came here to discuss terms."

Jonah replied quickly, "You know the terms. Free all religious prisoners. Abolish any law which limits religious freedom or the peaceful expression thereof. And free my wife, now."

The Blue Lords murmured and buzzed before Marcus replied, "Your wife is already free. Your attorney has her. But your other requests will take time. We're a large nation with hundreds of correctional facilities; you can't expect this to happen overnight."

Jonah furrowed his brow, and before he could verbalize a syllable, Marcus jumped back in to clarify, "However, we fully expect to have most, if not all of them released by end of day. And we will meet later today to overturn the law outlawing any faith other than the Blue faith. We are making a nation-wide announcement this morning to that effect. Actually, that broadcast should be going out right now."

"That's good," Jonah replied more in relief than anything else. Like a runner seeing the finish line, Jonah knew that he had, at last, fulfilled God's call on him.

A Blue Lord to Marcus' left stepped forward, "And what of you?"

Jonah smiled a bit, "Oh, I know my fate. This is my last day to walk the earth. I have seen my own grave."

Another Blue Lord spoke up, "So, you're just going to let us execute you for destroying the temple?"

"Well, I certainly don't want to die," Jonah answered and then continued, "But I have seen the future and I already know it is to be. I also know that many good things are to be as well. Besides, if I go free now, members in your own number will seek to carry on this fight and many more innocents will die."

Matasis smiled at this and chuckled to several of his allies on the board.

Jonah saw them in the back of the room and pronounced to them "Matasis, you laugh at the shedding of innocent blood, but this is an offense to God, more than any of you here realize. However, the rest of you, if you repent now, God is quick to forgive. But Matasis, I have seen the future and I know the number of your days. Your time on this world is short."

These comments angered Matasis, the lone remaining demon on the board, so much that he began to rush forward. He thought better of this course of action having seen firsthand just hours before, the Spirit of the Lord upon Jonah.

Chairman Marcus called them to order and requested that the body reconvene in one of the conference rooms upstairs. Most of the Blue Lords were, after all that had happened, afraid to execute Jonah. But they were more afraid of losing their hold on power. Jonah's demands were not public knowledge, so they could spin the change in laws as something unrelated to the execution of this fugitive. Even before the fire from the sky, Jonah was a real threat. And to be honest, more than half of the Blue Lords did not believe these acts to be God's works. They attributed all of them to Jonah, and getting rid of him would still spare them this threat. Freeing those prisoners and allowing religious freedom was, as the majority of them saw it, an inexpensive means to solve this "problem". Of course, the price of being evil is very expensive. In fact, there is hell to pay. I've seen it.

While Jonah's words that morning were lost on most of the Blue Lords present, it took root with several of them.

As the group turned to leave, several looked back. Jonah was their prisoner, but it was clear to all that he was not in the least bit hindered by those steel bars.

Shortly thereafter, Jonah's attorney, Dave, slipped into the holding area. He called, "Jonah, how you doing?"

Jonah answered him softly, "I'm fine. What about my wife?"

"We have Monica," Dave announced to Jonah.

Jonah sighed, "Thank you, Lord. Thank You."

Dave continued, "She was released this morning. They were holding her way outside of town. One of my interns has your wife and is headed back to my office. Also, I heard that they agreed to your demands. So that means we can blow this joint," Dave said.

"As in, leave?" Jonah turned his head up towards the standing Dave.

Dave replied quickly, "Well, yeah dude. There is no reason to stay here now. I mean since they've already made the announcement banning religious persecution."

Jonah stood and shook his head. "Besides the fact that I agreed to give up if they'd stop the bloodshed and meet my demands, I have seen the future. I was there and I saw with my own eyes that in that certain future, all whom I love that remain among the living today, live there also. How could I, in good conscious, do anything that might make that not so, not that I could anyway. So if today is to be my day, then I'm okay with that."

Dave approached the bars to make one final appeal, "I hear you, and yes, I do understand what you're doing. But how do you know that all of these things you've seen aren't just a dream? How do you know they're real?"

Jonah opened out his hands in a pleading motion for Dave to understand. "This is the substance of things hoped for, the evidence of things unseen. How can I say that I have this faith, if I do not act upon it? And it's not like I have it all figured out. There is still much that I don't understand. I don't understand why God allows us so many different faiths, but I do know that He loves us and has a plan for every man and woman. And I know that this is the path that he has placed me on, and I must walk this road as he has called me to do, and I must share the truth He has given to me, not just by speaking it, but by living it as well."

As the last of these words parted Jonah's lips, his right hand patted his chest above his heart. Dave could see a sense of recognition pass over Jonah's face as he felt something inside of his vestment. Jonah reached into that inside pocket and pulled out a greeting card. Dave asked him, "What's that, a Father's Day card? But you're not a dad, are you?"

Jonah smiled and said, "No, but I will be."

Dave spent the rest of his time with Jonah documenting his final requests. By lunchtime they were done. They said their goodbyes, although Dave said that he'd be back before the guards came to get Jonah.

From what we now know, Jonah ate what remained of the meal that Vicki brought him and then spent the balance of the day praying and writing. I've incorporated some of what he wrote in what you see here today.

Dave returned to Jonah's cell about 7:00PM, an hour before the evening's proceedings were to start. Jonah didn't expect that the Blues would allow Monica to see him, but he thought that perhaps Vicki would come back with Dave. Dave told me the upshot of what he told Jonah that evening. "Well, we debated that. Vicki wanted to come, but we felt like it might compromise her ability to continue working with us, or more importantly, protect Monica. At that time, anyone working in our office went on a list, but she certainly would have gotten a star by her name if she'd gone back with me that night. My office never sent interns or clerical staff to those last visit meetings." In making this statement to me, Dave acknowledged that even before these events, he knew that Vicki was undercover for the Circle.

The guards came for Jonah about 7:30PM. They did what little prep was needed and escorted him to a holding area just off stage. At 8:00PM exactly, the lights went up on stage, in the same Central Square where little more than a week before, Jonah had rescued Sara and the others.

The host of the evening activities, a long time favorite of the crowd, engaged in vulgar banter with the audience. He teased and demeaned the entertainment de jour. Jonah didn't respond to his taunts. To die as a fugitive must have seemed fitting to him. I could not have understood once upon a time, but my time in missions has taught me what Jonah and so many other saints learned more quickly than I. That is, to lose one's life in such a way is to gain.

About twenty minutes into the broadcast, the host brought up an audience member to spin the wheel to determine what form of execution Jonah would suffer. Jonah's lone desire regarding this matter that he expressed to Vicki, was that he hoped for one of the less painful methods of execution.

Gleefully, the woman spun the wheel. The least painful choice on the wheel that evening was the slow bleed, where they put you on the board, turn you upside down and slit your throat. The ravenous crowd loved it because more times than not, blood squirted into the audience. They literally licked it up. But from a physical pain perspective, it is the least painful method on the wheel.

Being only human, Jonah did look up to see where the wheel would stop. At first it appeared that it would stop on Slow Bleed, but at the last instance it clicked over to Drawn and Quartered. The host gave a devilish smile and a wink to Jonah and the crowd.

As the guards led Jonah to the upright board and began to tie him down to it, Jonah's face remained as stoic and unmoving as ever. But as Jonah was rolled to the front of the stage and he could see the crowd more clearly, his eyes flew wide at what he saw.

While most of the crowd was clamoring for his death, Jonah could see a column of red extending from the stage center and back into the masses. In the middle of all of this hatred stood hundreds of Christians, clad in red in the formation of a cross. Many dared to tie a red ribbon around their wrists. Some chose a red scarf to wrap around their heads. And still others were fully adorned in crimson. All of them stood in silence amidst the chaos around them. And there in the middle of the cross, Jonah could see Monica. She was the only one in red lifted up. She was sitting on Karun's shoulders, but around the two of them he saw Manisha, Jorge, Marta and all of the guys from his job at the electronics store. A couple of rows behind Monica he could see Vicki watching over her. Monica, seeing that Jonah at last could see her, climbed down from Karun's shoulders and made her way, along with those around her, towards the front of the stage. Monica led the way, and with each step another tear fell from her eyes. As she neared her destination, she caught sight of, for the first time in their marriage, a tear in her husband's eye. She called out to him, "Jonah!"

Jonah called back, "Monica! I love you."

Monica and the others tried their best to hold their positions in the frenzy that was brewing. The Blues always worked themselves up into a lather before the switch was pulled to initiate whichever means of death they sought.

But before they could reach their crescendo, Jonah looked to the heavens one last time and uttered "Thank you." Then his chin fell to his chest.

The lead doctor on duty stepped over to investigate. He placed two fingers on Jonah's carotid artery. He then motioned for a couple of his colleagues to come over and the crowd grew quiet. After a minute the lead doctor threw up his hands. The audience and host looked on as several suits strode over to the gathering. After another minute of discussion, one of the suits marched over to the host and whispered in his ear. The host spun around whimsically and said almost apologetically, "Oh well, it looks like tonight's contestant has checked out early. This one certainly has been a poor sport."

As the lights came up around the Square and the disappointed crowd began to disperse, the stage attendants began to remove the straps from Jonah's arms and legs. Before they could begin to move him offstage, Monica, followed by Karun,

Manisha, Marta, Jorge and several others, climbed up on stage. The security guards lining the front of the stage quickly reassembled to address the flood of red approaching and climbing onto the stage. But Chairman Marcus, who had been watching in the wings, stepped onto stage and motioned for the guards to allow Monica and those with her to have Jonah's body.

Tearfully, Monica and the others finished freeing Jonah's body. Karun took his place holding the back his friend's head off the stage. Monica, draped in flowing red veils, approached her husband's body and placed one last kiss upon his cheek. Her eyes were full of tears, but one could not say that she was crying even as her teardrops fell on his quiet face.

Monica then turned away from the stage to lead the procession away from that killing place. Karun and the other men lifted Jonah's body onto their shoulders. Monica had taken no more than five steps when she encountered a heavily draped woman kneeling before her, her head bowed. The woman looked up and pulled back her hood to reveal her face. A remorseful and repentant Vicki was bowed before Monica.

Before Monica could say a word, Vicki, who continued to look down, spoke loudly, "Don't urge me to leave you or to turn back from you. Where you go I will go, and where you stay I will stay. Your people shall be my people and your God my God. Where you die I will die, and there I will be buried. May the Lord deal with me, be it ever so severely, if anything but death separates you and me."

Monica knew those words from the book of Ruth, and she saw Vicki's spirit and knew right away that Vicki had put away old things and repented of all that had gone on between them. Monica walked over and stretched out her hand to her former enemy. As Vicki arose, Monica said to her, "Come, walk with me."

They took Jonah out of town to a meeting place where the body of believers often gathered before they had been outlawed those years ago. The next day the group, from which the campers we met on our visit would be drawn, took Jonah's body to a field near where Monica and Jonah lived. Monica did not want to bury him in the home or under the bridge, but she knew that her husband longed to be out of the darkness. So they buried him in the open field just outside of where we found them six months later. This was the same field in which we appeared.

The official word from the Blue government was that Jonah had died from heart failure. They said that the anxiety of the moment had brought on the attack. They say that he was scared to death, literally. But those who knew him knew that this was not true. Still others that were there, claimed to have seen angels descending to Jonah during his final moments. The implication was that they were there to escort him to Heaven. Having been through what I have, who am I to doubt this? However, there are yet others, who whisper in the shadows that the meal Vicki brought Jonah was poisoned. They argue that the first partaking of this meal gave him a near death experience, and that the second consumption took his life on stage before he could be executed. These people claim that either Vicki did this on orders from the Circle or she did this out of compassion for Jonah because she did not want him to suffer. Well, having married the woman, Vicki, I can say without doubt that she had nothing to do with it. This is what she told me, and I believe her. I fully recognize that some will argue that she had no reason to confess this to anyone, that this would be the kind of thing one would take to his or her grave alone. And while I will concede the second point, I take issue with the premise still. I knew the woman for her lifetime from the time we met to her passing, which for me, with my comings and goings, was centuries of my own life.

And I can say that if this had been her doing, I would know. I don't know what more I can say than that.

And while I conclude these notes here, I count the blessings that have been bestowed upon me. Having my wife for such an extended period of time was a true blessing. And the fact that I could work in the mission field for years and then return to her not having missed a day in her life, only made my joy more. I count the blessings of having such a wonderful family. At this writing only Akina, who is already in the throes of her coming madness and Kim and possibly Avis remain alive, but when you're a time traveler, that's really quite a relative statement.

At times Akina would pick me up, and on some occasions Kim as well, and we would slip back in time to see our loved ones from afar. We have sat in the trees outside of Sandy's window. We took in a baseball game one time at Turner Field in Atlanta just to sit in the upper deck so that we could look down on Reggie sitting below us having a hotdog, drinking a soda and yelling at the umpires. We visited Darnell when he kept vigil over people and places ravaged by evil forces. Sometimes we made ourselves known to him; sometimes we just sat. After Carla died, it became very hard to watch him waiting in the darkness alone like that. We have stood on the rooftop of a forty-story building just so that we could look through binoculars to watch Carla enjoying the Jazz Festival at Piedmont Park; any closer and she'd hear our thoughts. Our younger selves were there with her, eating chicken wings and potato salad. Since we have no memory of seeing our older selves that day, we have to keep our distance. But that was such a perfect day, that we've visited it often.

More than once during one of my visits home, I've made my way back to New Orleans where I first realized my gift, just to sit by the Mississippi and watch time flow by. It has so much more meaning to me now.

The blessings of my mother, aunties and Uncle Paul stay with me still. I continue in prayer for Avis. I have lived all these centuries to see her released from the unseen world of the Pit. Who knows how many years that translates into in the Pit? Back on earth she serves at a church, attending to the sick and hungry, healing those God calls her to touch. She moves from community to community, basically living off of only what people give to her and an odd job every now and then when she can find one. I can't imagine all she went through in the Pit; she has told me some, and I have my notes on that and some very interesting events since she returned from the Pit. But I don't know how I can truly tell her story. I will certainly try, if God allows me more time here, to do so. Although she returned to our world still in her mid-thirties, she has aged normally since then and at this point her days on Earth are short. Yet, her heart is full.

Not only Avis's story would I like to tell, but also that of the others. The service of my aunties, Darnell, Akina, Kim, Uncle Paul and my own grandfather, whom I never met, stir my heart even to this day. My mother and her sisters battled tremendous evil and prevailed, including defeating the Council of Nob, which still amazes me. Darnell fought demons here and in realms beyond our existence. Akina, like me but more so, has skipped across time and space more than any being of flesh and blood. Unlike me, she is not limited by extreme temperatures or lack of atmosphere. How can any mortal relate what she has seen, but given time here, I will dare to try. My cousin Kim's story is mostly an earthbound one, but her story is of a people, a legacy, a struggle. And Uncle Paul's story; where do I begin? Lastly, I feel compelled to speak of my grandfather, Hosea. Here was a man whose wife left him four very special girls to raise alone. A man, who by the world's account, possessed the least of gifts when compared to the rest of us, but fought the greatest evils, even against Uncle Paul during his wicked turn. If it is God's will that I share each of these stories before I leave this world then it shall be done.

The three children I had with Vicki have been a blessing to me. I have buried all three. To outlive all of one's children is a lonesome pain. Only one of them was blessed to have my gift of longevity, but as I will experience soon, as did my mother, simply not aging does not equate to being immortal.

I did not marry again after Vicki. Certainly, I would have liked to, but life amongst the stars does not easily lend itself to that pleasure of life. I married once, but got it right the first time for a lifetime of joy to me.

There are planet quakes every day here; sometimes there are two or three. The ones who are paid to know when this world is supposed to finally break apart, quibble on just how long we have. In Earth terms, the predictions range from a few days (their days are twice as long as ours) to just under six months. And still with their world coming to an end and their atmosphere already departing in some regions, they continue to fight and pollute the skies with marks of war. There is enough technology here that some countries and foundations have been able to send a couple of thousand children off world to uncertain destinations. They have no "terra" forming technology yet; so the chances are slim that the universe will ever know these persons or these forms of life again.

One regret I have about staying here to minister to these during their time of need, is that I can't be with Akina during hers, during her descent. Even being far apart, I still catch her dreams sometimes and I can see the madness coming.

And still I wonder. I wonder why the Lord allowed Jonah to believe his brothers were dead. Perhaps He needed Jonah to let go of this world so that he might claim the next or maybe work without fear in this one. I also wonder why the Lord called Sandy home so soon, although, in part, I think I have an answer. By her sacrifice we were reminded that we are to be free of fear and shame. The blues they bring are a travesty, an illusion of imprisonment. We are all free, despite whatever condition we find ourselves. Also, I think the hell that we went through with Sandy as she battled the demons of her past brought each of us closer to our goal in this life. Even all these years later her short life still resonates in mine. In all these years since, I've never known anyone else like her. Certainly Sandy had her challenges, but in the end, in spite of all of our heroic deeds, she who was the least of us, was the greatest of us all.

Still I pray for Akina, and I count my blessings. I pray for Kim, and I count my blessings. I pray for Avis, and I count my blessings. To have lived all these years in good health, I am blessed. To have traveled the stars, I am truly blessed. To have traveled to and from, through time and maintained my sanity, I am wonderfully blessed.

Some are gathering their families for one last meal together. And some of those are choosing to leave this life together on their own terms. I can't agree with those that choose this route, but I understand.

Surely, with my gifts, I could have found a way to be on one of the departing space crafts, but I've had my day and then some. It's time.

Something else holds me to this world besides my love for the inhabitants and my contentment with what God has done in my life. Here, in my own room, where I retreat when all is quiet on the floor, I dwell amongst my loved ones. In my chair or sitting on the floor, I am surrounded by fragments of papers containing whole people. Many are handwritten notes by those I have loved. Each one of them is precious to me, and they hold me where I want to be.

Some say that you can't catch someone's spirit in the words they write, but I'd say they're wrong. I sit here amongst letters and words from the long since departed; yet they are here with me in my heart and brought back to life with each word I read. Like anyone, I long to spend my last days with those I love.

In closing let me say that we are a golden tapestry of souls woven together by one Spirit. Moment after moment, day after day, life after life, may we lay ourselves open in service to one another, that we might lay claim to the Kingdom of Heaven even before our flesh is no more.

But this is not an easy war we wage, for sometimes it is against our own selves. And though we are children of the day, we are afflicted by the night. Still, like the light that chases away the shadows, so too are we forever called to wrestle with darkness.

PLEASE JOIN US AT:

WWW.TOWRESTLEWITHDARKNESS.COM

NOTES

NOTES

NOTES

NOTES

NOTES

NOTES

NOTES